HIGH
FALL

HIGH FALL

A Kiernan O'Shaughnessy Mystery

SUSAN DUNLAP

Delacorte Press

Published by
Delacorte Press
Bantam Doubleday Dell Publishing Group, Inc.
1540 Broadway
New York, New York 10036

Library of Congress Cataloging in Publication Data
Dunlap, Susan.
    High fall : a Kiernan O'Shaughnessy mystery / Susan Dunlap.
       p.   cm.
    ISBN 0-385-31024-2
    I. Title.
    PS3554.U46972H54   1994
    813'.54—dc20   94-6047   CIP

Designed by Rhea Braunstein

Manufactured in the United States of America
Published simultaneously in Canada

September 1994

10 9 8 7 6 5 4 3 2 1
BVG

For Mary and Judy Reardon,
warm friends,
women who make a difference

A book like this requires a great deal of research, and I am indebted to:

Chief Deputy Coroner Bob Siebe of the Sonoma County, California, Sheriff-Coroner's Department, for his expertise and ability to see what was needed.

Producer Mae Woods, for her knowledge, precision, and unfailing generosity.

Stunt woman Cheryl Wheeler Dixon, who answered my questions in the beginning when they were unclear—the hardest time.

Stunt coordinator Mic Rodgers, for giving me an insider's look. And to stunt doubles Sonia Davis, Jamie Jo Medearis, Steve Davison, John Meier, and Michael Runyard.

Chemist Ira Katz of Tri-ess Sciences, Inc., for his patience, knowledge, and enthusiasm.

Writer Phyllis Miller, for her help and support all along.

Phyllis Brown and Lewis Berger of Grounds for Murder Mystery Bookstore, and Ron Lynn, for their knowledge of San Diego.

Bob Greber, for his introduction to movies and money.

I am especially indebted to the late Dirk Petersmann, producer of *Heart and Souls,* who went out of his way to make sure I was comfortable on the set and got the information I needed. He was a gracious man who is missed.

And to my editor, Jackie Cantor, who has always been there for me with patience, enthusiasm, and insight.

CHAPTER 1

IT was a pickup shot. The rest of the crew was already back in the studio in L.A. Film for every other scene was in the can. Yesterday there had been a hundred people racing around the set at Torrey Pines—the whole first unit, the stars, the director, production assistants up the wazoo, and media pushing through the wall of fans, cameras ready for a last shot of the Big Names.

Lark Sondervoil glanced around the cliffside parking lot at the crowd. Five hundred people? This was awesome. Normally a new-girl stunt woman doing a gag would draw no one besides the grips packing up the cameras and cables, right? And Production—those guys were sweating bullets, panicked about the crowd getting in the shot, tripping over the cordon, and suing the studio, or one camera-happy tourist with a flash ruining the scene or spooking her in the middle of her first big gag. Worried that they'd have to do another take and throw everything one more day behind schedule.

The electronic press kit had gone only to the media outlets, to get them to come to the press conference afterward. She'd never dreamed the shot would draw a crowd like this, even with the footage of Greg Gaige doing the Move, and the teaser:

> THE GREAT GREG GAIGE IS DEAD, BUT HIS SENSATIONAL GYMNASTIC MOVE LIVES!
> NO STUNT *MAN* HAS EVER DUPLICATED GAIGE'S ARTISTRY.
> BUT A SPECTACULAR NEW STUNT *WOMAN* HAS BURST ON THE SCENE.
> LARK SONDERVOIL WILL DO WHAT THEY SAID NO WOMAN COULD: THE GAIGE MOVE!

Lark had read it in *The San Diego Union-Tribune* and *The La Jolla Light,* and the words were set in her memory like hard metal type:

> Nineteen-year-old Lark Sondervoil has recaptured the elusive Move that made Gaige the best stunt double of his time. But not even Gaige, once an Olympic hopeful, ever attempted the Move at a wild spot like Gliderport! Lark Sondervoil will perform the spectacular spiral flip Move and come to a stop at the edge of the bluff, nearly 400 feet above the beach!

"Even *he*"! Well, she'd set them straight about that at the press conference. After she wowed them with the Move. And the high fall gag that followed it.

The teaser ran on every TV station, in all the papers. The press loved all the connections—the film about a stunt woman, ending up with the Move a stunt man created for his Olympic gymnastic tryout years earlier, performed by the new girl in the business.

Now the set was mobbed. It was all Security could do to keep the crowds behind the ropes. Half of San Diego was here—with deck chairs, coolers, kids, and dogs—calling to friends, tossing balls, kicking up dirt, and gunning motorcycle and pickup engines. Whiffs of sweat and suntan lotion, garlic from the catering truck, and exhaust fumes cut the air. The production assistants were going crazy trying to keep enough quiet to shoot. Christ, they'd done twelve takes on scene 484! The Gaige Move, in 485, was next. But the whole schedule was so far behind, it'd be a miracle if they got to 485 and 486—the high fall—before the sun went down. Still, that wasn't her worry. She couldn't let this extraneous stuff spook her, not when she was going to do back-to-back the most important gags of her life.

She concentrated on her body, noting the hot southern California sun on her skin, the sharp afternoon wind scraping off the heat, snapping her hair in her face. She kicked at an outcropping of sunbaked sandstone and felt it hold momentarily, then crumple. SHEER UNSTABLE CLIFFS STAY BACK, the sign said. The cliffs she'd be falling off in scene 486. It must have taken centuries of wind to dig trenches that size in the bluff—like the spaces between a giant's fingers. So easy to stumble off those gnarled fingers. No, don't even think that! Worrying was a waste of time. You do your homework, then you're in control. That's how you survive in this business. There's no need, no *point,* to hamstring yourself by worrying, right? *Right?*

She was in control. She'd routined both gags; she'd gone over the plans again and again looking for flaws that weren't there; she knew what she was doing. For the high fall, she had checked out the sandstone; harnessed up, double-checked the harness attachment, then hooked onto the hundred-foot crane and rappelled herself over the cliff edge to check the catcher-trap that Cary Bleeker had constructed. Cary was compulsive about safety. He had to be, with his record. Still, she wasn't about to trust her life to him. You have to check everything you do and everyone else's work, too. Look at Brandon Lee, for chrissake; something goes wrong with the gun in a scene, and suddenly the blanks it's supposed to be firing are live ammo. Who would check for that? It's what you don't even think of that kills you.

She hadn't taken any chances; she'd lowered herself down, jumped into the catcher so hard, she thought she'd pull it off its moorings. Just as Cary had promised, it closed around her like a Venus flytrap—no chance of bouncing back out and down the 335 feet to the beach!

The high fall itself would be fine; it was the Gaige Move she was concerned about.

The wind tossed her hair, icing the sweat on her neck. Had Greg Gaige sweated out the last minutes on a set before the Move? Nobody asked that. They didn't care about Greg himself anymore. He was a legend now, and most of what was said about him was lies.

She had time for one more run-through on the Move, so the camera assistants could note where she touched down and put markers where they needed to focus. She strode to her start spot, three feet inside the inner cordon post, and stood, eyes closed, doing the Move in her mind step by step till she bounced to a stop and took the three stagger-steps back onto the camouflaged and well up-slanted cement slab three full yards from the bluff edge.

Now for the real run-through. She opened her eyes, looked neither right nor left, but took one breath and pushed off, running full out for the warning chain, leapt and cleared it, and landed easily on the ridge between two trenches. Two more steps near the fake ice plant that Special Effects had put down to cover the explosive charge that would "throw her" during the shoot. She jumped hard, pushed off into a double backflip away from the cliff edge, hit down on the balls of her feet, and flipped forward into a corkscrew twist—the Gaige Move. Feeling the hard ground under her feet, her arms grabbing air as if to catch herself, she did the three stagger-steps back to a stop, on the cement slab well clear of the bluff.

Perfect! She'd nailed the Gaige Move! The Move they said no woman would ever get! The sun blazed off the sandstone. Her heart beat so fast, she couldn't think, only feel. She felt full, glowing, invincible.

Then it was gone. The gag was over; life was ordinary again. She realized the crowd was clapping like mad, as if they knew they were watching history—the woman about to become the hottest stunt double in town.

'Course, if she screwed up the Move when the cameras were rolling, she'd never work again. No! She'd be fine. She'd nail it in one take.

She glanced quickly at the crowd. Maybe they weren't here to see the Gaige Move at all, but to be on the spot in case she muffed the high fall over the bluff and died in a broken heap on the beach below. Instantly, she shook off the thought. With the catcher on the side of the bluff and the wire she'd be wearing, the high fall would be almost a no-brainer. It was the Gaige Move that mattered.

"I'm going to miss it, Ez!" O'Shaughnessy grumbled to the Irish wolfhound in the back of the Jeep. "Okay, so it's my own fault. As if *that* ever made things better."

Gliderport was jammed with cars parked in double rows at the edges of the field and stashed every which way in the middle. People were pushing between them, rushing, half running toward the movie set at the end of the bluff. Half of San Diego is here for the high fall, Kiernan thought. Below, you probably can't see the beach for the people.

But it wasn't the high fall that Kiernan had raced to the bluff to watch. It was the Gaige Move that she couldn't bear to see again—and yet couldn't bear *not* to see. Her stomach roiled with the same churning she remembered from adolescence. It amazed her that Greg Gaige still had that effect on her. She had barely known him after all—had met him only twice, and the second time it had ended wrong. He'd been dead ten years now. But Greg Gaige had changed her life. In the gray of her childhood, with parents who spoke less and less, gymnastics had been her road back to the living; the road out. And he, who had been the star of Baltimore gymnasts ten years before she had, who had gone to Hollywood, had been the beacon. For years, her goal had been to match his gymnastic skill and share his Move.

Now the Move was to be done by neither Greg nor herself but by a nineteen-year-old girl. And Kiernan, used to weighing options, making informed decisions, and moving right on, had spent the day vacillating. At the last moment—*after* the last moment—she'd raced for the car and sped through rush-hour traffic to the bluff. And now, here, she'd be lucky to find a place to park before this girl attempted Greg's Move. Would she be rooting for her to nail the Move, or would she be hoping the girl fell on her face? That she wouldn't know till the first flip.

Pettiness was one of the things she really hated in people, and this eruption in herself—well, it wasn't making her day any better.

At the end of the parking area sat a line of wooden horses saddled with NO ADMITTANCE signs. Behind them, trailers and moving-van-size trucks blocked the view of the movie set. All that was visible was the arm of a giant crane. But peering between trucks, she could see people scurrying around—a good sign. The set wasn't yet silent, with the cameras rolling.

"How soon is the Gaige Move stunt?" she called out to a woman striding, walkie-talkie to ear.

"Up next!"

Oh, God! She couldn't be this close—and miss the Move!

Fifteen yards ahead, a station wagon's taillights lit. A gust of gray belched from the exhaust pipe. The station wagon was pulling out! "O—*kay,* Ez! We just may make it." She gave the big dog's head a pat. The wagon backed out into the narrow lane of traffic and started forward. She eased her foot down on the gas. The sweat running down her back turned to a shower of relief.

A motorcycle shot around her and into the space.

Kiernan jammed on the brakes. The Jeep bounced; Ezra hit the seat with a thud and a yelp. "Ezra! Are you okay?" she said, quickly checking his head and paws before she leaped out to deal with the motorcyclist.

But the cyclist was off his Kawasaki and into the crowd racing toward the bluff.

"Hey, come back here!" she yelled, furious.

He glanced back at her sheepishly, or maybe he was just squinting against the sun, and moved on. He was favoring his left leg, but not enough to slow him down.

"Probably *had* to learn to limp fast," she muttered, getting back into the Jeep and slamming the door.

She sped to the far end of the parking area and pulled in next to a pickup. "We can still make it, Ez. The run'll do us both good," she said, watching him for telltale signs of injury as he loped toward the bluff. At just over five feet, she wasn't much taller than the giant wolfhound, and while she was running full out, he was barely in second gear. She held the leash loose, her hand resting on his back, and felt the comfort of their communal motion. The dry air ruffled her short dark curly hair and flapped the legs of her green walking shorts and lemon-yellow sleeveless shirt. A fanny pack, filled more with Ezra's needs than her own, bounced with each step.

As she neared the sawhorses and the trailers behind them, she slowed, somewhat calmed by the run. Sweat dripped off her face. Within the cordon, people were still moving on the set. The shoot hadn't started. It's ridiculous, she thought, that this should matter so much to me.

Slowing to a walk, she peered between the shoulders of the taller onlookers. The vans and trailers, generators and limousines, that separated the set from the parking area were well behind her now. Near the edge of the bluff stood the huge crane. Poking the eye of God, her uncle Matt would have said. Closer in was a spit-shined classic Buick, with piercing predusk sun glinting off its portholes. Black-sleeved wires wove through the dirt. Groups of men poured over Polaroid shots. Cameras were everywhere: secured to a platform, balanced on shoulders, held in hands. Two dowdy women with plastic honeycombed bags of brushes and hairspray cans dangling almost to the ground ambled toward the catering truck. Skirting them, drably dressed young men and women clutching their walkie-talkies raced around the set like cars on funhouse tracks. "Keep behind the lines," the nearest admonished the crowd. "If you have to take snapshots, don't use flashbulbs."

In the narrow lines of space between the trailers, Kiernan spotted Lark Sondervoil, the stunt woman, her long silky blond hair blowing in the gusts. *Too delicate. Not tough enough for the Gaige Move;* the thought was in her mind before she realized it. She stared at Lark, in an electric-blue leotard that highlighted her small rounded breasts, her tight butt and sleek muscular legs. There was no room for padding under the leotard— but then, if she executed the Gaige Move right, she wouldn't need it, she'd land on her feet—something, Kiernan thought with a start, that she herself had never managed.

But then, neither had any of the boys in her childhood gym. And they had trained with the coaches for months on the Move. It was a strength and agility move; for men, the coaches had insisted, not for girls. Not even for her, the only student who had made it to the Nationals. She had tried, last thing every day after four hours of scissor lifts, of balance-beam backflips, of releases on the uneven bars, of handstands and tumbling runs. When the others had trudged sweat-covered into the dressing rooms, their voices damped down, and the coaches began shifting mats and packing up wrist supports, she'd moved to the floor exercise mat and stood at the corner, running through the Gaige Move in her mind. The smell of garlic, onions, tomato sauce, and frying ham from stoves in the row houses upwind had flowed in on the cold drafts of winter. There had been time for only one try before the coaches shooed her out. One flip, one push, one back twist, one landing on her shoulder or head or face. And the only encouragement she received had been from the image of Greg Gaige, and he was long gone from Baltimore even then.

No one had ever duplicated the Gaige Move. But the poster of him doing the Move—grinning in the midst of it—hung like an icon on the gym wall.

Lark Sondervoil was tallish, with the long sinews of a dancer or a yogi. She wasn't built like Greg Gaige. Greg had been a tough city kid, with a small muscular body that said: *Don't mess with me.* Gymnastics had been his life. When he wasn't doing a stunt—a *gag,* they called it—or thinking about doing one, it was as if the air had been let out of him. Kiernan recalled that wary, hesitant look from the second time she had met him, on a movie shoot in San Francisco. She was out of medical school by then, and he was at the top of his stunt career. Then his call had come; his shoulders had straightened, his eyes no longer had seemed to lurk at the back of his sockets. His lips pressed firmly together, his eyes on his start mark, he'd strode to it and nailed the gag in one take.

And Lark Sondervoil—so elegant, so lithe yet strong, and so focused—could she really do the Move? Kiernan could almost feel Lark's muscles straining to start, her mind pulling in all her concentration, sucking all her energy into one explosive ball. If anyone ever could nail it— She ached with envy.

The noise around her grew louder and thicker, like the jumble of calls and music at her childhood gym. Abruptly, she brushed away the memories. She was over forty years old. She had been a forensic pathologist, and now she ran her own investigation agency, which provided well enough for her to have a servant clean her house, cook her meals, and take Ezra for five-mile runs on the beach every morning. How could she be jealous of a nineteen-year-old girl?

But she was. She envied her the lead-in run, feeling the air skim her skin as she cut through it; the thrust of ramming into the push-off, the utter joy of spinning in air by the shift of her muscles, whirling with the earth and sky mixing into each other, and herself wrapped in the intensity of her own body, every muscle taut, moving together into the solid, certain stick of the landing. God, she missed it!

She looked back at Lark Sondervoil. If someone had to eclipse Greg Gaige, let it be a *woman*! And let her nail it! Maybe just one, tiny, noticed-by-no-one-but-herself misstep on the landing? No, dammit! Let her make it!

The voices grew louder, sparked off each other. Kiernan jerked her head to the right; her eyes opened, and she stared.

Back by the trailers, she could see the disputants. It was a scene that normally would have had her yelling "Bullies!" and racing at them. But now she smiled. Ahead, two burly guys in black had a smaller dark-haired man by the arms, half escorting, half pulling him toward the NO ADMITTANCE sign.

"Grow up, Yarrow! You haven't done a gag in years. You're not a stunt man anymore!" one of the bouncers yelled, as he shoved the smaller man between sawhorses. "Go over there with the rest of the tourists!"

The man squirming futilely, complaining in vain, was the motorcyclist who'd stolen her parking spot.

Lark Sondervoil shook off the intrusion. The guy looked familiar. Security was flipping out over him. Why? Who was he? She couldn't let that get to her—not now. She had to keep her concentration.

She stepped over the chain and strode the fifty feet to the edge. Now that she was moving, she felt light again, normal, almost good. She glanced down at the beach. The people were like dots, the breaking waves looked flat. She'd done high fall gags into water. She knew how to flutter and stretch out flat, to land full out on her back and use the buoyancy of the water to cushion her fall. The last time she'd done that, she'd broken only two ribs and hadn't spat up blood for more than a day. Well worth it for a $25,000 adjustment. And nothing compared with the adjustment they'd negotiated for this gag. But the water down there wouldn't cushion her this time. It was way too far out and way too far down. Everyone in the business knew the story of A. J. Boukunas doing a 321-foot fall. When he hit, his air bag had exploded. And that was forty feet less than this fall would be if she missed the trap.

But she wouldn't. She shouldn't even be thinking about the high fall yet; the high fall was scene 486. In scene 485 the Gaige Move finished three yards in from the edge of the bluff. She was just upping the ante with herself, she knew that. She loved it. If it hadn't been the trickiest gag, set on the most spectacular spot this side of Big Sur, she wouldn't have been caught by it. If she weren't about to prove she could do it better than the best—than Greg Gaige—she wouldn't bother.

She had time. She could tease herself with the high fall.

She stared down at the camera, set up for the high fall on the cliffside fifteen feet from the catcher, held up by steel ropes and pulleys, railings around the platform, girders propping it up, nets hanging under it in case the camera assistant dropped his lens or his teeth. He had so many ropes on him, he could have been a marionette.

She looked back at her own catcher-trap, hidden beneath the camouflage of bushes now. Even she could see nothing more of it than the white fake ice plant flower that marked the middle, which would be her guide.

Cary Bleeker had wanted to put a special effects man under the trap, ready to drop the dummy that would fall to the beach. She'd seen the effects guy sweat when Cary routined that plan. Cary was compulsive as hell, but the effects guy knew Bleeker's reputation as a bad luck director. Poor guy could see himself as Bleeker's bad luck in this picture.

She wasn't big time yet, but she had been big enough to shoot down that idea. No way, she'd told him. Too dangerous for the effects guy, with her slamming into the trap above him. The sandstone was too soft to run a beam into. Cary—give him credit—he'd seen sense quick. He'd had Special Effects rig the dummy with a spring release. Her landing would set that off. The camera on the crane would film her going over the edge of the bluff, and the platform camera would take a long shot of her and the dummy falling down the bluff wall. Editing would splice in a cover shot of the horrified crowd on the beach they'd taken yesterday to mask the switch. All illusion. She laughed. It was so easy when you saw beneath it.

Bad luck might strike Cary Bleeker again, but it wasn't going to strike on her gag!

*   *   *

From the closest-to-the-bluff spot behind the outer line of the cordon, Kiernan stared across the five-foot no-man's-land to the inner cordon. Inside that, on the set, flames spat from a trash can near the trailers. A man in coveralls grabbed an extinguisher and put it out. The walkie-talkie crew kept circling anxiously. Two men in jeans were pushing a mounted camera. Banks of lights worthy of a night game at Jack Murphy Stadium flashed on just long enough to make the bright afternoon look drab when they went off. Huge black tarps on tripods suggested a distant fleet of pirate ships. A tall paunchy man said something to Lark Sondervoil and patted her on the arm. Lark shook her head, and Kiernan could see that she had been startled out of her capsule of concentration. But the man was the city media liaison—or so his badge said—and Lark was doing her part for municipal relations. Behind them, a thirty-fiveish balding man with his remaining dark fringe caught in a ponytail braced a foot on the rung of a director's chair. Kiernan found herself grinning at the thought that real movie sets really had directors' chairs, and that directors—if that was what he was—really dressed all in black. He glanced at the mob of onlookers and back at a dumpy woman. She glared at the crowd, spat her words at him, and flapped her lapel, as if that would somehow transform her hot, brown office attire into beach clothes. They both looked ready to snap.

The crowd of onlookers had shoved forward, and now Security men lifted the cordons five feet in toward the set. Taking advantage of that, Kiernan moved the five feet forward and shifted half a yard to her left, nearer the bluff. It was only eighteen inches, but it meant an instant longer before the Move would pass her by.

"No no! Not even for a wolfhound, the guardian of kings, the companion of Brian Boru." The city liaison scratched Ezra's head as he motioned Kiernan back off the stolen eighteen inches and, she was sure, watched to see if she recognized the name of the tenth-century Irish king.

The man—McCafferty—was probably little older than she. Ten years ago, he'd have been tall and dark and might have had a look more soulful than Ezra's. But by now he brought to mind the bachelor uncle that every Irish family nurtures, the melancholy poet with the wee paunch he carries like a parcel of lost dreams. She looked from him to the dog. "I'm just giving him room."

"Much as I appreciate that, well, lass, ya can't. The city's responsible for these bluffs, and we've had more than one death off them."

The wind rustled her hair. Briny whiffs of sea water below mixed with the smell of the sunscreen on her nose.

McCafferty held a hand to the side of Ezra's eyes, protecting him from the gust. "Here, fifty feet back from the cliff face, the wind seems like a hard wall of warrior's shields, pushed double time across the sandstone by a line of conquering troops."

She restrained a smile. Melancholy poet, indeed.

"But over the edge, lass, it's entirely different. It's a rare year when no one dies on the Gliderport bluff. Scofflaws cut the metal chains and drive out to the edge of the bluff—where you were edging toward. Too late, they realize the sandstone's crumbling under their weight. Hikers in sandals traipse down the cliffside trails, illegal trails. Some of them freeze in fear three hundred feet above the beach; others aren't so lucky. And the hang gliders . . . the updrafts that they love so much, that sail them out over the green waters, turn without warning and smash them into the bluff." He glanced back toward the main camera dolly. "They're crazy to be doing a stunt up here."

Lark shifted to the other foot. She hated this waiting. It was like being bound, gagged, like huge magnets held her feet to the ground and every step had to pull the whole earth up with it. It was like iron weights compressing her mind. A couple of minutes to go. But a couple of minutes seemed like a lifetime.

But there was no way around it. The last scene had been shot at five twenty yesterday. The lighting had to be the same for this one.

She glanced over at Mavis Herrera, the script supervisor, standing like an anorexic schoolmarm with her big horn-rimmed glasses and ever-present notebook. Lark looked from her to the scene's old Buick parked next to the UNSTABLE CLIFFS marker. The sun was moving down its side. She didn't know when the magic moment would come, when the light would shine off the chrome exactly as it had in the last Polaroid that Mavis had snapped as yesterday's shooting ended, but she'd be ready.

She didn't look around to see which friends had come for her triumph. She couldn't afford to get distracted now. She gave Cary Bleeker a quick nod. Cary didn't notice; he kept glancing at the crowd as if they were about to charge over the cordon and steal the cameras. The city guy was fussing about the city's liability on the bluff.

She glanced at the small food trailer next to the catering truck. It was closed now—closed for her gag. The gray-haired cook stood in front, his white apron tied loosely over jeans, the nets off his hair and beard. Lark lifted a hand in salute. He grinned, doffed his sunglasses, and gave her a thumbs-up. Like a flash of lightning, anxiety shook her so hard she couldn't see—the Gaige Move! God, to capture that here, now, to make the Move live again! To stand before the press and tell them—

The assistant director was in place, ready to give her her cue.

The time for idle thought was over. Her vision squeezed in from the sides, tunneling forward. If there were noises out there—the crowd, the cameras, car engines, motorcycles—she didn't hear them anymore. In her mind she saw only her path between the trenches to the end of the rise, and the camouflaged cement slab three yards from the edge onto which she'd "stagger" back to end the take. Bleeker had talked harness, but there was no way to do the Gaige Move in a harness!

She closed her eyes. Fear hollowed out her inner core now. It swirled cold in her empty chest and stomach. She took her place on the start mark.

"Quiet on the set!"

Kiernan watched as Lark Sondervoil stood at her mark and the city liaison ambled to the far side of the set.

"That was you in the red Jeep, wasn't it?" There was a slight twang to the speaker's muted voice. It took Kiernan a moment to pull her attention from the set and focus on him. His curly black hair fluttered in the wind and his dark blue eyes shone confidently, but his mouth was poised half open, waiting warily for her reaction. He was, she realized with a start, the guy on the motorcycle. "Sorry about the parking spot."

"Sorry enough to move your cycle?"

He shrugged. "Got me. If I'd known it would be this long till the Move—"

"You wouldn't have had to ace me out of the possibility of seeing it?"

"Yeah, well, I'm really not a lout. It's just that—well, see, I knew Greg Gaige. I saw him do the Move," he said, the hesitancy suddenly gone from his voice. His dark blue eyes had a faraway look. "I saw it the last time, right before he died."

Her breath caught. She turned to eye him straight on, but she could hear the hesitancy in her own voice as she asked, "How exactly did Greg die?"

"How?" He was not looking at her but glaring at the black-clad man on the set. "He was doing another gag—one that Cary Bleeker coordinated."

"Lark. You ready?"

"Ready." It took all her breath to make that come out strong.

"Camera. Action."

Lark Sondervoil took a breath, pushed off, and ran forward, her long tanned legs thrusting into the sandstone, blond hair billowing behind. She ran feeling everything, nothing, eyes on the cliff edge, each step free, flying—hers. She sailed over the warning chain and drove her feet against the ground. The explosives shot up sand and dust and rocks. She flew backward, legs straight, ankles tight to keep her feet from pointing, from looking too sleek. The ground gave minutely when her feet hit. Relief shot through her and was gone. The second explosion blew. She pushed off, corkscrewing her shoulders, pulling up with her pelvis, fighting the need to bend knees to chest, fighting to keep her legs straight, to nail the last half-twist and bring her feet down on the mark. And then they were there, marshmallowing into the ground. The *ground,* not the cement block, but that didn't matter now. She'd nailed it! The Gaige Move! She'd done the Gaige Move on film! Relief rippled through her more fully, but slowly now. The wind seared her skin. Her heart pounded. She pressed her teeth together to keep from grinning ear to ear from the joy of it all. The shot wasn't over—she still had the stagger-steps.

She had to look terrified! Forcing her eyes open wide, she did the first of the three stagger-steps back toward the cliff. Then the ground gave under her feet! What was happening? She had to stop. But she'd blow the scene. The second step. The ground was—the ground was squeezing out from under her feet. The hell with the scene! She thrust her shoulders forward and grabbed. Her hands clutched air. She couldn't stop! She flung herself forward, facedown to the dirt. Her elbows hit and bounced her backward. She was over the edge of the cliff. Falling in air! Panic squeezed her heart. She tried to stare through it. She grabbed for her knees. Flip, goddamn it—flip to grab for the rim of the catcher-trap. She yanked all out. The turn was taking, she was flipping over, her head toward the bluff, hands out. She'd be okay; she'd make it.

The cliffside came in sight—no catcher.

She kept turning. She saw the beach exploding up at her.

CHAPTER 2

CARY Bleeker's eyes widened in horror as he watched Lark Sondervoil flail over the cliff. That wasn't in the scene. What the hell was Lark doing? He'd never have asked her to go right into the high fall—without a wire, yet. She could be killed. The camera crew hadn't checked their focus for that yet; the whole high fall could be one big blur.

He took a step toward the bluff, would have *run* out there like an idiot, but the burst of applause from the tourists caught him. The camera on the crane was at the bluff edge; it'd be fine. Thank God he hadn't called cut. Thank God they'd had the camera over the bluff rolling, on the off chance there'd be something to use. He was covered. Better than covered. A smile stretched his narrow-lipped mouth across his cheeks. Goddamn, Sondervoil was good. He couldn't even complain about that press conference of hers, and the fucking crowd the size of Pasadena—not with the shot she'd just given him. No doubt about it, Sondervoil was the best.

It wasn't until he turned to his production assistant and started to speak that he realized he'd been holding his breath. Sixty thousand dollars tied up in this scene, and the studio execs on the horn every day. If this gag had gone belly-up, his ass would have been hanging as if he were in a grocery window in Chinatown, looking more wizened than the smoked ducks on the next hooks. If some asshole in the crowd had . . .

But it had been okay. More than okay. The Gaige Move had been great, and better yet, the scene that followed it, the high fall, *looked* fine. If it was and they didn't have to reshoot it, they wouldn't have to hang around till five thirty tomorrow night. They could break set after the morning shoot tomorrow. It would save them a half day. With salaries, rentals, meals, hotels, what would it come to? Ten thousand dollars? He'd have to call the line producer. God, that was one call he'd enjoy making. *If* Buddy had gotten it on film.

"Super!" He grinned at Jessa Mann's serious little face. The kid looked like an amalgam of every production assistant he'd ever had in his fifteen years directing. Always eager, always earnest, with enough reined-in drive to create a full-blown ulcer or a director's slot of their own in five years.

"Perfecto. Lark added that great scream when she disappeared over the edge, didn't she?" As soon as the words were out of her mouth, Jessa flushed. He could have reassured her, told her that unlike her picture of "the director," he didn't have to have every subordinate pretend every idea and innovation had burst full-grown from his own genius. He could have told her he understood the Hollywood game as well as she thought she did. But he understood it well enough not to blow his own image. "What do you think?" she bubbled.

"It's a knockout." He gave her back a little rub. The Move had been terrific. Sondervoil had insisted she could pull it off. He'd seen Greg Gaige do it, and Sondervoil was almost as good. He hadn't believed her when she first broached the idea, or when she insisted. No man had ever copied Gaige. He'd never really believed a woman could pull it off, much less a novice like Lark Sondervoil. But he'd go to his grave with that secret. To Jessa, Sondervoil, and the studio, he'd known it all along, he was a prescient director who could spot a talent and squeeze the most from her.

"You want me to get on to Publicity, Cary, and get a mention in the trades?"

Bleeker nodded. All of Hollywood would be reading about this major gag in tomorrow's *Variety* and *Hollywood Reporter.* He hoped it wasn't too late to make their deadlines. By tomorrow, the words "Cary Bleeker" would be as prevalent at dinners as "More wine?" Nobody would be calling him Bad Luck Bleeker anymore. "Daring." "Innovative." That was what they'd be saying. By Wednesday, his agent would be piling up scripts, juggling lunch invites, and slotting in meetings. He glanced out over the set, his last set as second unit director. By this time next week, he'd be choosing his first film as director. "Write up the gag, and let 'em know if we break set a day early. Tomorrow do a follow-up on how much under budget that puts us." He'd taken a big chance on Lark Sondervoil; now she could share the credit for the early finish.

Don't get ahead of yourself, Cary, he reminded himself. Don't let the gods know your dream. "Jessa, wait till I've checked with Buddy on the camera platform." He lifted the two-way radio. "Buddy, you were rolling, right? You got the whole thing all the way to the beach?"

He could hear Buddy breathing into the phone. Dammit, the man wasn't answering! Why couldn't cameramen behave like craftsmen instead of goddamned *artistes?* A stab of fear punctured Bleeker's chest. Maybe Buddy hadn't been ready. Maybe he had figured he could space out while Lark did the Gaige Move and tune back in when the PA called for the high fall gag. Dammit, he *should* have been ready! He wasn't paid just to sun himself down there on the platform. "Buddy, Lark was spectacular. Did you get the whole fall?"

"Yeah." The syllable was barely audible through the phone's static. This was taciturn even for Buddy.

The cold knife in his chest twisted. What could have gone wrong? Once Buddy got himself lowered down and tied onto the platform, all he had to do was follow the action from top to bottom. A guy with a camcorder could do that.

"You get the dummy?"

"Unh-unh."

"No?" Cary was yelling. "You didn't get the damned dummy? How could you miss it? Didn't the spring work?" Dammit, he should have gone over that spring with Special Effects, made sure that that dummy would fly out twenty feet so it didn't bounce down the cliff and get hung up somewhere on the scrub. Calm yourself, Cary. Buddy's still on the platform. He can reshoot the dummy. There's time to shoot it today and still break set tonight. Calm. "What happened with the dummy?"

"Nothing." Silence. "Can't you see over the edge of the bluff?"

"No. We're all too far back. Why?" The icy knife cut back and forth through his chest, his heart.

"Cary, the dummy never ejected. Lark never hit the cocoon, Cary. . . . She went . . . off to the side. She . . . crashed all the way to the ground. Cary, she's dead."

Dead! Cary couldn't breathe. The glaring sunlight that had danced around him pressed in from all sides, squeezing his ribs. He forced himself to inhale slowly and speak carefully. "Tell me exactly what happened, and what you got on film."

"Like I said, she just missed her mark and went over too far north. Just a few feet, it looked like from here. I mean, you can't tell distance from this angle. But that's what it looked like. She never even touched the cocoon—"

"And it never ejected the dummy at all, then?"

"No. Dummy's still safe and sound underneath."

Bleeker was barely breathing at all. He could hardly force himself to ask the key question. "How did she fall? Did she hit the cliff side and bounce, or did she fall straight down?"

"What difference . . ." The cameraman's voice trailed off, and when he resumed speaking, his words were speared by anger. "She bounced off the cliff two or three times. Big bounces, Cary. Big, splashy, goddamned bounces, like you'd never get with a dummy. I got it all on film. It's the best action shot you've ever done, Cary. It'll make you a hero."

Bleeker folded the phone before he could hear the click of the camera operator breaking the connection. He pushed away the fury and disgust in the man's voice. He'd have plenty of opportunity to hear that again, from plenty of mouths. Half of Hollywood would call him a ghoul for using the footage. The other half would label him a fool if he didn't.

CHAPTER 3

"OMIGOD, she's dead down there," a man yelled. "The stunt woman—she went off the bluff wrong! Fell all the way to the beach!"

As one, the crowd of onlookers turned toward the cliffs. Kiernan stood stunned. Dead? Sweat coated her skin, and yet she felt icy cold. Her stomach churned with guilt. She'd half hoped Lark Sondervoil would take a wrong step, maybe blow the landing on the Gaige Move. She'd only wanted Sondervoil to not quite nail it—nothing worse than that. She hadn't wanted the girl to *die*.

She was shaking so hard, she had to press her arms against her ribs to steady them and squeeze her throat closed against a wave of nausea. *Nineteen years old!*

Across the cordons on the set, people were moving as if on remote control, or racing around aimlessly like the remote had shorted out. Beside her Yarrow, the motorcyclist, leaped the outer cordon, then the inner one, both times landing on his good leg. He raced up to the director just as the man was putting his walkie-talkie in his black shirt pocket. "What the hell's going on here, Bleeker?"

Bleeker glanced quizzically, then started toward the trailers.

Yarrow grabbed his arm. "Don't pretend you've forgotten me, Bleeker. We've worked together too damned much for that shit. Trace Yarrow. Now tell me, dammit—is she dead?"

Bleeker's small brown eyes narrowed; he looked down at Yarrow and shook his head. "Nearly four hundred feet down a sandstone cliff, where the softest thing is brush that would scrape your skin off—what do you think?"

"What the hell happened?"

"She went right into the high fall. She was supposed to stop"—he seemed to be pleading—"to hook on to the wire—"

"You're blaming *her,* Bleeker? *You're* the second unit director here! You're responsible. Where's the union rep?"

Bleeker stared, his head shaking again, but slowly, dazedly.

Yarrow grabbed his lapels. "Oh, no. You're not going to get away with it this time. Not like Greg Gaige, when he—"

Bleeker seemed to come alive. He shook free. "Get off the set, Yarrow. You've got no business here. And don't go laying this on me. Lark was supposed to be on the wire. She chose not to. The set was supposed to be empty—no one here but the crew—and she sends teasers out to every media outlet in San Diego. If she got spooked by the crowd, it's her own fault. The girl was out for publicity." He took a breath and said with disgust, "She was a daredevil."

"*Daredevil!* Listen, you—"

"No! I don't have time for this. We were already days behind schedule. By the time this business is cleared away, we'll be weeks late."

Two guards started toward the pair. Bleeker turned and strode off. Yarrow glared after them, then stomped back across the cordon next to Kiernan. "No stunt double would go off a cliff without a wire! Something's real fishy here. They're covering up. Just like when Greg died in the fire gag." He turned toward the bluff. "I've got to get out there and see—"

What about when Greg died? she wanted to ask, but there was no time for that. She grabbed his arm. "No, you don't. The cops will be here any minute."

"They don't know anything about gags. They won't know what to look for. By the time they have a clue about what they're after, they'll have trampled it into the ground."

The people around them who had stood alone in stunned silence now clumped together in threes and fours, murmuring, pointing to the bluff, eyeing the set, moving a step toward the bluff, but unwilling to leave the spots they'd staked out. On the set, the security guards backed away from the crowd, toward the unlit banks of lights and the cameras they were protecting. The production assistants she'd seen scurrying around the set huddled, hanging on to each other, their backs to the bluff. The shrill rise of a distant siren sliced through the nubby sounds of the bluff. Two men—directors? producers?—walked together by the cordon. The shorter one shook his head. "How far behind schedule is this whole business going to throw us?"

Kiernan jammed her teeth together to keep from shouting, *Hey, a woman is dead, and all you care about is your schedule?* A stunt woman, a *gymnast*, like Lark Sondervoil spends her whole adolescence practicing, half the time with bruises up and down her legs, her wrists or ankles so badly sprained they have to be taped, with shin splints, pulled hamstrings, broken bones, concussions, every day risking landing on her neck and never walking again, all to perfect something like the Move to do for your goddamned movie. Now she dies, and all you guys care about is your sacred schedule!

Lark's death had nothing to do with Kiernan; logically, she accepted that. But viscerally, she knew she owed Lark. She stared hard at the two men, still talking—hoping? *planning?*—to shove this inconvenient death under the rug! Her hands squeezed into fists. Dammit, they would not get away with it!

That much she could do for Lark.

She turned to Yarrow. "Yarrow, are you saying this was no accident? Do you honestly believe the director had something to do with Greg Gaige's death?"

"Two top-notch stunt doubles die a decade apart, and both times he's directing. What do you think?"

Kiernan hesitated.

"You saw her run through the gag. It was perfect, right?"

She nodded.

"And that time she landed a couple of yards from the edge of the cliff. So do you think when it came to the real thing, she suddenly decided to add a few steps in the middle and trot off the cliff?"

When gymnasts compete for a medal, they may be forced to drop a move, but they never take the chance of adding one. Surely stunt doubles were the same. "Yeah—?"

"Look, the whole setup is weird." His words came faster, his voice more urgent. "Stunt doubles—they're supposed to be invisible. Like the star did everything. But Lark, she contacts the media, gets herself a ton of publicity, all these spectators, and a press conference. That's crazy. You pull something like that, and you never work again. Lark knew that. So why take the chance, huh?"

Kiernan watched Yarrow, his foot tapping on the sandy ground, his thumbs looped into his pockets, as close to hands-on-hips as he could get, his whole body leaning forward, pushed so close she felt as if he were going to suck up her air. The last thing she wanted was to be allied with him. Still, she had to ask, "You think it had something to do with Greg?"

"Makes sense."

"When Greg died, were they upset only because it put them behind schedule?" She noted Yarrow's startled face; even she was surprised by the bitterness in her voice.

Yarrow nodded. "They got him in the ground as fast and cheap as they could."

The siren gulped and started another rise.

She couldn't walk away. "Okay." The word was barely audible. She swallowed and said, "We need to be sure. I'll check the bluff."

"You? And you won't be tramping over the evidence? What—you'll be hovering two feet above the ground?"

"I've handled plenty of investigations; I know how not to disturb the scene. I'm a licensed investigator." The siren shrilled.

From nearer the set came a low moan. Ezra! She couldn't leave him. But there was no time to take him back to the Jeep. She assessed Yarrow: trustworthy, but only marginally so. Enough to leave him in charge of Ezra? She pulled her key ring from her pocket and snapped off the Jeep's. "Take my dog back to the Jeep. You remember it, don't you? A red Jeep Cherokee parked at the far end of the lot."

Yarrow nodded, the hint of a grin tickling the tense set of his mouth and then vanishing.

She stared him in the eye. "If anything happens to my Jeep, you're in deep shit. If anything happens to my *dog,* don't plan to inhale."

A siren cut the air behind her. In the parking area she could see two policemen, busy dealing with the crowd. Damn—she'd waited too long. In a minute their reinforcement would arrive and clear the bluff. She turned and ran toward it.

Twenty feet from the edge of the bluff, she stopped. The sirens were closer. Exactly where had Lark Sondervoil gone over? One rise of dry bluff looked like the next: little ripples of land shoving up beside the trenches that the wind had cut into the bluff.

The ground was hard and scrabbly; only the heaviest of skids would mark it. Any mark Lark Sondervoil had made here had been destroyed by the special effects blasts. Kiernan bent over, scanning the edges of one hole, then the other. Both were empty but for the remnants of the light and sound devices.

She needed to rerun Lark's movements in her mind. No, no time for all that. But she *had* to. Quickly she scanned the Move, figuring where Lark would have landed after her final double backflip. From there she hurried toward the edge of the bluff where Lark had stumbled off.

Kiernan wasn't afraid of heights—if she had been, she'd never have admitted it, even to herself. *Especially* to herself. But she wasn't. She had never *not* looked down. Looking down had been the reward of climbing up.

But now she was moving flat-footed, cautiously, too slowly. The sand swirled around her feet, particles the wind had picked loose from the sandstone bluff.

Brakes squealed. The siren cut off in midwail. From the parking lot she could hear car doors banging. The wind ripped at her shirt, battered it against her ribs. She planted her legs hard and looked down, down the nearly four hundred feet to the beach.

The way down was smooth for this bluff. But it wasn't perpendicular. Knife-sharp protrusions dotted the cliff wall. On the nearest one, maybe a hundred feet below, she could see something blue. Lark's leotard had been blue. She swallowed against the too vivid picture and forced herself to look farther down, but there were no telltale signs on the cliffs beneath. Nothing till the blue blotch in the middle of a small crowd on the beach. Almost directly beneath where she was standing.

From behind her came the wind-muffled croaks of a bullhorn. She had to get off the bluff. They'd reprimand anyone traipsing across the crime scene, but a private investigator they'd throw the book at. She looked down, right and left. Her eyes widened. She wondered if Lark had seen and understood. There to her left, twenty feet below the next rise of the bluff, was a white cocoon, big and tough enough to catch any stunt woman.

Any stunt woman who had gone off that mesa.

Lark Sondervoil had stumbled off the wrong mesa.

An icy chill swirled in her stomach. She found herself looking from the fluffy safety of the catcher to the long, hard, and rocky fall beneath her.

On the beach, official cars (tiny black rectangles topped with flashing red-and-yellow specs) were converging from both directions. State park lifeguards—fully badged peace officers who were closer to cops than beach boys—were probably already in the crowd down there. Farther south on the beach she could make out an ambulance. And in the distance to the north, a helicopter. Life Flight, she thought.

By the time she could get down to the beach, the body would be gone. Quickly, she scanned the bluff.

For the first time she noticed the platform fifteen feet beyond the catcher. It held a camera and two men sitting with their backs pressed against the bluff. "Omigod!" she said aloud. They must have gotten Lark Sondervoil's fall on film. That was where the answers could be.

"Move back off the bluff," a loudspeaker blared. "This is the police. Everyone out on the bluff, move back behind the line. Now!" Two pairs of uniformed officers were running toward the bluff.

She glanced over at the set, trying to spot Bleeker, the director. The man was nowhere in sight. She needed to see that film. Fast, before the police confiscated it. She strode off toward the parking lot, restraining the urge to break into a run until she was well past the police.

Yarrow was standing by the Jeep, hands in pockets, his foot tapping. "Well?" he demanded.

"I was out on the bluff," she said panting, "at the spot where Lark . . . It was the wrong spot. The catcher is . . . ten feet to the south."

"Ten feet away? How the hell could that happen?"

"Maybe Lark panicked?"

"Lark? Never!"

"Maybe she just screwed up. Daredevils screw up."

"Daredevil? *Daredevil?!*" His face hardened. "Lark Sondervoil was no daredevil," he said, spitting out the term like an expletive. "You heard Bleeker, huh? Well, Bleeker's an ass. Where does he get off calling her irresponsible? He's the second unit director—the stunt coordinator— he's the one who's supposed to be creating these gags, directing them, the one who should have the expertise to plan them. That's *his* job!

"Hell, considering it's Cary Bleeker," he yelled over the wind and engine roars, "it's no surprise he acts like he just wandered onto the set with sandwiches. It probably *was* Lark who orchestrated the whole gag. But Bleeker is responsible. Lark was as good as they come, but she was only nineteen years old. The girl hadn't lived long enough to know she *could* die!"

"The Gaige Move was perfect," said Kiernan, "so either she shifted the angle of the line of approach, or she started at the wrong spot."

"The line of approach was straight at the bluff—no mistaking that."

"Okay. . . . But if she planned the stunt, wouldn't she have noticed the start marker was moved?"

That stopped him. It was a moment before he said, "Normally, I'd say yes. But here, when the start marker is the cordon pole—well, the cordon might as well be a solid wall; it's not something you would think might have moved."

"Once she started, wouldn't the ground feel different to her?"

"She'd checked everything herself," Yarrow said slowly, clearly thinking as he spoke. "Lark was always A-plus responsible. That gives you a feeling of confidence," he said in more of a question than an answer. "But," he said, looking sure for the first time, "the down side is, you trust that feeling. She'd checked it all. Why would she think the cordon might move between the check and the scene call?"

"But still, Yarrow, if it *felt* wrong—"

"She should have stopped the moment she sensed something was off. Of course. But look, here's reality. She's got one take to do the biggest gag of her career. If she nails it, she's a queen. They'll forget how pissed off they were about her publicity and all. But if she stops midway through or loses her concentration and muffs it, maybe she throws the whole schedule back a day, costs the studio a bundle. Then no matter how good she does the Gaige Move, all the studio remembers is a publicity slut who cost them an extra ten thousand dollars." The cracking in his voice betrayed him; he stopped and squeezed his eyes shut. "Goddamn it, Bleeker's been directing stunt work on and off for fifteen years. What was the matter with the man? What ever made him try a gag like this on location? He could have made a mock-up in the studio—"

"How?"

Yarrow glanced around, eyes lighting on his motorcycle as if he'd come on it by surprise. "How do you mock up, detective? Look, you can mock up anything if you're willing to pay for it. You hire an architect, he'll build you the world—and have it blow up in your face eight times if you need it to. And to do a mock-up of this set, it'd be a snap. Mock up the bluff with a ten-foot drop onto Porta Pits or safety bags, do a cover shot—easy with a gag like this. Cut from Lark falling, to the cover shot of what would be her view straight down the bluff, then cut back to the dummy falling out of the bottom of the catcher. Simple."

Kiernan nodded. "Like Butch and Sundance in their last leap."

"Yeah, sure. It's all illusion. All life's illusion, if you know where the breaks are."

Before he could change the subject, she said, "So why didn't Bleeker do a mock-up?"

"You're thinking logic. Forget it. Bleeker didn't care about that. He wanted a 'great' shot. You're not in the business, are you?"

"No, I just came to see Lark. I wanted to see the Gaige Move. And the high fall."

"You and goddamned Cary Bleeker. Only he wanted them on film. He wanted the high fall with the setting sun behind it. Artsy. So when Lark went off the bluff, both she and the sun were going down."

"Couldn't he have done that with the mock-up?"

"Yeah, sure."

"Couldn't he have done it better in the studio, under controlled conditions?"

"He could have. He *should* have. But look, you're missing the point."

"Which is?"

"If he had had Lark Sondervoil do the Gaige Move on a mock-up and she had performed that Move as perfectly as she told everyone she could, what do you think people—by which I mean influential people in the industry—would be saying when the film was previewed?"

" 'Lark Sondervoil performed an astounding feat.' "

"You got it. Or let me shorten that for you. They'd be saying: 'Lark Sondervoil . . .' Those are not the words that Cary Bleeker wants coming from their lips. Not to warm his heart, not like 'Cary Bleeker directed,' or better yet, just 'Cary Bleeker!!!' You getting it yet?"

Kiernan nodded acknowledgment. "For Bleeker, this film is like a résumé, right? The patient died, but the operation was still a success."

"Yeah, and if the patient died onscreen, in a spectacular fall, you can bet the operation was a success that Bleeker couldn't have hoped for. He says he figured she'd do the Gaige Move flawlessly. And she did. Not as good as Greg, but—but he never could have counted on her moving right into the high fall."

"What do you mean? Wasn't that in the script?"

"Sure. In the stunt plan. It was the next gag."

Kiernan tapped a finger on the motorcycle seat. "You mean Lark was supposed to *stop* with the Gaige Move?"

"And harness up before she went over the bluff. No stunt double would do anything as suicidal as a fall like that, no matter how many times they'd routined it."

"Except a daredevil."

Kiernan expected Yarrow to snap back at her. Instead he shook his head. "You got it. That'll be the official word."

Behind them brakes squealed, police radios spat out syllables, doors slammed. The parking lot was as hectic as it had been when Yarrow first cut her off with his motorcycle.

"So what'll happen now?" she asked Yarrow.

"Studio and everyone here will be covering ass like the queen was paying a surprise visit to Black's Beach."

She nodded. "The 'clothing optional' section."

"Yeah, and by the time they're finished, their buns will be under so many layers of clothes, you'll think they've been invited to the royal ball."

"But the police—"

He put a hand on her shoulder. "Honey, the cops may be good, but they're dealing with the masters of illusion here, with a crew that's so used to watching their backs, they can run full out with their eyes over their shoulders. And make no mistake about it, the last thing Cary Bleeker wants—any of them wants—is the truth. They've got their fall on celluloid. Already, they're thinking how to get the biggest splash from it. They don't want the police parceling out the news releases, showing the film before they can. With all the media here, it's a publicity bonanza for them. All they've got to do is keep control."

"And finding out what happened to Lark Sondervoil?"

"Dead is dead. In this business you only pack what you can carry on."

"And that is?"

"The spin from the gag. Gags don't get publicity. But this one, with all the media here, it could be a box-office bonanza. More to the point—the only point—it'll make or break careers. Hey, you're a detective, right?" he asked without a break.

"Yes," she said warily.

"Okay, I'm hiring you."

"Not so fast, *honey*. You don't buy me like a pound of meat." She caught herself before she went on about her medical expertise and her considerable fees. Or warned him that private investigators could not legally undertake murder cases without a police okay. That issue she could work around: no one else was talking murder yet.

And Yarrow—she knew he'd be trouble. She'd been attracted by guys with that raw intensity too often over the years; she knew its down side by heart. But none of that mattered; she owed Lark Sondervoil.

"We got a deal?" Yarrow demanded.

"Can I get a look at the film?"

"Sure. No problem."

"No problem? The police will be confiscating the negative."

"You think these guys are going to give up their only copy for something as inconsequential as death? The negative's already at the lab, believe me. And tonight they'll hold the postmortem over the dailies."

"At the hotel where they're staying?"

"Normally, yeah. But not tonight, not with the cops liable to trot in and confiscate that film. No, they'll find somewhere else."

"Yarrow, isn't there anyone you haven't ticked off too much to ask?" She sighed. Exactly the kind of trouble she'd expected.

She assumed he would snap back at her, but he laughed. "Not many. I call 'em as I see 'em. 'Course, there's Liam."

"Liam?"

"The city liaison. He and I go back more than ten years. I got him his first job in the movies. Took him away from doing the taxes for the head of Pacific Breeze Computer, a startup company where I was 'consulting.' He owes me. Besides"—he nodded in agreement with his thought—"he hates these slipshod bastards. This is his last dealings with the movie people. He's going to a snazzy job in the state treasurer's office. He says politics is the straight and narrow compared to this business. And this—Lark—it'll be the last straw. He knew her. He'd be glad to help you—and to screw them."

"Do I hear a *but*?" she asked.

"Alas, you're dealing with the one person on the set for whom a contract is a contract, a commitment is a commitment. He's still got a contract with them. He won't betray them to you."

"We'll see," she said.

CHAPTER 4

"THERE'S nothing more I can be telling you," Liam McCafferty said to the reporters, clustered behind the line of trailers at the edge of the set. A growing number, Kiernan was sure. From his tone, she was also sure it wasn't the first time McCafferty had made that announcement. In a tan suit and tie—the only suit on the bluff—he looked like an Irish schoolmaster dismissing an unruly class.

She waited until he had walked a few yards, past another trailer and a group of extras clumped together tearfully behind it, to catch up with him. "Terrible thing."

He glanced at her, a glint of suspicion momentarily visible in his brown eyes. Then a smile pulled his skin into folds that seemed right for him. "Ah, the lass with the fine wolfhound. Where is the noble beast?"

"Back in the huge vehicle I bought for his comfort."

"As it should be, lass. As it should be. But it is a wretched thing about poor little Lark." He glared back at the sorrowful trio behind him. "Not that any of them cares. Crocodile tears, they're shedding."

"Just because they're doing their mourning in full makeup in the parking lot, within camera range of the press?"

"Aye. They wouldn't recognize a real emotion—not in Hollywood. If it's not awesome," he said acidly, "earthshaking, five-star, it's not worth a thing. They think they mourn, just as they believe they love, but they don't love anything but their careers."

The man was quite an actor himself, with his almost stage-Irishman brogue. "Is that so different from politics?" she couldn't resist asking.

He paused, considered. "It is. There success is the only thing, but everyone understands the rules."

"But—"

"Liam," a woman called from across the set.

"Duty calls, lass," McCafferty said, and shuffled off, looking out of place among the young, layer-clad denizens of the set.

She started after him, but it was no use. She'd come up empty. Damn! McCafferty did remind her of her uncle Matt, and Matthew O'Shaughnessy was a born politician, a man who could respond to a question with such charm that few realized he'd trailed them down the path of his own disarming philosophy and led them nowhere near the answer they sought.

No, wait. She wasn't on empty yet. She caught one of the walkie-talkie crew. "Liam needs to know where the rushes will be tonight."

"That's not my area."

"Find out! It's important. I have to get back to him now! I'll be over there fending off the press." Without waiting for a reply, she strode across the edge of the parking lot. The reporters stood in a loose knot, as if they were in a moment of stasis before centripetal force whirled them in more tightly around their prey or centrifugal force spun them back to their offices. She recognized Jake Steingroot, the film critic for the *Union-Tribune*. She'd met him at the opening of the last Woody Allen picture. "Jake, do you have a copy of the press release?"

"Kiernan?" he said distracted. "Nah. Nothing in it."

"Then why are you here?"

"Sondervoil came to the paper in person." He paused, then shrugged. "Hey, it's not us Pavlov-ing around a pretty young face. The girl hinted there would be more than met the eye about this gag."

"More what?"

"Didn't say. But I, and they"—he motioned at the rest of the press corps—"figured what the hell, it's worth a chance. A slow Tuesday afternoon. Even if she didn't say a word worth quoting, the shot of her going over the bluff would be a front page photo. How about that for prescient thinking?"

"Got it!" The walkie-talkie boy eyed Kiernan conspiratorially, waiting till she moved away from Steingroot. "The dailies," he said, "they'll be at the UC campus theater."

She turned back for Steingroot, but the critic was ambling across the parking lot. And, she decided, he could no more answer the big question than she. Lark Sondervoil had gone to the media in person, a gutsy and time-consuming move for a nineteen-year-old. Why? Was she what the media called a publicity slut? Or was there something more to this gag, something that was connected to her death?

Kiernan pulled into the driveway of her duplex to drop off Ezra and grab dinner before the rushes—viewing the day's film from all the cameras—began at seven. She sat with the Jeep window open, her head sticking out next to Ezra's, the two noses alert for the same aphrodisiac —cooking odors flowing from Brad Tchernak's flat. How could she think of food when a young woman was lying in the morgue? She'd been asked a variation of that question often enough. But not at the coroner's office when she'd been there, nor in pathology rotation, nor by the cops in Homicide. In medical school she'd learned to grab a nap anytime, go without sleep for thirty-six hours at a stretch, and keep life and death separate.

Ezra leaped from the back of the Jeep and loped toward the kitchen— ever the optimist, she thought. It was well after six, time Tchernak should be chopping and sautéing, stirring—or whatever chefs did. It had been weeks since the last sauerbraten, or Tchernak's succulent paella with sea anemones, baby cherrystones, and Walla Walla onions. She listened for the whir of the blender, the clatter of spoon against mixing bowl, the sounds appropriate to the kitchen of her cook/house-keeper/dog-walker.

What sounds emerged through Tchernak's wide-open windows were clanking metal and grunting man.

Kiernan shook her head. Crashes of weight bars from Tchernak's parlor-cum-weight-room had jarred her ten or twelve times an hour, at any hour of day, seven days a week, for over a month now. Dammit, she didn't need to accommodate Tchernak in his lunacy. The man wasn't a husband; he was merely an employee.

But Tchernak was more than an employee. He was an employee who wanted her. At least sporadically. And one, she had to admit, with a sexy, rough-cut face and a cute little beard, and a body she wouldn't kick out of bed—theoretically speaking. You don't sleep with the men you work with, any sensible woman knows that. Those relationships are like quicksand: real soft to slip into, worth your life to get out of, and you're both left covered with muck. But in the same house, well, re-straint certainly wasn't easy. There were times when the lure of him was truly tempting. But he wasn't her type, and besides, there were reasons why their relationship was a business one, or almost just a business one —reasons on both sides.

A voice in her head said: What's the matter with you? A young, attractive guy with a body that's state of the art? A guy who tracks down bluefish caught in one of the few unpolluted areas off Jersey and bakes them as God would if He cooked; who brings you *doppio caffe latte* in bed, in a Thermos that keeps it warm till you wake up. A guy who loves your dog. What more do you want?

But then, no one ever pretended pathologists were normal.

She got out, opened the back door, and watched Ezra bound into Tchernak's half of the building. The clanking stopped, and the panting switched to eager canine greeting.

Kiernan leaned back against the fender. Why had she hired Tchernak to begin with? She'd wanted to simplify her life, stop hassling with housecleaning services, the takeout Thai, Vietnamese, and Mexican deliveries, and the pizza shop that would come through on the all-too-many nights when she forgot about dinner till everything else was closed. She'd been desperate to end the frustrating search for the perfect dog-sitter who would feed, walk, and fawn over Ezra and approve when his mistress called twice a day and asked "to speak to Him."

She had wanted an unobtrusive cook/housekeeper, a mature lady with fifty years of experience over stove and vacuum cleaner, and five-mile-on-the-beach thighs for Ezra's run. Was that asking too much? She hadn't planned on a six-foot-four, 240-pound thirty-year-old ex-football star who couldn't get it through his head that his days on the gridiron were over. Six years was the average career for an offensive lineman, she'd reminded him more than once. The average healthy twenty-eight-year-old lineman—if anyone could be considered healthy after being smacked around professionally sixteen weeks a year for six years— retired from the game or was cut from the team roster. What the hell made Brad Tchernak think that after three ruptured discs and three years out of the game, he could stage a comeback?

Tchernak grumbled amicably about being a servant, but for him, a job that provided free housing and didn't interfere with his training schedule was a coup. Maybe too much of one. The man was setting himself up for a crashing disappointment that would leave him hanging around the phone every day for the entire football season, sure the call would come each time an offensive lineman went down. With each phone-silent hour, he'd be plunked deeper into the black well of despair.

He'd gone through this same torture last March. And April, May, and June, before he was finally forced to admit that he wasn't free agent material. He knew it was illogical, the odds astronomical, but he couldn't give it up.

And she'd realized that she could do nothing to ease the pain he kept shoving into the future. Nothing except fire him, and she couldn't bring herself to do that. It might be kinder, but she wasn't that kind.

Maybe the Hollywood people were right about emotions. There was a lot to be said for celluloid emotions that didn't mire you down and leave you distracted when you needed to work.

She ducked into her flat to change into more businesslike attire, the tan pants and quasi–bomber jacket her dressmaker had created to keep her from the racks of bows and ruffles that pass for women's clothes in the world of the petites. "I'll be back late!" she called into Tchernak's door on her way out. "I'll grab a burger out."

That Tchernak didn't ask about her afternoon said something about his obsession. That he wasn't curious about her sudden evening plans said more. But his indifference to her grabbing a burger, possibly fried rather than grilled, brown rather than gently pink, with no accoutrements more exotic than catsup spoke volumes.

She pulled out of the driveway and was back on Torrey Pines before she realized she didn't have time for dinner at all.

CHAPTER 5

KIERNAN spotted Cary Bleeker at the screening room, a small theater on the campus of UC San Diego, across North Torrey Pines Boulevard. She was surprised to find the second unit director himself guarding the door. A flunky would have been her guess—and her preference. But if Bleeker was worried about the police, this made sense. She hurried along the cement path, past droughtscape tundra, a reminder of La Jolla before the days of well-watered Kentucky bluegrass lawns. Twenty feet from the glass door, she slowed and looked past Bleeker into the dim-lit lobby, where five people stood shifting their weight, glancing around. They were close enough to touch each other, but none were pressing flesh, none were speaking. They looked like distant relatives standing in the foyer of a funeral parlor, unable to leave but fearful of confronting the corpse. Going to a *funeral,* not a wake like the ones at Saint Brendan's back in Baltimore, where a brief decrying of the irreplaceable loss was a mere prelude to making the most of it. More than once she had glanced at a silent face in the coffin and hoped the deceased's spirit was not hovering, watching in frustration maneuvers that he could no longer influence.

Though the group here looked familiar, Kiernan couldn't say for sure whether she had actually seen them on the set or not.

And she didn't have time to think about it. She had only a few steps until she would face Bleeker at the door. She'd planned on employing the truth—not always her first choice—but the silent tableau behind Bleeker screamed wariness. The last thing these people were likely to do was invite in a stranger—a stranger with a PI's license.

So on to Plan B, the result of a couple of calls and a little luck.

In the lobby a man leaned over and whispered to the woman next to him. Kiernan almost smiled in recognition. His face had none of the fervent, guilt-free conspiring that centuries of Celtic wakes had imbued, but there was no mistaking that look of machination.

She rapped on the door.

Bleeker's forehead wrinkled. "This is a private affair."

"That's why I'm here."

"Who are you?"

"Kiernan O'Shaughnessy. SAG," she said. Screen Actors Guild—*union*—the last word anyone in management wants to hear. She flashed her PI's license, knowing that Bleeker was not about to peruse it, not at a time like this. "So how long do you expect the rushes to take?"

"What? You know we don't let reps in to see the rushes."

Oh, shit! What you don't know—it will kill you every time. "Normally, sure," she said, "but we're not talking everyday event here. We're talking accident, fatal accident to one of our members."

"No way. I've got enough problems without you." Probably he hadn't realized he'd groaned out loud.

"Look, one of our members died on the set, going over a bluff for chrissake. We're going to have a shitload of questions to answer. We're in this together. We all want the same thing, right? Make it easy on yourself."

Behind him, the quintet edged toward the screening-room door. The gray-carpeted, gray-walled, half-lighted lobby looked too sterile to be real. The darkened candy counter sported not cascades of soda pop but bottles of designer juices. Too *California* to be real! The odds were only fifty-fifty that she would manage to slither into the screening room; best to hit the other questions while she had the opportunity. She waited until the screening-room door closed behind the five, then said to Bleeker, "You're the stunt coordinator. What went wrong with this gag?"

Bleeker swallowed, bobbing an Adam's apple large enough to choke him. The black fringe of hair, goatee, and twill-and-denim ensemble accented the sudden movement in his pale neck. He looked like a second-story man caught with his glass cutter out. "Nothing, except at the end. She had no business going right into the high fall."

Kiernan put a hand on his arm. "Cary, baby, I'm going to need an answer a bit more incisive than that."

"Look, can we talk about this later? Show a little respect. Lark's only been dead a couple of hours."

She patted his arm. "You know I'd take that plea more seriously if you weren't here ready to go over the rushes. So, Cary, you coordinated the gag?"

He glanced behind him, but there was no one there to save him. "I sketched it, but you know how it is. Nothing in this business is one person."

"Yeah, unless it's a credit on the trailer."

"Well, *credit*'s not the operative word when you've got a girl dead. Look, I spent the last couple hours with the police asking me ten questions for every one answer they thought they needed. I'm already a week behind schedule, and if I have to do this gag over, I'm going to be so far over budget that I might as well have jumped over the cliff with Lark Sondervoil, so can we talk about this after the rushes?"

She wasn't about to be put off. "Let's get it over with now. Just tell me what part of the gag you routined."

"The concept. Over the bluff. It was a helluva high fall gag. Dammit, it could have been a helluva gag. All I needed was a competent stunt woman to go flying over the cliff." He shook his head. "I got her the best catcher built. The supports are drilled ten feet into the bluff wall. Do you have any idea what I had to go through with the city to get a permit to drive metal beams into their sandstone bluff? You'd think I wanted to climb up Mount Rushmore and sink two-by-fours in Lincoln's nose! Damned negotiations with the city took so long, it threw the whole location schedule off, even though we'd allowed double the time we thought we'd need. McCafferty wouldn't give us the okay until two weeks ago."

McCafferty? Liam McCafferty, the wolfhound lover? "Well, why didn't you just use a mock-up in the studio?"

"Verisimilitude." He shrugged. "We could've shot it against a blue screen and dropped in the background later, but there were things we'd have lost. Look, everyone discussed this ages ago. Lark herself was all for it." He shrugged again. "Okay, so her real reason was the notoriety of doing the Gaige Move, then going over a bluff. I'm no innocent; I knew she was using us. But that's the business. But no way did I realize she'd use it as a gimmick to draw the press."

"Did she tell them she was going off without the wire?"

"Who knows? The first I heard of the goddamned press conference was when a reporter banged on my trailer door this morning. By then, it was too late to cancel it. Left us with enough gawkers to watch the parting of the Dead Sea. Security was snowed under. So if you're asking what went wrong with the gag, I'll tell you. Lark screwed it up with that crowd. *She* got 'em here, the pressure got to her, and she freaked."

"All her fault, right? And tell me, Cary, just why would she do that? If she called the press on her own, *if* she created a security nightmare— and mind you, I'm not copping to that—then why? People never work again for lots less, right? A girl like Lark, she didn't need to be grandstanding. She was headed straight for the top." Kiernan was getting into her role. "So why risk it all? What could have been so important for her to say?"

He shook his head. "No idea. Nobody knows. If you don't believe me, ask anyone."

Bleeker tossed in qualifiers with the instinctive defensiveness of the perpetual goat, Kiernan noted. "You're saying she took fatal risks for a little publicity? Come on. Our members are careful. We remind them their lives depend on checking their equipment themselves. Special Effects screws up a wire; they're sorry. The stunt double is dead."

"Look, if you're thinking it was me who suggested no net or wires, you're crazy. I had a decelerator. Wardrobe made her outfit so it would conceal the harness. The wire would have come out her ankle. If she'd been hooked on to the decelerator, she'd have braked all the way down the bluff. By the time she got to the beach, she'd have been going slow enough to pick daisies off the wall."

"So?"

"She couldn't do the Gaige Move with a wire on. But she was supposed to be on a wire for the fall. I insisted on it." He put a hand on her shoulder and squeezed. "I'm going to be straight with you. Lark Sondervoil was not the best woman for the high fall, nowhere near it. But she came in under budget. And she was the only one who could do the Gaige Move. And she was happy doing it at the edge. With this film as far over budget as it is, and the studio brass chewing on me like I was lunch, I couldn't pass that up."

Kiernan shook loose of the hand. "Come on, you're the director. You're telling me that a second-rate stunt woman forced you to forget about safety? Our members will be delighted to hear they've got such power."

"Okay, not forced—she didn't force me. I could have insisted she do the Gaige Move back from the edge. She was wired every time she tested the catcher. She must have jumped off that bluff five times a day every day this week. If I hadn't seen her go over today . . . if someone had just told me she'd bought the farm, I would have guessed she'd slammed into the catcher so often, she broke the supports."

Kiernan shook her head theatrically.

He flung up his hands. "So I got greedy. No greed, no lead in this business. I knew we'd get a better shot the way she wanted it. I'd seen her do the Gaige Move. Done her way, it would be a show-stopper. Maybe a saint would have turned that down, but lady, I'm just a man, and I'm not about to give up a lead. And I trusted her judgment. Who could imagine she'd just go on over? I didn't think she was a daredevil," he said, spitting out the last words like a slur.

"Hey, Cary, we don't have all night!" a bushy-haired man in work shirt and bandanna called from the theater.

"Look—"

"It's okay," Kiernan said, starting toward the theater.

"SAG—just for Lark's gag," Bleeker said to the quintet as he and Kiernan entered. It was more of a warning than an explanation, Kiernan could tell. He motioned her to a seat on the far side of the aisle from them. Rejecting that, she slipped into one at the back of their section. Bleeker shrugged and moved to the front and was no sooner in a seat than the lights went out.

In the darkened room, the air seemed raw with anticipation and dread. And she had the feeling that the finger of fate pressed across each pair of lips. No comment was worth prolonging the suspense.

The door opened; the lobby light smacked Kiernan's eyes. As the lobby door swung shut, Kiernan could make out the form of a small, sturdily built woman in what was probably a business suit. She was eating a bar of something that smelled of garlic.

"Dolly!" Bleeker exclaimed, "I didn't expect—"

"You didn't expect me here when we could get slapped with a wrongful death? When I was down here anyway?" She flopped into a seat in the front and plopped the rest of the food into her mouth.

"We're not liable," Bleeker insisted in a voice so unsure of itself that it halfway belied his words.

"Sweetie, we're always liable if they can prove negligence."

"Dolly, the scene was scripted to end at the bluff. The girl did the fall on her own. We took every precaution possible. We had a catcher strong enough to stop a meteor, with a Porta Pit deep enough for her to have smothered in. She tested everything."

"Cary, Cary, such an innocent boy. Now let's see that footage."

"Tom, cue up the fall sequence," Bleeker called.

The room remained dark; no introductions were made. Kiernan wished she knew whether it was because they all knew each other or because Dolly Whoever was so important no one else mattered. Whatever the reason, she was relieved.

The film started. It moved at normal speed, but the room seemed to have slipped into slow motion. Kiernan felt as if she could see the breaks between the frames of film.

Lark Sondervoil stood, the lights shining on her long blond hair, on that blue leotard that would soon be the focus of the ambulance crew and Life Flight medics on the beach. *Nineteen years old!* Kiernan thought. *When I was nineteen, I was planning for medical school, sure that I had the Answers by the tail, just waiting for me to learn enough to reel them in. It never occurred to me I wouldn't Know, much less that I could die.*

The camera was behind Lark, not beside her where the onlookers had been. It showed her racing straight forward over the warning rope. The explosion seemed disconnected from the action. But the double flip of the Gaige Move was perfect. The second explosion was off too.

Kiernan's chest went cold. The Move was perfect. It could have been done by Greg Gaige! Her fingers dug into the armrests; her whole body was icy. She *was* the Baltimore teenager again, watching film of Greg over and over again, alive with adoration, with dreams of emulating him that she couldn't admit were built on nightmares of failure.

Lark staggered back—for the first time the camera caught her face. The focus was cloudy, but Lark's expression of panic was clear enough to be almost real. *Could they use that? With the cloudy focus, Lark might look enough like the actress she was doubling. With all the publicity they'd get, would they care?*

Lark took another step back. The edge of the bluff was less than a yard behind her. *How could she have done anything so dangerous?* The instant the thought was words, Kiernan knew the answer. It was the same answer she would have given twenty-five years ago: "I know what I'm doing." She'd have tossed her head defiantly. "If I die it will be worth it; I'll be as good as Greg Gaige!"

Another step. Lark wavered. Her arms jutted out to the sides. She was off-balance. The expression of phony panic vanished, replaced by all-too-real concentration. Her head jerked forward. *Braking the back-motion.* Her foot slipped. She thrust both arms forward. *Save it! Save it!* She jolted down a foot. Her concentration vanished. Terror filled her eyes. She clawed at the air. Her mouth opened, but no sound came out. She slipped over the edge.

The film stopped.

No one spoke. Only Dolly groaned. "Christ, half of it's out of focus."

The film started. "Same scene. Crane shot." Bleeker's voice was shaking.

When that take ended, Dolly cleared her throat. "She's running parallel to the inner cordon. Was that the way it was planned?" There was no hesitancy in her voice.

"Yeah," Bleeker said. "Now C camera three, on the platform over the bluff."

"*Over* the bluff? Why was that one running at all on this scene, if she wasn't expected to go over?" a male voice asked.

"The light would be failing fast. We decided not to take time between the Gaige Move and the high fall to lower the camera crew down there. So we got them there before. And since they were there, why not? I figured I might get a cover shot out of it. Roll it, Tom."

The camera focused on the beach. Dots moved. *People.* It panned up the side of the bluff. Wind fluttered the small, scrappy leaves of whatever it was that survived there. Hard brown stems moved grudgingly. A spray of dirt spat from one rough promontory. Spears of sandstone thrust up like stalagmites, only to be topped by the ever-climbing hard, dry wall. The ascent seemed endless.

The picture shook, as if an earthquake were jolting the camera platform. Kiernan's breath caught. The camera jerked upward, catching Lark feet first as she plunged over the edge of the bluff, arms flailing uselessly, head bobbing forward in vain. She fell straight down. The big white cocoon blocked her from view. She hit the wall and bounced out into nothingness. The camera lost her, momentarily focusing on the spot where she had been, then jerked down to catch the electric-blue leotard as it dropped and hit and scraped down the sandstone, bounced and dropped again and again, to a spot hidden by an outcropping on the beach.

No one spoke. It wasn't until she heard breath let out ahead that Kiernan realized they'd all been too tense to breathe.

"Omigod," Bleeker said slowly, his voice was barely discernible. "Surely, she wasn't conscious . . ."

"If we'd known she was going to go over ten feet from the catcher, we could have saved a bundle and had a great shot to boot." It sounded like the bushy-haired guy. No one laughed.

It was a full minute before Dolly said, "The whole damned thing's out of focus. How . . . wait, she went off the wrong rise, didn't she! How the hell—"

"It's not like she hadn't run through the whole routine ten times," Bleeker insisted.

The room was still dark. Kiernan hesitated, balancing her advantage of eavesdropping against demanding an answer. But it was the woman next to Bleeker who voiced her question for her: "I heard a rumor that someone had moved the marker, so she went for the wrong pick point— her point, not the camera markers."

"Who?" Dolly and Bleeker demanded.

"I don't know. I can't even remember who told me. There was so much going on by then. But she ran straight down by the cordon. The cordon had to be the mark she was using, right?"

Bleeker groaned.

"Well, who the hell would move a marker?" Dolly asked. "A—we'd better hope that rumor doesn't spread. Well, fat chance, right? In this business, rumor is truth. So then, B—we'd better hope if there was a mover, it wasn't one of our grips. It wasn't, was it, Cary?"

"No," Bleeker forced out. "No, of course not," he added with surprising conviction. Kiernan discounted that hard-hatched assurance as she was sure everyone else did. Confronting Dolly with corporate culpability now would require the steadfastness of an oak. Bleeker was more akin to a willow.

"C," Dolly continued, "we continue to tell the press when they ask— and we're damned lucky they're not outside already—"

"I got use of this place through a friend," Bleeker put in quickly.

"C—we tell the press we are distressed and horrified. 'Of course, we're cooperating with any investigation,' blah blah blah. Nothing more. Got that?"

The murmurs of agreement seemed hesitant.

The actual markers that the camera crew had placed on the ground wouldn't be on the film, of course, Kiernan realized. So if you didn't realize why the focus was off, you wouldn't see the evidence here.

It was a moment before the bushy-haired one said, "And the studio does—?"

In the semidark Dolly stood up. She turned to the group and took a deep breath, and Kiernan waited for her to explain.

"Cary," she said, "where are the fucking lights?"

Kiernan moved next to the door, ready to bolt before they had time to remember she was here. Bleeker started for the door and stopped halfway, clearly unwilling to miss the vital bit of information. "Tom," he called loudly, "get the lights on."

Kiernan reached for the door.

"What we will do . . ." Dolly said softly.

Kiernan stayed put.

The lights came on. All eyes were on Dolly. Kiernan remembered seeing her with Bleeker on the set. She'd looked out of place there, but here—if appearances told the tale, Dolly could have been expected to carry a mop and pail. She was squat, middle-aged, devoid of makeup, and dressed in expensive brown slacks and a well-worn sweater, but no one who saw the well-creased line of her jaw and the intensity of her dark eyes would have mistaken her power. Or passed up the chance to hear her decisive pronouncement on handling Lark Sondervoil's death.

"We will leak the word about Lark's drug problem."

"Drugs?" Bleeker was torn, but he was alone in that. The other four sighed. *With relief? Or admiration?*

Kiernan held her breath, waiting for one of them to object. Or even question. But apparently no one was willing to risk dislodging their deliverance.

"Hold it right there!" Kiernan demanded. "Lark Sondervoil did the Gaige Move. No one's been able to do that since Greg Gaige died. No *woman's* ever mastered it. It takes control worthy of a gymnast of Greg Gaige's caliber to do that move. Who's going to see that and then believe that she was on drugs?"

As one, the group turned toward her, their faces unified in shock and fear. Bleeker looked as if the rug had been pulled out from beneath him and he was embarked on a fall that he'd always known would be inevitable. Only Dolly seemed unperturbed. If anything, she looked more determined than before.

"Who are you?" she demanded.

"SAG."

"Out!"

"The operative point is"—she stepped toward Dolly—"I'm the one here representing our interests. And I have never heard word one about Lark Sondervoil and drugs."

Dolly smiled, pausing long enough to savor her victory. "Well, sweetie, I can't speak to your information network. But if you want the official word on Lark and her drugs, you can check with the California Highway Patrol. They nabbed her last week, got a urine sample—her choice—and bingo—opiates."

Swallowing her shock, Kiernan thrust her hands on her hips. "Last week could have been last year. That says nothing about today."

"In the media it's everything," the bushy one said. "Once a junkie, always suspect."

"We're clear," Bleeker murmured.

"What kind of opiates? How much?" Kiernan demanded.

"Sweetie, we've been more than open with you," Dolly said, turning away from her as she spoke. "But we've got business now. So, out!"

"That's okay. Our lawyers are outraged. I've got calls to make." Leaving the threat dangling, Kiernan stalked out. It took her half the distance to the Jeep to shake the union rep persona. She loved being that in-your-face. And the final threat—she'd just added that for the hell of it. Bastards let a woman die and come up with this cockamamie story about opiates. Well, let them sweat a little. Dammit, she'd have them sweating until they were begging for offices in the deep freeze. She'd . . .

She climbed into the Jeep and rested her hands on the wheel. The first thing was to find out who Dolly was. Yarrow could tell her that. Whoever she was, she had so much authority that in the land where beauty is power, she dressed like a hag. And without a second thought, she'd admitted her oversight in allowing a stranger in the room too long. What would it take to unsettle her?

It was going to be a damned hard case, but there was one good thing. Going face to face with Dolly—well, Kiernan was going to enjoy that.

CHAPTER 6

DOLLY Uberhazy tapped a short thick finger against her arm. "Cary, get Archie Lesher on the line."

Bleeker flushed. He wasn't a flunky. Goddamned studio production executives had armies of flunkies. Was she treating him like a production assistant, like some nephew of some has-been, some kid right out of college, to humiliate him in front of the others? Or was there more to it than that? Was she signaling them that he was going to take the fall for whatever came out of Sondervoil's death? Oh, God, of course. Of course. But he couldn't deal with that now. Now the question was how to handle this order. He shrugged. "Sure. I've got his number back at the trailer. Do you have it with you?" He held his breath. Make her root through her purse—that'd slice the feet off her image. Only the illusion, of course; he knew it and Dolly knew it. But the rest of them weren't worrying about that now, and when they recalled this meeting, at least they wouldn't think of him as a gofer.

Dolly pulled out a plastic-covered notepad. Bleeker glanced up at the projection booth to cover his reaction. Wouldn't you know she'd have a dime store pad; the woman never missed a chance to remind them that she was too secure to bother with image. She handed him the pad. "In here, under the L's. I'm just doing this to cover bases, Cary. If that woman is representing Archie Lesher, I'm a flying turtle."

Cary dialed and waited. Should he handle the phone or give it to her? "Archie, Cary Bleeker here. I'm at the screening— Yeah, we are devastated about Lark Sondervoil. Overwhelmed. Such a talent, and a sweetheart. Dolly's here, and Edgar, Sally, and Max." He didn't ask about the O'Shaughnessy bitch. It was a gamble; he was holding his breath. He exhaled in relief and said, "Yeah, terrible about Lark. We're all distraught. Look, Arch, we just wanted to let you know that there's a woman passing herself off as your stand-in."

He exchanged glances with Dolly. The woman could give approval with less muscle work than anyone on the West Coast. And she was impressed. If he played his cards right, he could come out of this smelling like a rose—instead of stinking up the place. "I figured you'd want to know, Arch." He kept himself from taking another look at Dolly's face. Had he gone too far with the "*I* figured"? "No, of course, Archie, we didn't deal with the woman. I don't know who she was. Probably a groupie in here for a thrill." He didn't buy that for a minute; neither did Lesher, he was sure. He'd worry about who she was later; so would Lesher. But they weren't about to do their worrying together. "Yeah, man, we'll see you."

He clicked off the phone. He could have summarized Lesher's half of the interchange, but he waited till Dolly was forced to ask.

"So?" she said.

"Says he doesn't know who she is." Bleeker shrugged. "Maybe he doesn't."

"He doesn't." Dolly said. "Mata Hari–ing isn't Lesher's style. He's too smart to try a stunt like this with me."

Bleeker started, then forced a half smile. "Let's call this a wrap tonight. We're all too shot emotionally to be worth a damn on rushes. The rest will keep till tomorrow. Thanks for coming, Max, Sally, Will, Edgar, Marve." It wasn't the smoothest dismissal, but that was fine. He turned to Dolly and asked about the schedule. And when the others had left and he heard the lobby door swing shut behind them, he said, "That woman was talking with Trace Yarrow earlier. Remember Yarrow?"

She shook her head.

"He used to be a top-flight stunt man. 'Course, that was over ten years ago. Don't think he's worked since *Bad Companions*." He paused, noting her flinch. "But he was on the set today. Christ, everyone who'd ever heard of Greg Gaige was there. Someone said they even saw Dratz."

"Carlton Dratz?" Her voice was half an octave higher. It was all Bleeker could do to keep from laughing. So he'd finally gotten to the bitch.

"Carlton Dratz, indeed. Haven't seen or heard of him since Greg Gaige died."

"What about Yarrow?" Dolly's voice was under control again.

"He'll still have a SAG card. I'll track him down. I'll see who this imposter O'Shaughnessy is and where Yarrow fits in."

Dolly walked to the door. Even now, when she was virtually empty-handed, she trudged like a rhino—with that big horn to skewer anyone in the way. She pulled open the door, glanced into the darkened lobby, and turned back to him. "Don't worry about Yarrow going off on a tack of his own."

Despite himself, Bleeker stood staring as the door closed after her. Had she known Yarrow all along and denied it so blithely that the possibility had never occurred to him? Did she recall who Yarrow was after he had told her? If so, how did she know Yarrow would be tame? Or was the woman just so goddamned sure of her power that she took it as a given she could control anyone with a third-cousin connection to the film industry?

He shut off the lights and walked into the half-dark lobby, pausing so he didn't run into Uberhazy again outside. He couldn't drive himself crazy trying to figure her out. What he needed to do was get on top of this Sondervoil business, and the first step would be to find the impostor and tame her.

CHAPTER 7

TRACE Yarrow put down the phone. He should have slammed it down; he'd wanted to from the moment he heard Dolly Uberhazy's voice. But he hadn't, had he?

He glanced around his studio cottage. The walls were bare but for the calendar from the cycle shop. The Madras spread on his single bed had bled so much, it was as if the color were racing the threads to oblivion. His table and unmatched chairs were from the Goodwill. Hell, no one could accuse him of being "into things," into acquiring, into status.

He had loved doing stunt work. That'd been the best time of his life. He'd been so focused, there'd been no space for thought; he'd felt *alive*. And afterward, with the guys, the foot soldiers, he had known he belonged. He'd paid his dues. He'd been a "new boy" for five years, so long that he was afraid somehow the "okay guys," the ones who'd made it, could see his secrets and know he wasn't good enough. He'd just about decided that he loved doing gags enough to put up with life as an outsider, when suddenly one day he found that he was an okay guy himself. And he knew that the same guys he trusted doing a motorcycle spinout, or a horse drag, or a car hit, could be counted on in his life outside the business.

And then he'd had to walk away. It had been hell.

Now he'd got himself caught between two women. That meant trouble. He liked the detective, good enough body to be in the business, and what a mouth on her. Well, he liked that in a woman. She'd trotted right over the warning rope and gotten onto the set as if the rules weren't meant for her. That he understood. All the time she'd been looking ahead, watching for chances, shifting, skirting, lunging, always in control. And he wouldn't mind being the guy who crashed the levee of that control, no indeed. He could imagine that firm little body, and all that controlled passion and . . .

But she didn't quite trust him.

His chest went cold; it was the same feeling he'd had when he'd been the driver in a car hit. The okay guy he'd had to hit had been running into the road. He was gauging the speed of the car, ready to jump and slide over the hood. If you're going to come out just a little black and blue, you have to be in the air when the hit comes; the guy knew that. But he jumped too late. No time to brake or even swerve. Guy ended up with broken bones like yesterday's chicken dinner.

Yarrow tried to shake off the cold. He hadn't let the guy down, but he'd felt just as bad as if he had. He'd hated being the driver. Taking the hit—that was his style. Being the guy you couldn't trust, or even *appearing* to be—well, you might as well be dead.

But the lady detective was right not to trust him. If she'd asked him an hour ago if she could count on him—the two of them scratching out the truth about little Lark Sondervoil, battling the greed and ego of the studio—he'd have screamed, "Yes!" It wouldn't have occurred to him that that bitch Uberhazy could phone him up with one of those offers he couldn't refuse.

She hadn't held out the moon to him—teased him with a stunt job he knew he could never again handle. She didn't offer him a coordinator's job that would have had everyone in the business asking why all of a sudden, after ten years away from the business, Trace Yarrow got that plum. She was too smart for that. What she had held out to him was just a simple position, a script consultant, but an on-staff position, with the one thing he couldn't get any other way.

He limped to the sink. Dolly Uberhazy had offered him medical coverage—the hope of therapy for the leg, of pills for the pain, of not waking up at four A.M. wondering what he would do if the leg gave way again.

He'd sold his soul for his body. Lark Sondervoil would have understood that. And dammit, so would Greg Gaige. Would Kiernan O'Shaughnessy? She was the one he'd be hanging out to dry. Well, she wouldn't know, would she?

CHAPTER 8

"WHAT'S the story about Lark testing positive for opiates?" Kiernan demanded as soon as she had crossed Yarrow's threshold.

It had taken her an hour to drive from the heights of La Jolla through downtown, past her own turnoff, on to San Diego's Pacific Beach where diners were still moseying across Mission Boulevard, and shoppers were skirting through the traffic at Ingraham and Garnet, and into the alleys of Ocean Beach.

Ocean Beach wasn't ten miles from her home, but she knew it only superficially as a remnant of the days of psychedelics—shops on Newport Avenue sported hand-painted signs in blues and purples, and merchandise leaned toward surfing wares and health foods. Volkswagen bugs still thrived, and long-haired, well-tanned blondes who ambled on along the sidewalks resembled the original owners of those automotive flower children. Keeping the bug in gas, the board afloat, a little extra cash to get high on, good music and good smoke or snort: the good life lived.

Trace Yarrow was older than the lotus-eaters Kiernan associated with Ocean Beach, but from the look of the single room he lived in—with its unmade day bed, TV, Formica table, and thrift shop chairs—he fit right in.

Occasionally, she had driven down alleys like Yarrow's, alleys that divided streets in the various "Beach" sections of San Diego, and wondered who lived in these one-room units the size of garages. Who would opt to sit behind a window overlooking a paved alley or back wall? Who slept so soundly or so little as to ignore the roar of cars and trucks and motorcycles forty inches away, at two, three, or four in the morning?

Who shrugged off the probability of a burglar coming in through an alley window with the ease of swinging his legs over a porch rail? Or did these tiny dwellings hold nothing valuable enough to be fenced? It was, she had decided, the bus-depot-locker style of living.

Yarrow's walls boasted a repair shop calendar and three flowered prints he'd probably been too uninterested in to bother taking down. Safe to say the man wasn't visual. Still, Kiernan found herself thinking of her own duplex and the view of the Pacific waves breaking on the rocks below her balcony. And her present decorative delight: a trompe l'oeil table painted with red straw placemats, bright blue-rimmed dishes holding servings of salmon steak, roasted red chili strips, and potato salad topped by bulbs of fennel. Off to one side, a basket of gold-buttered, red-paprika'd garlic bread, and in the corner, the head and neck of Ezra as he snatched a slice. Commissioning it had been an indulgence, as was her adored bluefish, flown in fresh from the East Coast, and Tchernak. She liked to think she wasn't dependent on indulgences, but the idea of doing time in a room like Yarrow's was one thought she pushed away.

This was the first case since opening the agency that she had started without promise of payment—considerable payment—and even this she chose to consider not a poor business decision but an indulgence.

"Opiates?" Yarrow repeated, still standing by the door as if he were undecided about whether he should have let her in. The harsh artificial light underlined the creases and pouches of his chipmunk face. She guessed he wasn't much older than she, but he'd played those years a lot harder.

"What're you talking about, O'Shaughnessy? A whiff of coke, or plungers full of heroin?"

"Either."

He swung the door back and forth on the hinges. "Where'd you hear that?"

"What is this, Twenty Questions? Look, Yarrow, you give me a song and dance about Lark Sondervoil being a sharp stunt woman—I take *sharp* to mean bright enough not to stumble over a bluff when you're loaded." With another potential client she would have come on easier, but Trace Yarrow was such an in-your-face little guy, he'd mistake courtesy for weakness. With him, the winner of the game would be the guy who shoved the hardest.

"I didn't—"

"Save the excuses. Just tell me what's the story on Lark Sondervoil."

His hand tightened on the door. "Skip it. I'm not Lark's keeper. And there are plenty of gumshoes dying for work."

"Fine. Run an ad. I'll cancel my order with the Maserati dealer." She grabbed the door. "Consider the hour I spent in the screening room a gift."

"You got in to see the rushes?" he asked, clearly so impressed he lost track of the game.

"Didn't you think I would?"

"So what'd you learn?" he asked, avoiding concession.

Kiernan restrained a grin. She loved the jab and run; the thrill of the game; always alert, all the chips in the middle of the table, all the cards facedown and nothing to do but psych out the other guy. It made her feel—well—alive. But she knew the pitfalls of guys like Yarrow, driven, single-minded, men who made love like there'd be no morning. There were reasons why they were ex-lovers, and reasons why after each one she'd sworn *Never again*. In a dark alley they were the best guys to have striding beside you—*if* they showed up. She ought to grab this *out*, press her palms together in thanks, and shut the door behind her.

But Yarrow knew things about Lark Sondervoil she'd never find out elsewhere—Lark, *and* the movie industry. She'd take the gift, but in the form she wanted. She'd pick his brain and then walk out the door. "My questions first. What's this business about Lark and opiates?"

Yarrow released the door, took three steps, and flopped into a dinette chair. "Anyone else, I'd tell she was crazy, but for you I'm searching my brain like a bum looking for butts in the gutter."

"How well did you know Lark?"

"Met her once at a party."

"Once! That's all?" Maybe Yarrow had too many cards facedown.

"Look, O'Shaughnessy, Hollywood's a small town, and the stunt world's one little block in it. I don't have to be in bed with the girl to know the word on her"—he paused, catching her eye—"but it's a nice way to find out."

Or maybe it was too many face up. She ignored the comment.

A woman not watching her opponent would have missed the slight tightening of shoulders, the quick sideward glance that preceded the steady gaze. "I could give you the rundown on anyone in the business. Just ask me—go ahead, ask me."

"Back to Lark. How come she trotted around to the media and hinted at more than the high fall? Was she a publicity slut?"

"No. The opposite. That whole thing was bizarre. Stunt doubles try to stay out of the limelight, to protect the illusion that the star does everything. Lark." He shook his head. "The studio was furious."

"What could she have told the press?"

"Nothing."

"Not *nothing*! Think! Did she talk about Greg? About doing his Move?"

"Not to me. But I did hear that she wanted the studio to acknowledge Greg in the trailers—the credits on the screen—and it was no go."

Kiernan nodded. Greg Gaige deserved that honor, small as it was. She liked Lark better for her asking. "Yarrow, tell me about Lark. What was she doing at the party?"

"I don't know why the hell—"

"No, not why she was there. Tell me how she behaved there. Close your eyes, see the scene, describe it for me."

"Look, I'll tell you what I know, but I'm not about to go weird to do it. Here's what I know about that night. It was maybe six months ago. I probably saw her for five minutes. She was just leaving when I got there."

"What time was that?"

"Eleven? Eleven thirty?"

Kiernan raised an eyebrow and let him make his own assessment of its meaning. He was trying to guess her hidden cards as much as she was his.

"I'd just gotten off work. I'd been troubleshooting and when the computer goes down, you gotta run no matter what time it is. I remember thinking I was lucky to be done before midnight."

"So you got to the party at eleven or so. Why was Lark leaving so early? Did she have a gag the next day?"

"That's what I asked. She was downright offended. She said she'd never have stayed out that late if she'd had to work the next day—even if the gag wasn't scheduled until the afternoon. She made a big point of adding that. The truth is, the girl was a pain in the ass. Young, eager, ready to pump you for everything you'd learned in twenty years. And then you realized that she didn't give a damn about you, it was just the gags—the stunt work—she cared about."

Kiernan laughed. "Little hard on the ego?"

"Anyone would be pi—" He shrugged. "Yeah, maybe."

She smiled. At least one of Yarrow's down cards was better than she'd expected. "What was Lark drinking?"

"Light beer."

"You sure it was a light?"

"Oh, yeah. You may think of stunt men as the beer-and-horse or beer-and-cycle set, and in the old days that would have been true. I'm not saying they don't drink now, but you won't see anyone seriously in the business downing a six-pack. A stunt double can't afford to put on an extra pound. You know why?" A grin tickled the corners of his mouth. His dark blue eyes twinkled.

"It makes the gags harder to perform?"

Yarrow nodded. "Good guess. That's the official line."

"And the real reason?"

Now the grin took hold. "The star would throw a fit if he thought that the stunt double standing in for him was a blimp. In this business, if you want to eat, you don't eat—or drink fat beer."

Another card revealed. Another card she liked. But that was only two in a five-to-seven-card hand. She knew better than to bet the pile on two cards and a feeling. Or she should. And right now she wanted to see Lark Sondervoil's cards more than Yarrow's. "But Lark did drink?"

"Yeah, but I'd be surprised if she'd had more than one. She wasn't showing any effects. And I'd come straight from work, so I was still clear enough to notice."

Thinking back to the question of opiates, Kiernan said, "Maybe liquor wasn't so much her thing. Maybe she'd done a line of coke?"

He shook his head. "Like I said, it's a small community. I would have heard if she was a sniffer. The handle on Lark Sondervoil was 'ambitious.' She talked gags; she hung around with whoever knew the most—"

"The people who were the most influential, or the ones she could learn from? There's a big difference."

Yarrow leaned back, balancing with ease on two legs of the chair. His own legs were extended, his feet off the floor. A guy in any other line of work would have landed on his head, but Yarrow was barely moving. Kiernan had to stare to find the minute adjustments of his hip flexor muscles with which he balanced. And the tiny adjustments looked so automatic as to be almost unconscious. She could do that, she thought, if there were another chair sturdy enough to balance on. *Not now,*

Kiernan. Trace Yarrow was begging to be distracted. But as soon as she got home . . .

"Lark was a smart cookie. She looked too pretty to have brains, too. But the one time I saw her do a long stair fall, she'd been called in to replace a woman who'd broken her arm. Lark asked every stunt double on the set, not only about what she should do, but how Lainey, the one she replaced, had screwed up. Was Lainey a daredevil? Did she prepare decently? Had she done stair falls before? Had she had time to prepare for this one? Lark was thorough to the point of tedium. Taking that job was a risk, but it was an opportunity she couldn't pass up. People have risked a lot more than limbs for jobs," he said with an edge to his voice that she hadn't heard before. "Not to mention, there was a good adjustment that went with it."

"Adjustment?"

"Pay for a specific gag. You don't go off a bluff for an hourly wage."

"What did Lark go off the bluff for?"

"Seventy thou for the Move and the high fall. Word of that spread like pollen. It wasn't the biggest adjustment in the business, but it was damned good for someone of her stature. It knocked her from novice to name. If she'd pulled this off, she would have been number one in high falls."

Outside, a motorcycle roared through the alley, its spray of sound bouncing off the cement walls. The screen door shook, the table vibrated; Yarrow flexed his hips abruptly to keep from losing balance. Purposely she didn't make eye contact with him, and she could see from the corner of her eye that he was looking away. In his place, she knew, she would have done the same. She hoped there would never come a point when she had to admit she couldn't balance in a handstand, couldn't walk on her deck rail without worrying about the rocks below, much less be seen losing balance on a kitchen chair. God, it must be hard to be a *former* stunt man.

"So if she'd gotten jobs with one day's notice, she needed to be ready?"

"Yeah, right. Lark Sondervoil was not a girl to miss her chance because she'd partied the night before."

"And yet, Yarrow"—Kiernan waited until he looked over at her—"the California Highway Patrol got a finding of opiates in her urine when they stopped her a week ago."

"You heard that at the screening room?"

"It doesn't matter where I heard it. That's not the type of story anyone fabricates; it's too easy to check. It's got to be true."

"No way. First of all, Lark wouldn't do drugs. And even if she did, she'd never go out and drive on top of that."

"What makes you so sure?"

"Her parents were killed in a head-on crash. Drunk driver. The word I heard was that she still clutched every time she drove. Whoever told me said that anyone else would never have driven again, but Lark, being Lark, couldn't permit herself that cowardice. So she made herself drive. On the road, I mean; in the business she steered clear of car gags—she did falls and fights mostly. But every time she got in her car, she checked the tires. And when she started the engine, she checked the brakes. My friend said he'd driven with her once and she nearly sent him through the windshield before they were out of the driveway. No way would that woman do drugs and drive."

"And yet the CHP got their finding," Kiernan insisted. She could feel herself tensing. Dammit, she liked Lark Sondervoil. "It just doesn't make sense."

Yarrow shifted forward. His chair came down with a bang. "Won't the autopsy answer questions like that? Isn't that the type of thing you get paid so much for finding out?"

She almost laughed. *If you're dealing, why don't you get all the aces?* "I don't make findings that aren't there. If Lark did drugs a week ago and hasn't since, there won't be any evidence."

"But if there's some other reason, like maybe some weird chemical imbalance or something, that'll show up, right?"

"If it's within the parameters of what the pathologist is looking for. The thing is, Yarrow, pathologists don't have time, and corpses don't have enough tissue or fluid to allow them to check for every chemical. If there's an abnormal finding in the area they're questioning, it will come up. If it's somewhere else, it won't."

"But drugs—surely they'll check for drugs in this case."

Kiernan nodded. "They'll check for drugs, but not for anomalies."

"And if they turn up drugs in her body, good chance everyone's off the hook."

She stared him in the eye. "And if they don't, Yarrow, well, there's still the CHP report."

He met her gaze and held it. The gaze they shared held the certainty that somewhere in the movie business, someone was cutting his losses and cashing in his remaining chips. And Lark Sondervoil was of no more importance than a plastic disk worth a dime or a dollar. Yarrow tapped his fingers on the table. "Grounds for a helluva reasonable doubt. No one's going to push."

"Her family?"

"Nope. The parents were all of it. That's why she took their accident so hard."

"Then you're right. The only people who care will be the ones eager to blame her."

"Yarrow, Lark Sondervoil's start mark was keyed by the inner cordon, right? After the first pole was moved, it'd be natural for guys to lend a hand moving the rest of the poles into line. The first pole is the key. Who shifted that?"

He shook his head. "The place was a madhouse. No one will ever tell you that." Yarrow glanced slowly around his room, as if inventorying his possessions.

For the first time since she'd arrived, it was silent outside, and in the silence she could hear his breaths coming just a bit too fast.

"So what's next?" he asked. "You bring a contract for me to sign?"

Despite herself, Kiernan laughed. Yarrow probably wasn't even good for bail. But the man did have connections. Using his name could open doors—or slam them. She'd just have to watch her toes on the sills. "No, this one's on me."

"How come?"

Because she'd once been one decision away from being a Lark Sondervoil? Because she wanted to know what Lark was so desperate to announce to the world? Or because Greg Gaige had changed her life, and this was the least she could do in return? She said simply, "I knew Greg Gaige."

He leaned forward, resting his elbows on his knees. She couldn't tell from his expression if he understood her commitment or if he was trying to assess whether he'd won with a pair of deuces. A motorcycle roared down the alley. He waited until the sound was no more than a distant hum before he said, "How did you know Greg?"

She shrugged. "*Knew* is too strong a word. I only met him twice. I've barely thought about him since he died."

Yarrow leaned forward. "Come on, we're in this together. Tell me how you met Greg."

It wasn't a memory she shared easily; it was too integral to her to be disbursed in casual words.

She could still see the gym the day she had met him—Greg Gaige Day. Blue and gold banners hung beside the poster of him on the newly painted white wall. The floors, scrubbed and relacquered, sparkled in the sprays of sunlight and were still sticky under her bare feet. The locker rooms smelled of paint and Pinesol rather than sweat. And as they awaited the arrival of the great one, excited girls fingered their braids, pulled strands loose and braided again; boys clasped and reclasped wrist braces and chalked their hands until white clouds floated through the room.

"He came to the gym the year after my older sister died," she said, brusquely enough to block questions. Yarrow didn't need to know that she had stormed out of the church when they refused to bury Moira in hallowed ground. Or that the neighbors in Saint Brendan's parish had warned their children away from her. She'd been thirteen years old. The gym had become her haven, but even there she'd been a stranger, a refugee among the public school Protestants, a tiny, spark-angry girl, with an emptiness held at bay with scissor lifts until her abdominal muscles ached, stretches until her tendons burned and her mind was numb. "I was much newer to gymnastics than most girls my age. I'd missed a lot of practice when my sister died, so I was awkward and unsure if I'd ever get the key moves." Unsure, too, she'd realized later, whether a girl like her *could* deserve success.

"It was Greg Gaige Day. The idea was that gym routine would be normal: student groups would go from vault horse, to bars, to rings or balance beam, to floor-routine mat. I remember that the cymbals in the floor-routine music crashed and jolted a girl off the balance beam; a boy lost his grip on the rings and clumped to the mat; one of the other guys tried a new release move and made it—barely. Everyday stuff. The whole place smelled of sweat and chalk dust that got thicker by the minute.

"But of course, it wasn't just any day. There was no chatter, no one missed a landing and shrugged it off. And every face there was turned to Greg Gaige as he watched the seniors." He'd pointed out a more efficient grasp on the high bar, a better angle on the pommel horse, a way to get more power from a punch back. Most seniors stood a moment too long after he spoke, waiting, or unclear, or unsatisfied. Even then, she could tell Greg was awkward one on one, and teaching was not his skill. His feel for gymnastics had been too visceral to be taken apart and given piecemeal to the next hopeful.

"I was too much of a novice to be among 'the observed.' When my turn came on the vault, I pushed thoughts of the seniors, and Greg Gaige, out of my mind—I was good at pushing things away. All week I'd been fighting form breaks in an elementary vault. I pictured executing it perfectly, held up my arm, and pushed off. When I came out of the dismount, I felt as if I almost had the essence of it, but I knew that that hadn't translated into arm or leg or hip movements; and to an observer I still looked like a clumsy kid who'd missed too much practice.

"But when I looked up, Greg Gaige had been watching. He said, 'Good feel for it.' " She smiled at Yarrow as if that ended the recollection.

But she could still remember hearing Greg's words, her breath catching in her throat with the shock and the glory of it all. She'd said to Greg, "It was just a beginner's vault; nothing like the seniors—"

Greg had put his arm on her shoulder, leaned over, and said so that only she could hear, "The feel is what matters; it's what makes a gymnast. You are a gymnast. This is where you live."

Then the coach had asked Greg a question or pointed out something —she couldn't recall what anymore—and Greg was gone. But she'd relived that moment with him every night until she was in college. It wasn't until years later, after she'd seen him in San Francisco, that she realized what he'd meant when he said, "This is where you live." He'd meant *live* as in *alive. This is where you are alive.* What he'd been admitting, even back then in Baltimore, was that gymnastics was the only place *he* was alive.

By then, it was way too late to ask him the question that had occurred to her only after she was in medical school: All those years ago in the Baltimore gym, had he picked her out because she was the best prospect there, or merely the loneliest?

Whichever, his words had been the spark that reignited her. She hadn't gone to the Olympics, but she'd come in second in the Nationals. She'd written to him each time she medaled; he'd responded with a sentence of congratulations. And when she chose premed over a gymnastics scholarship, she'd written him one last time. He hadn't answered, and so she never knew whether she had slipped from his interest, or he found it too depressing to think she could give up the thing that made him alive for a career cutting up the dead.

He couldn't know that the practice of forensic pathology *did* make her alive. She thought she'd chosen forensic pathology to understand the secrets of her sister's death. It wasn't until after she'd been fired from the coroner's office that she realized she loved uncovering the secrets of the body—every body. When she was discovering the truth, she felt alive. Then she understood Greg Gaige's passion.

She'd been lucky; she got a second chance, as a private investigator. And maybe Greg had been lucky, too, to die before his career ended, before he had to face life without being alive.

She met Greg again that time years later in San Francisco. But she certainly was not going to describe that night to Yarrow.

She looked across the table at Yarrow. He started to speak but stopped before a sound came out, for some reason choosing not to prod her. A sensitivity she hadn't expected? Or merely no desire to be dismissed? "Anyway, Greg went out of his way for me. I can do a little for him." She stuck out her hand. "So, I'm in."

He took the hand, shook officially. Then leaning back, he said, "This death of Lark's . . . I just can't believe Lark is responsible. It's too much of a coincidence. The last movie Greg Gaige was in, the one with the Move . . ."

He paused so long that Kiernan nodded.

"On the bluff today, there were five people who were on the set of *Bad Companions* the day Greg Gaige died."

CHAPTER **9**

"**F**IVE of the people on the set when Greg Gaige died were here today, Yarrow?" Kiernan repeated, amazed. "Who?"

"Besides me? Bleeker was the second unit director. Dolly was the line producer, the one responsible for the day-to-day budget of the movie. And Liam."

"Liam McCafferty, the city media liaison?"

"Yeah, I got him the job as accountant on *Bad Companions,* not that he'd thank me. The production coordinator was a ditz, and the location set was so small and isolated, he ended up saddled with all the office work. Poor guy was running twelve hours a day."

"And who else?"

"There was word of a spotting of the odious Dratz."

She made a "come" sign with her fingers.

Yarrow flopped in his chair. "Dratz. I can't remember the kid's first name, but he was the son of some studio bigwig. The wig had sent him down to the set to get rid of him. And I'll tell you, the kid hadn't been there an hour before—well, it was clear that the wig would have shot a movie he hadn't a prayer of selling if it meant getting his son out of his hair." Yarrow shook his head slowly back and forth. "Dratz was like a greased piglet, snuffling into everything, chattering on the set when the cameras were running—I can't tell you how many takes he ruined. He told the actors how to act, the directors how to direct. Christ, he even had suggestions for the Gaige Move! He couldn't touch his toes with a yardstick, but he carried on like the great expert. Like any fool off the street could do a high fall, or a car jump, or a stair fall. He couldn't understand why the star didn't do the fire gag. Dratz was so odious, his name moved into the vernacular: Dratz stuff."

Another time, Kiernan would have leaned back in her chair, gotten a beer, and listened to every one of Yarrow's stunt-war stories, or at least all that dealt with Greg Gaige. But there wasn't time now; she had to focus Yarrow. "Greg was the best in acrobatic stunts, right?"

Yarrow got up—not so much stood up as burst up—winced, and instantly covered that acknowledgment of pain. He leaned on the back of the chair, his foot tapping softly, as if he had chosen that pose for comfort rather than support, as if his weak-side foot were responding to a melody meandering through his head instead of kicking at the pain receptors.

If he could have paced, Kiernan was sure he would have. But in this tiny box of a room, pacing would have been akin to spinning. Still, he wasn't left sitting face to face with his thoughts. He had been able to handle memories of Lark unprotected, but not of Greg Gaige. Kiernan felt her skin prickling. She leaned forward as if to see into Yarrow more clearly.

"Yeah, O'Shaughnessy, when it came to acrobatics, Greg was the best once. He went straight from the Olympic trials in gymnastics to doing the Move as a stunt in his first movie. He was short for a guy, but he wasn't a pixie like you. No offense."

"None taken. Being short isn't offensive to me," she said with a bit more edge to her voice than she had intended. She didn't resent being short; what got to her was the towering world's belittling assumptions.

Yarrow hurried on, "Greg was probably about my height, or almost."

Five foot eight. She remembered that.

"He was incredible. He had muscles—there was no part of his body he hadn't toned. I saw him once—he was talking to a couple of us. He flipped up into a handstand, lifted one arm, balanced on the other—and never altered the cadence of his speech. And he could bend—it was like he was made of rubber. The man bent where other people didn't realize they had joints. He could touch his chin to his knees."

Kiernan resisted a shrug. A tight forward bend was nothing special. Even in medical school, when she hadn't worked out for months, she could place her palms flat on the floor.

"Greg would drop into a backbend and bring his hands to his ankles. It was like he just folded back."

Kiernan nodded in approval. That was impressive for a man, even a male gymnast. It meant stretching all the anterior muscles—the quads, the abdominals, the pecs—that he'd tightened with endless reps and lifts, and the scissor kicks and planches that made up the routines. It pleased her to hear he hadn't lost it. "How old was Greg then?"

"When he died? Hmm . . ." He stroked his chin from the sides, pulling his thumb and fingers down along the jawbone. "Early forties, maybe a few years older. Most stunt people don't do gags that long. By that time your knees are shot, you've messed up your legs and feet from landing wrong, or you've cracked ribs from the force of the falls, and you've spat up enough blood to keep a vampire for a month." He caught her eye and grinned, more relaxed now.

She smiled back, wondering what he'd managed to bypass. In a minute he'd be telling jokes about his operations. Still, it beat bemoaning them, or like Tchernak, pretending they'd healed two hundred percent. In an hour he'd be offering to show her his scars.

"See, O'Shaughnessy, there comes a point in your thirties when you realize that you won't last forever. After another trip to the emergency room or another six weeks in a cast, you discover that you don't heal as fast anymore, and that no matter how much you sweat in the gym, you're never going to get back to where you were before. You know it in your head, but you still don't believe it. So you negotiate another job on the basis of how well you did your last gag, and once you start practicing it, you realize that you can't manage the sudden moves as well, that you're just a hair less agile, a wink slower, and the moves that were second nature—well, now they take the concentration you used to save for the new stuff. No one says anything. You tell yourself they don't notice the difference, not yet."

Kiernan kept her gaze steady, pushing back the memory of Greg saying: *This is where you live.* She couldn't let her memories of Greg color Yarrow's. And she needed a good assessment of Yarrow himself, to evaluate those memories. Had one of the brakes he was talking about resulted in his shortened leg? She would have guessed the cause to be a congenital scoliosis, or if not a curved spine, at least compensation for the nerve damage and muscular imbalance that can accompany ruptured discs.

Yarrow pulled the chair toward him and balanced his elbows on the top rung of the ladder back. His hair was thick, dark, and wavy atop his sun-toughened face, but his tan torpedo arms sported a coating that had been bleached blond. And blond on his legs—any sensible person would have changed from shorts as the night cooled, but Yarrow, she was willing to bet, would freeze his hard-muscled right leg and its thinner mate to create the deception that he was unconcerned about the atrophied muscles. It was a foolish bravado, but for her it had the appeal of a wild card.

"In this business," he said, "what you've learned over the years—your experience—is your capital; when you get to the point that you're living off your capital alone, your days are numbered. If you've got any smarts, you start looking for a job coordinating the stunts, or maneuvering to direct the second unit."

"Wasn't Greg smart?" There was a time when even to mouth that question would have been heresy.

"Smart?" His foot tapped louder. "I'm not much with words; action's my thing. But *smart:* that's just not right. Greg was sharp in a quiet, cut-to-the-core kind of way. See, most of us athletes, we've gotten through school on sports alone. I played every sport. I'm five foot eight; I was the star of the basketball team, and the top-scoring wide receiver in football for the entire county. I didn't have to waste time with books. Most of us are like that. Some have the sense to study, too. We're not dummies, that's not what I mean at all. The irony is that after that free ride through school, we end up doing gags and having to learn about physics and mechanics so we can figure out what Special Effects is up to, so we can second-guess the stunt coordinator, and make sure we stay alive and with our bones in the places they started out."

"And Greg?"

"I never got the sense he'd been a bookworm. It wasn't like he read Shakespeare on the set. But he understood how the gags were planned. He didn't hesitate to make changes. And he always insisted on doing all his own prep."

Kiernan smiled. That was the Greg she'd known. She gave Yarrow an extra point for fair observation. "But he didn't try to move into coordinating?"

"No." His foot stopped tapping, and he slid the toes back and forth in an arc. "He wasn't interested in that."

She nodded; so Greg hadn't changed since he stood awkwardly with the seniors in the Baltimore gym. "Was he married? Did he have kids? Was he doing anything besides stunts? Back in school? Or working for some cause?"

Yarrow shook his head. "I don't know."

"Maybe someone who spent more time with him—" she said, disappointed.

"No!" The front legs of the chair hit the floor. "Look, I watched him work, I hung out with him on the set. I should know."

Why so protective? But she understood; there was something about Greg that made his fans protective. The lion with the burr in its paw? "What did he talk about? Besides stunts."

"That's tough," Yarrow said, repositioning the chair. "If he talked about people, it was how they did the gags."

Like Lark Sondervoil did, she noted. "Besides gags?" she insisted.

"The business. He laughed about that. I mean, there's plenty of weird stuff on a set, lots of crises and pseudo-crises, actors 'Camille-ing around,' Greg called it. Then there'd be the union rep racing down when we were on location to make sure all their working members were on the master list, and the producer'd be having a fit because the studio execs were on his ass. I remember Greg laughing that a movie set would be a great spot for an anatomy class. Students would get to see every body part in individual motion: asses balanced one on top of another sky high, heads rolling, tits in wringers, and balls"—he laughed—"balls in more danger than on any gridiron."

Headlights shone on and diffused in the clear glass bricks that passed for an alley-side window. The car roared past, leaving on the glass bricks a mottled pattern of blues. The glass bricks shielded more than they showed. Like Yarrow's laugh, she thought. His description of Greg warmed her heart; this was the man she'd hoped for, the stunt man who stood back and looked awry at the compulsions of the powerful. When she'd met him in San Francisco she'd hoped to find that kind of man. But . . . she hadn't.

She stared at the glass bricks, navy against black, like an empty night sky. Silently, she beckoned another car to splash the dark with color and life, Yarrow to offer something that would keep her from asking: "Are you sure it was Greg who said those things? Or was he the one who laughed at them, politely, halfheartedly, because he was watching how you moved rather than listening?"

Yarrow's head tilted to the right. He leaned more heavily on the chair back, the pretense of not needing it rousted from his mind by the question. Finally, he said, "It was Greg who said them. I think."

She nodded. Memories, she'd learned, were malleable animals.

Wishes blended with facts and cemented into histories that people were shocked to find untrue.

"Greg was almost ten years older than me," he said too quickly, as if to block out the altering memory. "He was an old hand when I was still green. I sat at his feet and admired him. You may have thought I was a pain in the ass with my motorcycle—"

Kiernan grinned. It was exactly what she'd thought.

"But back then, when I'd done a couple of gags, bought my first Harley, and figured I was the decade's James Dean, if my head had been any more swelled, I'd have burst my skull. And even I admitted that Greg Gaige was something special. He was the best," Yarrow said, softly. "When he was planning a gag, the rest of the world fell away. And when he was doing it, his whole body changed. It was like under his skin the energy was so compressed, so controlled, that there would be no way to stop it. But when he was doing a gag, his eyes shone, his jaw set, and it was like he wasn't just *doing* the gag, he was a part of it. No, that's not right. He *was* the gag."

Yes! she thought. Of course, Greg Gaige would have enmeshed himself in the gags, just as he did the gymnastic routines. He would have been always working out, practicing, figuring how to add new levels of difficulty, or so the legends in the gym had proclaimed. "And the rest of the time?"

"It was like he didn't belong. Like he didn't know how to fit in. Like he'd put so much into his craft that there was nothing left for normal life."

She could have asked Yarrow to elaborate, but she didn't need to. She knew. And when she had first learned that, the shock had slapped her the same way it did him. She, too, had assumed that the man who perfected the Gaige Move would rate a ten in every other aspect of life. She could see the residue of disillusionment on Yarrow's face a decade after Greg Gaige's death. She could feel it in her gut like a swirl of crushed ice.

"He'd wander around the set like he had a day pass. On *Bad Companions,* I remember people saying he spent his time sitting in the shade of the catering truck, talking—or more likely listening—to whoever came by, from the grips to the line producer. If I hadn't known him and you'd told me this guy was a tennis pro or a ski instructor waiting for the season to start, I wouldn't have questioned it, except I'd have expected them to be more savvy socially. But then he'd start discussing stunts, and it was like someone pushed the plug in the socket. He just lit up." He shook his head. "I was up and coming then, hot stuff. Figured that beam of attention was just for me."

"And?"

"I grew up." He let go of the chair. The front legs jumped and banged to the floor. Yarrow walked to the door in three uneven steps.

Behind him, headlights glowed white in the glass brick window. Kiernan realized with a start that she hadn't noticed the engine roar worthy of Cape Canaveral. What had it been about Greg Gaige that called people to nurture illusions about him? Was it his total commitment? His innocence? The odd purity of the combination? Most people could never attain that purity, and if they were like her, they were very thankful they couldn't. She forced herself to lean back in her chair and said, "You told me Greg died in a fire gag. But he did high falls and acrobatic stunts. Why was he doing the fire gag at all?"

"The stunt business is a small world, O'Shaughnessy," Yarrow said, easing back into the comfort of pedantry. "Everyone's got his specialty, but if you want to work, you've got to be able to do it all. Take me—I did great motorcycle gags, but if they needed a double for a cycle crash and a stair fall and it was a location picture, they'd have taken a guy who couldn't handle the cycle as well but who could do both, before they'd pay two doubles."

Kiernan nodded. "The bottom line is the bottom line."

"And Greg, well, he was over forty. I'm sure when they called him in the middle of the movie, he told himself he couldn't afford to turn down a job. And this one offered him the chance to do the Gaige Move—not in the fire gag, in an earlier scene. He hadn't done that onscreen since his first picture. It was one more time to do the thing that he did better than anyone else in the world. Fire scared him shitless, but he wouldn't have let that opportunity go even if it meant doing the fire gag nude."

Kiernan shivered. "One last chance to say it's not just a memory, that you're not a memory, yet."

Yarrow was staring at her. She realized she'd spoken out loud, and words he didn't want to hear. But retirement wouldn't have meant just the loss of fame, she felt sure, or even surrendering a way of life. For someone as consumed as Greg, it would have meant abandoning the rationale for living, watching what makes life make sense slip away. Leaving him with . . . nothing. She swallowed and forced out the words: "How exactly did he die?"

Yarrow trekked back, and as he was taking up his post behind his chair, he said, "I wasn't on the set then."

"But you think it's suspicious. Why?"

"Why? I don't know. It's just that he was too good to die like that."

"Too professional?"

"Yeah."

"Like Lark?"

His eyes widened. "Exactly. Like Lark."

"Then you think one of those five people killed him?"

His eyes widened in surprise. "I never considered that."

"Yarrow! What the—"

"Greg was meticulous about his preparations. He put everything he would need in that cabin the night before so it would be ready at whatever ungodly hour of the morning he needed to start smearing the fire-resistant gel—very pricey stuff—on every inch of his skin. You can't get that stuff in your eyes, and it tends to run, so you've got to be real careful. Then he put on a Nomex suit over it—he should have put more than one on. Each suit is an extra layer of protection. I've seen guys use six suits in a ninety-second fire drop. But Greg never did; he couldn't stand being confined like that. He dabbed flammable gel on the parts of the material farthest from his body. He should have . . ." He closed his eyes against the decision Greg had made. "Look, he should have been wearing three or four suits. He decided to wear only one. He had an oxygen bottle right there in the cabin and didn't use it. What does that make you think?"

"What did the autopsy find?"

"I don't know. Honestly. If they came up with anything fishy, it never made the trades—the papers—or the rumor mill."

"Yarrow, what is it you think happened?"

He swallowed. "There's nothing like doing gags. You've got friends you trust with your life, literally. Working gags are fun. Lots are challenges. There are always new skills to learn, vital things to figure out. Every day is different. I know what it's like to leave. My job now, computer troubleshooting, is fine. I don't hate it. Some days are more interesting than others, but none of them *matter*."

A truck roared down the alley. Yarrow didn't look up. "What would Greg have done if he retired? Sell real estate in San Bernardino? He'd been the best; how could he live without—"

"Without being the best? With being ordinary?" Kiernan said softly. "You think he chose to die?"

"Makes sense," he choked out.

"No!" she snapped. She was out of her chair, leaning across the table at him. "Not Greg Gaige! Someone else, another stunt man, might have figured his career was over, but not Greg. Greg Gaige would die trying, right? *Right?*"

Yarrow's mouth opened, but he didn't speak. He yearned to agree, she could tell, but by now he didn't even know what he really thought. She sighed, furious with herself. She'd pulled out his memories, twisted them to the shape she was desperate to see, and now they were worth nothing. Maybe Greg Gaige had gone into the fire the way suicides load their pockets with stones and walk into the sea.

But Yarrow had had a decade to reach his conclusion. If he'd considered Greg Gaige a suicide, he wouldn't have been so outraged about Lark Sondervoil. "If Greg planned to kill himself, Yarrow, he wouldn't have worn any fire suit at all. Right?" She waited till he nodded, then said, "Who was Greg's beneficiary?"

Yarrow looked up, startled at her change of tone. "His mother. She and Greg hadn't gotten along. She was probably happier with the insurance money. She only lived a few more years after he died."

Something still wasn't right about Yarrow. His eyebrows squeezed in toward each other, his cheeks toward his nose, his mouth was pursed. But he wasn't balancing on the chair legs or pacing the way an athlete would handle things. He was too wary. Too afraid of revealing something? "Yarrow, you were on location, working with the man you idolized, the best acrobatic stunt man in films, and you didn't bother to watch his final gag?"

He shrugged. "My work was done. When you're done, you're free to move on to other jobs."

"And did you?" When he didn't respond immediately, she added, "I can run a Social Security check."

"I had a meeting in L.A."

"I don't think so. You said Greg got the call in the middle of filming. He replaced another stunt double, right?"

Slowly, Yarrow nodded.

"You were the stunt man, weren't you?"

The glass bricks were night blue, the alley silent. A smirk passed across Yarrow's face and disappeared like an offering rejected.

"Yeah," he said finally. "I never did another gag." He stared at the bricks, his lips together but his mouth moving silently. What was he adding? "Because?"

"Because . . . because I'll never know if the fire gag was routine. Or if it was a killer and by rights I should be dead."

Her breath caught. She didn't have to worry about meeting Yarrow's gaze; his eyes were cloudy, and he was seeing only within. Slowly, she said, "Why would anyone kill Lark Sondervoil to cover up a ten-year-old death that no one was thinking about? It doesn't make sense." She let a moment pass, waiting, and when he added nothing new, she said, "Look, I understand your feelings. But I have to tell you, as the base for an investigation, emotion is quicksand."

"You mean you're backing out? I gave you everything I've got. I can't help it if it's not the kind of evidence that any beat cop could take to the Supreme Court."

She stood up and pushed the chair in under the table. "Yarrow, you don't have anything, in either case. No motive, no means of murder; you can't even say for sure that Lark Sondervoil wasn't too loaded to perform."

"Look, if you wanted certainty. . . . Shit, I guess an investigation like this is just too hard for you."

It was a moment before Kiernan smiled. "I am not quite that easy to manipulate. Got that?"

He shrugged.

"Okay, here's what I can do," she said. "I'll check out Lark's body. If she was snorting cocaine, there'll be evidence of nasal deterioration; if she was shooting heroin, there'll be tracks."

"Maybe not. Cary Bleeker's real fussy about drugs. He's had a lot of problems, and he's not one to take chances with anything as risky as a stunt woman on drugs. No stunt coordinator would touch her if they thought she was unreliable. As ambitious as Lark was—"

"Yarrow, if ambition precluded cocaine—"

"Yeah, I suppose. Especially in Hollywood. But my point is that Lark wouldn't do drugs. And if she did, she'd never have tracks running down her arms and legs."

"Which is what makes the problem so much harder." Kiernan walked to the door and waited for him to follow. "The places she'd use are the ones no one would notice—under the tongue, between the toes, in the armpits and groin where the tracks are covered with pubic hair. They are spots that even the pathologist misses, unless he's specifically looking for that evidence, and doing it with a microscope. Even then, the marks aren't easy to find."

"So you don't think he will?"

"I don't know. This is a big county. It depends on who does the postmortem. There's no way to tell."

"Well, hell, we can't take that chance." Yarrow grabbed her shoulder.

She patted his hand. "Exactly."

If she was going to find any kind of answer, she had to start with Lark's body. Tonight.

CHAPTER 10

SHE drove a couple of blocks and parked by the beach. The town lights were behind her; ahead, a rumpled blackness. She sat with the window open, breathing in sea air thick with brine and the smell of earth, of the life in it and the death. Behind her, cars started, motorcycles roared, auto alarms beeped. She heard them vaguely, muffled by the pulsing of the sea.

And she remembered Greg Gaige as he'd been that night in San Francisco eleven years ago. She'd just started work as a forensic patholo-gist. The day had been long, and she'd ended it with an emergency postmortem of a hiker just back from the Sierra. Her finding: sufficient indicators, pending lab results, to suggest bubonic plague. Probably he'd been infected in the Sierra. But he could have brought back carrier fleas. Bubonic plague was endemic in the wilds of the west. But it wasn't prevalent in her county, and her findings had alerted the health depart-ment and the sheriff. Bubonic plague was one of the few conditions still subject to quarantine. The smells of putrification from the autopsy room still cut the air, as if they were clinging to the inside of her nose. Her hands reeked of Clorox. The autopsy had taken hours. And when she looked at her watch, she'd discovered an extra hour had passed and she was likely to miss her one chance to see in person Greg Gaige do the Gaige Move.

She'd sped to the freeway, cut across lanes as if she were making a left-hand turn, and tailgated everything in the fast lane. She made it to the set with five minutes to spare. As it turned out, the scene had been delayed and she was hours early.

When she walked onto the set, she should have been exhausted, but instead she was striding on air, so excited that her thoughts bounced off each other in her head. The light over the autopsy table flashed against the banks of lights on the set, and she had to blink hard to black out her own triumph and concentrate on being a spectator at Greg Gaige's.

Trailers surrounded the roped-off street. Cameras and wires and chairs and padded boxes of equipment littered the sidewalk. Drab-dressed assistants scurried in and out. The whole place had had the look of a rock band abandoning its digs moments before the arrival of the sheriff. She had spotted Greg Gaige just as someone called out, "Lunch break!" A midnight "lunch."

It had been over twenty years since he'd been captured in the poster-picture doing the Move, but Greg Gaige looked like the same eager kid. Age had hardly changed him. His short straight sandy hair began just a bit higher on his forehead, and around his eyes and mouth lines were sketched so lightly, it seemed they could still be erased. And those startling blue eyes that had stared out from the poster still sparkled. They weren't as piercing now as they had been years before—he wasn't working now. But his walk was the same as if he'd been heading for the mat to start his floor routine; there was a bounce to his steps from those exquisitely toned muscles releasing, then tensing back. And when he stopped to swap sentences with one of the grips he was like a sports car idling. He grinned, slapped a shoulder, released into movement again, was stopped by the director and, Kiernan noted, greeted him the same way he had the grip. She stood, staring, mouth open, as if she were thirteen again.

But when she'd introduced herself, she could have been talking to a different person, an understudy to the real Greg Gaige.

"I'm so excited to meet you again," she had bubbled. "I wrote you all about my gymnastic successes afterward, but I never really thanked you for your encouragement to me that day in the gym. It came at a vital time, and it really changed my life. I had your poster on my wall until I was in medical school"—she laughed—"and it was in tatters."

He'd smiled then, but it wasn't the expression that blazed from the poster picture. Rather, it was a hesitant gesture, as if he were unsure it was the right reaction. "How have you been?"

"Mr. Gaige, I'm from KHBK News." A young blond man extended his hand to Greg. "We're doing a segment on aspects of the movie business. What's it like doing stunts?"

"It's fun," Greg said, and started moving again.

"But how do you plan?"

He shrugged. "The same way everyone else does." He put an arm on Kiernan's shoulder and kept moving.

"Don't cut that interview short because of me," she'd said.

"I'm not."

"But the publicity—"

He'd laughed. "I don't like doing interviews. They won't have trouble finding someone who does. Now you—do you still do gymnastics at all?"

"Only for fun. There was a time I thought I'd be able to do your Move. When I was sixteen, I came close. Well, not what *you'd* consider close— *you'd* have thought a certifiable spastic was doing it—but to me it felt like it was within the specs. By the next year, I was already too tall, too developed." She had tried to pass off the observation lightly, but fourteen years after the fact, she could hear her frustration that the day she'd come so close to nailing the Move had been a Sunday when she'd sneaked into the gym alone.

As they followed the cast and crew to the restaurant for the late-night "lunch," she found herself telling him about medical school and her residency and her new job at the coroner's office. "I never get over the thrill of uncovering the body's secrets. People assume that with their bodies they get a standard issue, like there are a few different models with some variations—short, tall, wiry, thick—but that basically what's inside is all the same. They all assume their spines are straight, their hearts perfect, that their brains fill their cranial bones like hard-boiled eggs inside the shells. They'd be shocked to discover how many women —maybe a third—have scoliosis, how many mitral valves are flaccid without their owners noticing more than the occasional heavy heartbeat, or that people with brains that look like the yolk is missing from the egg lead normal lives. In the case I had today, once I peeled back the skin of the forehead—"

It was at that point she'd realized he was looking away. She wasn't a blusher, but she'd turned red then. The only time she could recall feeling that humiliated was when she'd tripped over her feet in the initial run of her floor routine. She'd been fourteen then. At the state meet.

"Sorry, Greg," she muttered, "I forget that dead bodies aren't every-one's choice of dinner chat." But it wasn't his discomfort with the dead that bothered her; irrationally, she had expected him to be proud of her, to agree that she'd made the right decision abandoning gymnastics for forensic pathology, to give her a "ten" for her life. But she hadn't realized that then. Then, she'd just felt small.

"No, no. Go on," Greg had said, embarrassed. "I'm just having a hard time with the technical terms. There's so much I don't know."

"You?" she'd asked, ridiculously amazed. "But you do the Move that no one in the world can. When you do it tonight, will it be the same as it was back in Baltimore?"

His blue eyes looked up and to the left, as if he were searching distant space for the answer. "It's always changing. I'm always working on it, trying to squeeze more out of it, jack it around farther, do the punch back faster, harder, give it more zing." He grinned. "I'm going to surprise 'em tonight, show 'em I'm not just getting older; I'm getting better." He shrugged and turned away. She couldn't decide whether he regretted having admitted worrying about getting older, or was embarrassed at how tritely he'd phrased it.

She'd liked that, the artist ever in process. "Like it's alive, huh?"

"I guess." He was eating soup that he'd gotten from the cafeteria line —only soup, because he didn't know how soon the call for his gag, for the Move, would come.

She'd asked more about the Move, its evolution, but his answers were no clearer. He was entirely physical, she would say later, involved in the Move so viscerally that to talk about it was like translating what he was doing into hieroglyphs.

"The life-span of gymnastics seems eternal for men—compared to that of women," she'd said as she finished off a steak, potatoes, beans, roll, and salad and was eyeing the side table of desserts. "Still, what will you do afterward?"

"I don't have another picture in the works, but that's not unusual. I can't think about that till after the Move. Now everything, even this conversation, I'm afraid, is like it's behind the curtain of the Move."

"But after you stop doing the Move?"

"I keep working on it. I know I can get more out of the last twist— you'll see tonight—I can jack it around farther."

"But after you retire?" Suddenly it seemed vital to her to hear the answer she'd sought.

"My *father's* retired."

"But you will be someday."

"I'll have plenty of time to think about it then." He pushed away the soup bowl. "See, the thing with that twist isn't the hips, this'll come from the shoulders. Once I push off . . ."

She had stayed on the set for three hours huddling against the cold summer wind that brushed off the San Francisco hills, watching four takes of the scene before Greg's Move. Greg had found her a director's chair, but he himself had paced, wandered, and answered questions with monosyllables or shrugs.

But when the call sounded for his gag, the Greg Gaige who walked to the start mark could have been the Master of the World. Every step was sure, those blue eyes that had been vague at dinner seemed to take in the entire set, then narrow to a focus of such intensity, she half expected to see the set burn.

"Action!"

He ran surefooted. An explosion from Special Effects sent a fireworks of lights. Greg flipped like a rag doll, twisted as if he were out of control, landed and sprung back like a corpse, then abruptly, minutely shifted his shoulders and added a half twist and touched down with the ease of jumping from a stool.

The cast and crew leaped up and applauded.

Greg grinned, turned to the spot where he'd left her, ran over, grabbed her in his arms, and spun her around.

"Greg." The director put a hand on his shoulder. "Give the media a word, huh?"

She kissed him, and before he could ask her to stay—or not to—she said good-bye.

Then she watched him stride across the set, settle on the stool before the cameras, under the Clorox white lights, and grin. The sweat on his arms and shoulders shined the muscles, and joy seemed to bubble at every pore. Those blue eyes that had been piercing a minute before glistened opaquely as if reflecting inward.

She stared, imprinting the moment in her memory. *This is where you live,* he had said back in Baltimore. Then, watching him again, she understood that as she never had before. Doing the Move was the only time he felt alive. She hurried to her car and drove, unwilling to watch him struggle to translate his triumph into the language of words, to slide back from glory into the mire of the ordinary, where he walked flat-footed in the land of the dead.

That night she'd dreamed variations of the evening and awakened at four A.M. horrified at her intrusive questions. "Why was I so pushy?"

she'd demanded of herself again and again, when her standard answer—
I'm a pushy person—brought her no comfort. Greg hadn't wanted to
consider her questions. In the gray of dawn, she realized that she didn't,
either.

And then he called. Was it because of the question or the kiss? It
didn't matter, she told herself then. She could deal with neither. As a
teenager, a kiss from Greg Gaige had been the stuff of Olympian dreams.
Now it meant seeing beneath the laurel wreath, destroying her most
cherished childhood memories. And that she couldn't bring herself to
do, even for Greg Gaige.

Now, eleven years later, she felt a tear wet her cheek. Could the man
who had sat on the stool in the white light and wrapped himself in his
smile have walked into the fire gag as if he were walking into the sea? By
asking him her question, had she picked at a sore that would grow until
it killed him?

The night fog off the Pacific dragged across her back and shoulders
like rough raw silk, icing the sweat she hadn't realized was there. She
dug the heels of her hands into her eyes. There was no turning back; the
questions were too much a part of her. With Lark, she had to find out
who had snatched away her future. But with Greg Gaige, she had to
know *why* he had died.

CHAPTER 11

SHE pulled into her driveway at twelve thirty. Tchernak was already in his kitchen—a kitchen worthy of Sharper Image's front window, or so Kiernan called it, with every culinary novelty known to electrical outlet. She watched as he whipped the egg and milk for an omelet. The sun-dried tomatoes were already soaking in olive oil Tchernak got from a restaurant shipment flown in from Salerno. His nova of choice came via a connection in Seattle. Only the orange, whose peel he had grated, was local—and organic. "Garlic on a movie set? They have love scenes, they don't have garlic," Tchernak declared.

"Tchernak, I smelled garlic on the set, and in whatever the studio exec was eating at the rushes."

"Couldn't be real. Must be fake. Faux garlic, that's great. Find out how they make it!"

"Tchernak, this a murder investigation, not a recipe swap. I need to think about the morgue, not the kitchen. I need to see a body, tonight."

Tchernak handed her a plate.

"You're not eating?" she asked, walking back into her own half of the duplex.

"Carb day." Tchernak followed.

Ignoring the intricacies of his training regimen, she sat at her trompe l'oeil table, put her plate atop its painted likeness, and dug into the omelet. Ezra scarfed down his tithe of the food, then trotted over to Tchernak and plopped canine head on human knee. "He's giving you a chance to make up for moments you haven't been thinking of him," Kiernan said.

Tchernak stared in the dog's eyes, shaggy head to shaggy head. "You know you're always first in my heart," he said, scratching the hound behind both ears. To Kiernan he said, "So what is this crisis that draws a humble servant out of his bed at an hour for which he should be paid time and a half?"

"You heard about the stunt woman who died at Gliderport today?"

He nodded. "The one you went to see? I figured that's why you were so late. You investigating that?" Tchernak's brown eyes lit up. "Who's your client? What do you figure happened? What do you need me to do? Let me think who I know with the Parks Department?"

"No need, humble servant. It's the morgue where I need a connection."

"What do you need from there?"

"Entry. Tonight."

"That shouldn't be any problem for you. Surely you know someone there from when you were a forensic pathologist."

"Not well enough to call them at one in the morning and convince them to trot down to the morgue and twiddle their thumbs while I go over one of their corpses with a magnifying glass."

"Ah, to be a pathologist, formidable enough to be allowed to sleep," he said, glancing down at his own bathrobe. "Perhaps, Kiernan, they'd be more amenable in daylight hours."

"By then, Tchernak, they'll be dissecting Lark Sondervoil's body. I need to see it before they've cut it open."

"So delicately put. I'm just sorry I didn't have cold chicken, so you could be gnawing on a leg while you're talking."

She grinned. It hadn't occurred to her when she hired a former offensive lineman with a record of more surgeries than quarterback sacks that he would be queasy about autopsies. "To get in legitimately, I'd have to be under the umbrella of Lark's lawyer or next of kin, whoever that might be. By the time I track down either of them and convince them to hire me, the body will be in the ground. What I'm looking for is the minute indentation that a slender needle leaves, and I'll be searching in spots where the skin isn't smooth. As you know," she said, aware that she was moving into the area of more-than-he'd-wanted-to-know, "even in the freezer a corpse deteriorates, and we're talking about a body that was battered as it fell and then lay under the hot sun for some time. It wouldn't have been in too good a condition when it got to the morgue. If I have to go through channels and time passes, there won't be anything left worth looking at. So, Tchernak, I need to get in there tonight."

Tchernak leaned back against the green sofa cushions.

"I'm not about to endanger my license. . . . No professional suicide."

Tchernak ran his fingers down Ezra's back.

"There's no decent ruse I can use there at this time of night."

"Nope. No decent ruse *you* can use."

Kiernan stopped, her laden fork midway between plate and mouth. "What does that mean?"

"We all have our resources. Or right about now"—he grinned—"all but you."

"By which you mean you *do* have a resource?"

He sprawled back on the couch, stretched his arms, and clasped his hands behind his head. "I might."

"Tchernak! Who?"

"The morgue attendants."

"You know the morgue attendants? All of them?"

"Well, maybe not the new ones." He patted his knee, an invitation to Ezra. The big hound stretched his neck forward. Tchernak watched until the wiry head was on his thigh. "I could contact the senior guys."

"Because?" she prodded.

Tchernak grinned. "Well, Kiernan, you were a forensic pathologist; you were busy rushing into the autopsy room, cutting up one corpse, and rushing on to the next. You had the exciting job. But time hangs heavy for the poor morgue attendant. The morgue attendant is a contemplative man."

The light was beginning to dawn. Kiernan smiled. "And what he contemplates is football?"

Tchernak nodded. "You maybe recall five years ago, we had a defense known as The Morgue. The morgue for quarterbacks. They dissected the quarterback. The morgue attendants loved that. They sent us a body bag. The team got them a block of seats for the games. During one game every time we sacked the quarterback, the morgue held up a body bag. They loved it."

"Why'd they stop coming?"

"Defense stopped getting sacks. And the city fathers," Tchernak said with a raise of the eyebrows, "felt the body bag was insensitive. But the thing is, Kiernan, we had those guys to a team party. They loved being part of the 'team'—well, there's nothing like it." He gave his head a quick jerk as if to shake off the memory. "They joked about owing us—

offense and defense—offering us the best spots in the fridge, moving us to number one on the autopsy schedule. Getting a friend in for a free gaggle at one of their corpses will be a snap. Whoever's on duty, it'll make his night." Tchernak pushed himself up. "Of course, nothing is without cost."

"And what might that cost be to a servant who makes more than a first-year lineman?"

"A spot on the case roster."

Kiernan groaned. When she hired him, they both thought they knew what they wanted. She had wanted a servant; he had wanted a job that would give him time to get in shape for a comeback. It should have been a perfect arrangement. It wasn't. There were too many temptations on both sides, not the least of which was the lure of investigating. She understood the attraction it held for Tchernak. She loved the thrill of investigating—knowing she was dependent solely on herself. She didn't want an assistant. And if she had wanted an assistant, it wouldn't have been Brad Tchernak. Tchernak had once admitted that when he was a *starting* offensive tackle with the Chargers, he was forever after the wide receivers to run one more route and let him practice the short out, "just in case the team needs a fourth-string quarterback." She didn't want him protecting her flanks, much less greedily eyeing the ball and second-guessing her pass patterns. And yet the thought of never finding out about Lark Sondervoil, or Greg— "What about your training schedule?"

"I'll work around it."

"And if it conflicts?"

"It won't."

And if you fail a tryout by an inch? She didn't want to think of that possibility. Tchernak would never let on how distraught he'd be. But they would both know. Of course, that meant he wouldn't be dragging those three ruptured discs of his out onto the football field.

Tchernak grinned. "Take it or leave it, Kiernan."

She laughed. "How soon can I be in the morgue?"

Harris, the morgue attendant, was torn. His small, pale face shifted from his logbook to point up at Tchernak. He smiled, an expression that seemed ill-fitting on his thin, bluish mouth. Tchernak loomed over him, easily a foot taller, a hundred pounds heavier, and twenty years younger than the pale man with pen resting on logbook.

"I thought you might be interested in the huddles," Tchernak offered.

"You watch the game on the tube, it looks like the quarterback does nothing but call the play and give the snap count. Hardly." Tchernak laughed conspiratorially. "I'll have some time while she's inside."

Harris nodded, his long nose and pointed chin bobbing in anticipation. Nervously, he glanced down the corridor, his darkening expression belying the echoing emptiness. His gaze returned to his logbook. He shook his head. "I got my responsibilities here. I can't be letting a stranger, even a doctor-stranger, into the morgue at night. I got to list every single person who comes in and out." Tapping a wizened finger on the book, he added, "My log can be subpoenaed into court. I'm taking a big risk."

Tchernak nodded.

Behind him, Kiernan mouthed "Go on." Harris was raising the ante, but he was using the wrong bluff with Tchernak. Tchernak had protected against the strongest, fastest defensive ends in football; he was used to faking out big guys. But conning a little old guy who needed his job, a guy begging for his protection—it was like asking him to kick his own quarterback in the knee.

Go on.

"Harris, you remember the Cleveland game, when they intercepted and ran the ball back for a touchdown? The strong safety—who was that then?—changed the defensive alignment twice at the line of scrimmage. Fouts was watching like a hawk. What never came out in the papers . . . but you don't have time to hear that."

Harris glanced down the corridor, lifting his nose as if sniffing the air. He ran his tongue over his thin, bluish lips, glanced at the logbook and back at Tchernak. "The thing is, see, they got this inspection party scheduled to swoop in here tonight. I don't know when. Checking up on the cleaning crew. Stuff's been missing, you know what I mean? Could be the cleaners, could not. But they find I let someone in here, they're not going to be worrying about no cleaners, if you get my drift. I got my pension, my health insurance, my *dental insurance* to think of."

Tchernak paled. He'd missed the pitch of the morgue man's voice rising at the end of his sentence—Harris's ante. What he saw was the prospect of a superannuated indigent huddled outside the poorhouse doors. In a blizzard. Surrounded by wolves. The way things were going here, Tchernak would be throwing the inspection crew to the ground to protect Harris, and she'd still be standing here in the hall. *Go on!*

Tchernak glanced at her—Madame Defarge, that glance said.

Kiernan waited, and when Tchernak didn't speak, she said, "I don't want to get caught in the storage room any more than you want me to."

Harris jerked toward her, as if he'd forgotten she was there.

"Someone grabs me, they wonder if you took a leak when you should have been on duty. Maybe your supervisor chews you out. But me they haul off to jail and I lose my license. Without that, I don't work at all." That was an out-and-out lie, but what were negotiations for, if not bluster and deceit?

Harris, however, was not swayed. This man, Kiernan thought, was cagey enough to barter bones in the underground skeleton market.

"Harris," Tchernak said, "I suppose you heard about Ron Lynn's morgue award."

Harris didn't respond, but the twitch at the corner of his left eye gave him away. The Chargers' former defensive coach had been the nearest thing to a god in the cynical world of the morgue attendants. "Okay," he said slowly, "but I'm not kidding you about the inspection team. If they head in there, there's nothing I can do to stop them."

Kiernan nodded and followed Harris to the corner autopsy room, noting the door to the intersecting hallway, one she hoped she wouldn't have to use.

Harris flipped on the light, strode across the icy room, opened a drawer, and pulled out a double-decker gurney. "Okay to do your looking here?" he asked. "You can shove it back in quick if you got to."

Lark Sondervoil's body was on the top—higher than Kiernan would have liked. She nodded, waited for Harris to leave, then listened as the slap of his footsteps disappeared. Tchernak and Harris would be talking now, but she couldn't make out a sound. Not a good sign. If the inspectors came by, there would be no way for Tchernak to warn her.

Kiernan shivered in the icy room. Automatically she began breathing through her mouth to thwart the smell of decay that clings to the air in every autopsy room, no matter how many waves of Clorox wash over the walls and tables, the scales and the exhaust fans. By the end of her time as forensic pathologist, she had felt as if the Clorox no longer cleansed her but merely coated the smell of rotting flesh that nestled under her nails and in her nostrils.

She let her eyes close, as if changing the lenses through which she viewed life, and when she raised her eyelids, five years had been blinked away. As if she were in green scrubs, mask over mouth, hands gloved, staring down at the body of a man who had been found dead a week in his kitchen by an electric meter reader who noticed the smell, of the corpse of a boy pulled from the cab of his pickup. As if she were assessing this body before making the Y-shaped incision from the acromioclavicular joints of the shoulders, below the breasts, and straight down to the pubis. The room she was standing in slipped to the edge of her awareness, and in her mind she was in the small autopsy room that had been hers back then, a space large enough to handle one postmortem comfortably, two in an emergency. There had never been an occasion when they'd needed to double up. Even the crash victims in the case that had led to her firing she had done sequentially. If she had called in help and worked on them side by side, she might still be on staff there. Might still be a forensic pathologist. Now, five years afterward, she felt relieved in the certainty that pathology was not the highway to Truth she'd always assumed, and yet she also felt adrift, without that certainty that had shaped her life.

The picture of Yarrow staring at his deceptively clear glass bricks flashed in her mind. He'd left stunt work just as abruptly. She hadn't asked why. The man was limping around, hadn't worked in a decade, yet still clung to the lodestone of "the business." It still worked its magnetic magic, even though he'd seen Lark Sondervoil die in a gag a few hours earlier.

Lark looked small lying on the gurney constructed to hold nearly every corpse that came through. One size fits all. As many bodies as Kiernan had seen, this first viewing of them never became rote. The dead always looked abandoned by life.

The body was naked, the blue-white of death. When they brought her in, the staff would have taken her to the staging room, placed her on a gurney for weighing, removed her clothing layer by layer, photographing each piece of clothing, photographing the body in the remaining garments—the necrophiliac's striptease, they'd called it in medical school. The techs would have taken prints then, and the investigating officer would have turned in a receipt for any evidence and personal property he'd recovered at the scene of death. In this case, there wouldn't have been much of either.

Purposely she didn't touch Lark's skin. After hours in the fridge it would be cold; she'd learn nothing from a touch. No point in disturbing the evidence unnecessarily. Ragged abrasions laced the limbs, and to a lesser degree the torso and face. Sand had stuck in the blood caked around them. The skin wouldn't be washed until the pathologist had a chance to observe the skin as it was, then correlate those observations with his findings when he considered the tissue and organs beneath.

"Abrasions presumably from the fall," Kiernan mouthed silently, as she once would have noted into the microphone hanging over the autopsy table. "High density of sand mixed with blood on anterior surfaces of both hands." The blood there was closer to pink than anywhere else; the ratio of sand mixed in with the blood greater. The sand on the palms would have rubbed in as Lark futilely grabbed at the bluff wall for purchase. The redder abrasions on the backs of the hands would have come from being flung uselessly against the jagged wall.

Kiernan's breath caught. Uncharacteristically, she wanted to reach out, to put a comforting hand on those battered hands. She shook off the urge; she'd seen too many bodies to allow herself to get caught like this. She focused on the abrasions. The lines of movement on that outer forearm spread not up, as they would from being abraded while the body slid down against the rough surface. They spread down; Lark had been falling headfirst, and so out of control that her arms had been hanging useless, to be scraped on the outside. Had Lark lost consciousness partway down? God, she hoped so. She didn't want to think of the terror of falling to death. Never in the autopsy room had she let herself speculate on the emotions of the dying.

She glanced at Lark's face. It was pale, almost cyanotic. No, she hadn't landed head down.

Kiernan stood unmoving, listening for sounds outside. She heard nothing but her own breath. "Significant quantity of blood." Skin wounds and head wounds bleed heavily. Blood would have gushed until shortly after Lark hit the beach, until her heart stopped pumping. "Little ecchymosis visible." There wouldn't be much bruising—death had come too quickly for the heart to push much blood into the tissues.

But there was lividity. Without lifting the body, Kiernan could see the blood settled at both sides of the neck and lower thoracic area—and doubtless in between. Not the normal pattern for a decedent who died lying face up. Normally the blood would have been spread evenly but concentrated in the areas that were neither constricted by clothing nor pressed against a hard surface, areas into which gravity-pulled blood could seep easily. The softness of the beach sand would have allowed more lividity than the table on which she rested now. But too little blood had settled in the neck and shoulders; they were barely colored. The upper pelvic area was darker, and darkest of all were the feet. "Lividity

in the feet apparent from the superior posterior calcaneus to cuboid."
She nodded slowly. That line sloping from the knob of the heel down to
the arch meant Lark had hit the beach heel first and come to rest at that
angle in the sand. Bones would have shattered, spinal discs ruptured,
organs burst. The skin, a remarkably tough organ, had held, camouflag-
ing the extent of the damage beneath. Kiernan's teeth jammed together
so hard, her head hurt.

Angrily she shook off the emotion. If she couldn't be objective in the
autopsy room, she was useless. Dammit, she had never been like this. In
medical school she had been the one who scorned the squeamish, the
mawkish guys who wanted to wallow in what the decedents felt. "Leave
that to the forensic psychiatrists!" she'd told them. "We deal in facts."

Fact: If organs burst, gases escape into surrounding tissue. She
checked the abdomen. Already there was a slight greenish discoloration.

Again she stood still, not breathing, listening to the sound of the air
conditioner, the hum of the refrigerator, straining to hear stray footsteps
outside. But she could hear nothing beyond the heavy double doors.

She pulled out her magnifying glass and gazed painstakingly down
the inside of the arm, one of the easiest places to find a vein, an area that
recreational drug novices find appealing. Kiernan didn't picture Lark
tattooing her arms with tracks. If Lark had had a habit she managed to
conceal, she would have shifted her injection site quickly. But coming
across the tiny telltale indentations on the arm would have been a clue.
That there were none was no clue at all. Slowly, carefully, she checked
the left hand, peering through the glass at the webbing between the
fingers, an easily camouflaged site. No marks. None on the right hand,
none between the toes, none in the pubic area.

"Kiernan, you ready yet?"

She jerked up and spun toward the door. It took a moment for her
eyes to focus on Tchernak, and another to see him clearly enough to
note the pinched skin around his eyes and mouth. "You've been in here
over an hour, you know."

She would have guessed ten minutes. But that was the way it was with
skin scanning. Suddenly she realized her back ached and she was shivering.

"The cleaning crew's already here. Harris is getting jumpy."

"One more minute."

"Harris says the inspectors could be here anytime. He's shaking like a bad punt. I can't even distract him with the time I set Lawrence Taylor on his duff. I don't have any better stories than that."

"Lie." She couldn't let herself think of Harris, not now.

It was a moment before Tchernak said, "He says the thefts have been in here—equipment. When they come, the inspectors aren't going to stop and chat; they'll be trotting right in these doors. Don't fool around."

"I'll just be a minute." As Tchernak let the door swing closed, she could see the small, deadly pale man pacing in the doorway. He had made his deal; he knew the risks. *She had to push him out of her mind.* Turning back to the body, she bent down over the face. "Eyes show postmortem clouding with some scleral hemorrhage in the medial aspect of the left eye." Not surprising. Had Lark lived longer, her entire face would have been bruised from the force of her spine striking up into her skull. Had she lived, her mind would have been captive in a useless body—if she had any mind left at all.

She had to finish, to see inside Lark's mouth, under her tongue, the last camouflaged place she could have injected herself.

She pushed gently at the teeth. No give. She stopped. Not surprisingly, rigor had begun. It might not be set completely, but it began in the muscles of the eyelid and lower jaw, and the mouth was already quite firm. If she forced the teeth apart and broke the rigor, it would not reset. It might affect the autopsy, skew the findings, and announce to the pathologist and anyone who read his report that someone had been disturbing the body. She pulled a penlight from her pack and shone it under the edges of the tongue. She bent closer, then moved farther back. But there was no way she could see the entire area. Sighing, she straightened up.

It didn't matter, she told herself. All the other more likely areas were negative. No shooter goes straight to the tongue.

But it *did* matter. Even if it was a one percent uncertainty, it mattered. She needed to go into this investigation untethered by the slightest doubt.

"Kiernan," Tchernak called, urgency clear in his voice.

Quickly she moved around to the far side of the gurney.

"The cleaning crew is across the hall. You've got to get out of here."

Her gaze shifted from the tongue to Lark's teeth. Stuck between the two upper left incisors was a seed.

Footsteps resounded in the Harris's hallway. She pictured the inspectors coming toward Harris, hands reaching out, grabbing his pension and medical insurance.

She bent closer to the mouth. A poppy seed!

The footsteps grew louder.

Were there more seeds? No time to find out. The image of Harris filled her mind—outside the poorhouse, in the snow. "Damn you, Harris," she muttered, shoved the gurney back into the fridge, and raced out the far door.

CHAPTER 12

"HOW can you even think of breaking into Lark Sondervoil's apartment? Those inspectors in the morgue were close enough to tackle you and throw you for one big loss. Have you missed the concept of learning from your mistakes? What are you—the kid who repeats the first grade her entire life?" Tchernak said as the Jeep turned onto the main road.

"Look, I don't want to go there any more than you want me to."

Tchernak's traditional farewell to her was "No speeding! No baiting! No fenestration!" He glared in disbelief. "In that case, you won't go."

"I have to. If the pathologist finds the poppy seed suspicious, he'll have the cops running all over her place by noon."

"He won't worry about that. He's not thinking about the Highway Patrol report; he's wondering how she died falling over a cliff. Even you don't think a bagel would skew CHP's tests."

"Police do investigate, Tchernak."

"My point exactly."

She put her hand on his arm, "Lark had scheduled a press conference after her gag. She was killed before she could speak. What was she going to clarify, or announce, or reveal? There's some connection between her and *Bad Companions*. This is my only chance to see what. Even if the cops sift through her apartment, they could miss that."

"Miss *what*? You don't know there is any *thing,* much less that it's there! Or that the police will disturb it if it exists at all."

"Tchernak, I agreed you could be an assistant on this case, not an offensive lineman. You've got your arms up so high protecting me, I'll never be able to throw the ball!"

Tchernak stared at her openmouthed.

She restrained a grin. "Say the cops *don't* shake out the apartment. Then they let it go, and the landlord cleans it out and rents it by the weekend. Lark's got no family—or so Yarrow says—no one's going to bitch if the landlord collects double rent the rest of the month."

"Still—"

"No, I've got to get in there before anyone else thinks of it."

"And if the cops come and find you, then what?"

"Then I move to Nebraska and raise championship wolfhounds."

It was three in the morning in Pacific Beach, the section of San Diego just below La Jolla. Kiernan pulled the Jeep up in front of a row of Cape Cod garden apartments that hunched uncomfortably between a stucco six-plex and ersatz Spanish villas. Down the street a couple of stucco cottages sat on the same-size lots. Cars filled every spot of curb, legal and otherwise.

Tchernak had finally been willing to override his opposition to breaking and entering and come along. But Kiernan had not been moved. What she didn't need was another body to stumble over inside Lark's apartment; what she did need was someone at home in La Jolla with Ezra. He could sit guard outside the apartment, Tchernak had insisted. "Don't you think you might be a bit conspicuous at three in the morning?" she'd countered. "All I need is to have to come rushing out of an apartment I've just spent half an hour getting into so I can tell the patrolman you're not a potential mugger or burglar."

But, in fact, with the number of pickups, mini-Jeeps, and cars with surfboards still strapped on top, the party going strong across the courtyard of the Salem Harbour Garden Studios, the car alarm down the street warning the night wind: "Step back, you've come too close," Tchernak could have sat naked on the sidewalk and not been noticed.

Kiernan checked the mailboxes of the Salem Harbour Studios and found Lark's: number five. Number five would be at the back of the northside rectangle. She hurried through the narrow courtyard, past the colored lights that reminded her of the one vacation trip her family had taken. Leaving Baltimore in February when the snow covered the hubcaps and arriving in a Miami motel, they had paused just long enough to change clothes and race to the palm-dotted beach, to swim and sun the whole warm, soft, amazingly bright day—and spent the rest of the week huddling in the shade of umbrellas, applying tea and thick white lotion to their sore bodies, and watching their skin peel. Even so, that first day on the Florida beach had been a spot of magic in her childhood, and the memory of it was the unfilled wish that had drawn her west to the land of palm trees.

This courtyard looked as if it had been designed by someone with a similar Miami week. Tall palms, short palms, mixed with the night-closed flowers of bright yellow day lilies, orange hibiscus, and red and yellow fists of lantara. San Diego was desert, its water so hard, its citizens bought bottled—but here the grass was as long and green as any lawn in Miami.

Number five was a studio up seven steps from the narrow walkway. Decorative wrought iron barred the window next to the door. Window bars, the lace curtains of urban blight! They scarred the view, were a danger in fire, fostered paranoia in the neighborhood, and more to the point, created a major obstacle to her getting inside and—God forbid the door should be blocked by a foreign body—getting back out. Purposely, she did not turn around to check for paranoids on neighboring stoops or behind windows. Might as well wear a day-glo T-shirt that said "Burglary—and More!" on the back. She listened, but the only sounds were the salsa music coming from number seven, on the street a car engine refusing to turn over, and the rustle of the branches of a tall star pine at the rear of the property. She waited long enough to assure herself, then pulled open the metal screen door, peered through the stained-glass panel into the dark room inside, and tried the handle. Lark hadn't sounded like a young woman whose door would be open. It wasn't.

Despite the laid-back ambiance of Salem Harbour Studios, Kiernan knew she had a limited amount of time to get inside. She had considered bringing a set of picks but decided the dangers of being apprehended with them outweighed the advantages. Instead, she'd opted for a key ring that could have hung from the belt of a school janitor—guaranteed to provide entry to the twenty most popular locks.

Normally, this was a moment Kiernan loved, the instant before entry. She savored its seductive illegality, its warmly illicit promise of penetration; she forced herself to stand a moment on the threshold husbanding her urges, feeling them throb against her skin, delaying the moment of delicious release. Normally, she gave herself the luxury of running her mental fingers down the soft, sensuous walls of her victim's valuables, wrapping her hands around jewels, and kneading out their secrets.

But entering the home of a dead woman was not the same. And this apartment in particular, this rent-by-the-week studio that for all her effort would give her no more than a flaccid drip of information, hardly elicited that kind of foreplay.

A sharp breeze chilled her back. Across the courtyard a door opened and music rushed out. Against her better judgment she looked over her shoulder in time to see a young blond couple amble down the steps, looking neither at her nor back at the apartment from which they had come. Their gaze was entirely focused on each other; they seemed to be walking by instinct and luck.

Kiernan turned back to the door, trying the first four keys in rapid succession. She checked on the progress of the couple—halfway to the street—then went through the next six keys. Again, she glanced after the couple, not really suspecting them but suspicious enough to assure herself that their behavior didn't change when they thought they were out of sight.

As reassured as she could be, she inserted the next key. The tumblers fell into place, the knob turned, and she pushed the door all the way open till it smacked softly against the wall.

She readied her flashlight and stepped inside. After the tropically bright lights outside, the studio was black. The music from number seven pushed in the door after her, so loud she couldn't make out the hum of the refrigerator, which in the standard breaking-and-entering resounded like the heartbeat of a waiting giant. She gave her eyes one more moment to adjust to the dark, then peered ahead at a square of light, trying to make out whether it was a small window or a pane set in the back door, a back door that she might need. Stepping inside, she swung the front door softly shut behind her.

To her right, she heard the rasp of a breath. Movement. She pivoted. Too late. She could sense the blow coming at her head, but she didn't feel the pain.

CHAPTER 13

KIERNAN'S head throbbed. The frontal plate of skull hurt. And—oh, shit—she was going to throw up!

No, she was *not*! O'Shaughnessys did not regurgitate; that had been her parents' mantra on that family trip to Florida. She'd heard it after her first infraction on the D.C. beltway, after her second around Charlottesville, and as a sort of Greek chorus echoing every comment on any topic through Virginia, the Carolinas, and Georgia. She'd been an adult before she could see an advertisement for hush puppies, East Carolina barbecue, or key lime pie and not feel a swirl in her stomach.

She pushed herself up and leaned back against the wall. Where the hell was she? The room was black. In the distance, way in the distance she could see a fuzzy pale square. A window?

Then the memory of entering Lark Sondervoil's flat eased into focus. Anxiously, but in cautious consideration of her throbbing head and key-limeish stomach, she pushed herself forward onto all fours and felt around for her key ring, making larger and larger arcs with her arm, till she could no longer balance and sat back with a thump of disgust. Bad enough that someone had beaned her, but nabbing the keys she'd spent years collecting was adding insult to considerable injury. She'd get him, and—

Get who? Was she even sure the *who* was a *him*? She recalled realizing someone was in the room and instinctively turning toward the noise. The wound was just behind her hairline, which meant that her assailant had come up behind her and struck down. She sighed—big help; when you're just over five feet tall, a twelve-year-old kid could strike down on you.

But she could ponder that later. There were two boons here. First, her assailant had already struck her and departed; he was not likely to come back. She could search the apartment in luxurious leisure. And second, someone else had figured there was something worth finding here. Or there had been. One out of two wasn't bad.

She braced her hand to push herself up and felt a cylinder. Her flashlight! She turned it toward her watch: three thirtyish (as clearly as her still-dazed eyes could tell). She hadn't been out more than a few minutes. And whatever the other failings of her assailant, at least he'd been quiet enough not to disturb the neighbors.

She shone the light across the floor where it wouldn't be noticeable from the windows. The studio was a twenty-five-foot square, with a kitchenette area in the right corner (where the square of light was), a bathroom-size insert in the corner to her left, and a door, probably to a closet, in between. The rest of the floor space could have been furnished by the Tchernak Decorating Company—no furniture other than a double futon in the right-hand corner, dowels attached ladder-style to the front wall, a loop of heavy rope hanging from screws in the side wall, and weights of various sizes piled neatly next to a ghetto blaster. Someone unfamiliar with gymnastics might take the place for an S and M dungeon, but Kiernan could picture Lark placing a heel higher and higher up those dowels, stretching her hamstrings longer with each lift. From the loop of rope she would suspend herself upside down; or hanging on to the side loops, she'd walk up the wall till she was inverted, then flip down and start again. And the floor—not carpeted, but covered in springy, good-quality linoleum—was just big enough to practice simple drops and flips. She had suspected the studio had come furnished, but not furnished like this. This had the feel of Hollywood accommodation.

The room seemed to have as little to hide as did Lark's body. An illusion? Kiernan made another sweep with the light. Nothing on the floor, not even a phone book. She pushed herself up and braced against the wall till her light-headedness cleared, then walked unsteadily across to the closet. It was small—the average San Diegan who'd rent a studio in this loud and unprivate complex wouldn't need space for more than a string bikini and a surfboard. Lark had three sundresses, a black scoop-necked all-purpose dress, half a dozen shirts and T-shirts (ironed and on hangers), and a variety of shorts hanging from clips on a ladder hanger. On the floor shoes were paired and aligned in two rows.

Lark's mother would be proud, Kiernan thought sardonically, closing the door. Her mother would be escorted into a Heavenly viewing room, seated amongst her friends. From there they would all look down on Lark's closet, and Mrs. Sondervoil would delight in saying, "Such a good girl, my Lark. I knew she'd have her closet tidy." The late Mrs. Sondervoil's late friends would murmur in approval and envy.

There was quite a different viewing room for mothers of women like herself, Kiernan suspected. With a start, she realized her mind was wandering; the blow to her head was taking its toll. Concentrating hard on the job at hand, she walked to the kitchenette and checked the refrigerator—hiding place of choice in recent years. But it held neither secrets nor food. Bottles of Calistoga water and trays of ice cubes were its entire payload. The cabinets and drawers echoed the transitory and indifferent quality of dwelling here: a set of cheap stainless, plastic plates from microwave dinners, two plastic glasses, and two mugs from Starbuck's coffee, easily the nicest thing in the kitchen. Above the stove was a bag of loose tea. PERUVIAN COCA TEA, the label said! Another entry in the positive drug-findings sweepstakes. She poured an ounce into a plastic bag and pocketed it.

Beneath the counter, drawer after drawer was empty until she came to the row nearest the living room: One held phone books, another a scrapbook. Quickly she checked the phone books for turned-down pages or numbers noted in the front, but Lark had not personalized it.

Taking the scrapbook back into the living room, she smiled. In Hollywood a scrapbook must be as normal an accoutrement as a cellular phone. But in this utilitarian, impersonal room, it seemed almost whimsical. Had Lark Sondervoil lain here night after night listening to the salsa music, the roars of accelerating engines in the street, and the squeal of brakes and read clips about her own triumphs to lull her to sleep? Or perhaps she had savored the bursts of noise, assured that once she finished this picture and wowed the world with the Gaige Move, she would never have to stay in a place like this again.

Kiernan was shivering. From shock, physical shock, no doubt. But she didn't have time to deal with that now. She moved over to the futon, slipped her legs under the cover, and opened the scrapbook. A wad of letters fell to the floor.

Again she smiled. So this was where her predecessor had looked. The Lark Sondervoil who lined up her sandals and slippers wouldn't have *jammed* her correspondence into the only book she owned. These letters could be the ones her assailant had rejected, but their being jammed in here could also mean she had disturbed him before he'd had time to read them. Wouldn't he have taken them with him? Not if he'd found the thing he needed. But a mention of Greg Gaige, a telling comment on *Bad Companions*—that could be in the middle of a letter he'd missed.

She closed the scrapbook and used the slick, hard cover to smooth out the envelopes and the papers inside. Damn, no letters at all! They were documents concerning the apartment. She squinted, trying to make out the fuzzy print. Dammit, did she have a concussion? She squinted harder and looked quickly at the documents before the words blended together. The pages were the lease, running for six weeks, signed by Dolly Uberhazy. Dolly—where had she heard that name? Ah, yes, the woman from the Hollywood studio who had strolled into the film rushes eating the concoction with the garlic or faux garlic that so intrigued Tchernak. The bottom pages were contracts for the phone and utilities.

She put the documents aside and paused a moment before opening the scrapbook. This was what she loved about housebreaking. A scrapbook; better than a dozen desk drawers, more intimate than a hundred closets. "The most important things in my life," a scrapbook might be labeled. "The things that make up my image of me." *The* book that the Righteous Dead in heaven bring to the special room to show their friends over and over, eternally. And in heaven their friends have to murmur in appreciation, if not envy. (Envy? Would that be allowed, even in her unorthodox heaven? But without the possibility of evoking it, what was the purpose of displaying a scrapbook?)

Pay attention! Stop drifting!

This scrapbook, the only personal item Lark Sondervoil had brought with her—or the only one the assailant had left in the apartment, Kiernan thought with a shot of regret—this would provide an exquisite view into Lark Sondervoil's soul. She opened to the first page, and smiled.

The yellowed newspaper article was not a picture of a younger Lark winning a competition or signing a Hollywood contract, or a narrative piece on her experiences as a new stunt woman. No, this article was not on Lark at all but about Greg Gaige! Any clandestine knowledge Lark had about him, surely it would be filed away here. Quickly, Kiernan turned the scrapbook pages, but only the first two had been used, and three newspaper clippings were taped on.

On the first page a brittle and yellowed picture of a man suspended horizontal eight feet in the air, his body half twisted toward the camera, accompanied a column headlined GAIGE MOVE STUNS STUNT WORLD. The still photo failed to capture the vivacity of the Move. It was the height of the lift, the tight spiral of the twist, the explosive force when he landed and punched back up into the flip that made the Move so spectacular. It was the way he held his body ramrod straight, or alternately flailed his arms and legs to make the sequence look as if he'd been tossed out of control when the script called for that. . . . She remembered it so well. She and the other teenage gymnastic hopefuls had seen that movie over and over. When he'd done it on the set that night in San Francisco, it took her breath away. But even here, with the Move frozen in yellowed newsprint, it was clear that the young Greg Gaige had been something special. In the midst of the flip and twist, Greg Gaige was smiling!

That photo—the same publicity shot that had been on the gym wall— had been the icon of her childhood hope. It had been at the far side of the vault horse, the first thing she'd seen when she looked up from her dismount, the first look of approval, the shared smile from the joy of it all. No words, no qualifiers, just the illusion of approval from the best of the best. In the ever bleaker days after her sister's death, when her parents themselves faded back from life, the image of Greg and memory of him saying "Good feel for it. *You* are a gymnast," had been her comfort.

Champion gymnasts whipped on smiles the instant their feet finally struck the mat and their arms shot over their heads, but when they were performing the flip or vault, they were as concentrated as heart surgeons. What an athlete Greg Gaige had been to perform the Move with such aplomb, with such joy. How could he have . . .

Kiernan turned the scrapbook page. NEVER OVER THE HILL, SAYS 45-YEAR-OLD STUNTMAN said the headline on the left. Kiernan nodded. What would constitute "over the hill" for a man who could smile in the middle of the Move? She checked the date: ten years ago to the month.

Less than a year after she'd been with him in San Francisco. After she'd ignored his telephone call. No, *ignored* was the wrong word—she hadn't forgotten Greg. Every day after, twelve times a day, she'd started for the phone. But something for which she couldn't find words had stopped her. And after the movie company had left San Francisco, she'd called the stunt doubles' association in L.A.—and hung up without leaving a message. She never talked to him again, but the yearning never left her. It wasn't the raw, impatience of love or lust, when her insides twanged like guitar strings and her skin was eager to the touch. This had been different, an aching emptiness from her throat to her gut, a grieving for the loss of her icon, a fury at Greg's unknowing betrayal of his image. She'd been desperate to find some angle from which to view him, some way to find the answers she had always assumed he possessed.

The last article, dated a week later, was only two paragraphs: STUNTMAN DIES IN MOVIE SET FIRE. A wave of cold passed through her. She wanted to turn back the page and ask, "Greg, what is it like to be the best of the best?"

And: "How can you lose the thing that was life for you?" "How can you face being Greg Gaige without the Move?"

Or maybe you couldn't.

Kiernan shivered. God, she didn't want to believe that—not for Greg . . . or for Tchernak . . . or for herself.

She squinted hard and looked down at the article, datelined Hollywood: "Stuntman Greg Gaige, 45, was killed in a fire east of El Centro on the location set of the film *Bad Companions,* said the film's producer Dolly Uberhazy."

Dolly Uberhazy, again.

She peered closer at the yellowed page. Next to the article, in pencil, someone—Lark?—had written: *No Boukunas, not Greg!*

Boukunas?

The door burst open, the lights came on. "Freeze!"

Kiernan yanked the blanket up to her shoulders and looked up into the barrels of two automatics, with two uniformed policemen holding them.

Fear flashed in her stomach and was gone. No time for that. She glared at the nearest cop. "What the hell are you doing bursting in here?"

"We got a report of a break-in—"

"It took you long enough to get here. He's been gone half an hour. He could be in L.A. by now. Look at my head—I'll tell you about the burglar. He was hiding in here when I got home. Knocked me cold. I'm going to have a lump on my head the size of El Centro. Hurts like hell," she added.

"Have you had medical attention?" asked the shorter cop, a barrel-chested dark-haired guy with a bristly moustache. Melchior, his name tag read.

"Not hardly; I was waiting for you. If I'd gone to emergency, I'd still be there. The doctors there are busy with gunshot wounds and jump-starting dead hearts; by the time they got to my bump on the head, the sun would be up. In the meantime you'd be pounding at my door figuring some flake called you out to a false alarm."

"Lady, you could have a concussion, a cracked skull."

"So what are doctors going to do about that? Put my head in a cast?" Keep them on the defensive; don't give them time to think. "And while I waited there in emergency, I'd be picking up every germ in San Diego County. No thanks." She sighed and slumped back into the pillow. "Look, I'm a realist. What are the chances you're going to track down this burglar who hit me over the head before I got a look at him?"

"Did you see your assailant, Ms.—?"

"O'Shaughnessy. No. He came up behind me, knocked me out cold, and was gone before I came to."

"Well, you're not giving us much to go on," the dark cop said. Gun still drawn, he took a step forward.

"Another case of violence pays." *No baiting! No speeding! No fenestration!* She sighed, again. "Well, let's just forget it. Save you some paperwork, and let me sleep off my throbbing head. There's not a thing I can tell you anyway."

The policemen shared a glance. Melchior, the dark-haired one, wanted to leave; he could see the logic in her offer. The blond—Wycotte, his name tag said—still clasped his gun. He, too, would have left happy—*if* she'd let him think it was his decision. But she couldn't have brought herself to do that, could she? She'd *baited.*

The blond holstered his gun, but the movement was hardly conciliatory. Rather, it was a statement that the weapon was extra, his presence all the power he needed. "Lady, would you show us some identification." It was not a question. And definitely a request she did not want to deal with. "And then," he went on, "you can explain why, if you live here, you're sitting in the dark holding a flashlight."

She swallowed the urge to snap back at him. *Think jail,* she told herself. She raised her right knee to pull up the blanket, and catching the corner of the blanket between her shoulder and the wall, she slipped her hand underneath, as if to get it warm. "Like I told you, I need to get some sleep. I was just about to shut my eyes when you burst in here. My boss rented this apartment for me. It wouldn't have been my choice. No furniture, and if you look around, you'll see there's not one lamp." They couldn't resist a visual survey of the room, she was relieved to note. As soon as their eyes shifted, she moved her under-cover hand to her pocket. "I read myself to sleep. Now what that means is, if I put the overhead light on, I have to strain to read, and more to the point when I'm sleepy enough to doze off, I have to get up and walk across the room to turn off the light, after which I'm not quite sleepy enough anymore, and I'm cold. Reading with a flashlight's not great, believe me, but it's better than that."

Melchior nodded knowingly, but from the expression on Wycotte's face, moving eyes across paper was not an activity he considered valuable.

"Look," she said, "if you're going to be staying here, then pass me a bathrobe." Maybe that would decide them on leaving. Or at least the robe would cover her clothes. She didn't want to be in the position of obviously pulling her driver's license out of her shorts pocket. People may sleep in their clothes, but they usually empty their pockets first.

Neither of them seemed to be leaving. Restraining a sigh of frustration, she said, "The bathrobe is hanging inside the closet door." They both turned only momentarily, but it was long enough. She slid her wallet out of her pocket and up near the pillow.

Melchior handed her a white terrycloth robe, thick enough to soak up sweat from an Olympic workout. She slipped her arms into it, and when Melchior made his request, she passed him the license from under her pillow. "You're staying in an empty room in Pacific Beach when you live in La Jolla?" he asked suspiciously.

"Not really. My stuff's still there, but I needed to get away. The guy I live with says I'm too hard to get along with, can you imagine that?" she demanded, keeping eye contact and a straight face. She could almost hear the laughs they'd have when they got back in the patrol car. "So I'm here for a while."

Wycotte couldn't resist the smallest of snorts before saying, "You're certain you don't wish to pursue the burglary complaint."

"Certain. But thanks for coming."

He turned toward the door. But Melchior didn't move. His forehead was creased, his finger tapping against his equipment belt. "You said your boss obtained this apartment for you. Do you have some verification of that?"

Damn! Now she was moving onto thin ice. "To show that I'm not some vagrant in for the night?" she laughed, and pulled the lease from the scrapbook.

He glanced over it. "Dolly Uberhazy, you work for her?"

Kiernan nodded.

"In what capacity?"

Crystal-thin ice. She could take slow soft steps and hope to ease herself to the other side, or she could try it in one leap. If she miscalculated, she'd land in water up to the lump on her head. She leaped. "Background investigation on Lark Sondervoil. I'm an investigator."

His face hardened. Behind him Wycotte stiffened. The air in the room felt prickly. Their stances, their expressions said: *You played us; you don't get away with that.*

"Driver's license?"

She pulled it out of her wallet. "Look, if you have questions, call Dolly. She'll be at home in L.A."

"You have her number?"

"No. The studio would, of course. But you're police, you can get it. Call her. I can't spend the whole night on this."

Now it was Melchior who hesitated. Wycotte moved by the door as if to say to his partner, "You brought this up, you handle it."

Kiernan waited a beat, then offered, "Or I can have her call you in the morning." When he didn't reply, she chose between options—silence or sweeten the offer—and said, "She was here for this evening, so she'll have gotten back to L.A. late." How could the cop *not* go for the option of avoiding another cranky career woman in the middle of the night?

But, as if reading her, a knowing smile wafted across Melchior's lips and disappeared. "I'm sure she'll appreciate our protecting her property. I'll give Ms. Uberhazy a call to confirm"—his tone reversing the meaning of the verb—"her arrangement with our Ms. O'Shaughnessy here."

CHAPTER **14**

DOLLY Uberhazy smacked on the bedside light and reached for the phone. She'd had to drop everything and drive to San Diego to see the stunt they'd paid a bundle for. And then there'd been that awful accident, and then those ghoulish dailies. No lunch, no dinner, other than those wonderful polenta-garlic rolls (the one good thing in the whole day), and she'd spent half the night trying to keep Bleeker and everyone on the location set from falling apart—and doing it in front of the police and the press. Then it had taken another three hours to drive home, what with the tie-up on the Santa Monica Freeway. She never should have taken the coast road. But she'd had plenty of time to think about that while she sat a mile from the Malibu turnoff, a foot behind an organic vegetable truck filled with cartons of greens and a shitload of, well, shit. Stunk like a fifty-million-dollar box-office flop. Like *Edge of Disaster* could smell, if she didn't keep control of things. In the next lane was a carload of kids blasting their music so loud it felt like another earthquake. She could barely hear Bleeker whining over the cellular phone. Christ, it was bad enough to have the Sondervoil girl dead, without Cary Bleeker sniveling about keeping a low profile with the press—as if the press were going to give them a choice. As if she would leave to Bleeker a decision that could destroy the picture. He should have known that, as long as he'd been in the business. Too soon for a wave of publicity, he'd whined. By the time *Edge* opened, the public would be sick of hearing about it. Maybe so, maybe not. She glared at the phone. God, she hoped this wasn't Bleeker again, not at three thirty in the morning. No, whatever Bleeker's failings, the man wasn't that stupid.

On the fourth ring she picked up the receiver. Whoever was calling had better have a damned good reason, but she'd learned long ago not to snap before she knew what she'd find between her teeth. Her tone was neutral as she said, "Yes?"

"This is Officer Melchior, San Diego Police Department. I'm sorry to have to wake you. Are you Ms. Dolly Uberhazy?"

"Yes?"

"Are you familiar with a Kiernan O'Shaughnessy?"

Who? . . . Don't wake me up in the middle of the night to play guessing games! she wanted to shout. "Why do you assume I am, officer?"

"She says you hired her."

"She told you I hired her?" she repeated, tacitly demanding more information. In a business with egos bursting into bloom at every turn, she had made her way to senior vice-president by listening to the rants, forcing the ranters to explain more and more, a helluva lot more than they wanted to—and never exposing herself. She gave a little grin of amusement. For a woman in Hollywood, never exposing oneself was quite an accomplishment. But then to the boys in charge, there were men and there were women, and someplace in the murky area between, there were women studio executives.

"Ms. O'Shaughnessy is a private detective down here. She told us you hired her to do background on Lark Sondervoil, the stunt woman who went off the cliff, right?"

"Go on."

"Ms. O'Shaughnessy told us you rented her an apartment."

"Why did she tell you that, officer?"

"We got a call that a unit in the Salem Harbour Studios had been burgled. And when we got there, we found her in it. You rented that, is that right?"

"Officer, I am an executive with one of the busiest movie studios in L.A. I deal in a ton of paperwork. I can't possibly remember what specific units I rent out of town or for whom. Perhaps if you describe this woman," she said, buying time. If it had been any apartment but Lark Sondervoil's, she'd have been off the phone and back to sleep by now. But she couldn't afford to be sloppy about anything to do with Sondervoil. Sloppy was what she'd been when she'd agreed to have Sondervoil in the film at all. Or greedy. Or just plain stupid.

"Your name is on the lease."

"Then chances are I did rent it."

"For Ms. O'Shaughnessy?"

"Describe her."

She could hear a slight intake of breath from his end of the line, just enough to remind her that he wasn't an underling but a policeman whom she might need to use later. Then he said, "She's little, with short dark curly hair, probably in her thirties. I could check for you; we took down the data from her driver's license."

"No, no. Don't trouble yourself, officer," she muttered. She had heard enough. This housebreaker must be the woman who'd crashed the rushes. What did this woman know, and how had she gotten on the scent so fast? And how much of it involved the police? "Officer, you've got the lease, and you've apparently got Ms. O'Shaughnessy, but something is still bothering you. Just why is it you've called me in the middle of the night?" she asked, in the tone that had led more than one producer to believe that he was the one sane person on location that she had found to work with.

"Because, Ms. Uberhazy, she suggested we call you. According to her, you wouldn't mind being woken up at this hour," he said, with such clear triumph that she could have laughed.

She did emit a laugh, the same laugh she used with those producers. But Dolly Uberhazy wasn't smiling. She knew more than she wanted to about the intrigues that were the ebb and flow of life on the set. She hadn't heard the truth in so long, it could have been a nursery rhyme. But if this woman had broken into Lark's apartment, there was more going on than she realized. Particularly when she was dealing with a woman who had the chutzpah to get the cops to make her introductions. "Well, officer, Ms. O'Shaughnessy is wrong. I'm no more delighted to be up at this hour than you are to be wasting your time on wild goose chases. I suspect I did hire the woman, but I still can't say for sure. Could you leave that question open for twenty-four hours while I check into it? And Officer Melchior, would you impress that on her and have her call me? Right away."

"You can count on that, ma'am."

As she set down the phone, she smiled uneasily. She'd have Kiernan O'Shaughnessy up here before dinner. The woman might be a detective. But being a senior vice-president carried its own unwritten perks. She had her own ways of getting what she needed. And by the time O'Shaughnessy arrived on her doorstep, she would know what way to use.

CHAPTER 15

IT was raining. She ought to close the windows at the head of the bed. Instead, Kiernan squeezed her eyes tighter shut against the dull morning light and pulled the comforter over her ear. Rain was nature's way of saying "Sleep in."

The rain was heavier. It couldn't be rain; it must be sleet. But it smelled wonderful. Like roses. Eyes shut tight, she wriggled around under the covers until her nose was inches from the window. The roses must be growing out of the ocean. The sweet perfume wafted through her nasal passages into her lungs like a rosy sedative, leading her softly back into sleep.

Ezra let out a guttural moan. "Ez," she grumbled. Tchernak wouldn't have left without walking him. No, surely not. Even in the rosy sleet, he'd have taken him. "Hush, Ezra."

The sleet rapped harder on the window. Next to her ear, Ezra barked. Her eyes shot open. "Whatsamatter, Ez?"

The rain rapped again. Not rain. Somebody rapping on the window— her *second*-floor window, over the boulders on the beach twenty feet below the house. She looked out through the slats in the headboard. Into a bouquet of pale orange roses.

Holding it, and himself perched precariously on the wrought-iron railing of the window box, was Trace Yarrow. The Pacific wind was mussing his curly black hair. His lapis blue eyes were gleaming, and there was a grin on his broad, tanned face. For an instant she thought he was Greg Gaige.

But Greg was light-haired. And Greg was dead.

Yarrow proffered the bouquet through the open window. It wasn't raining, but the night fog hadn't lifted yet. "Like some company? I could stand to get warmed up."

"Yarrow?" she said, still sleep-dazed. "What the hell are you doing out there?"

"I'm propositioning you. Or didn't I make myself clear?"

"I figured the exertion of getting up here had clouded your judgment. Since you'd brought the flowers, I was going to overlook your momentary tackiness." Was her mother in the room in heaven, saying: "Who would have thought my Kiernan could handle any social situation?" Well, maybe not, considering the social encounter was taking place over her bed.

She squirmed into her robe, envisioning her mother complaining to her deceased friends: "I told her to wear a nightgown. Nice girls don't sleep naked. Would she listen to me? Now, when she has a trespasser . . ."

She motioned Yarrow in and to the bathroom sink with the flowers. The surprise was wearing off, and she found herself wavering between amusement and a prickling of violation. Tchernak, she thought, wouldn't waste time on amusement; fortunately he'd already be gone. And Ezra seemed to deem Yarrow an acceptable guest.

She needed to ask Yarrow something. What was it? Damn, she couldn't think when she was still half asleep. Settling on one of the padded wicker lounges across the room, she said, "How did you find my address?"

"Nothing's hidden from a guy who really wants to know. I called the Irish Wolfhound Society and said I was looking for a walkmate for my O'Toole."

Kiernan laughed. Her glance rested on the clock. Nine thirty A.M. "Yarrow, I am charmed by the roses. And the Tarzanship. But I've got to leave for L.A. in half an hour."

"Okay, okay. The offer of my body was just an extra. Are you going to L.A. to see Dolly?"

"How'd you know?"

"A guess. Bleeker's still on the set here, so you're not driving to L.A. for him. You should have taken me up on my offer." Before she could protest, he held up a hand. "Would have given you something in common with Dolly."

"You slept with Dolly Uberhazy?"

"No, no. Not me. I always made it a point to keep business and pleasure separate. You don't sleep with sharks." He sat on the other chair. "But the first couple of weeks on the *Companions* set, Dolly was gaga over some hunk there."

"Who?"

Yarrow shrugged. "Dunno. Don't think I knew then. My gags weren't scheduled until the end of the second week, and then I got canned three days later. So I'm telling you what I heard—but on good authority—not what I saw. Anyway, *who* he was wasn't the point. The funny part was Dolly carrying on like a teenager. I mean Dolly, for chrissake. The stories about her were worth the trip out there. One minute she's shouting down the union rep, the next she's fluttering her fan and making eyes."

"This from a man who's just scaled my wall with roses."

"I just don't want you going in with your eyes shut."

"Yarrow, I don't shut my eyes."

"Ever?" He grinned.

She looked him in the eye. "Only when I sleep."

"I'll wait and see." The grin faded from his face. "Look, I just want you to be prepared for the kind of people you're dealing with. Dolly Uberhazy has elbowed her way to the top, over the bodies of guys who were bigger, louder, and better connected. She's not about to admit that when she should have been paying attention on *Bad Companions*, she was making eyes at the hunk. Now she's the one with the power. This is Hollywood. Everything's magnified. Success is the sun and the moon, and failure's a pit as deep and cold as the ocean. There are actors, directors, writers who would kill for Dolly's approval. Literally. What's running a stranger off the road compared to seeing your name in the movie trailer?"

She didn't quite believe him, but she wasn't clear enough to say why. And there was still that question she needed to ask him, something from last night. From Lark's apartment. What?

"Take Jason Pedora—"

"Who's he?"

"Greg Gaige's half-brother. Been working on the story of Greg ever since he died. He didn't kill him—I'm not suggesting that—but if he'd thought there was a story in it, he might have. Guy's a nutcase. If Dolly said she'd buy his screenplay, he'd be willing to mow down everyone west of Burbank."

"Was he on the set yesterday?"

"Can't swear to it. Then again, can't imagine he wouldn't be. You want me to check?"

She nodded, and stood up. "Yarrow, I appreciate the warning. I was a gymnast, I'm used to scoping out things before I make a move. But Dolly Uberhazy hasn't called me to her own office to blow me away."

"Not literally. What she's going to do is try to co-opt you." He walked to the casement windows, the limp apparent. "She's going to tell you that she got me to agree to tell her what you find."

"She bought you!" Kiernan snapped.

Yarrow turned. "She *thinks* she bought me. I haven't told her anything."

"You don't have anything to report. Lark's been dead less than a day!"

"Look, I didn't have to let you in on this. I could have just taken my studio job and my health coverage and let you walk blind. But I'm risking the last chance I'll get for good medical and telling you the woman's a viper. A viper with friends and lackeys." He headed for the door.

"Yarrow! Wait! Who or what is Boukunas?"

"A. J. Boukunas? A stunt man. Died in a three-figure high fall. Designed a new air bag to land on, smaller, less expensive. Did a three-hundred-twenty-one-foot high fall onto it to prove its worth."

"And?"

"Proved it wasn't good enough. It exploded. He died. Why?"

" 'No Boukunas, *not* Greg!' Lark wrote that in her scrapbook. What did she mean?"

Yarrow shook his head. "Greg didn't do three-figure high falls."

"And? Come on, Yarrow, this is our only clue. They were both stunt men. They had different specialties, used different equipment—"

"But Greg never experimented with equipment. Never. He never took a chance on equipment that wasn't proven. 'The risks are in the illusion, not the props'—that's what he said."

She watched Yarrow walk out. He'd answered her question and told her nothing. Lark Sondervoil hadn't put her career on the line for a press conference to announce what the stunt community already knew, that Greg Gaige was careful.

CHAPTER 16

J ASON Pedora was not standing at the bar. He didn't do that kind of thing—too much of a Hollywood cliché. He was damned if anyone would call him a failed screenwriter, draped like a dish towel over the bar, trying to impress ingenues with tales of his dead half-brother. He sat at a corner table by the railing, his espresso with a twist just far enough past the center of the small red-clothed table to pass for a NO ADMITTANCE sign. A drink—straight Tanqueray—was what he needed, but he didn't allow himself liquor before eleven thirty in the morning; he wasn't about to be the Betty Ford prospect cliché, either.

Pedora ran his fingers through his wavy gray hair. Still thick if not still black. And he had a lot more of it than that little prick of an agent of his. Last time he did lunch with him, he was sporting a rug and drinking Perrier like all the yuppie Puritan post-boomers who ran Hollywood. Whole scene was so uncomfortable, he could hardly taste the Tanqueray without thinking that every ginny breath reeked has-been. Or never-was.

He swallowed the rest of the espresso. He could pick up one of the wannabes. Venice was full of them. To hear them tell it, the movies were peopled by B-list actresses with A-list luck, while they, au contraire . . . They were full of it, but he didn't care; the dreams, the delusions, the outright lies—it was all material for a writer. And *Venice Nights*, his screenplay, had almost made it. Even before Greg died, there'd been studio people in Creative hooked on that one. Or almost hooked.

He eyed his watch: eleven fifteen. Damn! He could break his rule. He laughed to himself: he'd broken more than rules in the last twelve hours. Why not a drink? He needed it this morning; hell, he deserved it, after what he'd been through yesterday: the whole bit in the apartment, and before that, seeing Greg's Move again. He'd had to see it, to catalog his own reaction to it. That second script guy in Creative, the one who'd called him—not vice versa—after Greg's death—damn, Greg would have been proud if he'd known about that interview—studio'd come within a hair of buying *Venice Nights* then. . . . Not enough guts, emotion, Creative had said. Well, how could he be expected to create emotion on paper after his brother had been burned to a crisp? 'Course, he shouldn't have expected a twenty-five-year-old in Creative to have any compassion, he knew that now. He should have cottoned to it then. Youth and nepotism, the twin horsemen of Hollywood!

Well, he for one had never traded on his youth. And there'd never been any big Pedora back at the studio to open doors for him, like that little prick Dratz on Greg's set. Not even Greg had really been any help.

Well, not a total loss. In fairness he'd gotten some of his insurance money, but only because his mother—their mother—had given it to him. Hardly what you'd call brotherly love. He'd helped Greg perfect the Move. Fat lot of credit he got for that. The Gaige Move. Not the Gaige-Pedora Move. But no use in telling that to anyone now. Just sounded like whining. Even when he'd wowed the young, lithe stunt hopefuls with his tales of Greg, he'd had to watch it, to make sure he came across as not whining. And now, it was so long since the fire, none of these girls even remembered Greg.

Until now.

When he went to La Jolla yesterday, he'd expected to spike the creative juices by seeing Lark Sondervoil do Greg's Move. Who the hell was *she* to do the Move that he and Greg had created! There had been something fishy on that set. Just like on *Bad Companions*: trucks sneaking onto the set in the middle of the night. They'd barred him from the *Bad Companions* set—Greg's fault—but in the last ten years he'd learned how to keep out of sight. Yesterday they hadn't even noticed him on the set. Ten years ago, if he'd been as smart as he was now, he'd have had proof about what was in those trucks. He saw them driving onto the set and pulling back out half an hour later. PACIFIC BREEZE COMPUTER, they'd said. Shit, they don't deliver computers in the middle of the night, even in California!

He had put it all in *Midnight Cargo*. And they'd called that screenplay unbelievable! In Hollywood! Well, he'd give them believable. That trot over the bluff yesterday, that was believable. And that little blonde, how had the little bitch learned so much about Greg? What else did she know? Had Greg told her what was going down at *Bad Companions,* when he hadn't let on to his own brother? There'd been no letters from Greg in her apartment. No diary. Nothing. He could have landed in jail, and all for nothing.

Of course, the cops wouldn't have caught him. They *didn't.* He was too smart and too quick; the bitch who walked in on him found that out. Even afterward, when he'd stood under the window and listened, neither one of San Diego's *finest* had heard a sound.

Pedora turned to face the ocean. The water was too far away to see, but he could hear the crash of waves and smell the brine that seemed to come directly from teahouses on the shores of Yokohama.

No, wait—damn!—this Lark girl had been nineteen years old. She was nine years old when Greg died! Greg wouldn't have talked to her or written his secrets to her; he wouldn't have *known* her.

There *had* to be some connection.

That fall over the bluff had been no accident. Of course she had had it coming, stealing the Move he and Greg created. How had she figured out the tricks no one but Greg knew?

Notes—maybe she did have notes stashed away somewhere else. Somewhere the little dark-haired bitch discovered after she'd forced him out of the apartment. If she had let the police see them— Sweat poured down his sides. The cops wouldn't understand the value of those notes. They'd leak them to the press! His material! The final touch for *Midnight Cargo*!

He lifted the small white cup and waited for the last brown drop to roll down the inside into his mouth, then swung his long legs over the wrought-iron fence that separated the café from the Venice sidewalk beside the beach. The morning fog still hung over the sidewalk and the beach. He eased his hands into his jacket pockets. A block beyond the café, the sidewalk was empty, the sand as bare as some tropical island. Some *cold* tropical island. Even the beach houses that faced the canals like rows of stamps in a five-dollar book—rows of stamps, that was a good image, he'd have to remember that—even the houses seemed attached to the canals rather than the beach. If it were night, cops would be driving by on the sand, warning him not to walk alone. But he didn't worry; he'd lived here too long, knew too many of the guys that the cops were warning him about, knew too much for them to mess with him.

Hell, he could have written a blockbuster about some of them—if he didn't mind it being published posthumously.

But no time for that now. Lark Sondervoil's notes; he had to find them. He could get back in her apartment. . . . Dangerous; the cops would be watching it. . . . But no, no need to risk that. The little dark-haired bitch, she had had time to hunt around in there—the time she'd robbed him of. She'd know.

A smile spread across Jason Pedora's narrow face. Her, he knew just where to find. She and Dolly together—he liked that. Should he take her down right there, in Dolls's office, or wait and get her alone? No need to decide now; when he had her face to face, his gut would tell him what to do.

He'd let his chance get away before and had paid for it with ten years of living like a bum. This time nothing and no one was going to stand in his way.

CHAPTER **17**

KIERNAN pulled up to the Summit-Arts Studios gate at twenty to two. Hot valley air oozed in through the open window; spears of light reflected off the chrome of the Miata ahead, pricking at her eyes. The sky was an opalescent blue, a million miles away, with no connection to this exposed platter of a city too naïve or distracted to shade itself with more than a palm tree. She leaned forward, shaking her shoulders to free the sweat-stuck blouse. Every time she left the ocean breezes at home for L.A., she dressed too warmly. Now she could have done without the gray linen jacket and the long sleeves on her green silk blouse.

While the guard checked his list for her name, she glanced ahead. The studio looked like a boomtown grammar school. In layout it resembled a dead flightless bird, its body the sound stage, and its low, limp wings the stucco block offices that wrapped around to create a courtyard filled with lines of prefab units, and between them, trailers. Apparently, Kiernan thought, Summit-Arts Studios had had a burst of good fortune.

"One car pass, name of O'Shaughnessy." The guard waved her through. "Ms. Uberhazy's in the second building on the left."

She had allowed herself fifteen minutes to get a feel of the studio. Walking toward the bird's belly, she found herself amidst the airplane-hangarlike sound stages, and warehouses so ordinary they could have held cartons of cleansers or sides of steer. Or M-16s. The only thing that distinguished them from any other storage facility in Burbank was the absence of traffic. Unmarked eighteen-wheelers were parked in front of a couple, but what commerce there was on the alleys seemed to be handled by baggy-pantsed bicycle messengers on old fat-wheeled Schwinns with big wire baskets in front. The town that time forgot.

She stared through an open door at paintings one above another up the warehouse wall, furniture stacked like the spoils of a distress sale. A messenger screeched to a stop inches in front of her, grabbed a manila envelope, and raced inside.

Around the corner dust floated thick, as carpenters hammered and sawed on a black wooden cave. Across the alley an open-sided slice of submarine sat aground on cement. She turned another corner and was abruptly at the corner of New York's Fifty-second and First Avenue—the back lot—with dark-red-brick four-floor walkups, street-level boutiques and delicatessens, an alternate side of the street parking sign, and cans of Pabst and BLACK COFFEE $.60, REGULAR COFFEE $.65 posted in the delicatessen window. The small, splinted street trees looked as if they'd spent their frail lives battling carbon monoxide, and a copy of the *Times* was pressed against the wire mesh of a trash can. But in the hot California sun nothing moved, and Fifty-second and First looked as abandoned as a city after the plague. And it seemed fitting to glance through the East Side Cleanette's open door at an empty shell holding nothing more than worn sawhorses and plastic makeup cartons so brittle and dusty, the potions inside them were doubtless drier and more fragile than the skin they'd been bought to save.

She shook off the thought, suspicious that Yarrow's warning was tinting her thoughts. But still there was an emptiness to the studio that made the facades seem thinner, the bicycle messengers look as if they were riding to nowhere. The people she saw could have worked in a third as many buildings. So Summit-Arts's burst of good fortune had bloomed and—burst. Lark Sondervoil could be the focus of a helluva wrongful death suit, maybe one big enough to scuttle the studio. Ambulance chasers and "next of kin" would be popping up like crocuses. No wonder Dolly Uberhazy was a little jumpy at the thought of a private investigator.

Kiernan walked into Building Two, one of the stucco block affairs, five minutes early. A larger-than-life, brighter-than-sight poster from a film she hadn't seen dominated the room. The receptionist in front of it was not harried by phone calls, and there were only two other people waiting. As she asked for Uberhazy, Kiernan had the feeling that both of them—a woman Lark's age, and a man in his fifties—were straining to hear not her words to the receptionist, nor the receptionist's into the intercom, but those coming back out of the intercom.

And when the receptionist announced that Dolly would be "right with her," Kiernan turned and nearly smacked into the man.

"I've been here forty minutes," he whined, slapping his white plantation hat on the desk. His long, thinning gray hair bounced and resettled to show the hat line around his head. With his pursed lips and the slump of his shoulders, he could have been wearing a T-shirt emblazoned BORN TO WAIT.

The receptionist gazed at him as she might at a mendicant dropping in on the Pope. "If you'd had an appointment, Mr. Pedora—"

"Appointment? Death doesn't make appointments!" He paused momentarily, as if savoring his last sentence.

Kiernan stepped back. *Jason Pedora! This* man was Greg Gaige's half-brother? They both must have gotten all their genes from their not-in-common parents. Pedora looked every bit as crazy as Yarrow had said.

"Well, Ms. Uberhazy does expect appointments. Look, I've told you—"

The intercom buzzed. In a moment the receptionist said to Kiernan, "Dolly'll see you now."

Pedora glared from the receptionist to her.

"Kiernan O'Shaughnessy," she said, extending a hand.

He jerked back, eyes narrowing. "Jason Pedora."

"Jason Pedora, the writer?"

"Why, yes . . ."

To Kiernan's right, the office door opened, and Dolly Uberhazy looked out. Kiernan handed Pedora her card. "Where can I reach you?"

Pedora froze, turned abruptly, and without a word hurried out the door.

"Crazy as a loon," Dolly said. "I don't know how the hell he gets onto the lot. He's been barred from sets for over a decade, but the man's a gopher, you can't keep him out." Resting her gaze on Kiernan, she said, "You'll regret giving him your card," and trotted back across the expanse of her office.

Kiernan followed, past a huge fish tank housing a sunken Fifty-second and First Avenue and a platoon of black and brown fish floating in and out of the empty apartment windows. A watery midtown Pompeii.

"Yesterday evening you were the union rep. In the middle of the night you were a gumshoe. So, sweetie, what are you this morning—a talent scout for third-rate writers?" Dolly motioned her into one of the hard boxy chairs on the low-rent side of a maharajah's table—remarkably ornate, but still squat like its owner. Dolly Uberhazy was wearing the same ensemble she'd had on at the screening the night before—brown silk slacks and chocolate cloak-sweater—the kind of expensive garments the mother of Kiernan's college roommate had favored, insisting they would last a lifetime. From the looks of her, Dolly was determined to find out. The creases and lines that wadded that sweater suggested Uberhazy had spent the entire night flopping in and out of chairs. Now she sat behind the maharajah's table, in the only straight-backed chair in the room.

Bad back, Kiernan thought, and too much time behind the maharajah's table. Don't let her take charge; keep her on the defensive; set the pace. "You were the producer of the film Greg Gaige died in."

"You work fast. Or were you investigating me before yesterday?"

"*Before* Lark's death? Why would you suspect that?"

The suggestion of a smile rolled down Uberhazy's face, over her sharp brown eyes, the nose that hung a millimeter too close to her thin lips and a narrow chin that jutted minusculely forward as if to say: *I'll take your shot, roll it around in my hands, and smack it back at you.* "Look, here, sweetie, I didn't invite you up here to answer *your* questions. So tell me, just what are you after? You can skip the union rep story—I've got a few investigators of my own. I know your history and that you're licensed *now*." Her right forearm rested on the table, but she neither fiddled with a pencil nor tapped her fingers. She had too much control for that.

Choosing not to be distracted by the implied threat, Kiernan said, "Lark drank coca-leaf tea; she ate poppyseed bagels. That's nowhere near enough opiates to toss her over the cliff, but it's ample to skew a urine test. Before Lark began the Move, the cordon markers were shifted on the set—"

"So what are you saying—that that was deliberate—meant to kill her?"

"I don't know yet why Lark died. But it's certainly suspicious—doubly suspicious after Greg Gaige died in a fire after doing the same Move. And you were a power in both films."

"There's no connection," she said too quickly.

Kiernan leaned toward her. "What do you know about Lark?"

Dolly shook her finger. "No, no. You don't seem to get it. I'm not here to answer *your* questions. Besides, the answer is 'nothing.' She's Cary Bleeker's find. He asked all the questions about the stunts she'd done for her promo reel. I just viewed the reel."

"I thought most senior vice-presidents had more power than that."

"Right, detective, I could have overruled Bleeker. But Lark's reel looked great. I saw Greg Gaige practice the Move. When Cary Bleeker offered me another chance, I couldn't resist."

"For yourself or the box office?"

"Without the box office, sweetie, there is no self." She leaned back against the slats of the wooden chair, then added quickly, "If you want to know more, you'll have to get it from Bleeker. If he's in any condition to talk."

"He seemed okay last night."

"Shock can have delayed effects."

"Why should Bleeker be so distressed?"

Dolly was silent. Considering? But no, she was not a woman who needed that long to make a decision. She was a judgment-a-minute woman, one who'd rather be wrong than indecisive. So why the hesitation?

Dolly leaned forward, elbows on the maharajah's table. "I want you working for me."

"Or you'll take your ball and go home?"

"Or I'll call back the San Diego cops and let them haul you in for housebreaking."

Kiernan laughed. "Choose between jailers? No, I don't think so. Besides, there are too many questions about Lark's death; you're not going to direct police attention back to the case on another front." She waited a moment, accepting Uberhazy's silence for acquiescence. "I'll be straight with you. I want to know about Lark Sondervoil's death as much as you wanted to see her do the Move. But in this case my services aren't for sale."

"The door's behind you."

"What I can tell you," Kiernan said, making no move to leave, "is that I'm as good an investigator as you're going to get. You've checked me out; you know what I can do and what I earn doing it. I know gymnastics, I've evaluated the insides of more dead bodies than you want to think about, and I am going to find out why Lark died—not because my rent depends on it, but for a much more pressing reason, because I want to know. So if you're looking for the answer to why she died, all you need to do is wait. But you won't have to wait as long if you tell me what you know."

"I don't plan to help you so I can read about this in the paper."

It was capitulation. Kiernan smiled. "I'll make you this much of a promise: I'll give you first crack at my findings, before the press. Unless, of course, you are culpable."

Dolly nodded.

"So why was Bleeker so distressed?"

"He knew the girl."

"And?"

That challenging smile appeared on Uberhazy's face. "Cary Bleeker's had a string of bad luck, enough that I had to think carefully about hiring him. I was taking a chance."

"But *you're* not immobilized by all this."

"I'm an executive. I can't afford to go to pieces. And to be fair"—she laughed—"fairness is not exactly the main concern in this business. But to be fair, I'm not anywhere near as far out on the branch as Cary Bleeker. This is his last chance. When I first heard of Bleeker on *Bad Companions,* he was the golden-haired boy."

"But?"

"After *Bad Companions,* he got the reputation as a bad luck director."

"What kind of bad luck?"

"Hunt-and-peck kind of stuff. Engine caught fire on a crane, and the crane rolled back into the set. No one was hurt, but it took two weeks to get the set back in shape, and between the cost of rebuilding, paying actors, and the crews sitting in the sun with nothing to do, not to mention repairing the crane itself, it ran high enough so that the picture never got out of the red. That kind of thing."

"And do you know what happened on the set of *Bad Companions?* Or were you too preoccupied with your tryst?"

Uberhazy nodded. There was no sign of that challenging smile. "The problems on *Companions* were a lot more benign, until the fire, but that had nothing to do with Cary. That truly was bad luck—"

"Tell me about it." In her mind Kiernan could see the picture of Greg Gaige smiling as he did the Move. She pushed it away.

"Most of the things were small stuff, pain-in-the-ass nuisances like people leaving their cigarette butts in their napkins to smolder."

"What people? Dratz stuff?"

It was a moment before Dolly said, "You know what a Dratz is?"

Kiernan couldn't resist a grin. "I told you I was good at my work. A Dratz is a schlemiel sent by the studio brass, who talks on the set, second-guesses directors, instructs actors, and feels anyone is capable of doing any stunt short of the Gaige Move. And who's got to be tolerated because he's a bigwig's son."

Dolly nodded approvingly, but her eyes were drawn in, wary. She wants me to be good, Kiernan thought, but not too good.

"Okay, sweetie, Dratz drove Cary Bleeker crazy. Word of his screw-ups flew through the industry like wildfire. And then there's the real fire, Greg Gaige dies, shooting's delayed, scenes have to be redone, and the whole thing sends *Companions'* overruns into the stratosphere. And Bleeker's name is tied to both: fire and Dratz."

"So he hasn't worked in all these years?"

Dolly shrugged. "Cary had some friends who had him coordinate no-brain stunts or direct run-of-the-mill second units. But Dratz is an alba-tross perched on his head. Look, things go wrong on every set. With that many people, all watching out for number one, there are bound to be screw-ups. Accidents happen, directors fume, producers throw tan-trums, actors are hysterical—and then life goes on. But if Cary's on the set, every problem is a disaster, and it's caused by Bad Luck Bleeker. So no one's willing to put his ass on the line to hire him."

Uberhazy's shoulders were pulled in tight, and those fingers, which had lain perfectly still in her early show of control, now made indeci-pherable patterns on the maharajah's table. In a minute she'd be finger-ing her phone, and in another, ending the meeting. There was time for one, maybe two questions.

Lark Sondervoil was killed in front of many of the people who had been present at Greg Gaige's death. Could Lark have been on that original set ten years ago? Seen something? Was that the connection? "Where was the *Bad Companions* location?"

"West of El Centro, almost spitting distance of Arizona and Mexico. Why?"

No time for explanations. "Were there any children on the set?"

"Not unless you count Dratz."

"What happened to Dratz after that?"

"Out of the business. Even with a veep-Dad, a turd's a turd."

Kiernan leaned forward, making no attempt to hide her assessing gaze. "Dolly, you are a woman who has made it to the top in a tough business, a man's business. You didn't do that by being nice. And yet you are the only one to hire Cary Bleeker. You didn't sign him up to direct background shots—you made him the director of a second unit that would be doing some very visible things. Then you let him hire an unknown to do an extremely dangerous Move, a maneuver intimately bound up with the movie that tarred his reputation. You took a risk, not a small one to begin with, then you compounded it. Why?"

Dolly's dark brown eyes seemed to sink back into her head, as if she were pulling into a cocoon of thought.

"Give me the truth on this." Kiernan didn't need to add "or we have no deal."

Dolly stopped the circling of her fingers. Hitting the table with one decisive tap, she said, "Unseemly decency? Guilt? Or hunch? Fact is, I was the producer on *Companions*. I'd seen Greg Gaige do his Move. It was a knockout. When Cary offered me Lark doing that same Move, I could see the possibilities." She paused, and Kiernan had the feeling she was assessing her response. "Okay, no gag is going to carry a film; but this one, with its connection to Greg's death, could be just enough to get notice. *Edge of Disaster*'s a good film. It could be a sleeper. Or a little notoriety will goose reviewers to the previews; they review it, which gooses the studio to advertise, which draws the public, and bingo—a hit!"

"A phoenix from Greg's ashes?" Contempt rang in her voice.

"That's Hollywood, sweetie. I gave you the truth; I'm not asking you to love me." Her gaze met Kiernan's fiercely. *Don't you dare condemn me,* it silently demanded.

Deliberately, Kiernan didn't reply to that. This was an opportunity, not to save Dolly's soul, but to make use of her unease. "I need Lark Sondervoil's personnel records."

Clearly relieved, Dolly opened a drawer in the maharajah's table and pulled out a manila folder. "She's not a studio employee. She's a day player for *Edge of Disaster*. You won't find much in there."

Kiernan opened it. She had ordered background reports on Lark, Bleeker, Dolly, Yarrow, and Greg before she left. But there hadn't been time for BakDat to respond. It made her uneasy. She scanned the pages, and stopped at Beneficiary: the High Country Gymnastics Academy. "Do you know anything about this?"

"No more than you see. But for that little school, wherever it is, it's going to be a boon. I just hope—"

"—they don't sue?" Kiernan finished the thought. "Is there any way they would know about the bequest?"

"Not from us." She looked from the folder up to Kiernan; her eyes narrowed. "And I'm not paying you to tell them."

Kiernan laughed. "How many times am I going to have to remind you that you are not paying me at all? But for what comfort it is, I collect information—I don't disseminate it without reason. What about Greg Gaige? Was his mother his sole beneficiary?"

"As I recall."

"What about Pedora?"

"Even Gaige had had it up to here with him."

"Maybe he thought he'd still inherit. Any chance he affected the fire gag?"

Dolly leaned back in her chair and laughed. "Sweetie, if we could pin it on Jason Pedora, the Red Sea would part. But by the time *Bad Companions* went on location, we'd had to post a guard to keep him out."

"Guard or not, he could have gotten onto the set."

"On a location like that, of course. But could he have turned up the gas spigots or changed the fuel? What do you think Special Effects is going to tell me? I've got power—I insist and men jump. But that power comes from the studio, and believe me, the studio did not want to discover any cause other than—"

"Idiopathic?" Kiernan offered. "Spontaneous eruptions of unknown origin is a popular medical diagnosis, too."

"And probably for the same reason."

In the fish tank an automatic feeder spewed flakes of food. She watched as they floated down on the miniature Fifty-second Street like acid rain. The air conditioner hummed louder; a draft chilled her back, or perhaps the draft was merely dread. She had to know, but God, she didn't want to ask: "One more thing—"

"Yes?"

"Tell me about the fire."

Dolly jolted up straight. She looked ready for attack from any direction, ready to spin and strike. It was a moment before she spoke, and then her tone was all business. "*Bad Companions* was a coming-of-age film—spoiled city kid defies society, runs into *Deliverance*-type hicks in the back country with a hole in the road the size of a boxcar to catch strangers. Of course, by then the hole had been filled in, but that's off camera. In this scene she forgets about the coal stove—"

"She? Greg was doubling a woman?"

Dolly let out a bark of a laugh. "Sweetie, men run stunt work. They get the stunt coordinator's jobs; they do the hiring. And who do you think they hire? When there's a nondescript job—one like this where the double's supposed to be all covered in a fire suit—ninety percent of the time it goes to a man. Women with thirty years in the business can't get enough work coordinating to make a living."

So Lark Sondervoil's matching the legend of Greg Gaige was more important than she'd realized. And the rumor that she'd been incompetent enough to cause her own death could set a stunt woman back—well, back farther.

Dolly lifted her head, stretching out her back. "Okay, so he sets the cabin on fire. The script read that the fire engulfed the house, and he escaped—at the last minute, of course. Pretty routine as these things go."

"He did the Move earlier, right?"

"The Move saved a dog of a scene. Had only been done on film once since Greg's first movie, and that was so long before, no one but stunt buffs would remember. It was a knockout. And Greg's adjustment was half of Yarrow's."

Trace Yarrow had negotiated himself twice what Greg Gaige would get? "Yarrow was that hot?"

"Wrong again. Greg was so desperate, he would have worked for free."

A cold wash of sorrow flowed over her. She thought of Greg in San Francisco, unwilling to admit there *was* a future after gymnastics. Greg's mounting desperation didn't surprise her. But it shocked her that he had let himself become so transparent.

"He *had* to do his Move," Dolly went on. "Forty-five years old, he wasn't going to get many more chances, not with a maneuver like that."

"You talked to him on the set, right? You sat outside in the shade of the catering truck with him."

"Possibly, who knows?"

She slammed her fist on the desk. "You *know,* dammit! Greg Gaige wasn't someone you forget. He could do what ninety-nine percent of the world couldn't dream of and smile while he was doing it." Dolly was staring at her as if she were a groupie. What did Dolly take her for? Of course Dolly had—

But no, she was letting her feelings block her vision. In movies, spectacular was the norm. Stunts, even the Gaige Move, were just another day at the store. And away from the set, away from gymnastics, Greg Gaige had been just another person. She'd let herself forget that. Greg hadn't been easy to talk to. She'd chosen to forget that, too. But for someone like Dolly who wanted to talk *at,* he might have been fine.

"Maybe you talked to him about the affair you were having with the good-looking hunk."

Dolly brightened. "Jeez, I'd forgotten about that myself. Couldn't dredge up the guy's name if it meant a million gross."

"Try."

"No way. It was just a fling. You've been around. I don't need to tell you it doesn't pay to get involved. You make a commitment, you hang your ass out. And, sweetie, it gets kicked every time."

"But Greg—?"

"Nah, the affair was over before he got there, or I wouldn't have had time to shoot the breeze with him. We sat outside the catering truck, nibbling, drinking gallons—it must have been a hundred degrees out there. But I needed to get out of the smoke inside the catering truck. The location out there was on top of a mountain with one winding unpaved road up to it, so we didn't have a big catering truck like you saw at Gliderport, or the usual honeywagon—"

"Honeywagon?"

"Sort of a house trailer the crew uses to freshen up in. It's got small dressing rooms, bathrooms. Actors can wait there for their calls. Like I said, the road up to *Companions* was too bad for big vehicles, so we had a couple of smaller ones. Dratz started storing his day gear in the honeywagon that Greg was using, and soon Dratz was in there every free moment screwing one of the extras. Greg didn't want to make waves. So he and I sat outside and joked about being runaways." She paused, and the expression on her face seemed to change, as if she were pulling something from a deep internal reservoir to soften the tension lines. The approval was clear in her voice as she said, "He was a professional, a man committed to his work and willing to make sacrifices for it."

"Sacrifices of himself and others." Kiernan said slowly. The one person he had sacrificed without a thought was Trace Yarrow, and Yarrow had never worked again.

Why did Yarrow still care about Greg's death, much less his successor's? Steeling herself, she asked, "So the fire gag, what happened?"

Dolly's eyes half closed, the skin that had just relaxed stiffened. When she opened her mouth, the movement looked painful. "Everything went wrong. The day before, there'd been a Santa Ana-type wind blowing in from the east, pushing that dry desert heat. The grasses were brown, there were big cracks in the ground. People had seen Santa Ana brushfires take out entire canyons of homes. No one had slept well, tempers were on edge."

"And Greg got there early to do his preparations?"

"He insisted on doing it all himself. Great for us—one less Special Effects guy needed. By the time the rest of us staggered up there, Greg was in the cabin, ready to go. You could see him through the window, sitting in the rocker, waiting."

"How did he look?"

"Okay. He had a fire hood and the wardrobe dress on. They'd already done the close-up of the star sitting there in the dress. When it all got to editing, they'd be interspersed with the long shots at the beginning of the gag." Dolly rolled her pen slowly back and forth on the maharajah's table. That control of hers, so evident before, was gone. "There could be only one take. It was dawn. The A.D. called: 'Scene five-sixteen, take one.' You always do a take number. Special Effects turned on the gas jets; flames leaped up the front and sides of the house. The dress caught. Greg was supposed to get up, bang at the window, then go to the door and burst out—twenty seconds max. There were three cameras—all rolling. The A camera was on a crane, moving upward and in toward the cabin. The air was dead still, and hot as day; the birds were silent. The camera kept moving in. The flames were thick as curtains. We were all staring at the window; Greg should have been there. He wasn't. He didn't make it to the door. The flames shot higher—they weren't controlled by the jets anymore—the house was going up. Flames were shooting toward the camera. Still Bleeker didn't call cut; he was counting on Greg to pull it off. 'He's a pro,' Bleeker was thinking, 'he's stretching the gag.' The flames were all over the house, catching faster and faster, higher, nearer the camera. Then they hit a wire, sparks flew everywhere. Bleeker yelled for the emergency crew. Too late. Fire was out of control." She squeezed her eyes shut. "Greg never came out."

The air conditioner groaned, and the water filter in the fish tank chugged. Outside, an engine started and a car burned rubber racing away.

"The cabin was engorged. By the time our emergency crew realized what was happening, the building was embers. And when the town firemen got control and went inside . . ." Dolly swallowed hard. When she resumed her voice was barely audible. "They said the intense heat and the lack of oxygen would have killed him almost immediately. Maybe they were being kind; I don't want to know. They figured he must have gotten disoriented, thought he was starting through the door and walked into the wall. It was like lying facedown on the broiler." She swallowed again. "He just burned to a crisp."

Kiernan tightened her muscles, forced her concentration onto the sequence of questions. No personal thoughts; no feelings; she couldn't allow that. "Dolly, what do you think happened? Could someone have substituted diesel fuel for gasoline? Diesel is sticky. It'd catch on the fire paste on the outside of the dress."

Dolly sat staring as if she had heard nothing. Behind her the dirt-brown fish swam through their empty windows and along the glass walls of their world.

A mistake, Kiernan wanted to reiterate. She was offering Dolly an out. Why wasn't the woman leaping for it? How could a mistake be more damning than the alternatives? "Dratz? You suspect Dratz screwed up the gag?"

Dolly squeezed back against her chair. It was probably as close to cringing as she came. "Possibly. He'd been discovered in the cabin a couple of times. Once screwing that extra of his."

"Dolly, you would have been delighted to pin this on Pedora. Why so unnerved about the hated Dratz?"

"Who knows?"

"You do! Tell me. Now!"

Dolly's shoulders pulled in. She sat staring at the fish. Finally she said, "I've never admitted . . ." She swallowed. "The whole time I was on the set Dratz was dogging me . . . like I'd been rubbed down with hamburger. I couldn't have him barred from the set. Couldn't send him back to L.A. Can you imagine what it's like to try to carry on a clandestine affair with Dratz on your ass? Half the reason I cut the guy loose was Dratz—I knew he was telling his father every detail. I wasn't about to be the laughingstock of Burbank. But even then, Dratz didn't let up. I couldn't stand the sight of him one more goddamned moment. So"—she swallowed again—"I told him there was a can't-miss gag first thing in the morning. He would have to be up at five A.M. Figured he'd be bushed and out of my hair the rest of the day. Told him they'd need extras; maybe he could get himself on camera. They all want to be in the movies, every visitor on every set." Momentarily, her face relaxed, as if comforted by the respite into the normal. "Cary wasn't using extras in the fire scene, of course." Uberhazy breathed in deeply. The lines between her brows dug in bone-deep. It was a moment before she said,

"I'm not liable. It's not my fault. Even if Dratz did . . . I'll pay you twice your normal fee, and I know just how much that is, if you can assure me that Dratz didn't screw up the gag somehow and . . . kill Greg."

CHAPTER 18

A MERCEDES convertible pulled out in front of Jason Pedora. Pedora's foot hit the gas pedal. *Let's see how that rich asshole takes a dent! 'Nother nick in the fender wouldn't cut into the VW's resale value. That's right, baldy—move your fat ass out of the lot before I get you!* It wasn't that bitch Uberhazy, but what the hell. He lifted his foot off the pedal and leaned back in the unmoving car. He didn't need to watch the Mercedes and Maseratis in the parking lot. It was the red Jeep Cherokee he was waiting for, and that was right across the aisle. No way the little bitch— he glared at her business card for the fiftieth time—O'Shaughnessy— could escape him.

Dolls thought he'd sit outside her office and just wait. Wait while she talked to the other bitch. Well, he'd waited ten years. And Dolls, she owed him. She knew it. He'd given her plenty of chances to make amends. But no more.

As for the other one—O'Shaughnessy—she'd stared him right in the face, had the gall to give him her card, then shove in front of him into Uberhazy's office. He looked at the card again. No address, just a phone number, as if she were daring him to find her, search her house—which meant she didn't have the stunt woman's notes there, right? She'd stashed them somewhere else, or— Oh, no, maybe she was giving them to Dolls. Should he key into Dolls instead of her?

But no, she was the one who'd challenged him. And here was that Jeep of hers sitting in front of him like a big red duck. He could take his shears and run the tip from bumper to bumper—one long scar. How much would her insurance nail her for two doors and two fenders? A grand, easy. Or the tires—a couple of flats would keep her in the lot a helluva lot longer than she planned. Or maybe a slow leak that would land her on the shoulder of the freeway for an hour. He smiled. Or maybe the brake lines, a quick cut. . . . No, too pedestrian—he giggled at that, *pedestrian*—he'd only stoop to that if he had time for nothing more creative, nothing worthy of him. The tension was building within him, making him strong. He could wait, let his strength grow till it . . . but he couldn't wait too long.

If only Greg were here. Greg understood his—had he called it genius? Greg knew his screenplay would make the Move hot. He would see it was a natural, box-office magic, from the horses and the drugs, the whole international conspiracy, to the movie set, and then the murder, *Greg's* murder! He'd been the only one to spot the conspiracy. And to see its potential for an Oscar-winning screenplay. With his genius, his brother would have been the most famous stunt double ever.

They had killed it, just like they killed Greg. They were so smug that they teased him with the new blonde doing the Move. But he wasn't rigid; he'd given them another chance. The screenplay could be revised for the blonde.

And they wouldn't let him near her.

They owed him!

And then they killed her, too.

Studios kept screwing writers. Well, not anymore.

He glared at the red Jeep. *Come on! Come on!*

CHAPTER **19**

KIERNAN pulled out of Summit-Arts Studios lot. It was already too late to be in L.A. Ten-lane roads through the center of the city should have made driving a breeze. Breeze indeed. More like dead air. She pulled onto the freeway on-ramp and sat waiting as the entry light let on one car at a time. Behind her, a Mercedes driver talked on his cellular phone. Behind him, an old blue VW bug with a board for a bumper edged to the left, as if seeing ahead to the front of the line were going to make it move faster.

She cleared the light onto the freeway and settled into the second gear pace. She reached for the phone. Two cars behind her, the Mercedes pulled into traffic, followed snout-to-tail by the bug. Bug must have cut the light. The fine for that was more than the car was worth.

She called Tchernak. The line was busy. Was Persis at BakDat calling with the results of the background checks? Or was it Tchernak's agent with an offer from the Rams?

She dialed again, this time to Modoc County information, and once more.

"High Country Gymnastics Academy."

"I need to speak to the owner or the coach."

"One and the same. Jerry Talbot. He's almost through supervising beginners' warm-ups. Hang on."

In the distance she could hear the gruff calls of a male voice. Gymnastics had come into its own since she spent phys. ed. periods in the corner of the high school gym, struggling with handstand variations on the balance beam while the basketball team practiced twenty feet away. But High Country would hardly be a major player on the national scene.

She pictured the facility as similar to her own gym: full of tiny girls with silent, serious faces who looked like they'd have to be taught to smile. They'd be on the mats, balanced on their buttocks, legs jackknifed up by abdominal muscles hard as a judge's stare. Or standing to the side, vibrating in place as they waited to learn to mount the uneven bars. Another mat would hold older boys proudly chalking their hands before being lifted to the still rings.

"Jerry Talbot here. How can I help you? I've only got a couple of minutes."

Good. Brevity would save her explanation. "I'm working with Summit-Arts Studios. We need some background on Lark Sondervoil for the memorial book. Personal information to go with the wonderful publicity shots we've got of her." She felt a pang of guilt, but there was no time to rationalize now. "I'm sorry to have to call you so soon after you've heard the tragic news, but—"

"No, no . . . that's all right."

"Did you train Lark?"

"Her last two years. Before that, it was Liz Putnam, but she retired and moved to Sacramento."

"What kind of student was Lark?"

As she'd expected, he said, "The best. A real hard worker. She'd go over and over anything you taught her until she got it firmly in her mind. Then she'd practice it hour after hour, day after day, until it was second nature."

"Needed to get away from home." The words were out of Kiernan's mouth before she realized it; it hadn't even been a question. She could see the padded corner of the gym in Baltimore and feel the relief that had swept over her each day as she walked in.

Talbot hadn't replied.

Quickly, she added, "I won't put anything negative about her family in the book. I'm just trying to get a picture of her, a jumping-off place for myself so I can capture the real Lark."

"Well, okay," he said slowly. "You know Lark was her real name. Guess that gives you an idea about her parents. Old hippies. Musta done a lotta drugs early on. But when I knew them, it was liquor. They weren't abusive or anything, but they didn't pay on time. If they said they were going to do something, like provide cookies for one of the fundraisers, you could count on them to flake out—and be pissed off if you brought it up. Stuff like that. Who knows what else? Lark was real protective of them. As soon as she was old enough, she worked to cover her tuition. But parents like that—well, it had to be hard on Lark, as meticulous as she was."

And working there extra hours had given her a valid reason to be not at home, Kiernan thought. Had Lark, like herself, stayed out too late, flirted with boys in leather jackets with slicked-back hair, taken on every dare and stretched it farther? "Did she have a wild streak?"

"Far from it. She was the most responsible kid in the gym. With those parents, I guess she'd have to have been."

Kiernan felt a flash of separation, and disappointment. The good kid, one of those she had scorned. "Was she a natural athlete?"

"No way. She had a sort of physical dyslexia, like there was a road-block between the concept of a trick and getting her body to do it. Good athletes don't even have to think about most of their moves. But Lark couldn't even dribble a basketball without watching both the ball and her hand. And even then anyone could have made a steal."

"How did she survive in gymnastics?"

"Determination. Lots of personal attention. Centuries of repetition. With that roadblock of hers, we had to build bypass highways—that's the way we talked about it—but once they were in place, they were as good as any other road. When she finally 'got' a trick, it was so well-etched into her map that she could do it on automatic. She wasn't particularly creative or imaginative, but she was a craftsman par excellence."

A craftsman. She *was* disappointed. But maybe that was why Lark had mastered the Gaige Move when she hadn't. She had always been the kid who took chances, the one who had to leave her imprint on whatever she did. She could have been the kid to take the Move farther, if she could have gotten the Move itself. And yet Lark . . . "So once she'd practiced a routine and checked the layout, she'd go into automatic?"

"More like she'd go inside. If you're not an athlete, it won't make much sense to you."

Kiernan's jaw tightened. She hadn't competed in over twenty years, but still, to have him assume she was on the outside with her nose pressed against the glass . . . even though he thought he was talking to a publicist, not to Kiernan O'Shaughnessy, who had taken second in the Nationals . . .

"Look, you said you were with the studio. Lark was very good. Why do you need to know more—"

"Sorry," she said, shifting back into persona. "I know you're busy. I'm afraid I got sidetracked, because it's so impressive to know she could have accomplished so much with that handicap. Inspiring. She would have been a wonderful teacher."

"That was our hope for her. But she was too good to stay up here in the mountains. She wanted the Olympics, of course. They all do. She wasn't that good, but she thought she was. Too bad she never got to the trials."

Never even got the chance to try for it! God, she felt for Lark. It was like finishing college only to be told they'd stopped giving diplomas, or stopped giving them to people like you, or just to you. "Why not?"

"Her parents." The disgust was clear in his voice. "Ray," he called, half muffling the receiver, "cover for me a few minutes, okay? Sorry," he said, returning his attention to the phone conversation. "I guess you're aware that Lark's parents were killed in an auto crash. Happened the week before the trials. Lark was devastated. I don't know which bothered her most—their deaths or missing the trials. Well, at that age all that stuff mixes together, and kids don't know themselves what they're over-whelmed by. But Lark was never quite the same after that. In a way her life was easier without her parents to worry about. But I guess it was too late for her to have a childhood. She threw herself into practice with as much determination as before, but the hope was gone. And why not? She had no goal. And then she decided on Hollywood, a career in the movies. I had my reservations, I'll tell you, but the girl was a beauty, and I figured that would get her the extra time she needed. Guys will always give a pretty woman a break." He lowered his voice, and Kiernan had the feeling he had his hand cupped over the speaker. "We've got one little girl now—plain as porridge. But good; she can do release moves on the uneven bars like no ten-year-old I've ever seen. Do you think the judges ever give her a break? The cute ones they give the benefit of the doubt, an extra tenth here, an oh-five there. But this kid—it's like they think she made herself plain just to spite them. You'd think adults would have a little compassion; or fairness."

She sighed. "Yeah, you'd think. Mr. Talbot," she said slowly, "you had hesitations about Lark coming to Hollywood. Why? Did she seem too trusting?"

"Hardly. Look, the girl had had a lousy childhood. It made sense that she was locked up emotionally, like she lived inside a moat. But that doesn't mean she didn't *want* to trust someone. She was probably afraid;

maybe she didn't know how. In some ways she was an adult; in others a kid. You know how teenagers are. She'd have a crush on a guy, and she couldn't set limits or see consequences. Guess that was her parents coming out in her. They had no sense of limits at all. Luckily, Lark was a busy kid, so she didn't have time to go off the deep end much."

"Did you talk to her a lot after she got to L.A.?"

"Never. I was hoping to hear from her, though. Kids in the gym were dying to know what it was like to be a real stunt woman."

"I can imagine. Did you ever call her?"

"Had no number for her. I thought she'd call us, or maybe I just hoped. I guess I wasn't surprised. You know how kids are," he added, as if fearful that he'd said too much.

"Just one more question. How did Lark get to Hollywood, into the movie business?"

"She called someone down there for a screen test. Then she just up and went. Said she wasn't going to miss out again."

"They don't do screen tests for stunt doubles. Stunt players get known by word of mouth. If they're called, they send in tapes of their work."

"Guess Lark knew the right mouth."

"Whose?"

"Got me. You're with the studio. I assumed he must be one of yours."

"Did you know," she said quickly, "that Lark added an extra twist to the Gaige Move?"

"Really," he said, the pride clear in his voice. "But you mean up there on the bluff, when she died."

"Right. But she did it. She took the Move to a new level. But how did she do that? You yourself said she wasn't creative."

"Got me. She must have learned it down there." From the gym came sounds of a crash. "Gotta go."

Was Cary Bleeker the man Lark had called? If not, he'd know who was, or he damned well could find out. Replacing the receiver, she glanced at her watch. It was after three. No chance of her making La Jolla before six, or more likely seven. Now the big question was, would Bleeker and the film company still be there.

CHAPTER **20**

"Y OU'RE home, Tchernak?"

"You calling from the car?" Even though he didn't mention his oft-repeated dictum—phoning and driving should be mutually exclusive—Kiernan could hear the censure in his voice.

She didn't approve of the distraction for other drivers. And she tried to avoid it herself, but not, as she had been quick to point out to Tchernak, because she wasn't competent. Her goal was to keep both hands on the wheel in case she could slice into the left-hand lane, whip around a four-wheel slug, or block an eighteen-wheeler from cutting in front of her and plodding along in first gear, or do any of a number of things Tchernak tagged "adolescent." But the lure of speeding was not a temptation that she was likely to face on the I-5. "If it weren't for lifting the phone, there'd be no movement here at all."

"Huh? Oh, you're on the freeway and you didn't give the CHP time to clear a lane for you?"

"Sarcasm is so unattractive in hired help."

In the background she could hear panting. She smiled. Tchernak himself sounded short of breath—the familiar "doing reps" breath pattern. "How was the *Edge of Disaster* set?"

"Didn't shoot today," he got out between great heaving exhalations that almost blocked out the increasingly enthusiastic panting.

"Summit-Arts canceled the day's schedule? Because of Lark's death? More sensitivity than I would have expected."

"Had to. Police questioning."

"Rats, so we're back to the start." She slammed on the brakes inches from the fender of a vintage Corvette that had jerked to a stop. "The

Mercedes behind me's been riding my tail since I got on the freeway. Volkswagen behind him's just about in his trunk. Guy in front of me's squirting suntan lotion and he's got his head tilted back so far he could be looking me in the eye. He's so busy slathering his face he can barely handle his phone."

"He driving with his knees, Kiernan?"

"He's not driving at all. A pickup just cut in front of him. Oh, shit, look at that! A panel truck floated in behind the pickup. With the amount of room he's left in front of him, the Queen Mary could cut in!"

"Maybe he'll grease the phone and drop it in the fast lane. No, wait, what was I thinking of? You're in the fast lane, right?"

"There is no fast lane. I'm merely in the more easterly line of seats. But the guy in the Corvette, he could have had his face lifted in less time than he's been working on it. I've been watching that face for half an hour, Tchernak; the only thing his work is doing is proving the Law of Diminishing Returns." She edged the car forward.

"Fortunately, the opposite is true here." Tchernak's breath sounded more normal. In the background the panting was more evenly spaced but no less insistent. "You are about to appreciate how valuable an experienced offensive lineman is in our investigative business."

Our business—just what she'd been afraid of. "*My* business."

"Offensive linemen don't give up," he continued as if she hadn't spoken. "I hung around the set. Never got near Bleeker, but when the grips—the heavy-duty movers, to you uninitiated—needed help, who do you think they were thankful to have?"

"What about their union?"

"There were no reps on the sets. And the grips thought I *was* union."

"Good work." She eased off the brake a bit, balancing it against the gas on the slight upgrade. Ahead, the Corvette driver was lathering his neck. "And so you found . . . ?"

"I cocked an ear when the cops were around. They're still real comfortable with the drug theory. They didn't react when Pete, the sort of middling grip, mentioned the markers on the bluff. They didn't ask about them being moved."

"But you did?"

"Right. Pete's sharp; he's been a grip on four films, but he's not the key grip. So if something wasn't up to snuff, it's no skin off his nose."

"Gentlemanly mixing of metaphors there. So Pete said?"

"Anyone could have moved the markers. There were so many people rushing around that nobody would remember where they were when or who else was with them. There'd been a flood of reporters earlier, then the last line of trailers had to be moved forward to accommodate the city; everyone was jumpy. The scene right before Lark's ran to seven takes. They were scurrying to get hers in while there was enough light."

"What was his impression of Lark? Savvy? Naïve? Competent? Careless?"

"Well, he found her physically desirable—"

"Euphemistically put?"

"Believe it! His take was, she was good, but she was getting a helluva chance in *Edge* and she didn't seem appreciative. *Driven* was the word he used. Like she was on a mission. Like it would all bloom at her press conference."

"What kind of flowers was Pete expecting to bloom there? Something Dolly or Bleeker didn't want revealed?"

"That was his guess, but it was only a guess. He was halfway across the set when she was talking to the city press liaison. What Pete did say was that with all the media fuss and the waiting, Lark was edgier than he'd ever seen her. Her and everyone on the set. Makes sense."

The traffic began to move. Kiernan eased on the gas, wedging the phone against her shoulder and poising her hand on the gear stick to shift into second. The Corvette shot forward. She shifted and hit the gas just as a stretch limo cut in front of her and screeched to a halt. Simultaneously, she hit the horn and the brake. The phone banged to the floor.

"What was that?" a small voice yelled up from the rubber mat.

She scooped up the receiver. "Traffic." Before Tchernak could reiterate his cellular phone axiom, she said, "Have you gotten the backgrounds from BakDat?"

"Persis promises she'll have them to me before you get home." The panting was louder, faster, more insistent.

"Well, Persis is in luck. I've got to catch Cary Bleeker first. So she's got about four more hours. Do you have any idea where Bleeker is now, or will be by the time I get to La Jolla?"

"In his trailer on the set. At least, that's what he told the cops."

"Okay. I'm going directly there. I'll be home for dinner afterward."

"Uh, Kiernan . . . ?" Tchernak began in an uneasy tone, entirely too hesitant for a man used to butting into defensive linemen.

"Yes?"

"As long as you're going to be there anyway, do me—do *us* a favor."

"What can I do for *us?*"

"Well, see, I tried a couple of the spiced garlic rolls. They're great, and there's something in the herbs and spices that takes them to a new realm. The chef should forget this movie nonsense and market them nationally. But that's his lookout. I just want the recipe, so I know what those spices are. And I couldn't get the cook out of his kitchen to tell me."

"Tchernak, you want *me* to ask for a recipe?"

"They don't know your history; they won't laugh at you."

Kiernan chuckled. "And I was worried you'd get so involved in the investigation, you'd forget your job at home."

"You laugh, but the next time you want a lasagna before you meet a client, you'll be sorry I don't know those herbs and spices."

"I'll see what I can do. Now, let me speak to *him.*"

"Geez, Kiernan, you're not going to do *that.* You know you're using a cellular phone; anyone could hear."

"Tchernak!"

"Okay, okay. It's your funeral. It'll serve you right if the Corvette's listening. Here *he* is."

Ignoring Tchernak's familiar plaint, she listened for the happy slurp on the receiver and said into the mouthpiece, "Ezzzzraaaaaa, what a fine dog."

Ezra gave a little bark.

"Such a good dog. Ezzzzz . . ."

The sun was lurking low on the water by the time Kiernan pulled up —rumpled and grumpy—at Gliderport. The sea wind had tossed over one of the black reflectors, leaving the panel balanced precariously against a trailer, its dark shadow snaking beneath the trailer bed. Her jacket, which had been too hot for Los Angeles and the car trip, was inadequate now, and the wind ran icy fingers down her sweaty back. Her face felt gummy, her legs rubbery from the drive, and she would have given her right arm—well, no, not a whole limb, but a carpal digit —for a bourbon on the rocks.

Had Dolly called to warn Bleeker? She would have had ample time. She stopped by the Summit-Arts security guard and flipped open the pass she'd gotten from Uberhazy. "Which trailer is Cary's?"

"Last one on the right."

The set, which yesterday had looked like an over-deadline construction site—with people racing back and forth, hauling equipment, driving equipment, and yelling about equipment and lack of equipment—now seemed like a still photo. The giant crane was gone, no longer daring ambitious stunt doubles to climb up its slick arm, all the hundred feet to the top, to balance there high above the earth, and there feel the wind in their hair, know the decelerator wire was hooked onto their backs, and step off into nothingness. The giant catering truck was gone, probably back at the local production offices for the night. The canteen wagon–size hitch trailer in which Tchernak's coveted garlic polenta rolls were fried was still there but closed, its metal awning fastened. She felt a pang of regret about the recipe. She would have enjoyed giving Tchernak something. Their unspoken agreement was give and take; it worked for both of them, and it didn't work for either. She put in as much as Tchernak, but her offerings were the easy ones—money—or an okay for an abrupt week off to work out with a specialist in Arizona. Tchernak had pulled a psoas muscle the day he'd arrived in Tucson and limped painfully home. It had taken more than she'd thought she had to ease the pain that stretched from his spine to his thigh, from anger to frustration, and hovered just above the scalding surface of fear. Giving up gymnastics had been wrenching, but she'd been stepping off the giant crane into a net of promise. And there'd been college. She'd offered Tchernak her knowledge of the pain and terror—silently, the only way she could, the only way he could accept it. But stepping off the crane was one thing; being shoved off, and without any net, was another. It might be that nothing would keep him from crashing to the ground.

Not a good role for a woman with no bedside manner.

Two rows of silver trailers formed a sort of picket fence, demarcating the hard sand set from the hard sand beyond. Bleeker's trailer was in the far row—an indication of low rank, Kiernan figured. The more valued "names" did not have windows at the edge of the parking lot into which an adoring fan might peer.

"Who?" Bleeker demanded wearily in response to her knock. He sounded as if he'd spent the day being rolled under every piece of equipment he'd yelled about the day before. And now, his tone indicated, he was going to have to face one more bulldozer.

"Kiernan O'Shaughnessy. Dolly sent me." She was gilding the lily invoking Dolly's name. Nothing in Bleeker's voice suggested he had the authority to refuse anyone. Even the guard hadn't bothered to call and warn him.

And when he opened the door, he stood slumped in defeat. His black shirt showed signs of a long day in the sun. Deep horizontal wrinkles across the hip joint of his black jeans told of hours spent sitting in sticky-hot chairs. Inside his fringe of dark, sweat-damp hair his bald dome shone an uncomfortable sunburned pink. Clearly he had been too preoccupied to remember a hat. For a man whose pate indicated years of baldness, that was a notable oversight. "What does Dolly need now?" He squinted at Kiernan; his hand tightened on the door. "Wait a minute. Last night you were the union rep."

So Dolly hadn't contacted him. Not even a courtesy call. "Private investigator, working with Dolly." She flipped open the pass.

A groan escaped Bleeker's lips. If he was making any attempt to hide his reaction, it was a failure. He might as well have had a ticker tape running across his forehead: *Why did Dolly hire a private eye? Why didn't she tell me? What does she know that I don't? Whatever, she's getting ready to stick it to me.* "Just what does Dolly Uberhazy's private eye want?"

"I need a few answers," Kiernan said, offering nothing but fuel for his paranoia. "Easy answers, preferably inside in the air conditioning." Air conditioning was the last thing she needed, but that was no reason to miss whatever the production trailer might reveal. He eased back, and she moved past him to settle in one of two leather swivel chairs. The trailer, more of an office than a mobile womb, looked like any too-busy office. There was nothing personal in it.

Bleeker flopped in the remaining swivel and took a last swallow from a Sierra Nevada bottle.

"Dolly said you made her an offer she couldn't refuse with Lark Sondervoil. How did you find Lark?"

"She called me."

"She herself?"

"Right. She called me cold."

That didn't fit with the picture Talbot had painted of Lark Sondervoil at the High Country gym—not a girl who would stride into L.A., know who to call, and have the chutzpah to do it. But Bleeker no longer seemed capable of making it up. The man looked like a collection of leaderless parts. His brown eyes were tense, his lids awkwardly half-closed, and his body was slumped in the chair as if someone had let the air out. "A cold call, Cary? Isn't that pretty unusual, particularly for a nineteen-year-old novice?"

"Trying's not rare. Succeeding is."

"Just how did she manage that success?"

"I don't remember."

Despite the air conditioning, the trailer was muggy, and as she looked at the papers scattered atop the desk, she could make out a thin coating of white powder that could have been powdered sugar from a morning's doughnut, talcum, or the result of a more expensive mishap. Given Bleeker's state, if she let him slip out of one question, he'd be lost to her. "Cary, you're exhausted. I have a job to do. Don't make every question a tug-of-war. Why did you see Lark Sondervoil?"

"The Gaige Move." He shook his head. "Like I never learn. You'd think that would have been one action sequence I never wanted to set eyes on again."

"You hired Greg Gaige for *Bad Companions,* right?" She leaned forward in anticipation.

"Right."

"For the Move?"

"Then? No. I just needed to cut expenses. The Move was gravy. Shit, I thought I'd made the deal of the century. I was a hot commodity."

Kiernan felt her face flush. Her face never betrayed her like that. But *cut expenses* as a rationale for hiring the best acrobatic stunt double of his time? She'd heard it from Dolly, but this offhand comment from a marginal second unit director . . . By the time Bleeker contacted him, Greg must have been clinging to the crane arm with both hands and both legs. "Yarrow had a contract. How could you fire him?"

Bleeker shrugged. Clearly, it was not a question that ignited his waning bit of curiosity.

"Cary!"

"Look, you want an education on film financing, get your friend Dolly to give it to you. But take it from me, contracts can be changed or broken, and when they do, it's not the studio that loses money."

"And Yarrow had no viable recourse?"

"Not unless he wanted to mortgage the farm for court costs. And never work again."

"Is that kind of double-dealing standard in this business?" The Greg Gaige she knew wouldn't have been prepared for that. He'd grown up doing the required number of release moves on the bars, honing floor exercises so he stayed inside a forty-foot square. The most duplicitous thing he'd encountered had been the random bias or provincialism of judges, and everyone on his gymnastic team would have been complaining about that. But to be hit like an old croquet ball, used to knock another off the field . . . She squeezed her eyes shut against the picture. When she opened them, it was to face an even more depressing question: How bad had things gotten with Greg that he accepted the offer? "Why did they even assume Greg Gaige would accept that kind of offer?"

Bleeker laughed limply. "Why? Because he *made* the offer."

"Greg solicited Yarrow's job?" she asked, so stunned that her words seemed to flow out of a stranger's mouth. "Why?"

"Gaige was too old. He'd lost a step. He was living in the past."

"But he could still do the Move so you wanted him, right?" It wasn't a question but a demand.

Nodding in acquiescence, Bleeker shrank back into his chair.

Her chest went cold. She could still see Greg Gaige that time in San Francisco, striding across the set with the lightness and surety of a cougar. It had been twenty years then since he'd posed for the poster photo. The years had begun to line his face, push back his hair, but that didn't matter. He had still been the same eager, excited, sure-he-could-do-it guy. But *Bad Companions* hadn't come long after that. In San Francisco he must have known how precarious things were with him— even then, when he refused to acknowledge her questions about the future. She pushed the picture away and stared back at Cary Bleeker. *Tell me Greg Gaige didn't sink to the level where he was begging for work, stealing jobs from his friends!* She forced out the words, "Angling for a job that someone else is already on—is that unusual?"

"Not unheard of. If it were the studio doing the double-dealing, no one would bat a lash. Look, there's nothing in this business that can't change like that." He snapped his thumb off his little finger, making only a dull thud for a snap. Momentarily he stared, surprised, at his hand. "On the *Bad Companions* location, things were changing all the time. I'd come back from lunch and find the studio had hired a new actor I'd never heard of. Or they'd need one of the stars back in L.A., so they'd move up the shooting time of their scene that used the same set as my scene, so mine got shifted backward. Did they tell me, a lowly second unit director? Fat chance. Got so I didn't even bother complaining."

"But the stunt community—?" she prompted.

"That's a little different. It's small, and the guys who've been around awhile have a little more honor among themselves." He lifted the Sierra Nevada to his mouth. It was empty. "You want a beer?"

"Yes."

He reached over to the fridge, pulled two bottles from the door, and handed her one.

She opened it and drank, but her throat was so taut, it was hard to swallow. "And Greg, didn't he have honor?"

Bleeker stared at the green bottle. "Yeah, he did. But he had only a few more good years left, anyone with any sense could see that. It was like the shorter the time, the more desperate he got. When he died, I thought . . ." Bleeker leaned back and took a long swallow of his beer. His eyelids shut. He took another drink. Kiernan was just about to prompt him when he spoke. "It was lucky he died before he lost the Move."

Kiernan picked up her beer, but it was a moment before she could make herself drink. "I saw a still of Greg in the middle of the Move—smiling."

"I know the one you mean." A spark of enthusiasm flickered and died, like a match beneath thick green logs. Bleeker's voice was without inflection. "It was from his first movie, the other time he did the Move. When I saw it, I was blown away. I mean, it was the most important publicity shot of his career, and he was *enjoying* it, as if he'd missed the line between work and play. I mean, I love directing, but I know it's work."

"Right. But it's a fine line. And you've probably enjoyed it less since the bad luck incidents," she said, aware that she had built a bond between them and now was snapping it back at him with an ease that was almost automatic. "They started on that set, *Bad Companions,* didn't they?"

He reached for his beer, then let his hand drop. "Christ, does the entire world know about me? Or did Dolly inform you? Dolly, hell—she's probably the only exec in Hollywood who'll still take a chance on me."

"Why did she?"

"Who knows? Maybe it was the Gaige Move. Hell, maybe it was something as quirky as my finding the polenta rolls she's so crazy about."

"The menu was in the contract?" Kiernan asked skeptically.

"I sent a box of them with my agent to spice up the deal," he said with a wan smile.

"Or to remind Dolly that you recalled her eating them last time—on the same set she had an affair on?" Kiernan wanted his reaction to that affair.

"Listen, if I sent food to commemorate every affair on a set, I could feed Bangladesh."

"Who was the guy?"

"If I could remember every guy—"

"Right," she said giving up on that. "Dolly did tell me about Greg's brother having to be barred from the set. And about Dratz. Do you think one of them is behind your 'bad luck'?"

"Pedora? The guy was a nutcase, a paranoid would-be screenwriter who figured all Hollywood was united in one great campaign against him. Sure I figured it could be him. Or Dratz. Or Yarrow. Or anyone else on the set. Who knows? Don't waste your time trying to figure it out. I've spent ten years. There's no rationale. I've checked payroll logs, but there's no one person who's been on every set. I've turned my mind to mush thinking about motives. Was Yarrow pissed off at being fired? The guy was operating on a bum leg. He should have seen that coming. And Pedora, did he lose his mind because his meal ticket was killed? Like I said, the guy's a nutcase."

"But you're not sure he's *your* nutcase?"

"I only wish. If I could prove it was Pedora, or Dratz, or anyone else, I'd take out a full-page ad in the trades. My career would be reborn. Do you know what it's like working my ass off year after year, directing second unit after second unit, never getting to work with a star? And waiting, always waiting for the disaster that's coming?" His voice rang with emotion.

"Does it happen on every picture?"

"No. It's almost worse that way. Intermittent reinforcement."

"What kind of things do you mean when you talk about 'disasters'?"

"Short-circuit in the wiring burns out a couple of banks of lights."

"Couldn't that just be an accident?"

"Of course." He sat up straight. "But it had never happened before. And then, suddenly, two banks. One we could have done without. Two cost us a couple nights' shooting."

"What else?" Kiernan said, her shoulders tightening with excitement.

"Malicious pranks. Look, when you're a second unit director, in charge of a lot of technical and mechanical devices, there's a myriad of stuff that can go wrong."

"Give me another example. What happened in your last picture?"

He started to protest, then shrugged. "Flowers. I don't remember what they were called. They were some kind of delicate pastel things flown in from the end of the earth. The greensmen stuck them in the ground the day before the shooting. Next morning they were gone, the whole damned lot of them. Nothing but singed leaves. And you know what that means."

"You have to wait to shoot till you can fly in another batch. In the meantime you pay people to stand around?"

"Exactly. Producer was so furious, I'm lucky to be sitting here with my balls in place. And my wallet. He threatened to take the overrun out of my check. I should have been making so much." He shrugged. "Nothing wrecks a career like going over budget."

"Singed leaves." She leaned forward. "The plants were burned?"

"Yeah. Somebody threw a roll of paper towels over them and lit it."

"These incidents, did they all use fire?"

"Yeah. Every one."

She leaned forward, bracing her elbows on her thighs. She'd been so sure that moving the marker was the latest of the pranks, a prank that had gotten out of hand. But whoever spent years intermittently harassing Bleeker had been obsessed enough to include fire in every incident. Obsessives don't suddenly drop their MO and opt for the easiest means. "Cary, the fires in these pranks, were they always central to the result?"

He shrugged noncommittally.

"Yesterday there was a fire in a trash can by the trailers, remember?"

Slowly, Bleeker nodded.

"And right after that," she said, "the marker was moved."

CHAPTER 21

THE beer can fell from Cary Bleeker's hand. Bleeker leaned forward in his chair and clutched his head. Normally, Kiernan would have classified the reaction as theatrical. But now she, who'd been known to remind people of her lack of bedside manner, had the urge to scoop Bleeker onto her lap like a small child and hold him safe till the pain went away. Victims fell apart, but perpetrators carried on, too. She wasn't sure in which category Bleeker belonged.

Either way, a wound like this one could throb for the rest of his life, and no amount of comforting would provide an opiate. If he was innocent, the most she could do was to give him time to let the initial shock pass. But if he had moved the cordon posts, she had to take advantage of his unguarded state. The truth came first. "Cary, maybe moving the marker doesn't fit with the other pranks?"

Bleeker pushed himself up. Momentarily, his dark eyes brightened, then he shook his head and slumped into the leather chair. "No, it fits his MO."

"Have there been injuries in the other pranks?"

"No." He clutched his head again, but he didn't sink forward, and in a moment he gave up the awkward position and let his hands drop. "This is it. He wins. I'm out of the business. I'll never direct again. I quit." An ironic smile flashed on his swollen features and was gone. "Who am I kidding? I won't have the chance to quit—no one will ever hire me. Bad enough I've cost hundreds of thousands of dollars over the years, but now I'm responsible for killing people."

"Cary, there isn't time for self-pity."

His head snapped up. "What kind of woman are you?"

Bleeker was angry, but at least he was alert. "Let's look at this practically," Kiernan said. "Who have we got as suspects? The pranks started on the *Bad Companions* set—"

"Christ! Carlton Dratz—someone spotted him on the set! How fucking fitting. Lark's death has the earmarks of Dratz. He moves the marker —because he isn't thinking, because it's in his way, because he wants to see what will happen, who knows?—and ends up with a killing, for which someone else suffers."

"By 'someone else,' you mean you as opposed to Lark?" So much for jolting him out of self-pity. "Where is Dratz these days?"

"Who knows?"

"Where did he go after *Bad Companions*?"

"Off with one of the extras—the girl he was so busy screwing in the honeywagon."

"Her name?"

"I don't know."

"Cary, we're talking about the man who might be ruining your life, and you haven't even bothered to track down the woman he went off with?"

He jolted up. "Look, the guy wasn't the center of my life. He was like a cold sore on your lip, you know? When it's blooming, it's all you can think about, but when it goes, you forget about it, and one morning you realize it's been gone for days. When Dratz left, I was just relieved to have him gone. It wasn't until three or four pictures later that there were enough incidents to form a pattern, and I began to think about Dratz. But by that time, no one remembered who *Companions*' star was, much less who all the extras were."

"Wasn't there a crew list?"

"Sure, but it didn't include local hires; it wasn't updated. It's useless."

"There has to be some way we can find out," she insisted.

"I haven't found one, not in ten years."

"Bleeker, you are not an investigator. There have to be records from that set, contracts signed, salaries paid."

Bleeker's face brightened. "Yeah, of course. Hey, this is going to be easier than you thought."

Kiernan scowled. If there was one thing she hated, it was civilians telling her her work was going to be a snap.

"Here's why it's going to be so easy for you to find out about Dratz. The accountant from *Bad Companions* is here." Bleeker beamed at her.

When she didn't respond, he nudged: "He can get the payroll records from *Companions*."

"After ten years? You don't even save tax forms that long."

"Yeah, but see, accounting is so boring. It was a thrill for this guy to be on a movie location. All the hassles and changes, it was Hollywood with a capital H, and he loved it."

"And that accountant was Liam McCafferty, the city media liaison, right? I talked to him on the set yesterday."

Bleeker beamed brighter. "See, I told you he loved it."

CHAPTER 22

JASON Pedora stood next to the little food trailer, panting from the double-time run in from Torrey Pines Boulevard. He wasn't meant for that. Nobody'd asked Isherwood or Fitzgerald to jog.

But the bitch's Jeep was still here. Jeep with a gas tank the size of Ventura. *She* didn't have to gas up. So *she* chose a route where you had to sell your soul for a gallon. Damned bug's tank only held ten point six. Took him half an hour to find a station that didn't want the family jewels.

But she was still here. In Bleeker's trailer. He heard her voice through the window. The trailer sat at the edge of the set; the guards didn't bother to patrol it. As if they knew what Bleeker was worth. He could have doused a rag with gas and tossed it through Bleeker's window, and no one would have been the wiser. Would have been easy, a no-brainer, a Dratz move.

Pedora smiled, thinking of Carlton Dratz and Bad Luck Bleeker, and all the "misfortunes" that had come to pass when Bleeker was on a set. He'd heard Bleeker whining. If Bad Luck thought *those* hits were big time, he hadn't seen anything.

Not now. He made the rules, and the rule was one hit per production and *Edge* had already had that. And he had more important things on his mind.

Still . . . he'd learned a lot in the last decade, about wiring, and light and sound devices, and flash fires, and cables and brake lines, and grease fires. Hell, they could have had a fire department devoted to him. He laughed.

But no, this was serious. He hadn't wanted to do fire. But this was the right thing. In memory of Greg. How long would it take the imbeciles to get that?

"If they weren't so fucking cheap," Greg had said, "Bleeker would have a fire safety crew. Wouldn't depend on the regular, all-around, no-specialty crew, and the town fire department who couldn't get their asses to the set on time." Greg had had his own safety crew, but there was no question of them being on payroll, not with the tightwads in production cutting every corner and Bleeker too lame to put up a fight. A penny saved . . . for Greg's life.

Well, Bleeker, the cringing wimp—the set could be burning around him, and he still wouldn't get it.

He looked back at the Jeep. It was her he had to watch. Couldn't let himself be sidetracked. She would come right by here after she left Bleeker's trailer. But he could slip around the side of the trailer out of sight. He rested a foot on the trailer hitch. It gave a slight bounce in reaction to the pressure. Pedora looked down. And smiled.

A padlock secured it to the next trailer. But the tongue hadn't been pushed into the groove.

The O'Shaughnessy bitch was coming out of Bleeker's. He couldn't lose her, not now, not after all he'd had to do.

He looked back at the padlock. Trailers like this, they were so easy. They were asking for it. How could he not . . . ?

Pedora pulled off the lock and loosed the chain. Give it a shove, just a little one.

But no, he had his rules.

Besides, he might have to break them later.

CHAPTER 23

"THE movie business, I hated it. It was a quagmire then, and look, now ten years later it's still taking up my time." Liam McCafferty laughed. " 'Course, there's no saying I didn't leap at the chance and make the most of it. And when the city offered me its media liaison spot, I wasn't about to give them a no." McCafferty was a big man: big waves of faded red hair, features too big for his face, which seemed too big for his body, which in itself was big. He appeared to be in his midfifties, but she suspected closer to fifty was the truth. The disparity came from the sag of his body and the brogue he'd chosen to affect. He reminded Kiernan of one of the old ward pols who used to corral her father for meetings in the basement of Saint Brendan's. And Uncle Matt, who'd been one of them.

It had been after nine when Kiernan called McCafferty at home, but once she identified herself as the woman with the Irish wolfhound, McCafferty insisted she come right on over. Now, at almost ten o'clock, he was seated in one of a pair of brown leather mission chairs facing a wall of windows that looked down from the top of La Jolla's Soledad Mountain. Below, lights around Mission Bay shone like yellow crystals against the royal blue of the water. Party lights twinkled white from the masts of ships in the bay and San Diego Harbor beyond. Concentric cords of white and red, the warnings and memories of cars, surrounded the water like ribbons on a holiday package.

Delighted, Kiernan settled in the other chair and accepted a drink in the kind of Waterford crystal glass she recalled being in the locked cabinet of her mother's sister, who had married above herself.

"I'll bet your family's proud of you," she couldn't resist saying.

"That they are, Ms. O'Shaughnessy. Now I don't want you to think I go around spouting this to everyone I meet, but you being back-east Irish—I can hear mid-Atlantic in your voice—I know you'll understand. I'm the only one of my generation to finish high school—of all the cousins, and there was a heap of us kids. I worked my way through college; it took eight years. But when I graduated, with honors yet, you'd ha' thought John Kennedy had been resurrected. And then, years later, for me to come out here to the Golden State and get a job in the movies." He shrugged in an attempt at modesty that couldn't cover his pride. "Well, when I went back home after that, the likeness of myself was on the wall between the Kennedys and the Pope."

She smiled comfortably, able to picture the scene without effort. She mentally filled in the background Tchernak had been able to squeeze from BakDat's tardy—and guilty—Persis in the half hour it had taken her to drive to the top of the hill in La Jolla—Soledad Mountain—then added, "And now that you're in line for assistant to the state treasurer—"

Her raised a meaty finger. "Hush now. Nothing's firm yet."

"I'm sure that my small mention of it won't alert the gods. You'll be in Sacramento before the gods know you're available. And with the wind at your back," she said with a laugh.

McCafferty smiled, sipped his drink—a pale rye and ginger—and sat back comfortably in his soft leather chair. Like the watered drink, he was an interesting mixture of the old and the new, of traditional Irish and the competitive edge of California. At ten in the evening he might well have been dressed in sweats or jeans, but he was in corduroy slacks and a tweed jacket, and his pale blue shirt still looked fresh.

"So why were the books for *Bad Companions* such a quagmire?"

He glanced accusingly at his desk in the far corner of the room, as if it were responsible for his past errata. "I'll tell you, I wasn't a natural for accounting. If I'd been the son of a rich man or grown up with educated people, I would have relaxed in college and taken classes in sociology, and theater arts, and who knows what. But just getting to college was such a big step, and I was working so hard to pay my way through, and afterward to repay the loans, that I felt I had to take classes that would lead directly to work. Thus accounting, and later computers. For an insecure kid like me, the rules were a comfort. With them, I felt as if I could go anywhere and I'd be able to make it." He smiled expansively. "Well, you can see how innocent I was. Which is what I realized in spades when I got a look at the cost runs on that film. I'd just finished doing the taxes for a startup company, and they were a breeze compared to that."

The startup company where he'd met Trace Yarrow.

"Rules? I'll tell you, Kiernan, these folk don't deal in fantasy only on the screen. To them contracts mean nothing. Salaries are changed more often than the weather. People were hired for two months, and after a week they were gone. The studio accountants were screaming—literally screaming—on the phone that we were over budget, then the next thing I knew there were two new limousines for the stars. I'd go to do the payroll and discover there were three people working I'd never been notified about. No one kept receipts for anything. It would have been easier to plan the budget for an emerging nation." He shook his head. "I did the best I could. In retrospect, I'm sure I stuck a lot closer to the truth than they wanted. They got to the point where they were virtually swatting me away with all my questions. But then, it was me those cost runs were going to reflect on, and I knew from the second week there that I'd be moving on."

"Because you'd found another job?"

"Not yet, but I knew I would. They'd loaded the whole of the office work on me. I was so busy taking messages, ordering envelopes, and running the copier, it's a miracle I had time for the cost runs at all." He lifted his drink to his mouth and held it there, tapping his teeth on the glass before taking another sip.

Watching him, Kiernan wondered if those small sips were signs of caution, adjustment to the California mores of wine or mineral water, or merely indications of distaste for the weak drink. As the saying went, the Irish were divided into drinkers and teetotalers. Her own parents had been the latter, and for her the lure of liquor had been mixed with the lure of freedom. There had been nights she couldn't remember the next day, and ones she wished she couldn't. School and then work had limited those nights. And once she'd started postmortems, pictures of gnarly liquor-hardened liver tissue seemed to float in each glass.

He rested the glass back on its coaster. "I was a token in the movie business, a poor straitlaced bean counter in a rich game run by people with fewer rules than lovers. I could see early on that no matter how hard I worked, I'd always be an outsider."

"I know the feeling," Kiernan said, though it had been many years since it had bothered her. Smiling suddenly, she said, "Why is it that the name Carlton Dratz comes to mind?"

McCafferty did a momentary double take then threw his head back and guffawed. "Say no more. The twerp was a poster child for nepotism. He burst through the set like a greased pig, leaving a bog of mire and sh— of droppings wherever he went. I'll tell you, when he started through my books—him without so much as an accounting course to his name, and not enough sense to keep the pages together—he fouled me up for weeks and got both the union and the studio screaming. 'The next time you stick your head between the covers of my books,' I said to him, 'I'll mash it like a pressed flower.' I could ha' done it, I must have been twice his size." He shot a glance at his midsection. "Or at least I am now."

"But you restrained yourself?"

"Indeed. Provoked as I was, I knew that if I waited, he'd take care of it himself. He was instructing the director how to direct, he was chatting aloud on the set—I don't know how many extra takes they had to do because he couldn't keep quiet. You can't believe how much money that runs! A week into shooting, he took a nap in the 'fire' house, woke up, and strolled into the middle of a scene out in front of it. He 'borrowed' a guy's motorcycle and tried to jump it across the trap in the road, and it ended up a pile of metal at the bottom of the hole. All that, and there wasn't a thing anyone could do about Dratz, what with him being the anointed one. I'll tell you, Kiernan, I grew up in a family where people talked about 'the Troubles' as if they happened half an hour ago instead of over half a century ago and an ocean away, but I never understood what it is to be 'in an occupied land' until I dealt with Dratz. We were way over budget, but when Dratz finally left, Cary Bleeker ordered cases of champagne."

"Dratz went off with one of the extras. Bleeker told me that. He said you never forget a name and you would remember hers."

"I do. But alas, not so much because I've the memory of an elephant, but because she passed on a few months ago. Jane Hogarth was her name. I don't recall *her,* but she couldn't have been very old even now, ten years later. She'd been working in the costumes department of some studio; that's the only reason she merited an obituary." He glanced over at Kiernan. "I suppose in your business, you need to check for foul play, so I'll save you some work. The obit called it death after a long illness."

Kiernan sighed. "I'm sorry for her, and sorry for me." She lifted her glass but stopped abruptly before it reached her lips. "Jane Hogarth? What did she look like?"

"That I don't recall."

"There must have been pictures," she said. "Publicity photos, newspaper shots."

"Not of her, an extra. Only the stars are in the papers."

She smiled at him, understanding the unspoken half of the sentence. "But you do have pictures of the stars, then."

Lights flashed outside the window.

"Ah, Kiernan, the fireworks from Marine World! 'Tis the joy of living on Soledad Mountain. Better than the Fourth of July. They're usually set off only in the summer. Tonight must be some special occasion down there. Or," he said with a smile, "perhaps it's in honor of yourself being here."

A veiny mushroom of lime and silver spread above the black bay water. She moved closer to the window. Fireworks had always entranced her; no matter where from or how often seen, the spray of sparkles, the glittering foam of color bursting one upon another dazzled her. Watching, she became a child again, the child who had begged, cajoled, sneaked out, and later stomped out to Gunther Hill on Fourth of July nights to see the once-a-year magic in the sky.

Roman candles burst higher in the air, still well below McCafferty's window. The Fourth of July was a season away. Memorial Day wouldn't come for months, but fireworks streaked the dark starry sky, reminding viewers on the hills of La Jolla, Claremont, and Linda Vista, in the flatlands of Mission Beach, Ocean Beach, Pacific Beach, and south to the rising land of Point Loma, and the high rises of downtown, that every day in San Diego is a holiday, every night spent there a cause for celebration.

"Liam, I envy you. It would be worth living in a treehouse to see this every night. Better even than the fireworks by the Lincoln Memorial."

" 'Tis grand, indeed."

"But you haven't diverted me from your pictures. What do you have from *Bad Companions?*"

"Nothing," he snapped. It was a moment before he forced a smile and added, "You'll have to take me at my word. I wouldn't be telling untruths, not to you."

Kiernan matched his smile, in length and insincerity. McCafferty was certainly lying, but she wasn't willing to call him on it, not without a fallback position. The man was a pol, a professional Irishman who tempered his cadence with the resin of the old sod and burnished his statements with reminiscences true or useful. His whole demeanor insisted that he was a charmer with old-fashioned standards. It was an affectation, or more likely a mere exaggeration, that would warm the hearts of transplanted Irish as well as those who had never been east of Reno. And it would pull the wool over those who had not grown up surrounded by Aran sweaters.

She walked to the window and looked down Mission Bay at the gold spray of fireworks. And closer, at McCafferty's street.

Parked fifty feet in front of her Jeep was the blue Volkswagen bug with the wooden bumper. The same car that had been behind her on the I-5! Who the hell—

She turned and was into the motion to race down the stairs and yank open the Volkswagen door, when she caught herself, turned back, and took another look at the street. A jogger was chugging down the sidewalk. In less than a minute he'd be next to her Jeep. In a minute he'd be beside the bug. "Hey! Hey! Get away from that Jeep!" She started toward the door.

McCafferty caught her arm.

"What's going on?"

"A guy followed me from L.A. In a Volkswagen. Now he's fiddling with my Jeep. I'm going to drag him up here and make him—"

"A little thing like you? No, no. You let me handle this." McCafferty, ever the old country gentleman, headed down the stairs, no doubt grateful for the excuse to escape her questions.

McCafferty should be gone for a good five minutes, but she couldn't count on that.

Quickly she surveyed the room. Where would his pictures be? Obviously somewhere he figured she wouldn't find. The man was an accountant, an orderly person. He would keep all his records from *Bad Companions* together. And whatever these photographs were, they would be with those records. But where?

His desk? He had glanced in that direction earlier. Not *in* his desk, though. A desk is for today's problems, not last decade's memories.

She hurried across the room and eyed the three cases of shelves above the desk. On the top left shelf were eight books with *Accounting* in their titles. On the shelf below was a file box, followed by *Bookkeeping* titles, *California Government, California History, Car Repair* . . . "Alphabetized!" She smiled. Would that every house she searched were kept by an accountant. The movie records could be placed under *Movie, Summit-*

Arts, or something more obscure, but that file box on the second shelf was just where *Bad Companions* belonged. She climbed up on the desk and hauled it down.

Outside, tires squealed. McCafferty was shouting.

Wedging the box against her chest she jumped down, opened it, and leafed rapidly through the file folders inside. She opened "*Bad Companions* Miscellaneous" and, ignoring the papers, pulled out the one photo. It was not a publicity picture, nor one of just the stars, as McCafferty had suggested, but three rows of grinning people, arms over neighbors' shoulders, beer cans in hand. It could have been the picture from any company picnic, if that company had hired for looks. With youth and hair, Cary Bleeker had had a bit of star quality. Trace Yarrow stood uncomfortably inside the arm of a man of similar stature but with a smirk that suggested he'd nabbed Yarrow unawares. And even Dolly Uberhazy, smiling happily, seemed caught by the communal glitter. Or maybe her reaction was to the tall man under whose arm she stood.

Kiernan's smile widened. She had been right. Unless Uberhazy had had a profligate life, this was not a man she'd forget. He was a knockout —tall, with waves of red hair, and eyes that rested on her alone. Kiernan held the picture closer.

"What the hell—?" McCafferty yelled. "Rooting through my papers like a common criminal. While I was out there protecting your car from some hot-rodder who took off like a rocket! Don't you have any sense of decency?"

"Of course not. You knew I was here on an investigation." Covering her shock at not hearing his steps, she smiled and held out the picture. "People told me about Dolly Uberhazy's handsome lover. I didn't realize he was you."

His full lips pressed hard together. He shut his eyes and breathed in deeply, and when he spoke, it was without the easy sociability, and Irish lilt, of earlier. "I asked you not to—"

"Liam, two stunt doubles are dead. No secret is more important than that—particularly a ten-year-old affair. Or is it?"

"No, of course not," he said a bit too quickly. Turning, he walked across the room, picked up his glass, and took a sip—a sip too small to ease discomfort, Kiernan thought.

She restrained the urge to look from the man to the photo and back. The decade of good life had transformed McCafferty from a gangly god into a middle-aged accountant. The stars in the middle of the photo probably looked much the same now. Your tires are your life, she thought inanely, recalling her Jeep salesman's pitch. For stars, their skin was their tires. For McCafferty, the tire was around his middle. She walked to the mission chairs, glad she didn't have to repeat that clutch of observations. "Liam, did you really think I wouldn't be able to find this? Why did you make such a point of keeping it from me?"

"That was a bad time in my life. I'd been sheltered. You know how it is, the good Catholic boy."

She nodded.

"Looking back, it's hard to believe I was ever so naïve, and at so late an age. I did a whole life's worth of growing up in a month. Ah, the heady thrill of being chosen, being pulled into the center of 'The Movies.' When I told my parents I was 'dating' a movie producer, they pictured the grandchildren they'd been hoping for since I graduated from college, and me the next CEO of the studio. I was on top of the world. And when the end came . . . one moment I was the apple of her eye, and the next . . . She went back to L.A. and—bingo! Nothing. She didn't return my calls." He set the glass down in the center of a coaster. "It's not pleasant to be tossed aside like—like yesterday's contract."

"That's Hollywood."

He shrugged. "That's what they all said. A bucket of cold water, I'd have said. It sure woke me up. Give me politics any day, where friends are friends and enemies are remembered."

"Liam, forget it. That was ten years ago."

"But this—you," he said with an icy anger that was the first thing about him she'd been certain was real, "you sneering at my hospitality, that is today."

She pointed to a figure in the photograph, "This is Trace Yarrow, right? Who's the guy with his arm around Yarrow?"

McCafferty hesitated, then shook his head. "That is Carlton Dratz."

"Dratz? Was he friends with Yarrow?"

"Dratz didn't have friends."

"Was there maybe more—"

He snatched the photo out of her hand. "Nothing more! Trace Yarrow didn't even recognize Dratz on the set yesterday. That's how much there was between them. So don't go calling them fags. Now you've abused my hospitality once too often. It's time you're going."

"*I* wasn't judging; I was just asking."

"Enough!" He grabbed her arm.

She shook him off, pulled out her card, and put it on the table. "In case you change your mind."

"No, not for someone the likes of you. I'll give you one word of warning, though you're nowhere near deserving it. The city's already got calls about you. In budget crunch times like this, movie money's a handy extra. The city's not about to thumb its nose at Hollywood, not for the likes of you. You step one foot out of line, one mile over the speed limit, and—"

"And since you're the city's media liaison, when Dolly Uberhazy laid on the pressure, she called you?"

McCafferty didn't reply, but his stony glare told her that Uberhazy had indeed called.

She walked down the stairs wondering just how much of McCafferty's threat was true. *One mile over the speed limit;* she could be in jail before she got home.

The VW bug with the wooden bumper pulled away from the curb.

CHAPTER 24

T HERE must be a jet engine in that bug, Kiernan thought as she yanked the Jeep's steering wheel hard around and swung a U across four lanes of road. The Volkswagen was almost out of sight. And she, still in view of Liam McCafferty's window, couldn't afford to go one mile over the speed limit. Yet.

In the distance the bug's taillights, two small red ovals, shifted closer together and disappeared. He'd turned right. Uphill. Back into La Jolla. She floored the gas pedal, veered to the left, and as she neared the corner, cut across the empty left lanes to make a wider turn. She started up the steep hill, jerking the clutch lever into third with one hand as she let the wheel spin back.

Ahead, the only lights were the blurs from windows and intermittent splashes of streetlights. No taillights! Where was he? Dammit, he must have turned off on a side street. She downshifted, slowing as she reached the first corner. No sight of him either way. But he could have turned off his lights. He could have—

No time to ponder. No, go on. Try the next street. Nothing suggested she was dealing with a stunt driver. At this speed it would take a normal driver more than a block to get his bug under control. She pushed harder on the gas and as she neared the corner glanced both ways—no sign of him. To the left the street went downhill. She pulled the wheel to the right and headed up the sharp, narrow incline. He wouldn't know the area, he'd take the streets he could see, not the dark downhill drops.

"Where are you, dammit?" Sweat dripped down her back; the ridges of the steering wheel pressed into her hands. The road curved steeply up to the left. Glancing quickly back and forth, she checked the parked cars along the curbs.

The headlights hit the side of a car—twenty feet ahead! She slammed on the brakes. The Jeep squealed to a stop inches from the car. Sweat ran down her face; she was shaking. She backed up and looked around the car she'd almost hit. It was parked! At the curb! The road had ended at the cross street.

She sat in the middle of the street, glaring at the car, her skin quivering, her mind a muddle of anger and frustration. The driver had spent half the day following her; what was he after? And now when she was offering him his prey, he couldn't get away fast enough.

It was a minute before she saw the Volkswagen easing silently out from the curb nearly a block away to the right. She yanked the wheel to the right. Ahead, the bug popped into gear and raced down the hill.

She hit the gas.

Near the corner, the bug veered into the left lane. Headlights came at it. The oncoming driver hit the horn. Kiernan held her breath. The car slid by the bug and moments later passed her, something in its window shaking—a head, or more likely a fist.

The bug turned right.

She swung right—onto Soledad Mountain Road. No houses faced the road. It was steep, dark, empty. At the bottom on the hill was the red light at Felspar Street. A short block beyond that, cars whizzed by on Garnet, the feeder to I-5.

The bug was halfway down the hill.

Closer, she realized with a start, was an amber traffic light. She shot underneath it just as it turned red.

Ahead, Soledad Mountain Road was black. The bug was gone. This time she smiled. "Amateur." She veered to the left, ready to swing a loose right. *If you were smart, you'd have gone on to Garnet and merged into the traffic. I'd never have found you then.* Before Garnet, the only exit was onto Felspar. She hung a left.

The bug was a block ahead, speeding down a flat street of cottages and apartments. Parked cars dotted both curbs. He was a couple of blocks from Lark Sondervoil's apartment.

Kiernan slowed. *Go ahead, lead me there.*

The bug slowed at Noyes, then jerked left.

Damn! He must have seen me.

At the corner she made a left, just in time to see him turn right and into an alley and hit the gas, swinging too wide to the right, trying to compensate. Houses backed tight into the narrow alley. Garbage cans poked out from garages. The bug was doing fifty. It wove left, then right, barely missing a storage locker. He was in the middle of the block, jerking frantically from side to side. Metal scraped metal. He'd sideswiped a parked car. Oblongs of white cut the street as house lights came on. A woman in purple ran into the alley. The bug reached the corner, turned right again, then left.

Kiernan followed, a third of a block behind. She floored the pedal. She'd have him before he made the next turn.

In the middle of the block he screeched right and bounced between parked cars, two wheels on a lawn, two on cement steps leading to a walkway. Kiernan slammed on the brakes. Ahead on either side were two garden apartment buildings. The bug was on the pedestrian walk, between the two buildings, inches from the stucco walls on both sides.

Dammit, the driver was maneuvering as if he were on a Harley. Was the space big enough for the Jeep? Could she make it?

Hardly. Too dangerous. *Much* too dangerous, picturing apartment doors opening. *One mile over the speed limit,* indeed. She backed up, hit the gas, and drove around the block, jumped out of the Jeep, and ran to the walkway.

Garbage cans lined the walk. The bug had slowed down. He was inching past the last can when she got to the car, pulled open the driver's door, grabbed his ponytail, and yanked. "Pedora!"

He yelped and hit the brake. The car bounced. Kiernan held on to door and hair.

"Leggo!"

"Shut up or I'll rip your head off." Her heart was banging against her ribs, her palms so sweaty, she could barely hold on. "Now, ease this car over to that driveway and on down to the street. There—over there— put it in that parking spot." She said, balancing on the running board.

Pedora inched toward the curb, moving with such caution that she was sure he was seeing not the grass and cement in front of him but every danger he'd managed to avoid in the last fifteen minutes. Death in a dozen forms winked at him. The man was terrified. Her own head throbbed with tension, fury, and frustration.

"Get out!" she said to the shaking figure. "Walk across the street, in front of me. Go on! To the apartment." *Her* apartment, as far as the police were concerned.

At the apartment door, she said, "Take out my key ring." *Her* assemblage of keys for clandestine entry that he'd taken after assaulting her. "Come on, come on! That's it. Use the key next to the flashlight. Let's get inside before anyone connects you"—or me, she thought—"with all the laws you've broken."

Hands quivering, he unlocked the door.

"Hold the keys out behind you, and walk on inside. Leave the light off."

As he pushed open the door, she grabbed her keys. "Over on the bed, facedown. Go on!"

"Hey, I'm not planning to run out on you!"

"How do I know that?" she said, making a snap decision. He wasn't going to be a shaking leaf, following orders, forever. "Do I have your word?"

He hesitated.

"Your word?"

Finally he said, "Yes."

"Okay," she said, turning on the light. "I'm going to believe you. But you make one wrong move, and I'll have the cops here. You are in a shitload of trouble."

As he got up, Kiernan checked him more closely. His long gray ponytail was tangled, and the teal chambray shirt he wore unbuttoned over a faded blue T-shirt and jeans was so faded, it looked as if it had been washed every day for the last decade.

She looked at his hands. They were what her mother had called artist's hands—long, narrow, with just enough padding to keep the smooth skin from hugging the tendons. He didn't look out of place at all in the little studio. She could picture him sleeping on the futon, and using the ladder of dowels on the wall for—well, not for exercise.

"Sit down." She motioned to the chairs by the kitchen counter. And when Pedora had folded and unfolded his limbs onto one and she had climbed up onto the other, she said, "What were you doing outside Liam McCafferty's tonight?"

"I wasn't—"

"Don't insult me by lying. You followed me from Los Angeles, didn't you?"

His fingers twitched, paused, moved again, and stopped dead. "Okay, okay. So I was on the same freeway you were. It's a *free* way. I have as much right to drive it as you do."

"You followed me to Gliderport and then up to McCafferty's, right?"

The fingers moved slightly right and left and made little tapping motions. "So? That's not illegal, either."

"But assault with a deadly weapon is. We're not going to talk about your attack right here last night, not for the moment."

"You burst in on me. What else could I do?"

"Jason," she snapped. "Why—were—you—following me?"

"Because," he said, with the sharp nod of the righteous, "you're nosing around into Greg's life. Greg's death. I've got the right to know what you're finding out about him."

Damn. Could that really be the whole reason? That was nothing! "And what do you assume I'll find?"

Again his fingers moved. The man was *typing* on his thighs. Despite her frustration, she almost laughed. Pedora was so much in the persona of a writer, he could only think through his fingers! She was surprised he hadn't asked for time to jot down notes on the car chase for a screenplay. Was it possible he had chosen the route between the apartment buildings for that reason? Reality and the movies, how different were they in Pedora's mind?

His hands stopped. He stared at her. "They killed Greg."

"They?"

"The movie people."

"Why?"

"He knew too much."

If this was the quality of his screenplays, it was no wonder they hadn't sold. And yet . . . talking as she assumed someone in Creative might, she said, "Can you flesh that out? What did he know?"

"About the horses, and the drugs and the trucks."

What? "You're going to have to be more specific. Set the scene for me."

"It was the location site for *Bad Companions,* the place Greg died."

"Describe it."

"Out in the desert, way east of here. Not sand desert like the Sahara, but scrub desert."

"Trees?"

"Short ones, maybe twenty feet. Thin foliage, like Jacaranda but not so pretty. Mostly just dirt and cactus and plants so brown, you couldn't tell what they'd been. Hilly. A cabin in the middle of a high, wide, flat knoll —like a mighty god had sliced off the real top and left that. Land dropped off behind and to the right."

"What kind of cabin?"

"Three-room house, weathered wood. Special Effects had treated the wood so it looked old. Sort of like a big outhouse. It was supposed to have been deserted."

"Was it sitting on bare ground?"

"Yeah. No grass or anything. A couple of trees behind it, like it had been built in the one shady spot. That's what settlers did out here. I've researched that."

Common sense, she thought, could have saved him that research time. "The land dropped off on two sides. What was in front of the cabin?"

"The cameras. It was always shot from that direction."

"So the land continued flat to the left?"

"Oh, yeah. All the trailers were parked there."

"So if you took in the whole scene, was it like the cabin was—comparatively speaking—like an outhouse to the rest of the trailers?"

He typed that idea onto his thighs, paused, typed again. Was he expanding her image, she wondered, or typing over it?

"Yeah. Like an outhouse, set back in the yard behind the courtyard and an aluminum villa and an aluminum garage."

"What was in the courtyard?"

"The food tables, and the cameras."

"And what was in the garage? Cars?"

"Personal cars? Oh, no. They didn't let them park their own cars there. There was a big stink about that. You shoulda heard Carlton Dratz. He'd just gotten a Corvette, and did it piss him off to see that baby covered with dust and dirt. Only he could put his car in the garage. He used to get it washed every time he drove into town, like it never occurred to him that there would still be dirt when he got back to the set." Again he laughed, and this time Kiernan joined him, using the time to consider what he might know about Dratz.

Dratz and a stash in a garage? She could feel the answer getting closer. But she'd have to ease into questions about him. "So what else was in the garage then?"

He leaned forward conspiratorially and lowered his voice. "The horses."

"Horses?" she said. *Horses!* An aluminum garage in the desert—it must have been over a hundred degrees in there. Trying to keep the skepticism from her voice, she said, "Why would they keep the horses in the garage?"

He leaned closer yet. "So they could load the wasted ones onto the trucks and unload the fresh ones and no one would see them."

They couldn't merely have been mistreating their animals. The SPCA had people on sets to protect animals. "Tell me about that."

His fingers were poised above his thigh but didn't move. Nor did he speak.

"Give me the story line," she said, hoping that was the right jargon.

He shifted back, added a paragraph to his legs, then leaned forward and whispered, "Drugs. See, the set is right by the Mexican border. Border guards can't be everywhere, right? It's easy to run these horses across."

Horse-rustling! I can't believe it! I might as well be on the porch at Bellevue! Her thighs tensed; she was ready to stand up and walk out. On the wards in medical school, she had dealt with delusional paranoid patients —it had been the final factor demonstrating she had no bedside manner and underlining the advantages for her of working with the dead. The dead are quiet, and their bodies reveal the truth. The living are loud and deceptive. And the unhinged don't even realize they're lying. But her dealings on the wards had taught her that as bizarre and far-spun as delusions might be, woven into them were bits of truth.

She took a breath and forced her throat to relax, and when she spoke, it was calmly. The room was cold and stuffy from being closed. "Why—motivation?"

"Well, see, it's not just the horses. Horses are a dime a dozen. They're like toothpicks in a film budget. So nobody would smuggle in horses just for horses, right? It's what's *inside* the horses."

"And that is?"

He leaned farther forward. She was afraid he'd fall off his stool. He whispered so softly, she was almost reading his lips. "Cocaine. The Mexicans sewed the cocaine inside the horses' skin and smuggled them over the border. And then the trucks came at night and carted them off to the dealers in L.A."

"And they were replaced by a new batch of horses smuggled from Mexico?"

"Right."

She hesitated, wondering how far to follow this delusion. A band of

Mexican drug smugglers providing an endless supply of identical equines? She wanted to grab Pedora and scream, "Give me the truth!"

But she couldn't scream, not here, not without the neighbors calling the cops. If Dolly got another middle-of-the-night call about her "tenant," she might retaliate with a answer different from last time.

Besides, Pedora was too far gone in his own world to know the truth. What bits in Pedora's tale were real? Horses stuffed like galloping turkeys? No. But horses? There must have been horses. And trucks. "Where did the trucks come from?"

"The drug lords."

"The drug lords. What did they say on the side: 'Los Angeles Cocaine Company, home deliveries at any hour of night'?"

" 'Pacific Breeze Computer.' "

"What?" she said, taken aback.

"See, that's how I knew. I mean, they didn't need truckloads of computer equipment on the set. Why would computer trucks come in the middle of the night, once a week for three weeks? Doesn't make sense, does it?"

Bingo! "No, it doesn't. But if they came in the middle of the night, they must have done that to avoid being seen, right?"

He nodded, a small smile stretching his lips.

He knows he's got me, she thought. "So how did you come to spot them?"

"They don't let anyone on the set at night. They drive the actors back to the motel. That was fine for them. But me, I was sleeping in my car off the road at the bottom of the hill. It's not real comfortable in a bug. I'd wake up two or three times a night all stiff and have to walk it out. After the time I spotted the 'computer' trucks, I started getting up on purpose to watch for them. I *knew* there was something clandestine going on."

"What made you think it involved the horses?"

"They wouldn't let me near them. Because the bags that the coke was in leaked, see? The Mexicans didn't realize the horses would be running up a lather in the hot sun. They figured the horses were like mailing envelopes for their packages. They didn't pack for action, if you know what I mean." He didn't wink, but his eyelid twitched. "The coke got into the horses' systems, and the horses went wild."

"Is that what Greg thought, too?"

He shook his head. "Greg didn't have the mind to spot a conspiracy.

He was too caught up in his Move. When I told him about the conspiracy, he looked at me like I was crazy."

Probably not for the first time. "Jason, do you have any proof?"

"Sure. It's in the hole in the road out there."

It took her a moment to regroup, so sure had she been that Pedora would begin waffling when facts were required. She made a "go on" motion with her hand.

"The dead horses. They buried them in the road behind the cabin. The coke is still in them."

"They did that during the day?"

"Of course not. They buried them at night, when the trucks came and they were making the switch."

"And did anyone but you see this entombment?"

He sat up straight, eyes open wide. "You don't believe me, do you?"

"Did anyone else see it?" she insisted.

"Yeah. Dratz was right there. Ask him."

"Carlton Dratz?" *Perfect. The conspiracy theory supported by the person no one could find!* "Was he involved in the conspiracy?"

"Oh, yeah, he was running the whole thing. You don't believe me, I can tell. But it makes perfect sense. See, he was working for his father, Kurt Dratz, head of production at the studio. Look, his father sends him down from L.A. There's no real reason for him to be on the set. All he's doing is hanging around bugging people. Usually, Greg was willing to listen to anyone. But Dratz even got on Greg's nerves."

"Is there anything besides just his presence that makes you suspicious of him?" *Besides your paranoia?*

"Yeah, look, here he is, the son of a studio exec. He's got a room paid for at the motel. Does he sleep in it? Not on delivery nights. You know where he was then?"

"Where?"

"In the wooden house on the set!"

"The set house—the one that Greg died in?" Kiernan asked, amazed.

"Yeah." Pedora nodded slowly, smiling as if Kiernan were a particularly slow student who had finally gotten the point.

"How do you know that?"

"Because," he said, staring her in the eye, "I looked in the windows one night after I'd woken up the third time in the damned car. It was just an empty structure, but I figured it would be better than sleeping in my car. And it would show them, when they woke up and found me plumb in the middle of the set—sleeping! Hot-shot security!" He leaned forward and grabbed her arms. "You see now why they won't buy my screenplay. Not just Summit-Arts Studios. None of the studios will touch it. They don't want the country to know how they finance their movies with smuggled drugs. Truth"—he shook his head—"it means nothing to them."

Kiernan removed his hands from her arms and leaned back against the edge of the bar. What was worth saving of this tale? What could she believe? Cocaine-stuffed horses? Hardly! Yarrow and Pacific Breeze Computer—more likely. In the morning, Yarrow'd have plenty to explain.

"Just like *them*," Pedora muttered, his eyes twitching side to side, fingers typing on his thigh. He looked as if he might disintegrate at any moment. "Don't believe me. I showed them. I showed . . ."

"Showed who?"

He pressed his lips into a pout. His head shook faster.

She reached out and put her hands over his, pressing his palms onto his thighs, choking off the movement. "Bleeker? You showed him?"

He didn't reply. But his hands relaxed.

"You orchestrated Bleeker's 'bad luck'—the short-circuits that blew out the lights, the lighted paper on top of the flowers, all the 'bad luck' that threw his films behind schedule. Very ingenious," she said.

Pedora nodded, smiling. "Greg . . ."

"Would Greg have been proud of you?"

"Of course," he snapped.

"But Jason, why did all those 'bad luck' incidents include fire? Did Bleeker cause the fire Greg died in?"

"He's responsible. Greg told him he needed a special fire crew. 'Too expensive,' Production said. It wasn't Bleeker's decision, but Bleeker didn't complain. Stunt coordinator! He should have been called the death coordinator! They used the regular emergency crew, which didn't know fires from first aid, and the local fire department. And then—" He pulled his hands free and grabbed her arms again. "And then he couldn't even give the fire department the right call time. Greg was already dead, and they were still driving to the set."

Her shoulders hunched forward, her breath caught. For a moment she felt at one with Pedora and his fury and frustration. No special fire crew—that explained how a cabin could burn in the midst of a crowd and a man could die before anyone got him out.

And it explained why Cary Bleeker had taken no aggressive action about the pranks. The man was party to the guilt. And from a practical point of view, he wouldn't have done anything to resurrect notice of his failure.

She freed her hands and said more softly, "What happened to Carlton Dratz?"

Pedora shifted back away from her, his face more relaxed than she'd seen it. He looked almost normal, as if her acceptance of his story had removed the turmoil outside. "Dratz took off with the extra. He saw me watching him that last night, and he got scared. The extra was finished, so no one cared if they left. No, not true—everyone, everyone was glad."

"Where did they go?"

"Mexico, of course," he said lightly. "It was the perfect escape route, all planned out and well traveled. He gassed up his 'Vette and headed south. With the help of his business partners down there, see?" he added. "Look, you're supposed to be a detective, right? Well, that's the only reason I've told you this. Don't even think about writing a treatment of it. I've got my screenplay registered. You steal this, and I'll sue you from here to the East Coast. I'm the one who's suffered. I'm not going to have someone else collect."

Kiernan slumped forward; suddenly, all the exertions of the day caught up with her. *And for this!* she muttered to herself. *Definitely time to go home and sleep it off.* "It's all yours, Jason. Write in peace." She stood up, walked to the door, and opened it.

A policeman stood on the stoop.

CHAPTER **25**

"**B**AD luck? Or the law of karma?" she asked herself as the patrol officer escorted her into the police station. He had ignored her explanation, kept her waiting half an hour until a backup unit arrived to take charge of Pedora, and he only grudgingly agreed to call Tchernak once he deposited her here.

Her question arose again as she looked around. It might not be ill luck that the station serving Pacific Beach was an old, brown, one-story building at the Eastgate Mall in inland La Jolla, closer to her duplex than to the accident site in Pacific Beach. But walking into the white lobby and coming face to face with Officer Mark Melchior definitely suggested poor karma. Here, behind the scarred wooden counter, that round face with its deceptive halo of dark curly hair looked distinctly less benign than it had in the half-light of Lark Sondervoil's Pacific Beach apartment. Under the interrogation-bright bulbs, his eyes looked not just dark but piercing, his brow not furrowed with miscellaneous worry but wrinkled in suspicion. And in his pale, round face there was definitely nothing jolly.

Melchior poised his pen over a printed form. "Do you go out of your way to conduct all your lawbreaking activities in my district of the city, Ms. O'Shaughnessy? Or do you spend your daylight hours also careening through Point Loma or breaking into hotel rooms downtown?"

"I told the patrolman and I'm telling you—*I'm* not the one who hit that car," she said, taking a step back from the counter, which was almost chin high for her. The reception area was empty but for a couple of other cops—presumably business was slow here on Wednesday nights. "Check my Jeep for scratches; you won't find any. I'm not the offender. *I'm* the one who tracked him down and kept him busy until your men could find us," she said with a straight face. "Is this the kind thanks a citizen gets in San Diego for putting herself in danger? Or just here at the *mall* station?"

Melchior hesitated just long enough to signal to the cognoscenti that he had heard enough cracks about the station's Eastgate Mall address. "In danger? I assume, Ms. O'Shaughnessy, that you've been offered transport to a doctor?"

"I *am* a doctor."

"A private eye and a doctor. My, oh my!"

Glaring at him, she let a beat pass before saying, "I'm not a lawyer, but I'll definitely call one if this keeps on. Now tell me what you need, and let me get out of here."

"Relax. You don't make the rules here."

Her back tightened; her neck felt as taut as if it were in a brace. She pulled out her address book and began paging through it. If she called at this hour, Ardis Ramaswami would take her head off. And having disposed with that, she'd race down to the police station like a hungry tiger and not be mollified till she'd chewed off every head that poked out of a tan uniform. It was not a call to be made lightly.

"We need your statement. In my office."

"I gave it to the patrol officer. I'm too exhausted to do it all again."

"Let me remind you, Miss—*Doctor* O'Shaughnessy, that we can charge you with reckless driving, reckless endangerment—"

"No one saw me driving."

"Harboring a fugitive . . ."

I didn't know he was a fugitive, she started to retort. But she'd already blown that one. Melchior, she realized, had not yet gotten the official word on her. If the forces of Hollywood and municipal San Diego were already pushing him, he wouldn't be wasting words like this. Either McCafferty had been leading her on—and she doubted that—or she had to get out of here before the word reached Melchior. "Look, I'll come back in the morning and give you a statement."

"No, you won't! You're not leaving till you give me a damn good explanation of how you got hit over the head last night in an apartment rented to some woman in L.A. and ended up there tonight with the Evel Kneivel of Pacific Beach paths."

How much to tell him? The years she had worked in the coroner's department, the police had been her allies. But it had not been a natural alliance. Trusting the authorities was something she would never do easily. Their job was to protect the status quo, and she was by nature a perpetual threat to that quo. "Like I told you, I'm checking out the accident at Gliderport yesterday."

"*With* who?"

No one, she almost snapped. Technically, Lark's death wasn't a murder. And the place where Lark had died wasn't in his jurisdiction. The area around Gliderport was a quagmire of jurisdictional disputes. The land on top—the parking area—was city owned, the bluff itself was a state park, and portions of the beach belonged to each. "The cliff is the Parks Department's. It never occurred to me you'd be involved in their case."

Melchior hesitated.

Damn. She shouldn't have baited him.

Melchior glanced at his phone list, then apparently thought better of disturbing the overworked rangers. He opened the gate in the counter and motioned her to a hard chair by the metal desk behind. "So, Miss O'Shaughnessy, just why were you following—at whatever distance and speed you say—Mr. Pedora?"

She didn't move. "Because he tailed me from L.A. Finally, when I saw him sitting outside Liam McCafferty's house—"

"You're involved with Mr. McCafferty?" Clearly, the words had escaped Melchior's lips before he could censor them.

With an effort, Kiernan restrained a smile. "You know Liam?" She hoped she wasn't laying it on too thick.

"We know city officials."

Melchior was doing his best to pass this off; she had every intention of letting him. The last thing she wanted was Melchior in contact with McCafferty and talking about her. But the interchange did tell her that McCafferty was more important than she'd realized. The assistant-designate to the state treasurer was a powerful man. A bad choice for an enemy. She stood. "So if that's all then, I'll be—"

"Sit down!" The typewriter across the room stopped; the patrolman at the desk froze. Even the phones ceased ringing, as if every con in La Jolla and Pacific Beach had called a momentary work stoppage. "You'll do the statement now!"

The front door opened.

Momentarily, Tchernak filled the empty space. Then he strode forward, eyeing the defensive team behind the desk like a line set to blitz his quarterback. He leaned his six-four-240 on the counter. His deep raspy voice was frighteningly quiet as he said, "I need to get this woman home."

Melchior looked at Kiernan and said in a stage whisper, "Is this the boyfriend you moved to Pacific Beach to get away from?"

"You're Brad Tchernak, aren't you?" the patrolman blurted out. "Hey, I saw you play against San Francisco when you smacked Haley into the mud. You were great, man. And the Raiders' game that year . . . you know, my kid would go crazy over an autograph. His birthday is next week, and—"

All four phones rang. The outside door opened, admitting a loud argument and the couple creating it.

Melchior threw up his hands. He stepped in front of the patrolman. "Okay, Mr. Tchernak, take her. Get her back here in the morning. You're responsible." To Kiernan, he added, "You get involved in one more thing, I'll jail you as a public nuisance. I can do it." He turned to Tchernak. "You were a great tackle, the best, but if you can't keep her out of trouble, I'll pull you in, too."

Kiernan glared. "Look—"

Tchernak grabbed her arm, shoved her through the gate and on outside.

"Don't you know the first thing about taunting? In football, you can break a guy's back and go on playing. But taunting—that can get you thrown out of the game."

"I don't play team sports!"

"You ever see the offense or defense down on one knee on the sidelines in communal prayer?"

"Yeah, so?"

"Ever wonder what that prayer is? It's thanksgiving that you're not on their team." He motioned across the parking lot to the Jeep. "What's this about a car chase through Pee Bee?"

"I got tired of Pedora following me. Where's the Triumph?"

"Changing the subject, eh? Well, Little T's at home. I caught a ride up, because a good servant never knows when he'll be called upon to chauffeur his mistress."

The hairs on her neck bristled, but she didn't retort.

"And I figured you wouldn't want to wait to know what I've discovered about Jane Hogarth," Tchernak added quickly. He climbed into the driver's seat. Silently, she opened the other door.

"Well, chief investigator," he said as he started the engine, "your humble assistant had already pressed Persis at BakDat, right? I could have decided that it was late, that Persis had been staring at the screen so long, her eyes were crossed and the only thing that would lighten her mood was taking a bite out of me. I could have waited until tomorrow. That's what the average guy would do. But the professional investigator" —he paused momentarily, daring her with a glance, then went on— "plans every move. He—or she—thinks ahead. And what's ahead, you may ask. For Persis, it's the prospect of some good jazz to unwind to, and sleeping till noon. So I started in about how bad I felt about ruining her morning tomorrow, and how I'd just give her the order now and at least it would save her that much shut-eye later and—"

"I get the picture." Tchernak, she had to admit—to herself, certainly not to him—had good instincts. Better assessments of people than she would have expected. Maybe all those years of pass blocking, of keeping a step ahead of the defensive end, guessing which way he'd move, guessing how he'd react and acting first, had honed his skill at reading an opponent.

"Not quite, you don't. Persis decided she'd save herself the trouble and run Hogarth tonight—at day rates!" The hairs on his chin were virtually quivering with delight.

"Give yourself a bonus."

"I've already added it to the Oregon cherry budget. Anyway, what Persis came up with was that Jane Hogarth shared an apartment with her sister Joyce, who cosigned a loan."

"So you got Joyce's Social Security number."

"And, oh employer mine, her address in Los Angeles. Where I am heading in the morning. I figured she'll be more susceptible to my charm in person. Right?"

Tchernak's question hung in the air. Kiernan considered it. He de-served the chance; he'd earned it. And he could save her a lot of time. Chances were, he'd charm Joyce Hogarth. Women warmed right up to Tchernak's sexy, unfinished face. There was a dangerous, exciting feel to the man. He loomed, but something about him made people think he loomed *for* them. Tchernak was the guy to have beside you in a dark alley, and the one you could bet your last breath would show up there. Maybe it was all those years of protecting the quarterback, of keeping the defensive end at bay no matter how many seconds it took for the quarterback to throw the ball. Or maybe it was his habit of concentrating intently on each person he met—flattering to those who didn't realize that he was sizing them up, and that he'd have no qualms about using everything he gleaned against them.

But she wasn't willing to give up being quarterback. And the idea of anyone, even Tchernak—or perhaps especially Tchernak—having the right to be involved in every case made her want to rip off her skin and run into the night. In her lexicon, *consensus* was synonymous with *jail*. On the other hand, she needed Joyce Hogarth's information. And, hell, how could she tell Tchernak no? Another time, maybe, but not now. She shrugged. "Once you've gotten Joyce to tell you where Dratz and her sister parted company, call me."

Tchernak looked over at her. "You okay?"

"Yeah. Why?"

"You're so—well, down. I mean, like almost normal."

She laughed, but as soon as the sound came out, she realized it was halfhearted.

"Is it the case? You frustrated? It'll pick up. You've just started. You've got to be patient, make your plans, and wait."

She leaned back against the seat, glancing absently at the lighted store windows on Girard Street. Tchernak turned left at the corner, and she peered at the black of the ocean each time she could see between buildings.

When Tchernak pulled into her driveway, he said, "Ezra could use a walk. Come with me. Unless you're too tired."

Kiernan laughed. A nighttime walk on the beach, next to the throbbing of the waves—the heartbeat of the earth—the briny smell of endless possibilities had never ceased to cheer her. The Elavil out the window, she'd called it. "Do I sound that bad?"

"Every bit. I've never seen you like this on a case before."

"It's not the case," she said letting herself out of the Jeep and waiting while Tchernak got Ezra. "It's, well . . ." She rubbed the big wolfhound's back as he loped by to the sidewalk.

"Greg Gaige? Is that it?" Tchernak prodded.

"Well, yeah. I just hate to think Greg sank to stealing the job from a colleague and then died."

Tchernak rested a hand on her shoulder. "Kiernan, job-stealing goes on all the time in business."

"Of course," she conceded. She stopped, rested her arms on the railing over the staircase to the beach, and looked out into the darkness.

"It's not just that Greg did it, Tchernak, it's that he must have felt he *had* to. How could he *have* to? He was the best in the business." She started down the cement steps to the beach. Ezra eyed the steps and chose a path beside it, half stepping, half slipping his way down.

"Maybe," Tchernak said cautiously, as they reached the beach, "because of what he meant to you when you were younger—"

"No!" Kiernan snapped. Digging her heels into the sand, she strode across the beach to the water line. "Look, I don't want to wallow in that, like I'm a member of Survivors of a Less-Than-Perfect Childhood. I'm over forty years old; I don't need to blame my moods on my parents or parent-substitutes."

Tchernak jumped back; she suspected it was not just to avoid the breaking wave. The water chilled her ankles; it felt good. Tchernak was right in part, but she didn't want to get into that. "Look, you have to get up early. I'll take Ezra the rest of the way."

Tchernak laughed. "Very gracious offer. But I've defended myself against better tongues than yours. Down in a three-point stance on the line of scrimmage, you want to know what some of the ends have labeled me, my family, my friends, my sexual habits, my intelligence, or my chances of surviving the next play?"

She wrapped her fingers through his in the thanks she couldn't choke out in words. It was foolish, this inability to put feelings into words. She'd strode so briskly through her adolescence, through the lines of neighbors who scorned her because of her sister's suicide, that it had been a shock to discover she'd grown up and that people who knew nothing about the scandal were jumping back to avoid *her*. "When I saw Greg in San Francisco, he was as caught up in his work as Ezra is in running on the beach. He could have done TV interviews—the film company wanted him to. Instead, he went to dinner with me and figured someone else would like the limelight."

"He was the best, then, right?"

"He was the leading gymnastic stunt man. He'd created gags no one could match."

Tchernak sat down on a flat rock and rested his elbows on his thighs. "He was the best. He didn't have to consider taking another guy's job, not then.

"But when he got older, he didn't move as fast, he'd broken too many bones, maybe he'd lost a step. You scramble and scratch—anything so you can hang on, just a bit longer."

She settled next to him, watching the waves swell, pause momentarily balanced between before and after, then gush forth into frothy spray that spread like the lace doilies covering the backs of chairs in Rohan Street houses. She let her thigh rest against Tchernak's.

"You can't believe it can be over," Tchernak laughed humorlessly. "Read the sports columns—they say smart athletes plan for the future. Sure. Makes sense. Sounds easy. But look, if you were thinking about broadcasting or writing your memoirs, you wouldn't throw everything you've got into *this play*. You'd never chance it all to take down a guy who's bigger, taller, smarter, and ten years younger. It wouldn't matter more than the world that you toss him on his butt so your quarterback can make the play." He looked over at her. "If it wasn't all-important, you wouldn't be great to begin with.

"Your whole life has been focused on playing sports, being in high school games that the entire town comes to see, getting a scholarship. In college you choose your classes so they don't conflict with practice, because it's the team that matters. All with the dream of someday playing in the pros. And then, there, football is your whole world. You can do something hardly anyone else can. You're part of the team. When you're away from the team, it's like you don't completely exist, like someone cut off your foot. But back on the field with all of you working together, eleven against the world—God, there's nothing like it. You come off the field, and the next day you ache all over, but you can't wait to get back into uniform." He let his hands drop. "And then one day, like any other day, you walk in and you've been cut. Fired. Dumped. It's like they've cut off your legs." He swallowed and, still looking toward the ocean, said, "Suddenly you're nothing. The guys are in there, but you're outside pressing your nose against the glass. They could see you out there, but they don't want to, don't *dare*. And you hobble off, knowing you've lost the one thing that makes you feel alive."

Ezra ambled back, wet, panting, sand coating his whiskers. He sank into the sand and eyed Tchernak until Tchernak stretched out his legs and provided a shelf for the dog's chin. He scratched the dog's neck, and Kiernan rubbed behind Ezra's ears, letting her hand come to rest on Tchernak's. When Ezra stood, she wove her fingers in with Tchernak's and walked back home, letting the sound of the ocean cloak them.

There was no comfort she could give him. After she'd been fired from the coroner's office, she'd spent months with the drapes pulled, and two years in India packing her days too full for thought. And now investigating, and Ezra, and friends, and books and classes . . . maybe she was running to avoid the shadow Tchernak was staring at. But she couldn't let herself slow down enough to find out.

As she thought of Greg Gaige and gymnastics, she realized this was the first time she didn't envy men. Their careers in gymnastics were based on strength, agility, and the use of an adult body. For women, gymnastics ended with puberty, however long that could be postponed. But girls always knew their time was short. They were never given the illusion of forever; they didn't wait until middle age to realize it had been a lie.

Greg Gaige had never faced that. And yet, for Tchernak, for herself, she wished he had lived to come head to head with it, had pushed, fought, scratched his way through, and shown them how.

CHAPTER 26

KIERNAN woke on Thursday morning and looked at the bare wall opposite the bed, momentarily surprised to find the poster of Greg Gaige missing. But this wasn't the Baltimore gym, and it had been in a dream that she'd tried vault after vault—the simplest ones—and landed on her face. In the poster, Greg Gaige—his sandy hair thinned, those startling blue eyes of his faded to gray—shook his head sadly and looked away.

It didn't take a psychic to figure out the meaning of that dream, she thought as she pushed up and leaned against the chilly windows. Below, the Pacific inhaled and spat against the rocks. She wondered if she'd spent the whole night dreaming of Greg Gaige, guessing what the loss of his life's focus would have done to him.

Tchernak was on his way to L.A., but the coffee he left for her was hot in the pot, and one of his fresh many-berry corn scones was waiting in the toaster oven for her to push the lever. (Tchernak, who felt she was operating at capacity just to find the toaster oven, had already set the timer for the correct period of reheating.) When it was ready, she took the tray with juice, vitamins, and fruit from the fridge and carried it into her flat. She sat looking out over the ocean, drinking coffee and sharing food with Ezra.

She thought of Greg and of Tchernak facing the ends of careers for which they'd spent their lives working. But what of Dolly Uberhazy? What if she were fired? She'd find other work. But after making movies how could managing a Payless or directing personnel in Paso Robles compare? And Bleeker—would he care any less? He was nearly a pariah in the trade, and still he hung on. The movie business—the glamour, the pressure, the multimillion-dollar gambles, the days of split-second decisions—it was the Indianapolis 500 of job scenes. After that, anything else would be like driving a bus. Or fixing computer glitches, like Trace Yarrow.

Yarrow, who had lost his job to Greg and never worked again. The man with the now-and-again limp. The man who worked for Pacific Breeze Computer.

At ten o'clock in the Ocean Beach section of the city, boys in cutoffs and girls in bikinis balanced body boards and coffee cups as they migrated toward the beach for the local equivalent of nine to five. They passed an apartment building with a wooden facade and geranium-filled window boxes, called Alpine Manor. And a pagoda-roofed building named Samurai Sunset Condos. In Trace Yarrow's alley, the rear walls of the Manor and Samurai Sunset stood, devoid of decoration, like pastel ends of shoe boxes on a shelf. Inside, the tenants would have to look out the window to tell whether the cube of living space they inhabited was ersatz Swiss or Japanese. But in the alley it was all southern California, with the unfiltered sun bouncing brightly off the lime, apricot, and banana-tone stucco.

The shades of Yarrow's tiny cottage were still drawn, his windows sealed tight.

Kiernan knocked and moved closer to the door as a Suzuki Jeep sped by, a brace of surfboards strapped atop it, pagodalike.

Yarrow opened the door, rubbing his eyes with his free fist. His dark hair was tousled, and the black and white Happy coat he wore was barely held together by a loose belt. "Kiernan, I didn't realize detectives made their reports in person." He put a hand on her arm. "But I like it."

"It's not a social call," she said, pushing past him to one of the kitchen chairs. She had intended to demand an answer about the Pacific Breeze Computer trucks on the *Bad Companions* set, but seeing Yarrow, she changed her mind. She'd been suspicious of him, never sure he hadn't sold his loyalty to Dolly Uberhazy. Maybe the feeling was right and it was just the source of his commitment that she'd erred on—not Dolly, but Pacific Breeze Computer.

He grinned. "So, let's do business."

"That's exactly what we'll do. And you can start by telling me why after ten years you decided to hire a detective."

"Well, Lark—"

"No, not just Lark. Lark's incidental. The death you want to know about is Greg Gaige's. Why?"

"I told you—"

"You told me you were scheduled to do the fire gag. Maybe you would have died. Now you think that fire was suspicious?"

"I don't know. That's what I hired you to find out. I'm heating water for coffee. You want some?"

"No." She watched him move to the stove, the sink, and back. "Pour your coffee and give me the truth."

"Or?"

"Of I'll find out anyway, but you will never know."

The procedures for instant-coffee-making seemed to consume Yarrow's attention. He made each trip slowly, poured each liquid without spilling a drop, stirred, washed, and dried the spoon. He pulled out a chair, sat, tasted the coffee, and said, "Okay."

"Start with your limp."

"Small stuff. I broke my leg ten years ago. I've got a pin in it. Just like Greg Gaige, a very exclusive club. I'd be limping if I hadn't done rehab. I still favor the leg if I'm tired, or not thinking about it. But while I was limping big time, I learned the side benefits, like my own social blue curb." A grin crossed his chipmunk face.

"You're really a slime, Yarrow. If this is the way you treat people, it's no wonder you question whether the fire was meant for you. On *Bad Companions,* you must have been the emotional equivalent of Dratz. Who else have you 'gotten' with your little acts?"

"No one. I didn't do that then. I didn't have to."

"And what made you *have to*?"

He was in the same chair he'd used to balance on two legs Tuesday night. But this morning all four legs were solidly on the floor. Yarrow leaned forward onto the table with his hands cupped around the coffee mug.

"Ten years ago, when *Bad Companions* was filmed," she prodded, "Greg Gaige snatched your job. And you were pissed, right? Anyone would be."

"Yeah, but anyone wouldn't stomp off, drive back to town in a fury, get out of the car, trip up the curb, and break a leg. So there, you've got my secret."

She nodded. To an accountant or a physicist, she would have commented that accidents happen. But Yarrow'd been a stunt man. "Doesn't look good on your résumé, huh?"

"Believe it. If you're labeled 'delicate,' you're dead. *Delicate* is usually a euphemism for drugs, but if you're likely to break bones, it adds up to the same thing for them—you don't show, and it costs them money. Nobody's going to take a chance on a delicate stunt man. No reason to, when there are plenty of other guys around. And if they heard that I broke my leg because I was so pissed off about the job, well then, I'd be delicate *and* a jerk."

"So you laid low?"

"Right. I didn't call anyone in the business. But the damn leg took forever to heal, and by the time I got back in shape, I'd just been gone too long." He downed the coffee, stood up, and took the cup to the sink.

"What about stunt coordinating?"

"I said I'd been gone too long." His voice was as bitter as the coffee had smelled.

Kiernan sat back glancing at the tiny studio. Yarrow would have made good money when he did gags, but here he was living on the edge. He'd moved from gags to . . . this.

There was a piece missing here. Clearly, he wasn't going to reveal it. Did he expect her investigation to shed light on it? Was it something to do with Greg Gaige's death? Something to do with Pacific Breeze Computer? "Tell me about the *Bad Companions* set." She waited until he sat down again, and watching his reaction, she asked, "How were the horses?"

"Fine. Why?" His brow wrinkled in question, but nothing indicated wariness.

"I heard they were uncontrollable." She wasn't going to go into Pedora's paranoid fantasy about the Mexican cocaine.

Yarrow shook his head. "Hardly. There's a reason why stunt coordinators pay the money they do for trained horses, and it's not the desire to contribute to the well-being of the animal kingdom."

"Specifically?"

"They don't have time to waste with untrained animals. Look, the bottom line is, every day over schedule runs them a fortune. And stunt sets cost a bundle. They're not going to take the chance of a horse screwing up the gag, running the film over schedule, maybe having to replace the set because part of the gag included getting the set destroyed."

"Like the fire scene?"

"Exactly. They had to build another house just to shoot the exit."

Kiernan stared at him, incredulous. "You mean they used the footage in which Greg Gaige actually died? It's part of the film? People sat in theaters all across America watching Greg Gaige die?"

If Yarrow caught her horror, he certainly didn't reflect it. His tone was matter of fact as he said, "Oh, yeah. It was touch and go whether they would—but not because Cary Bleeker or anyone above him in Summit-Arts had any ethical qualms. The only reason they hesitated was that the footage was pretty ordinary, not the spectacular gag Cary expected when he thought Greg would race out the door of the burning building and do a flashy flip. Instead, what they had to go with were shots of arms pounding at the windows as the cabin burned. See, the plan was for him to race out the door all covered with fire and then cut. When the director edited the film, he'd splice in a cover shot of the explosion, with dirt and debris flying. So when he comes back to Greg, the house is pretty much destroyed, right?"

Kiernan nodded.

"In fact, the next shot of Greg would be after he got out of the fire suit. Special Effects would set up the fire behind him so it looked like it was still on his skin. He'd cover himself in the fire-resistant gel and then put a couple of dabs of flammable liquid on top to get a partial burn going. He'd have to move fast. If the gel dries, it's not much use. Then Special Effects would do the bang, spread the dirt, and he'd do the flip with the backdrop of fire behind him, where it wouldn't get in his face. It's easy, once you realize you can stop whenever you need to. It's all a matter of planning."

Kiernan nodded slowly, noting the transformation in the man. The frustrated man of minutes ago now leaned forward, eyes shining with pride.

"What went wrong? Surely Greg must have checked it out?"

"The timing was way off. I went over and over the film. There's no way he should have stayed in that burning house so long. The gag wasn't routined for that long. In full burns like that house, the temperature can get into the thousands of degrees. And covered in a suit like that, your sweat will turn to steam and you can end up with second-degree burns. If you didn't have the hood on and you breathed the air, the heat would burn your lungs. So usually there's a bottle of compressed air inside the suit."

"Usually?"

"Right. Greg didn't use it. He had it there; he just didn't use it."

"Why not?" she demanded.

"Who knows? Arrogance? Whimsy?" He seemed to discount the reasons as he offered them. "Oxygen bottles are awkward; they make it harder for you to move. He should have made it out in plenty of time. Look, we had an emergency crew, not a fire crew, but still—the gag wasn't supposed to run more than twenty seconds. The suit held enough air for a couple of minutes—ample time to cover suiting him up, the gag, and getting him out. The emergency guys could have sprayed him down and slit the suit in plenty of time."

"But?"

"He just never came out of the building. The fire got hotter and hotter. It was like he was dazed."

"Or drugged? Like Lark?"

"Exactly. Too much of a coincidence. That's why I hired you."

"But Yarrow, why didn't you tell me the firemen in town had the wrong call time?"

"What?"

"You didn't know?"

"No."

Maybe. She was past the point of believing Yarrow on anything. "What did the autopsy say?"

"There was no autopsy."

"What?" she said amazed. "I can't believe that. Here in California? Even in a rural area that doesn't have a pathologist on staff—"

"It had nothing to do with the place. Greg had some kind of religious thing about autopsies. He'd signed some form refusing to be cut up."

Greg Gaige with a religious objection to autopsies? Frantically she tried to recall any hint she'd heard in Baltimore, anything he'd said in San Francisco. But she had to admit, it was a topic not likely to arise either in the gym or at dinner. "Oh, shit! California government code 27491.43," Kiernan said, recalling her frustration when she'd come up against it in the medical examiner's office. "The deceased has signed an affidavit indicating he does not want to be autopsied because of a religious belief. It's not like applying for conscientious objector status where you have to convince the court of the validity of your belief. Here the deceased just has to have stated he has one. And the only circumstance under which the court can order an autopsy is if there is suspicion of homicide or contagious disease. I take it there was no suspicion at the time?"

"Wouldn't have made much difference. The fire got so hot it split the suit, and by the time they got to him, there was nothing left but a skeleton that looked like it had been on a barbecue spit."

She stood up, willing the vision to dissipate. After a moment she said, "Yarrow, where is Greg buried?"

"In a little cemetery out by the set. Last thing the studio wanted was a big Hollywood funeral. They wanted it quick, cheap, and over," he said with such undisguised bitterness that she believed him.

"And the location set—where was that?"

Yarrow stood and shoved the chair under the table. "East of here, in the mountains."

"Can you be more specific?"

He shrugged. "It's been years. I can picture it, outside a little town. But ten years in San Diego County"—he shrugged—"ten years ago half of San Diego didn't exist."

"What was the town like then? You must remember something about it."

"No. Well, wait. It was a military place."

"A base?"

"No, I never saw that. But the town had a military feel."

"Why do you say that?"

"I don't know. The only place I ever stopped was the cemetery. Look, that's the best I can do."

Maybe so. But Dolly Uberhazy had been the line producer on that set. She could do better.

CHAPTER 27

FROM the Jeep, Kiernan called Dolly Uberhazy.

"I'm sorry, Ms. Uberhazy's in a meeting," an uninterested voice said.

"Tell her it's"—she discarded *important*—"vital. I need to talk to her now."

"I'll give Ms. Uberhazy the message."

Half an hour later, when Kiernan came to her own street, the phone hadn't rung. She wasn't surprised. She kept going, heading north through the still sleepy morning of La Jolla, past Wipeout Beach and the more benign Children's Pool behind the breakwater wall, and her favorite tourist attraction, Sunny Jim Cave, which was more than a hundred wooden steps beneath the middle of the La Jolla Shell Shop. She drove north along Torrey Pines Boulevard, past dazzlingly white stucco walls overhung with vermilion bougainvillaea. In the unshaded sun the red and yellow hibiscus seemed to glow, the fronds of fan palms preened, and the orange and blue birds of paradise looked ready to take wing. And the short, wind-twisted Torrey pines, which grew nowhere else in the world, seemed gleeful about their choice of home.

She turned left into Gliderport. Had it been only two days since she'd been here watching Lark Sondervoil die? Summit-Arts should be doing clean-up shots today, but from the look of the parking lot, they might have advertised another spectacular killing. "Like a necrophiliac's convention," she muttered, driving between cars till she found a spot large enough for the Jeep. Spectators in shorts and cycle shirts milled around the edge of the set, staring at the cordon line, peering at the banks of lights, snapping photos of the giant crane that still sat at the edge of the bluff.

The set itself was calm. Under the awning by the catering truck wagon, twenty-five or so people—some Kiernan recognized as production assistants—were drinking Calistoga waters and eating salads, burgers, polenta sticks. The place smelled of chili and garlic.

She'd planned to beard Bleeker about Greg's stunt time and the fire department crew who hadn't arrived in time, but Bleeker was in no condition to answer. Leaning an elbow on the catering truck counter, Cary Bleeker looked in danger of crumbling slowly to the ground. He was wearing the same black ensemble, more wrinkled and farther from clean than the night before. His fringe of dark hair was stringier, and even his skin seemed to have lost its connection to his face, so that it hung like a too-big mask bought in desperation for Halloween. If he'd been up all night, drinking till morning, she wouldn't have been surprised. When he spotted her, he groaned. "Ms. O'Shaughnessy, you, too? Everyone else has been here today. Every reporter in San Diego and a bunch from L.A. have been tailing me. Did you see the trades this morning?"

She shook her head.

"I knew they'd dredge up the 'bad luck' business. I just never figured they'd find it so soon. I'd better stock up on this food while it's free—I'll be on unemployment for the rest of my life." He turned and watched the gray-haired cook flip a hamburger. Out of the corner of his eye, the cook glanced at Bleeker and then at her.

"Which are the garlic polenta things Dolly Uberhazy loves? I've got a friend who would kill for the recipe."

She expected the cook to answer, but he concentrated on burger and roll with the attention Tchernak might have given his cilantro, Italian fontina, and expensive-mushroom soufflé. It was Bleeker who said, "Here, the garlic polenta sticks with herbs, so you don't smell like a garlic-mouth. Sounds like nothing special, but if it's your thing, you'll never forget them. Would that Dolly had, that she'd never heard of this set, that she'd never thought of me."

Ignoring his whine, Kiernan took a bite of the polenta stick. It was wonderful. "The recipe would really make my friend's day," she said to the cook.

"Leave me your card," he said as he added lettuce and tomato to the burger. He pocketed her proffered card, passed Bleeker his burger, and walked out the back door.

"I wouldn't count on making that recipe for dinner," Bleeker said. He picked up his burger, and she followed him to a table away from the others.

"Have you found anything about Lark's death?" he asked, in the tone he might have used for *Is it really cancer?*

"I know that Greg Gaige was real uncomfortable with Dratz. How come?"

Bleeker shrugged noncommittally and took a bite. "If all you've come up with was that someone didn't like Dratz, your job prospects aren't any better than mine."

"What about Dolly and Liam McCafferty? Do you remember them as a pair?"

He shook his head, then said, "Could have been, though. An affair with any two people on any set could have been. How could I remember? I'll bet even Dolly couldn't. Affairs, they're like Fourth of July sparklers—you can't take your eyes off them, and then poof, they're nothing more than black sticks." He took a drink of his coffee. "Like my career."

"I need to see the location set from *Bad Companions*. Here, I've got a map. How do I get there?" she said briskly.

But Bleeker was not spurred. "Map's not going to be any help to me."

"Think!"

"Okay, but it's been so long." He rubbed the side of his chin. "We started on that road through Balboa Park and then skirted southeast for an hour or so. Maybe two. The set was a few miles outside a small town. Christ, what was the name of that place? I can't remember."

"It was a military place, right?"

"No."

"You sure?" Military was the one thing Yarrow *had* remembered about it.

"Yeah. If there'd been a base nearby, there would have been stores in the town. But there was nothing there; the only thing worth buying in the town was gas to get back to San Diego." He took another bite of his burger. Finally he said, "Let me call Dolly. She was the line producer; she'd remember." He walked a yard away, unfolded his phone, and dialed.

For him, Kiernan noted irritably, Uberhazy wasn't in a meeting. She had to keep herself from demanding the phone, confronting Uberhazy, and getting her answer directly. Or *not* getting it. Better to see what Bleeker came up with.

He was back in two minutes.

"You got her?" Kiernan asked.

"Yeah. But she doesn't remember the location site."

"Doesn't she have records?"

He fingered the rest of the burger. "Not that she could get to. Records that old could be anywhere."

"She must have remembered something."

"No," he said to the burger.

Damn! She *should* have grabbed Uberhazy when she had the chance. Damn! "Okay, so you took the Cabrillo Freeway through Balboa Park. Did you go through Dulzura?"

"I don't remember."

"What about—"

"I said I don't remember. Leave me alone."

She grabbed his arm. "You remembered five minutes ago. What did Dolly say to black out your memory?"

He shook off her grasp.

"Cary, what's she afraid I'll find out there? Think. There's plenty of guilt to go around. If she can escape her part, she's going to leave all the more for you."

He tossed the rest of the burger in the trash. "There's nothing she can do to me. I'm finished in this business." He glared at Kiernan. "There's nothing anyone can do anymore."

"Damn, damn, damn," Kiernan muttered as she strode back to the Jeep. What, specifically, was Dolly hiding?

She climbed into the Jeep. She'd have to have Tchernak track down a videotape of *Bad Companions*. But that could take weeks. She didn't have that kind of time. She had to see the location where it was filmed. And now the only two remaining people who'd been there were Jason Pedora —whose memory might include anything true or false—and Liam Mc-Cafferty, who wasn't likely to tell her.

At two in the afternoon, Kiernan paced from the shale slab fireplace to the glass brick interior wall of her former-kitchen-now-office. "I know the law is the law, Tchernak, but it is insane to have a professional stunt man die in a gag and not even check out his body for drugs. Pedora's a loony, but even so, when you've got suspicion of drug-running on the set and then a death that screams 'Drugged!' and no one bothers with an autopsy . . . even if Greg was burned as badly as Yarrow says, there could still have been clues."

Tchernak looped his aviator's jacket over a hook hidden beneath a frond of the pygmy palm tree next to the door. "Listen, I got ahold—"

"The body doesn't burn at the same rate all over, not in a situation like that, when he's in a fire suit. There could have been organs intact, plenty of tissue to check for cocaine. How could they—"

"Listen to what Joyce Hogarth told me. Joyce—"

"Now the body's been buried ten years, probably in the cheapest of pine boxes. By now, there really would be nothing left but bones. Not that it matters if I can't even find the location set, much less the body."

"Joyce's sister, the extra, knew Carlton Dratz, all right. She—"

"I've got to get a look at that location, Tchernak. I've been calling McCafferty all afternoon, and all I get is his machine. I'll bet he's sitting right next to it, grinning self-righteously, dreaming of a meteoric rise to the exalted spot of state treasurer itself. I'm going to drive right up there—"

"She had an affair with Dratz. She—"

"Even if I could find the body, I couldn't get it exhumed. The only way they'd exhume is for suspicion of murder or contagion. Damn. He's hardly going to be contagious after a decade. Even if he was positive for plague ten years ago, it won't matter now. No, I need to see if there's anything buried on that location out there in the country that no one seems to remember."

"Not no one."

She stopped midpace and stared at Tchernak. "What do you mean?"

"That's what I've been trying to tell you. So if you'll listen . . ." He plopped himself onto the big yellow-sunflower couch and patted the other cushion in invitation.

Kiernan sat and crossed her legs under her. "So?"

"Probably no other operative in San Diego County could have gotten past Joyce Hogarth's door. But—"

"Don't tell me Joyce Hogarth was a Chargers fan?"

"Nope. Wouldn't know the side of the football from the end. I borrowed a red 'fifty-six Corvette from a buddy."

Kiernan slapped her hands together. "Give that man another bonus! A red Corvette like Carlton Dratz's! Did Joyce Hogarth make the connection?"

"At first she just stared. But that baby's a crowd-pleaser, so I wasn't sure if she was just ogling. I didn't want to lead the witness, right? So I let her circle it, pat the fenders, finger the steering wheel, all the time me saying nothing leading, like I'm just the proud parent, until she said her sister's boyfriend used to have one."

Kiernan nodded, already sorry she hadn't caught herself before encouraging Tchernak in this "second career." "Did she confirm that her sister was attracted to Dratz?"

"Well, she didn't actually say that. I got the impression that the attraction was to Dratz's money and the fact that his father was a big shot. The sister did plan to go to Mexico with Dratz. But here's the thing; they weren't going to go to Mexico until they finished shooting. That was the plan."

"But?"

"In all the commotion after Greg died, someone mentioned seeing Dratz near the gas nozzles—seems they used butane spigots to simulate the fire. They looked around for Dratz, but he had split. Had taken that little red 'Vette of his and vamoosed."

"And didn't take Jane with him?"

"She was already gone," Tchernak said smugly.

"Gone?"

"Yeah, seems she'd gotten a message that there was a casting call back in Hollywood, and she telephoned Joyce to come get her under cover of dark. All very hush-hush. Joyce arrived before dawn and carted Jane away, so Jane didn't have to face a scene with Dratz. The story is Jane was fed up with him, realized he wasn't going to be of any use to her, and wanted to dump him but was afraid he'd use his father's influence to get even."

"So she snuck out." Kiernan shrugged. "Not how Dear Abby would have advised, but a method of problem-solving that has years of tradition behind it. And what about the casting call?"

"A bust. Director didn't show. But Jane was so exhausted from the *Bad Companions* experience, Joyce said she'd never have gotten the part anyway."

Kiernan nodded. She could imagine Jane, the extra, sneaking out for the lure of a better part, particularly since her work on the location set was over. She could certainly picture Carlton Dratz schlemieling around the gas nozzles by the set house, turning a knob too high so the gas jet blocked Greg's expected exit, or managing to wedge a door so he couldn't get it open—whatever. She could almost see the bumbling

Dratz watching, horrified, as Greg died, as the realization burned into him that his fumbling had killed Greg. Jumping into his sports car and heading across the border seemed perfectly likely. And once he was gone, the production company closed ranks, buried Greg without question, and got back to the business of mass entertainment. All the parts fitted—but not *together*. "It's too fortuitous that Jane Hogarth got the casting call just before Dratz ran out. Are you sure there was a casting call?"

"I saw the message."

"Who from?"

"Bleeker gave it to her."

"Joyce is sure of that?"

"Yeah, because Jane was flattered that he recalled who she was."

"Okay, so there was a note—if Bleeker didn't write it himself. Then there was a—Tchernak, how many other people came to the casting call? Did Jane hang around with a bunch of other hopefuls until she realized the director wasn't going to show?"

"I don't—what Joyce said was that Jane had to be in Burbank at ten in the morning, knew she'd get caught in all the rush-hour traffic so she left at seven, which meant she had to get up at five thirty, and then she was back at ten thirty."

"Ten thirty! No hanging around, then. Either it was canceled—"

"Wasn't canceled. Jane groused that the bastard didn't even bother to call in. She said—wait—she said everyone else in the room was there for another part, a clown. She said she'd already been a fool, she'd be damned if she was going to be a clown, too."

"So odds are, her casting call never existed," Kiernan said triumphantly. "And Tchernak, Dratz was a sleazy little playboy. He'd irritated everyone else on the set. It's not likely he'd send his only companion on a wild-goose chase for no reason. Everyone figured he'd taken off with her. Why would he get rid of her, even if he expected to leave the next day? And we don't have any reason to suspect that he planned his departure."

"But if he screwed up with the fire," Tchernak postulated, "and panicked, it was convenient for him not to have to deal with her right when he wanted to take off."

"He wouldn't have known the day before that he'd ignite a killer blaze. If Jane's note was planted then, that means someone premeditated Greg's death—his *murder*." She sat a moment, feeling as if a heavy marble had rolled off the tip of her tongue. Greg murdered—the idea didn't come as a shock to her, rather as a legitimization of a concept she had pushed out of her consciousness. Bad enough to die in a fire. Accidental death probably followed a fall, a hit on the head, unconsciousness. A bad death, but nothing like the terror of being trapped in a burning house, of being scalded to death inside your fire suit. Kiernan's throat tightened; she couldn't swallow. How could a stunt man, with bodily control that normal people only dream of, die because he couldn't walk out of a cabin? Her voice was only a little shaky as she said, "Was Greg killed because he heard something or figured out what was going on in the garage? If Dratz was dealing drugs there—we need to know the whole works on that. And Tchernak, if Joyce Hogarth had to drive out to the set at night, she had to have had good directions. And I'll bet she'll be glad to give them to you."

Tchernak grinned. "Just my point! And you, oh primary detective, what will you be after?"

"Pacific Breeze Computers."

It was midafternoon before the print search turned up an article on Pacific Breeze Computer: LA JOLLA COMPUTER COMPANY FINED FOR DUMPING TOXICS. And three thirty when she reached Martin Jameson, vice-president of PBC.

"Karen Sherman, with the *Union-Tribune*." Kiernan said. "I'm doing a story on local firms that are now conforming to the EPA guidelines. Sort of an other-side-of-the-coin from our story about your infraction ten years ago."

"That! You're still on that?" Jameson's outrage certainly sounded genuine.

The original scandal must have been a major one, Kiernan decided. And Jameson must have been with PBC long enough to be involved personally. "Like I said, I'm presenting the other side of the coin. Readers aren't going to care what you did back in the dark ages. They'll be impressed by how you're conducting yourselves now, right?"

"I suppose so."

"Great. So let's start right after that infraction. That was April twenty-fourth, ten years ago. Along with the fine, you got a cease and desist from dumping your toxics in north county, right?"

"Your own paper made that real clear, Miss Sherman."

She could hear Jameson's irritated breaths against the receiver. Ignoring them, she said, "So then you started complying. First you had to dispose of your waste elsewhere. Where did you find?"

"Moss Valley."

"The municipal government there?"

"Actually, the scavenger service—you know, the garbage company."

"How did you find it so quickly? You must have been in a great rush."

"Miss Sherman, surely you know court hearings take forever. We could have built an incinerator in the time it took to appeal the desist order."

"But the desist order held while you appealed. You had to stop dumping immediately."

"Obviously you've been over these facts. All I can tell you is, we have complied faithfully ever since then. Check with Moss Valley."

"Very well. Thank you, Mr. Jameson."

It was another twenty minutes before Kiernan got off the phone and sidled to the trompe l'oeil table where a platter of hors d'oeuvres— braised crab on jalapeño zucchini bread, topped with a sharp cheese— sat atop the faux French bread. Atop the faux Ezra head was the real one, the real canine eyes eyeing the real hors d'oeuvres. She scooped off the crab and cheese topping, held it out for him, and plopped the zucchini bread into her own mouth, all before Tchernak, across the room making Tanqueray and tonics, could see. Then she picked up another piece.

"What we have," Kiernan said, "is an unexplained gap. Jameson at Pacific Breeze Computer says they stopped dumping illegally April twenty-fourth. But Moss Valley has no record of accepting their refuse until June first."

"So what did they do with five weeks' worth of toxic waste?" Tchernak demanded, clearly caught between interest in the solution and his environmentalist's outrage at the likely answer.

Kiernan plopped the crab into her mouth, chewing slowly to savor the sharp taste of the cheese and the peppers. "No one has an answer for that. But we do know that out there on the *Bad Companions* set, there was a big hole filled with something in the month of May that year. Have you got the directions from Joyce Hogarth?"

Tchernak got up, walked to the office, and silently walked back with a print-out in hand. "Yes, I have the directions."

Kiernan held out a hand.

"No, no. This is nothing so mundane as that. This, mistress mine, is one of those connections you love so much. It closes one of the gaps. It—"

"Tchernak!"

Tchernak grinned. "I got the background check on Trace Yarrow. Seems he does some consulting, troubleshooting new computer programs."

She nodded. That she knew.

"Doesn't work steady, doesn't work much. But would you like to guess where he's worked on and off for the past fifteen years?"

"Pacific Breeze Computer," she said, almost as an afterthought. "Doesn't work much. . . . I wonder just how much Pacific Breeze paid to get rid of their embarrassing five weeks of toxic wastes."

CHAPTER 28

K IERNAN came downstairs at five A.M. A steaming plate of eggs, scrambled with fresh salmon and fresh dill and sprinkled with freshly ground and roasted sesame seeds, sat next to a basket of popovers, a glass of orange juice, and a Thermos of coffee. Tchernak and Ezra had just left. She pictured them loping sluggishly on the beach. Ezra was not an early-to-rise hound. He could have been a pub or café hound, wandering among the brethren until closing time, and after a brief morning walk, happy to devote his A.M. hours to watching his person peruse the *Times*. And Tchernak, she felt sure, was slogging through the sand because nothing but distance could keep him from commenting on the foolhardiness of a solo trip to wild country where a murderer could misbehave.

She ate quickly, barely tasting the scramble. Her mind was on the trip ahead to the town no one could remember, and on Trace Yarrow, who was suddenly not home. She wouldn't have admitted it to Tchernak, but it made her uneasy. Yarrow had double crossed her, triple crossed Dolly; had he been back in contact with the producer for the quadruple cross? The lines of communication were too easy for all the suspects. Anyone she'd talked to could know where she was headed. She pulled a piece of paper off her desk and wrote: *Tchernak, see if you can find out just how much Pacific Breeze paid for their illegal dumping.*

She propped it amidst the breakfast dishes and headed out for the desert.

The road east out of San Diego changed rapidly from the downtown neighborhoods of white stucco and Jacaranda trees, comfortable fourplexes, and stark new high rises softened by patches of purple Mexican sage bush, golden day lilies, or the salmon-colored pods of Chinese flame trees, to shake-roofed suburban tracts so new, the landscape bushes still wore their burlap sacks. The developments butted up to four-way, four-lane stoplights with left-turn lanes and green-lighted arrows for each direction. At six thirty A.M. all four turn lanes were occupied, and Kiernan sat through the entirety of "Sunday Mornin' Coming Down," followed by "Monday, Monday," before her turn came.

Then, as if she had turned a page, all signs of suburb ceased, the last fifty years vanished, and she found herself on a two-lane blacktop winding between the gnarly lumps of hill. She grinned with delight as she pulled the steering wheel right and left, testing the curves at a speed nearly double that posted. The joy of desert driving. In the distance the land resembled the mounds and creases of a wadded bedspread that the cat had tracked dirt on. There were sprinklings of clover here and there on the spread, but mostly it looked as if the cat had been left in charge for a week. It said something about just how intrinsically dry the desert was that even after an abnormally wet winter, the ground cover was already tan. With the window down an inch, the air was still cold from night and smelled of straw and dirt.

She passed through Dulzura, under tall canopies of palm fronds and fenced-off stacks of hay. Any trace of fog had long gone, but a haze still covered the sky. From time to time she slowed—once she stopped at a café that surely had sat unchanged since the twenties. Inside she asked if there was a military town along the road. The only official force was the border guard, the waitress assured her.

Back on the road, she checked the mirror for cars. There was dust in the distance—maybe a car, maybe not. But a car on the road didn't mean she was being tailed. Still, she slowed, trying to make out the car; but it was always too far away.

The whole trip could be a bust, as skimpy as her directions were. The sun glared off the rocks, the land grew drier, the radio station faded and died out. She turned off the road, checking out small town after town, asking the military question, getting the same nonplussed reply. There was no army, navy, or air force base; no military town.

It was still early morning, but she felt as if she'd been driving for hours. Bleeker had told her there was no military base near the movie location. And yet why would Yarrow have lied? Or been mistaken? What would have made him think: military? A tank in a park? A statue? He hadn't been on the set long enough to recall the town as Bleeker did. For

Yarrow, the town would have shrunk to no more than an image in memory.

She drove on, windows open wide, feeling the dry air scraping against her skin, the sway of the Jeep as she leaned into curves Tchernak would tell her she was taking too fast. One more hour, she told herself, and she realized as she did that the possibility of not finding Greg Gaige's grave was as much relief as frustration.

CONROY 1M., the sign said. She signaled to the empty-looking road behind. Then she saw it. Atop a bare hill, on what was clearly the side of the town, was a giant flagpole with the biggest American flag she'd ever seen. At the base was some sort of monument. She was willing to bet it and the flag were lit at night. Yarrow's military image.

Despite its spot in a valley between hills, the town of Conroy was flat and dry and consisted of a clutch of weathered buildings—houses converted into stores—and the low, large stucco rectangles that are home to supermarkets and discount stores. Beyond the two blocks of "downtown" were splatterings of wood and adobe bungalows on lots too dry to sustain grass. For a number of the homes, the landscaping consisted of cars on blocks. Atop the far hill sat a water tower. On the near one was the flag. She headed toward it, eager to see what the monument commemorated.

The hill was thinly shaded by wispy trees. On the ground beneath was grass, sparse and pale, but apparently it was the best that perpetual care could provide. The place was a cemetery. This would be where Greg Gaige was buried.

She stopped the Jeep a block away and sat thinking. Now that she'd found the town, Joyce Hogarth's directions to the movie location would be easy to follow. It was not yet nine A.M. She could get out there, dig up a sample from the dumping hole, and be back before the sun was too hot. She could get to La Jolla by early afternoon, in time to take soil samples to a lab. She could nudge the lab so they'd give them priority. By tomorrow, she could know something. She could . . .

Her shoulders were hunched up against her neck. She was breathing in shallow puffs. She looked down at her hands squeezed white on the steering wheel, and she had to keep herself from twisting the wheel hard to the right and heading out of town. Away from the cemetery. Away from Greg Gaige's grave.

No. That, she could not allow herself to do.

Gritting her teeth, she shifted into first and drove the block to the tiled-roofed, single-story white stucco mortuary. The heavy wooden doors were unlocked, and she walked through a beige hallway with a worn brown carpet that reminded her of an arroyo, the dry stream bed of the west in which the only water that flowed was in memory. Here the mourners had flowed to the right, into a plain chapel with worn wooden benches, a place where more than ashes-to-ashes would have seemed ostentatious. The air conditioner rumbled, and the air smelled of freshener.

"I'm Edmund Halsey. May I help you?" a surprisingly cheerful-looking gray-haired man asked. "We don't get many strangers."

"I've come to see Greg Gaige's grave."

"Gaige?"

"The stunt man who died on the movie set ten years ago."

"Oh, sure, sure. That was before my time, but I can take you to the grave. You a relation?"

She nodded. *Always better to start out as a relative.* It was one of her rules. *Relatives can become very distant cousins if family responsibilities start to press in too close. But nonrelations can never move up to family.*

"Well, you're the first of his family to come by. 'Course we're pretty out of the way. Still . . . well, it's nice of you to stop in. Here, now I'll take you—"

"I'm sure you're busy, Mr. Halsey. Could you just tell me where the grave is?"

Halsey hesitated only a moment before saying, "No one is more important than our deceased and those who loved them. But you'd rather be alone. Of course. Many people feel that way. Through the doors, down the path. Once you pass the stone wall, it's the last grave on the right." He patted her arm.

Kiernan tensed at the touch but restrained the urge to pull away. She walked outside into the dry heat, along the unshaded path to the low stone wall.

Scraggly desert trees poked up like whiskers on a dead chin. Close up, the grass was even sparser than it had seemed from a distance. The small shade from the trees only made the sun seem stronger. But as if in reaction to nature's penury, survivors of the deceased had gone all out for stonework: angels, obelisks, mausoleums. Monuments listed families of names. Low, black railings surrounded the groupings. Kiernan was tempted to climb the hill and see what the large monument at the top commemorated, but she knew she was merely stalling. Taking a deep breath, she walked along the wall to the right, past the Montoyas and the Marshalls, the Lesters' vault with a spray of gladiolus at the door, the Tieros lying in the shade of a granite angel's outstretched wings. Then the graves, and the grass, stopped. She hesitated, running through Halsey's directions in her mind, and walked on twenty yards, around an outthrusting of hill to an unshaded spot almost barren of grass. A dirt-strewn metal plaque on the dry ground said: GREGORY GAIGE.

Her breath caught. "Not even a birth date." Trace Yarrow had said the studio wanted a swift and low-key funeral, but this? This was like throwing out the trash!

Despite the heat she shivered, as if her stomach were filled with ice, her lungs shrunken and atrophied. She wrapped her arms across her chest and stood staring at the cracked ground, seeing not it but the macadam of the San Francisco street as she and Greg had walked back from that midnight lunch on the movie set eleven years ago. "What about the future?" she had asked one last time.

She heard Greg swallow abruptly. They walked on, the slap of her leather shoes loud in her ears, the night city suddenly seeming empty of anything but her question and his desperate wish to avoid it. They rounded the corner onto the set. The banks of lights turned the street brighter than day but sucked out the color, leaving a dreamscape from which the giant crane protruded ten stories up.

Greg stopped, put an arm around her shoulder. "It's like shimmying up that crane. Not many men could do it. Few would want to. But I do, and I want to get to the top."

"And?"

"And keep adding new tops."

"And when you have to come down?" she'd insisted.

"I don't deal with down." There was no bravado in his voice. In that moment she'd known that he didn't look down because he couldn't. Then she'd pushed away the question. From time to time later, she had wondered what he would see down below, from whence he came and would eventually have to go. Would he have seen the competition clambering up? But she had held the question gingerly, looking at it out of the corner of her eyes. Or would he have been so startled he'd have let go and fallen to—she stared at the barren grave—to this?

She turned and started back to the Jeep. Greg's answer hadn't been the same as Tchernak's—that you can't get to the top if your focus is half on the earth beneath. Nothing so sensible.

She walked faster, and once in the Jeep, she sent up plumes of dust as she headed out of town.

The *Bad Companions* location site was five miles south of Conroy, on a road that had been paved years ago. The surviving hunks of macadam merely added to the height of the ruts. It was impossible to tell whether it had been used in the last year or the last hour. There were no houses or barns alongside, no orchards, fields, or water towers. Just a clump of gray-green bushes and spindly trees at the foot of the hill, where the meager water runoff collected. The road must have been paved, she decided, by Summit-Arts. There was no one else around to care.

She followed the broken pavement around a sharp turn and up a breathtakingly steep hill with hairpin turns much too close together. From each straightaway the view below was of sharp boulders and a single dry stream bed curled near the bottom like the corpse of a snake dried out by the sun. No wonder Summit-Arts had chosen the location for a picture that dealt with death and bondage. It was as close to hell as California could offer.

Atop, the only buildings in sight were a couple of trailers, sagging, rusted, one toppled to the side. They were small compared with those at Gliderport, but it must have been all the drivers could do to get them up that miserable road. No wonder, she thought, they didn't try to wrestle them back down it afterward.

Feeling overcautious, she parked the Jeep behind a stand of live oak on the far side of the hill from the trailers. The dying rumble of the engine trumpeted against the lone rustle of a leaf as a single bird flitted away. The swish of grasses hinted at unseen rodents. But there was no wind, no distant sound of traffic, no whir from hilltop power lines. The only regular sound was her own breathing.

The trailers sat to the right of the road. No one unfamiliar with the script letters of Summit-Arts Films would have been able to decipher the surviving black smudges amidst the rust and dents on their sides. Starting with the upright trailer, one that probably would have been a small one-bedroom home in a trailer park, she pulled open the door. Inside was air so stale and hot, it seemed unable to move through the doorway. She pulled her head back into the fresh air, took a breath, and peered in. She had suspected the trailer had been left here because of its size. But if the studio had left any furnishing, appliance, knickknack, or decoration inside, it was long gone. Even the interior paneling and walls were missing. The trailer was nothing more than an aluminum box.

A glance through the door of the toppled trailer showed an interior the same but for a doorless wall that divided the main room from another, presumably the bedroom. She poked her head inside and squinted against the dark, trying to discern the walls of the bedroom. There could be something in there, but she doubted it. I am not, she thought, hopping into an aluminum box, a coffin, in the middle of the desert when someone could be following me.

If some building were left here, why couldn't it have been the barn where the horses were kept, or some scrap from the cabin where Greg died? But she couldn't expect to have that much luck. After all, she did have the cemetery.

Fifty yards beyond, she found the remains of pole holes, but nothing else of the barn. The ground around was only slightly barer than the hillsides. If there had been horses scraping hooves on the dirt floor of the barn, a decade had done its work in covering up their traces. But the dumping hole—surely that would sport a different surface—lush from the churned earth beneath, or bare from the burn of the toxins. She moved on, fifty feet, then a hundred beyond, looking right and left as she went. But no rectangle of earth stood out.

She felt the cold draft of fear. If she couldn't pinpoint the hole, she'd be at square one again.

She walked back to the trailers. The sun was getting hotter now. It hit the shiny creases in their aluminum sides and seared her eyes as it reflected off. To the south the surrounding hills were a quarter of a mile away. Closer—halfway between—was a knoll and what appeared to be a sharp, deep valley beyond. The knoll would be where the filming had taken place.

As she neared it she could make out the burnt foundation of the house. Fifteen feet square, somehow smaller than she had imagined. As with the barn, metal poles had been sunk into the ground, and it was to them that the few remains of blackened timbers clung. The rest of the burned siding was gone, and the ground within and around the house was covered with the same variety of dried brown desert grass as the rest of the hills.

If Yarrow was right about the intensity of the fire, she thought, there wouldn't have been much left when it happened, let alone ten years later. Still, she surveyed the ground, moving toward the house. As she stepped across the line between the corner poles, a shiver traveled deep inside her back. Briefly she wondered, "Is this the spot where Greg was when he realized he couldn't get out, that he would smolder inside his fire suit? Or was he conscious at all?"

Shaking off the question, Kiernan moved on, across the rectangle to the slope beyond. She had gone thirty feet when she stopped. "So it's here!" she said aloud.

Running, she came to a nine-by-twelve plot, totally bare. She stepped gingerly onto the bare earth. It felt no different from the hard, grass-covered dirt around it. But then, it had had ten years to settle.

She crossed to the other side with relief, stood on the grass there, and scanned the ground ahead. There were no demarcations other than those caused by the terrain. No road south to the Mexican border, as Jason Pedora had said.

Walking back to the Jeep, she wondered at how little fact was the basis for Pedora's fantasy. How long had he repeated the story to himself before it blotted out the question of reality?

A motion picture being filmed is a big deal, even in a major city. For Conroy it must have been the event of the decade. Very little that the actors, directors, even the gaffers and accountant did would have escaped notice. Every shirt any of them bought, every stroll they took, every piece of mail that came their way would have been meat for discussion in town. No way could daily trailers of horses from Mexico, driving right through town to the set, have gone unnoticed.

But a couple of trucks from Pacific Breeze Computer would have raised no comment at all.

Feeling better than she had since she'd left the cemetery, she walked back toward the trailers. Maybe one more look inside?

She could hear Tchernak's appalled voice: "What kind of crazy woman, who knows she may have been tailed, hops into a metal box in the desert?" Dammit, the man was running not only her house but now her mind, too.

Why not give Tchernak this one? Take the safe route for once. She didn't need a second look. She glanced around her, and assuring herself she was alone, she strode across the mesa to the stand of live oak and pulled a shovel and bag from the back. She headed back to the hole where—allegedly, she thought with a smile—whatever had come out of the Pacific Breeze Computer truck had been dumped.

She checked around her for movement, and finding none other than a slight rustling of leaves, she poked the shovel into the hard earth. There are many things a woman can do better than a man, she thought half an hour and a pint of sweat later, but digging in hard ground is definitely not one.

It was another half hour before she had scraped and dug far enough down to get a decent soil sample, bagged it, and headed back across the mesa to the Jeep.

With relief, she tossed the shovel into the back, climbed in, turned on the engine, and pushed the air conditioner knob to high.

As she eased toward the road, she considered calling Tchernak. If he had the lab ready to move on this soil sample, it could save a day. Still, she thought as she turned onto the road and started down the steep, winding incline, getting proof that the soil was contaminated would be pro forma. What she *needed* was to find out what had happened to Greg. Had he died from the fire, or had he been dead before? For that she needed to see his body. And that, she didn't want to discuss with Tchernak.

As she drove back toward Conroy, she realized that she'd suspected that all along and hadn't wanted to face it.

No good-bye slice. That had been a joke in medical school during the pathology rotation: the good-bye slice they'd laughed about and promised each other, as they held their breaths against the unavoidable smells of rot and Clorox and began the Y-shaped incision.

The rule had never been called "No Good-bye Slice," but pathologists did not do postmortems on friends. Pathologists were notorious for being "not normal." They themselves admitted they didn't handle feelings well. But they weren't so totally without emotion that they could cut into the body of a friend and see nothing but bones and flesh, organs and fluids, and when they looked through a microscope not find it clouded by a tear.

But the water rolling down her own face was sweat, surely. She could handle seeing Greg Gaige's body. It was probably years too late to find more than bones and the metal rod in his leg. Still, if the coffin were lead-lined; if the drainage were a whole lot better than it looked down at the bottom of the cemetery, then maybe there would be something left of the nares of the nose, the throat, the esophagus, the lungs. Maybe she would be able to tell if his lung had been seared by steam or smoke, or if Greg Gaige had stopped breathing before the fire.

But how to get those remains exhumed? She could still quote from memory the California code on that, number 7500: "No remains of any deceased person shall be removed from any cemetery, except upon written order of the health department having jurisdiction, or of the superior court of the county in which the cemetery is situated." Practically speaking, the only reasons for exhumation were suspicion of murder and contagion. Here there was no question of contagion, and the suspicion of murder existed only in her mind. The lab report on the soil could take weeks. And even if it were positive, it would implicate Pacific Breeze Computers—it wouldn't *prove* Greg was murdered.

Ten minutes later, she was sitting across the mortician's mahogany desk from Edmund Halsey, saying, "Greg was a man who lived to be at the top. He talked about climbing a crane higher than your flagpole and feeling the wind in his face up there. I can't leave here knowing Greg's body is down at the very bottom of the hill." She'd meant it as an act, but as she said the words, she realized they were true and that the cold hollow in the pit of her stomach had never filled. "Don't you have a free plot at the top, near the pole, where I could feel like his spirit was climbing?"

"Well, yes," he said slowly, "but it's one of our more desirable locations—"

"Money isn't a problem." She expected him to eye her dusty, rumpled slacks and shirt and allow a subtle look of suspicion to cross his face. But apparently Edmund Halsey had seen the poor and disheveled pony up for burials often enough to believe her.

"The remains have been in place for a decade. Our caskets are quality resting places, but—"

"I'd like him to have a new casket. A suitable casket."

Halsey nodded approvingly. "Very well then, we can schedule the relocation for early next week."

"No!" she said letting her frustration come out as distress. "I can't leave until I see him moved. And I have to be in L.A. tomorrow."

"I'm sorry, Ms. O'Shaughnessy, but I'm sure you'll understand that our men have other jobs and commitments." Halsey looked truly sorry. Thousands of dollars sorry.

"I'll pay them double time. They can do the work after they get off from their other jobs."

"Well—"

"And you, Mr. Halsey, I know I'll be taking time you've allotted elsewhere. I'll just leave it up to you what is fair recompense. Whatever, it will be worth it to me."

"Well, I guess—"

"I'll be back at six P.M."

"You're going to watch?" Halsey's eyes opened wide, and he stared at her. It was the first time she had seen his professional composure fail.

"Oh, yes, Mr. Halsey. I missed Greg's funeral. This is what I have to do. But please make sure this procedure is very low key. I don't want gawkers."

"Of course."

Restraining a great sigh of relief, silently giving thanks to *Always start as a relative,* she pulled out her checkbook.

"It's a formality," Halsey said, "but I will need to see proof of your relation to the deceased."

Damn! She didn't have a backup plan. She *always* had a backup plan.

Halsey was within his rights, legally. Remains can be exhumed only on orders of the coroner, the county health director, or the next of kin. She allowed herself a sigh. "Mr. Halsey, Greg was my cousin, my mother's sister's son. Our names are entirely different. You don't carry proof of that kind of relation in your purse. I'd think the commitment I'm making to his well-being—"

"I understand, Ms. O'Shaughnessy, and I'm sorry to have to bring up this problem at a time like this, but I'm afraid it is necessary." He leaned forward, and his strained face said *I feel every bit as bad about this as you do.* "You could contact the closest surviving relative and get a notarized statement."

"Which relative approved his burial?" With an effort she kept her voice soft, merely questioning.

"That was before my time. Let me check. Oh, hm. I see this was authorized by the brother of the deceased, Jason Pedora."

"No problem," she said, smiling to cover the lie worth a decade in purgatory. "We'll be here tomorrow."

CHAPTER 29

J ASON Pedora looked older and thinner than he had the night before. His matted clothes smelled of sweat; his face was lined with weariness and frustration. And there was a feverishness to his eyes. As he walked out onto the sidewalk, he stared at pedestrians in the same way he might have, had his incarceration been ten years instead of overnight.

"What about my car?" he demanded for the fourth time as he climbed into Kiernan's Jeep.

"You can deal with that later. Now you can thank me for bailing you out."

"Thank you! You're the one who got me thrown in jail to begin with."

"I'm the one who forced you to sideswipe a car? Grow up, Pedora."

"I wouldn't have had to go so fast if you hadn't been after me."

"I didn't force you to follow me from L.A."

"If you'd—"

"Enough! Blame whoever you want! Spend the rest of your life blaming everyone else, I don't care. But right now we need to deal with Greg." She hesitated. Pedora was on the edge. In a more perfect world he would be under professional care and living in a safe and stress-free place. Instead, he was in the land of slippery truths, sliding on his own new scripts of his old events. She had to find a story line that fit with his. If she didn't, she'd be the villain in his piece.

Pedora sat, his back to the door, ankle resting on knee, seat belt dangling loosely on his lap. He glanced at it and back at her, daring her to remind him that unbeltedness was illegal in California.

She started the engine and headed west toward the beach, driving in silence until he asked, "What about Greg?"

"It's probably not worth it," she said, hoping to sound offhand.

"Worth what?"

"The funeral director has a spot vacant where Greg could have the kind of monument he deserves. He could be on the top of the hill, where he should be." Watching out of the corner of her eye, she could see his mouth tighten. Quickly, she added, "On top, where you put him when he was alive."

Pedora's mouth relaxed, but he didn't comment.

"You're his older brother, right?"

"By five years."

"So you were always there for him, making things easy for him, right? I had an older sister. She used to give me tips on how to deal with our parents, how to handle teachers in school, how to act cool."

Pedora still didn't reply. They were at the top of Soledad Mountain Road. Ahead were the tree-muted lights of La Jolla, and beyond the black of the Pacific. Her fingers were squeezed tight on the steering wheel. This was the part of being a private investigator she hated the most—this coaxing, ingratiating, this bedside manner stuff. If only she could be done with Pedora and get back to the cemetery.

She swallowed and said, "But you've done so much more. You've taken care of Greg when he was an adult. People don't realize the sacrifices that helpers make. I'll bet even Greg didn't."

"*Even* Greg?!" he shrieked. With an obvious effort at control he went on. "Especially Greg! Like he was doing me a favor allowing me to be his business manager!"

His business manager! Kiernan tensed her face to keep from reacting.

"Like it was a blast for me to go to the bank, and run the house, and go to the dry cleaner. And talk to reporters when he couldn't be bothered. And make sure no one disturbed his sacred practice schedule."

"Practice schedule?"

"Christ, even as a child nothing came before that. I had to work my way through junior college so there was money for him to have gymnastic lessons. I got a scholarship to college, but I still had to work every day because Greg needed money to travel to gymnastic meets. And when I got him his first job out here—"

"You were here first?"

"Oh, yeah. I was a screenwriter."

Was that true, or was it an olive tree of dreams built on a shriveled seed of fact? "And you helped Greg?"

"Got him his first job, helped him set up his practice schedule and his house and—hell, his life. He had no idea how to live. Had never cooked, never washed clothes. He didn't even learn to drive until he got out here! Everything had been done for him, everything in the family was arranged so Greg wouldn't have to interrupt his almighty practice schedule!"

"And your screenwriting?" she prodded.

"How did I have time for it, you're asking? I didn't, that's how. You can't write when you've got to stop and run to the laundry, stop and take Greg's calls, stop and race up to the location because Greg forgot something, stop for weeks because someone has to fly back east and put Mom in a nursing home."

"But Greg—didn't he care?" she found herself asking more earnestly than she'd intended.

"Care? He didn't even notice. His whole mind was on his schedule, his work, his Move."

"You sacrificed your life for him, right?"

"Yeah."

"And he didn't even notice, right?"

"Never!"

"Year after year after year!"

"Yeah!"

"And you got so mad you could have killed him, right?"

"Damned right!"

Softly, she said, "And then the chance came on that set, in the fire house, right?"

He started to reply, then seemed to mentally slam on the brakes. "Hey, what's the matter with you? I didn't kill Greg."

"You okayed the shoddiest of burials for him."

"I didn't have any choice about that," he insisted.

"They held a gun to your head?"

"They might as well have. *I* didn't have money for a funeral. His insurance wouldn't come through for weeks. And anyway, he'd always said that money was to go to support Mom."

"The last big gift from her son, the star?" She felt her shoulders tighten at the need to go back into the act.

"Right," he said with some hesitancy.

"And he didn't even think about you, about what *you'd* live on then."

"No."

"And you hadn't worked as a screenwriter for years."

"Hmm."

The lukewarm response stopped her. "What did you do after the funeral, Jason?"

"Went back to screenwriting," he said to the side window.

"At Summit-Arts?"

"As a consultant." The words were so low, she could barely hear them.

"As a consultant at Summit-Arts. Suddenly, after you haven't written in years, Summit-Arts offers you a job. Just at the time they want to bury your brother post-haste." She pulled the car over to the curb and looked directly at Pedora. He was hunched against the door, arms folded defensively, chin pulled back into his chest. "Why, Jason, would they do that? Why were they so anxious to get Greg buried? You must have asked yourself that. What were they hiding?"

He let his arms drop and stared at her, his head shaking with bewilderment. "The Mexican horses, and the drugs."

"Okay! And they're hiding the evidence with Greg's body. Let's get that evidence, okay?"

"Well . . ."

"We can get it when we have Greg's body moved. You just need to sign the release. We can get it notarized right here." She indicated the house in front of them.

She waited until she had the signed form in hand, before saying to Pedora, "Maybe Summit-Arts didn't kill Greg, but their failure to get the town firemen on-site allowed that fire to burn out of control. How could you agree to go to work for them?"

He stared at her, as if she were the crazy one. "Because they said they'd do my screenplay."

She shook her head. "Still—"

"No, listen," he insisted, and for the first time he looked and sounded totally clear. "I worked my entire life in the background. Finally someone offers me my one chance, the thing I've always wanted, and you think I should be too noble to take it? Mom's walls are covered with Greg's pictures. You don't think I'd like to see my face up there in just one?"

Before she could reply, Pedora turned to her. His whole body gave a quick shiver, as if dislodging a sharp stick that had penetrated too deep, and he said, "What about my car?"

Next to the cost of exhumation and the new headstone, Kiernan thought, getting Pedora's car out of impound would be a small price to pay.

CHAPTER 30

ΑT six P.M. Friday night the crew of workers and observers were assembled with a copy of Jason Pedora's notarized order, the burial contract, and a cemetery map. They walked along the path by the stone wall. A new grave marker sparkled in the last searingly bright light of day, belying the lifelessness beneath it. Ahead was parked a sturdy pickup truck that looked as if it had just been through the car wash. Painted yellow and with the proper insignia it could have been an AAA road service vehicle.

Wind swept down the hill like a cloaked skier. It flicked branches against one another and rustled leaves—funereally, Kiernan thought. She wished she had remembered to bring a jacket. She wished Greg— no, no names now, just "the deceased." The corpse. The body.

She hunched her shoulders against the wind, which would get colder as the light failed, and the gusts of air, which would grow stronger, and she thanked the powers that be for it. Not even standing upwind of the corpse would protect her from the overwhelming smell of putrification. Like meat left out on the counter for a month, or a year, according to the first pathologist she had studied under. There should be virtually no meat on the body, not after ten years in the ground in a cheap and hasty grave. Would he be in a steel-lined coffin that would preserve properly embalmed remains? Not likely. She glanced at the ground under the tent. It was not sunken, and that surprised her. It suggested an extra that she hadn't expected from this interment. Perhaps the cemetery had insisted. Whatever the reason, the smooth ground meant the coffin probably was in a concrete liner, to protect the casket from being collapsed by the heavy ground above, and not incidentally to keep the cemetery free of unsightly (and in grassy graveyards, difficult to mow) potholes.

Taking a breath of cool evening air, she pushed aside thoughts of interment procedures and concentrated only on the corpse. What should she expect from a body that had been steamed inside a fire-resistant suit? How much had remained of that suit at burial? What was left would have been stuck to the skin, buried with the corpse. And how much would that suit have kept the flesh, and the water sloughed off, in place? Some flesh would have been charred where the fire burned through the suit, and the bones would be brownish. The fire would have given decomposition a speedy takeoff.

Kiernan shook her head. The body would be bad. No need to predict how bad; she'd know soon enough.

As she watched the younger men digging, she found herself breathing through her mouth, as she had automatically in the autopsy room. She had assisted at one autopsy on an exhumed body when she was a resident in the medical examiner's office. The other residents, all men, had stood outside the door, watching her, one of them holding the fifty dollar pot for their bet on how long she would last. Then, even with exhaust fans strong enough to pull the air out of the autopsy room before it could cause contamination, the smell had been sickening. Later, she wondered if she would have taken breaks in the corridor had she not been aware of the bet. But then, she hadn't left the room at all. Instead, she'd damped down the nausea, breathed so shallowly through her clenched teeth that she wondered how oxygen had made it to her brain, and at the end forced herself to smile as she walked through the metal door into the hallway, extended her palm to the gaggle of residents, and demanded every dollar in the pot.

Then it had been a struggle to work through the adipocere, the yellow waxy mass to which damp had solidified the fat of the corpse. Now she'd be lucky to get that close. If the casket held, it would be moved unopened into the funeral home autopsy room to await reburial; she wouldn't even see the body.

What was her backup for that? Getting Pedora down here to insist that his representative see the body that was being transferred? That could take days, and there was always the possibility of another job offer in Creative to halt his willingness. Her shoulders tensed; despite the breeze, she was too warm.

The group stood silently as the light faded and the lamp under the tent shone brighter. Simultaneously, Kiernan wished she'd eaten dinner and was glad she hadn't. It seemed hours before one of the diggers called out, "That's it. We're down to the liner." And another aeon before they hauled up chunks of concrete. And a third before they had cleared sufficient space on all sides and were ready to shift the straps under the casket.

Kiernan eyeballed the cemetery crew—three bejeaned guys in their midtwenties muttering to each other and smothering nervous laughter as they moved around the casket. They'd protected themselves from the reality of the event as effectively as if they'd sealed their own bodies in freezer wrap. Give them one surprise, and they'd fall apart—and compromise the evidence. Kiernan eased beside Halsey and asked, "Has this crew worked with a casket like this?"

"Not likely. We run a quiet cemetery here. A *final* resting place. We haven't exhumed a body in twenty years. That long ago, the only bones these kids were pulling were wishbones."

Before Halsey could launch a full-force display of undertaker's humor, Kiernan said, "Maybe we should warn them not to get rattled."

Halsey stared a moment—trying to decide whether she'd attempted a mortician-worthy play on words, she suspected—then moved next to the blond ponytailed guy in charge of the winch.

The blond listened, then nodded, effectively discounting Halsey's warning. He stood, his face frozen in an expression of blasé disinterest that advertised how recent had been his adolescence, his bare-muscled arms folded across his chest. The rough edges of the sleeve-holes on his gray sweat shirt flapped in the cold wind.

Halsey stepped to the edge of the hole, eyed the straps, turned to the blond, and said, "Okay, lift her up—easy."

Halsey took a step back, as did the sheriff. Only Kiernan took a deep breath of clear air and moved closer. The blond flicked on the winch. The metallic whir of the motor cut through the rustle of the leaves like a hacksaw. The loops of the belts tightened from circles to ovals to triangles. The whir grew faster, higher pitched. But the coffin didn't move. The engine strained; the belts pressed in against the wooden coffin sides. Kiernan held her breath.

And then the coffin jerked inches up. The wood had doubtless been lacquered once, maybe stained deep brown. But now it looked as unfinished as a deck chair left in the snow all winter. Inch by slow inch, the coffin lifted. Halsey sighed. Kiernan took a quick breath, her eyes never leaving the coffin. The blond at the winch grinned, eyed his fellow diggers, and turned up the winch speed.

The engine strained. Halsey whirled toward the blond; "Hey—"

The coffin jerked like a fish on a line; the old wood bowed inward.

"Turn that thing down, you asshole!" Halsey yelled, just as the side of the coffin gave way.

The lid banged down on the side, cracking the flooring.

"Lower it! Lower it, you moron!"

But the blond was staring transfixed as the coffin lid slid down what remained of the sides and into the grave, exposing to the wind pink ash that had once been the coffin's silk or satin liner.

The coffin floor cracked in the middle. The belts went slack, then tightened. Both ends of the floor rose in a V. And the gray-white skeleton sat half up.

CHAPTER 31

MORE than an hour had passed, during which Halsey alternately shouted at and calmed the cemetery crew, directed them to lower a palette and shift it under the failing coffin floor, and transferred the ensemble to the holding room in the mortuary basement. Shards of the coffin clung tenuously to the palette; a tarp covered the corpse. A ceiling fan groaned ineffectually. The cemetery crew, green and shaking, made for the door. Even breathing through her mouth as shallowly as she could, Kiernan fought to keep from gagging at the putrid odor.

"Save the remains of the coffin," she said to Halsey.

"Why?"

"We may need to run some tests."

"Tests? Tests, when you're just moving remains to another site? Just what's going on here?"

"I don't know. But what I can tell you is that this is not the remains of a man who died with his head inside a fire-resistant suit."

Steeling herself so that her chest was barely moving, she walked to the palette and lifted the tarp off the body.

Bones. No flesh on the feet, nothing visible in the joints between the metacarpals and carpal phalanges of the hands.

She choked back a gasp. The skull still showed signs of being singed. And the teeth were blackened and chipped. Chipped from the heat. Blackened from contact with the flames. How had Greg's face burned? What had happened to him? He was a professional—how could he have gotten himself burned like this?

She turned away, shut her eyes. *The remains, just the remains. No names.*

Turning back, she looked more closely at the metacarpals and up the arms along the radius and ulna of the forearm to the humerus of the upper arm. The body was lying supine. Still sifting the air between her teeth, Kiernan pulled a magnifying glass from her bag and leaned forward, moving her gaze from the acetabulum of the shoulder slowly across the clavicle to the sternum and up over the mandible and maxilla of the jaw to the frontal plate of the skull. The thick bones of the skull were intact; only the smaller ones were broken. Deeper cracks showed in the ribs and the sternum, stress lines marked both iliac crests. From the intense heat of the fire? The breaks were not new, not caused by the exhumation. No section of the anatomy had taken disproportionate insult. But there was no indication of bones broken and healed.

Why was the breakage most prevalent in the head?

Why no signs of bones broken and healed? Greg Gaige had been a stunt man. He'd done high falls from buildings, horse falls from saddles, stair falls down flight after flight, not to mention the myriad of falls so ordinary in stunt work as to be unworthy of mention. Kiernan shook her head. There was no way Greg Gaige could have spent fifteen or more years of his life as a stunt man and never broken a bone.

"You satisfied?" Halsey demanded from a spot by the door.

"No." She moved to the foot of the table and, magnifying glass in hand, moved from the tarsal phalanges up across the small knobby bones of the ankle to the tibia and fibula, across the patella to the femur.

No breaks there, either. And no metal rod in the femur.

She stood up straight, walked to the door, took a deep breath of hallway air, and said to Halsey, "This body was not entirely in a fire suit. The head was unprotected in a fire. It's singed directly from the flames."

Halsey nodded without interest.

"And it's not Greg Gaige."

CHAPTER 32

NOT Greg Gaige.

Whose remains were lying in the cemetery's holding room? How had they gotten into the grave with Greg's name on it? The sheriff asked her those questions, but she had no solutions—at least, none she was willing to pass on to him. Her speculation she kept to herself. She answered his questions in the mortuary, again at the Sheriff's Department, and went over them a third time for her official statement. When she got free, it was after ten P.M., and she hadn't had a moment to ponder the revelation that had stood at the edge of her mind all evening, its blinding golden light casting all lesser thoughts into darkness. Greg Gaige was alive! Or at least, she cautioned herself, he had been alive a decade ago, *after* the fire gag. Was he still alive? If so, where was he? How was he? *Who* was he, now that he could no longer be Greg Gaige?

A chill shot through her. A man had died in Greg's place; could Greg have been responsible? She couldn't bring herself to believe it, but she knew the sheriff wouldn't hesitate. If he found Greg before she did, it would be too late.

She pulled up on a hill outside of town and tried her phone. The quick call to Tchernak was the easy part. Then she dialed Dolly Uberhazy at home. She waited through the answering-machine spiel with relief. The answering machine, the electronic means to say: I tried. "This is Kiernan O'Shaughnessy. We've exhumed the body in the Conroy cemetery. The body is not, repeat *not* Greg Gaige's. The sheriff will be—"

"What?" Dolly yelled.

Kiernan repeated the message.

"You had them dig it up?"

"You're getting distracted, Dolly. The point is the body isn't Greg Gaige."

"Oh, shit!"

"The body is someone else."

"Why the hell—"

"And that means that someone else did the fire gag."

"I can't believe this is all coming up again. *Bad Companions*—God, was that aptly named! The companion from hell. I thought I'd finally gotten clear of that film. I might as well have been Bleeker, for all the years it shadowed me."

"Because of the fire gag?"

"Because the damned film was so over budget, and because I was an easy scapegoat."

"An *easy* scapegoat? You were the producer. Weren't you *supposed* to be keeping costs in line?"

"Yeah, and I did. It wasn't that far over budget. It wasn't *Bonfire of the Vanities,* for chrissake."

"You used the footage from the fire. It's not like you had to stay and reshoot that scene. So what threw the film over budget?"

"Look sweetie, the script didn't call for the hero to burn up three-quarters through the story. We had the fire on film, but we didn't have him getting out of it. So we had to rebuild the whole damned house and shoot some makeup scenes with it. And that was the small part. Then there was the funeral, and there was a holiday weekend, and we couldn't get the lumber for the house for a couple of days, and by the end of it all, we were looking at a ten-day delay, with the whole damned payroll sitting around on location. You know what that costs, sweetie? Close to a hundred thousand dollars each and every day. All the leases needed to be renegotiated. The release date had to be postponed, which meant the distribution contracts had to be adjusted—not in our favor, I'll tell you. It was a nightmare."

"Did they blame you for Greg's—or whoever's—death?"

"No, of course not."

"Then why were you the scapegoat? Just because you were the producer?"

"Because, dammit—and don't you repeat this—I was a woman."

Dolly was the last person to cloak her failings in accusations of sexism. It was a moment before Kiernan said, "Ah, the affair you had on the set!"

"You got it, sweetie. A guy screws around, it's normal extracurricular activity. Doesn't affect anything—not his marriage, certainly not his work. No reason why it should, it's not like he's dealing with anything above the short hairs. But a woman has a fling, a fling so minor I couldn't have told you the stud's name a month later, and everyone in the business is saying: 'Oh, yeah, Dolly was so head over heels, she let the set go to hell.' My whole career could have gone down the tubes. It took me five years of the tightest-budgeted shoots to live down a reputation for negotiating every contract on the casting couch. And now, you —*you* dredge it all up again. Jesus, why didn't I let the San Diego cops lock you up when I had the chance?"

"Hey! Pay attention to the problem at hand here. You're going to be talking to the sheriff in the morning. And he's going to be asking who's in that grave." Kiernan could hear Dolly taking a deep breath.

"How would I know? That was ten years ago."

Dolly had been straight with her; the woman had been too angry to concoct stories. But now that she was getting herself under control, Kiernan couldn't read her as well. "Dolly, whoever is in the grave also did the fire gag."

"And made a bloody mess of it."

Kiernan let that drop. No need to push Dolly for an opinion on the deceased. Ten to one she herself knew who it was. She looked across the dark desert sky. The lights of Conroy were dim and low, like worn beige broadloom. On the top of the cemetery hill, the flagpole was, as she had suspected, lit brightly like a beacon for extraterrestrials. Or maybe a beacon for her. "Dolly," she said slowly, "the last time I saw Greg Gaige, he talked about his career being like climbing up a hundred-foot pole. He'd been at the top for years, but still he had no intention, no *thought,* of ever getting off."

"Why would he?" she asked. "That's the way it is in the business. You're not on top, sweetie, you're nothing."

"And if you're not in the business?"

"You're dead."

It was just what Greg would have said—only for him the business was doing stunts. Whether his stunts showed up on celluloid was secondary. But Dolly wouldn't understand that.

"Dolly, if you're concerned about staying on top of that pole, start asking yourself who could have been in Greg Gaige's grave. Who could be gone for ten years and not missed at all? Get ready for the sheriff to ask: 'Where is Carlton Dratz?' Do you really *know* it was him harassing Bleeker year after year? And how much better has your life been without him?"

CHAPTER 33

ΙT was nearly midnight when Kiernan got home. She opened the door to Tchernak's kitchen and was greeted by sounds of Beethoven, the aroma of garlic, and a canine yawn and guttural yip she took to mean: *Don't you humans ever sleep?* Ezra might have made it as a pub hound, but he wouldn't have approved of the two A.M. closing hour.

Tchernak, however, was definitely not sleepy. "Fifty thousand dollars! That's what informed environmental sources contend that Pacific Breeze Computer paid to get rid of their embarrassing toxic waste."

"Whew! People have murdered for a lot less than hiding fifty thousand illegal dollars."

"Plus undermining the environment," Tchernak insisted. Tchernak had been the spokesman for a group opposing offshore oil drilling. He took environmental insults personally. "Looks real bad on the old résumé."

"Even in the movies. Bad publicity." A whiff of garlic and spices teased her. "What's cooking?"

"The garlic polenta rolls with no-longer-secret herbs and spices. Hot from the oven." He waved a hand at the baking pan. He was in gray shorts and sweatshirt with the arms cut out. But the proud grin on his craggy face beamed gold.

"Dolly Uberhazy's beloved snack? How'd you ever get the recipe? I certainly couldn't."

"Wasn't easy. I drove up to the set this morning and bearded the cook. My working MO is charm," he said, grinning. "Okay, so it doesn't work as well on guys. But with Correra, the cook, it was zip. Correra relates to food, not people—or as much as he can manage in the midst of a hundred people on a movie set. In the end I think it came to nuisance value. He realized the only way to get rid of me was to hand over the recipe."

"Did you ask if he was the cook on *Bad Companions?*"

"Three times before I got an answer. No, he wasn't. And no, he doesn't know who was. Not the woman he got the recipe from; that he did say." He scooped a polenta roll from the pan and held it out to her, watching as eagerly as the now-alert wolfhound.

She took a bit, chewing slowly, savoring. "Great. A creation worthy of your own self, Tchernak. I can see why Dolly remembered them for a decade."

"A miracle." Tchernak inhaled deeply, smiling so broadly, he had to stop and reposition his face before he could eat.

She held out a taste to Ezra. Normally she loved being in Tchernak's kitchen with its chaos of green sauce and golden batter-coated bowls, its Eiffel Tower of used and abandoned pots, wooden spoons, stainless spoons, spoons that were round, oval, shallow, deep, full of holes or edged with lips, and knives and saws the like of which she hadn't seen since she'd left the coroner's office. She loved the smells she couldn't possibly have named. It pleased her to watch Tchernak moving from counter to stove in one long stride, humming the Beethoven he insisted was essential to the culinary art. Every time she walked in on him cooking, it comforted her at a level too deep to touch that someone was cooking just for her.

But now the memory of the broken and charred body in the funeral home shoved everything else to the edges of her mind. "By tonight, the sheriff will have identified the body."

"Carlton Dratz," Tchernak put in.

"In the meantime all I've accomplished is putting Greg Gaige in danger—and I can't save him. Dammit, I can't even find him to warn him." *Or discover if he is responsible for Dratz's death,* but she couldn't bring herself to say that aloud. Tchernak's expression told her he had the same unspoken thought. "What happened the day of the fire? Who was responsible? Where is Greg Gaige—"

"And where does Lark Sondervoil fit in? What made her worthy of being murdered, huh?"

"Lark was going to have a press conference. What did she know? What was she going to reveal? It had to be something connected to *Bad Companions* and the toxic dumping. Something that would touch off the kind of investigation they should have had ten years ago. But dammit, how did she find that out?"

Kiernan picked up another polenta stick. "How did Carlton Dratz get into the fire gag and die?"

Ezra nudged her arm. "Okay, I'm eating as fast as I can and still think." She dropped him a piece. "On Dratz's remains, there was no indication of a blow to the head, nothing to suggest he was assaulted and dragged into the cabin to die. Besides, Yarrow recalls seeing him standing inside the window." She ate the other half and said, "Dratz was fascinated with the set. He was even found camped out in the set house one night—who knows how many nights he was there and not spotted? He could have been in the fire house one or more of the nights when the toxics trucks made their dumps. He thought stunt doubles were paid too much for stuff that was just sleight of hand. So you can imagine how easy he figured the fire gag would be. And what a triumph it would be to do it and then whip off the hood and show everyone on the set that he had been right all along."

"But the suit's tight like a diver's suit, isn't it? How could he get in that by himself?"

"He couldn't. Greg was the only one who managed that. Not even other stunt doubles could do it. So Dratz needed help."

Tchernak held up a polenta stick like a finger. "Bingo! So Dratz co-opted the person he'd seen dumping the toxins?"

"Right," she said, reaching for another polenta stick. "And his helper —no fool—must have realized that Dratz was the kind of blackmailer who would never let up. He might never want money, but there'd always be something he'd be after, just because he'd love jerking some-one around. He faces the prospect of Dratz carrying on until the police get called in. He must have lived in terror. Every time Dratz walked near the hole or mentioned 'night' or 'truck,' he must have figured the end was near. And then, suddenly, Dratz decides he wants to do the fire gag. He wants a little help. An offer he couldn't refuse, right?" She broke off half a dog biscuit for Ezra and took another bite of the polenta stick. "So the helper dispenses with the town firemen by giving them a later call time. He creates a phony message to get rid of Jane Hogarth. Thus, no witness to Dratz getting up; no adoring girlfriend who might want to come along and who later would reveal all for the offer of a bit part in a B-movie."

"But if he had help, why wasn't Dratz wearing the hood to the fire suit? Even Dratz wouldn't let his face burn."

"It's not like his skin was exposed. There was the mask that the wig was attached to. It wasn't fireproof, but to a novice it must have seemed like protection. Easy to whip off at the end, like he wanted. And there was the fire-resistant gel. Dratz probably figured that was the elixir that allowed stunt doubles to create their overpaid illusion. Of course, fire-resistant is not fire-proof." Kiernan finished the polenta stick. "And Tchernak, there's the question of the oxygen. Why didn't Dratz use the oxygen? Yarrow wondered why Greg didn't. It was right there in the cabin."

"So why didn't Dratz use it?"

"Because, Tchernak, he wouldn't have known how. He could have learned, but learning wasn't his style. So you can see him figuring: Why bother for twenty seconds? After all, he wasn't going to have a fire hood blocking out the air. . . . Hoods are hot; they make people claustrophobic. He didn't know how long he'd have to wait. All for twenty seconds of action. Twenty seconds is nothing."

"But any halfway sensible—"

"We're talking Carlton Dratz here. You can just see him planning to run out, whip off his wig, and show them all up."

"So why didn't he?" Tchernak said, herding the remaining polenta sticks together on the serving dish.

"Because," she said, heading through the door to her own flat, "someone who doesn't know what he's doing can apply too little gel, expect it to do too much, or they can mix up the fire-protection gel with the fire-heightening gel. They don't know that when they breathe in air as hot as it gets in a fire like that, it will burn their lungs. They don't expect to panic." She reached for a polenta stick but stopped halfway. It was a picture too awful to think about. "The person who could and would tell me is Greg Gaige. Damn, I can't sit here eating. I have to—look, Dratz was planning to go to Mexico. An escape of sorts. Maybe he had false identity papers. Joyce Hogarth could know. We can call her."

"Kiernan, it's one in the morning."

"For a man's life, she can lose some beauty sleep. Besides," she said, breaking off half of the last polenta stick, "you can use some of that charm you didn't expend yesterday."

"I see by *we* you mean *me*."

"She'd rather talk to you, Tchernak. It's the least you can do after waking the poor woman up," she said, grinning. "I'll take Ezra out and leave you two alone."

By the time she reached the rocky beach, her smile was gone. Ezra's nails clicked against the rocks, seeming to dance above the drumming of the ocean. She was so close to finding the key to Dratz's death and Lark's murder, and yet the suspects, they were so incestuous, all of them so busy staring at the top of the hundred-foot pole, they didn't care who they kicked off beneath them. And Greg—was he out there, too, not in L.A. or back in Baltimore but somewhere in the thousands of miles between? Or had Dratz's killer killed him, too? So much life had been taken to cover up a couple of loads of toxins dumped in a spot no one cared about. To protect fifty thousand dollars and a career. A chance to get to the top of that pole.

She turned and started back. Murders so vicious, so desperate . . . Lark's murder was calculating, but Dratz's was the work of an angry person, one so enraged, he could decide to keep the Fire Department at bay while a man burned.

And yet both were what the police called clean-hands crimes—not ones where the killer had to face his victim as he died. Murders scripted by one used to directing the action from a distance, to budgeting time and creating an end to fit the script.

"Nothing," Tchernak announced when she walked back in her flat. "If Dratz had an alias, Joyce didn't know. And she did not want to discuss it in the middle of the night."

"That's okay," Kiernan said excitedly. "Listen, I realized that the question is not what happened on the *Bad Companions* set. But *why* it happened. Think about why. Not why the murders—they came as a result. But why would someone take the chance of dumping the toxins?"

"Fifty thou?"

"An incentive, but still not worth mortgaging a career for. The dumping and the fire—what was the actual result of both those actions? Not what *might* have happened, but what *did*?"

Tchernak settled on the sofa, sprawling his legs into the room. "It threw *Bad Companions* over budget?"

"Right. And who suffered?"

"Bleeker?"

"No. The Bad Luck Bleeker legend didn't take hold till the later films.

No one could have predicted that. No, Tchernak, the one who suffered was Dolly Uberhazy. And that, anyone could have foreseen."

Kiernan stood up and paced to the glass doors. "Tchernak, give Persis what you have to to move you to the front of the line. We need a Social Security check on Greg. It's a long shot, but maybe he's worked under his own Social Security number in the last decade."

A hint of a smile twitched Tchernak's wiry moustache. He let a beat pass and said, "Done. And zilch. And what I gave Persis you'll never know. But, alas, she came up with *nada*. Nothing but this little homily: You just don't pluck things out of the air because you want them."

"Great, just what we need—some pop philosophy from Baba Persis! And inaccurate yet! Because plucking wishes from the air is exactly what Lark Sondervoil did. She got the Hollywood job that everyone knows you can't walk in and demand." She paused, reconsidered, and flounced on the sofa beside him, bouncing him in her wake. "Tchernak, you are superb. And Persis is a gem!"

"Those are words I never thought I'd hear from your mouth."

"Look, here's the link for Lark Sondervoil. She didn't just call Hollywood and get a screen test sight unseen, like she said. We all know that doesn't happen. Someone had to see her perform first—at the High Country gym. Some man came, saw her, and told her about Hollywood. And someone, Tchernak, taught her to do the Move."

She grabbed the phone and dialed the High Country Gymnastics Academy. The phone rang six times before she put it down.

Tchernak was laughing. "Gym not open at two A.M.?"

She was already calling information for the gym director's home number.

"Talbot here," the sleepy male voice said. "What's the matter?"

"Jerry, this is Kiernan O'Shaughnessy. We spoke a couple of days ago about the memorial for Lark Sondervoil. I need the names of the people who taught her. There was yourself, of course. And before you?"

"It's the middle of the fucking night!"

"Wait! Don't hang up! This is connected with Lark's death, her *murder*, Jerry."

"The *movie studio* is checking out her murder! Come on!"

"I'm an investigator, hired by her friends who were afraid her murder would be covered up. It's a long story. I can explain it now, if you insist. But every moment we spend here means her killer may be getting farther away. Trust me, and I'll call you when we have the suspect and answer any question you want."

His breath beat against the phone; he didn't answer.

"Jerry, if you'd seen the panic on her face when she went over the edge of the bluff, three hundred and thirty-five feet above the beach . . ."

"Okay, but you better be dealing straight with me."

"I am."

"Okay, Liz Putnam. I took over High Country from her. She'd been in charge since it opened."

"And wasn't there someone else? Another man?"

"No, just Liz and me."

"Another man who worked with you briefly. A guy from out of town? Within the year before Lark left?" She was holding her breath. Talbot had to remember. Greg had to have taught Lark; there was no other way she could have mastered the intricacies of the Move.

"I don't—"

"Would you check your records? It's important."

"Well, okay, but I'm going to have to go across the yard to the gym office."

"Thanks." She paced to the deck doors and stood looking at the tail of the moon as it floated atop the green-black waves, disappearing before the breakers could smash it against the rocks. The movement of the great waves almost always pulled her into its own pace, calming her at the most frantic of moments. But tonight she found herself silently urging the waves to ebb more quickly and flow harder into the rocks.

"You know, you were right," Talbot said, clearly surprised. "There was a guy, came through here a little over a year before Lark left. Just showed up one day and asked about a job. I was skeptical. He looked kind of seedy, you know. But when he did a routine on the mat, he was something else, and not just for an old guy. Something else, period! So I took him on."

"But he didn't stay long?"

"No—thing was, he wasn't much of a teacher. He tried, and he was responsible, but his heart wasn't in it. Didn't really seem to care about getting the basics across to the little ones. I'd forgotten about him, because he didn't leave much of a mark."

"On anyone except Lark?"

"Right. He spotted Lark the first day, and he zeroed in on her. Well, hell, we'd all like to spend our time teaching kids like Lark. That's what you do in heaven. But when you're running a business, you have to take the clumsy with the good."

"You've got his name?"

"Yeah. It was Luke Correra."

CHAPTER 34

"LUKE Correra," she said as she put down the phone and grabbed the keys to the Triumph. "Correra, the cook! The big catering truck leaves every afternoon. Will he still be on the set, Tchernak?"

"Maybe. It is the middle of the night, Kiernan. He might be asleep wherever he's staying. People do sleep. The set was shutting down today. But when I saw him, he was cleaning out the small food trailer. I got the impression that he'd leased it himself. He could still be at it. Or he may have folded down his flaps and be gone."

"And if he's gone, he'll slip back into the netherworld he's been in for ten years and we'll never find him. Tchernak, you're going to have to get the Social Security number he's been using, and then check every record that exists: lawsuits, small claims, tax liens, assessor's records, credit cards, the whole schmeer. We've got to get an address on him, now. If he's not at Gliderport, he might make one stop at his home before he vanishes. We've got to be there."

Tchernak hesitated—biting back the words "protect you," she was sure—then nodded.

She ran for the Triumph—it was faster than the Jeep on curving roads —screeched out of the driveway, and raced for Torrey Pines Road. The top was down, and the damp night wind off the Pacific grazed her face and neck. She should have stopped to put the top up. And chance missing Greg by minutes? She turned on the heat, made a left from Pearl Street onto Girard, and hung a right onto Torrey Pines. It was some-where after three A.M.; she felt no touch of weariness at all. Her body quivered to run, to leap, to grab the answers before they got away.

She'd assumed she knew who Greg Gaige was when Greg was "dead."

The Greg who had died preparing to do the Move she could understand. But the man who had walked off the set into oblivion, abandoning the thing that made him *alive,* she couldn't imagine.

When she had still believed in forensic pathology as the path to Truth, and the findings of the sectioned stomach, the well-worn patella, the results of exhaustive toxicology tests as the scientists' Stations of the Cross, what would have been seductive or terrifying enough to drag her from it? And even when she had realized that forensic pathology was just a tool, a stage in medicine no more absolute than the therapeutic bleedings of centuries past, a tool subject to the failings of the machines involved, she was loath to renounce her faith. It wasn't until she had been fired and knew she'd never work as a forensic pathologist again, not until she'd spent two years adrift in India, that she had been able to start to think of life without the thing that had given it meaning.

And Greg, who had been the best stunt man in the business—had he changed? Had he lost interest in the thing that made him feel alive? She couldn't believe that.

The wind stung her face as she turned off Torrey Pines into Gliderport. She pulled up at the night chain, turned the Triumph inland, and headed across the empty parking area at a run. The moonlight turned the ripples of the empty dirt lot into hillocks; the wind sprinkled her jeans with sand and dirt. The cordon that had encircled the film set was gone, as were all the cameras, lights, and most of the trailers. Only two trailers, and the food wagon—a small affair that could be hitched onto the back of a car—remained, standing icy silver in the bright moonlight, their black shadows quivering in the wind.

If there was a guard—and she couldn't spot one—he'd be by the crane at the edge of the bluff. The trailers looked as abandoned as a back-lot set. On the food wagon a loose hitch clattered in the wind, hitched to nothing now.

She rounded the back of a trailer and was twenty feet from the food wagon awning before she spotted the gray-haired, ponytailed cook stretching up to fold in one of the support poles—as if he were reaching up for the high bar, ready to take his mount and swing up on it into a perfect handstand.

She stopped, staring, her breath too shallow to feel. She had never let herself dwell on his death. When she thought of him since then, she'd been quick to tell herself it was stupid to wallow in grief for a man whom in fact she'd barely known. O'Shaughnessys did not wallow. But now the years of unexperienced sorrows bubbled over, washing her with a swirling mixture of emotions she couldn't begin to understand. She felt full, flushed, as if the joy of it all were too much to contain.

Greg had stopped, too, listening but not turning to look. For an instant he stood stone still, but it seemed as if every muscle, every fiber in those muscles was idling at full speed, ready to leap the highest, the longest, the best.

She longed to forget about investigating, about Lark Sondervoil and Carlton Dratz, and revel in her own good fortune. She let herself wallow another moment, then walked across the blowing dirt to the wagon. "I'm Kiernan O'Shaughnessy. Remember me?"

Greg turned, smiling. "Kiernan O'Shaughnessy! You disappeared on me in San Francisco."

"I pushed you farther than you wanted to go in San Francisco; you were probably relieved I left. I'm a private investigator now, and, Greg, I have to have answers."

She was braced to cut off a run, but she didn't expect Greg to make a break for it, not now.

The wary, fearful eyes that she'd come to associate with him had relaxed. "So you're the one investigating Lark's death. I wondered if you would find me out. Come on inside here while I finish up. There's room for two old friends."

Two old friends. There had been times when hearing those words from Greg Gaige would have made her think she'd died and gone to heaven. She followed him into the trailer, blinking against the sudden light, and noted again how small a space a cook required. The whole trailer was hardly bigger than a good-size station wagon, with its entry through the passenger door, a restaurant-size stove midway down the driver's side, a sink and counter, and the pulled-down awning across from that. Cardboard boxes filled the floor by the door and beyond the stove, and there must have been a greasy towel hanging from every cabinet handle in the place. Greg shrugged. "It's a work in progress."

It had been eleven years since that night in San Francisco. Then, in San Francisco, it had been as if time had passed over him. Now, in the brash light of the trailer she could see the cracks, crumblings, and discolorations that had been unable to erode the granite of his greatness back then. They'd been restrained only temporarily, and then attacked with the vengeance nourished during their wait. His impish widow's peak had disappeared into a hairline well back on his head. The shiny sandy hair was now wiry, gray, and caught in a rubber band at his neck. Worry lines marked his forehead and ran so deep between his eyebrows, they looked painful. But beside his mouth the skin was still barely marked, a reminder of the shyness that had kept him silent. And those blue eyes that had seemed to stare out of the poster in the Baltimore gym and into the soul of the observer, sparkled all the brighter from their faded surroundings.

How long would it have taken her to recognize Greg, here in a role where he didn't belong? To see the older face of a man who "died" a decade ago and even to stop to wonder? How many times had Bleeker grabbed a sandwich or a Diet Coke and never looked at the man serving it? And Dolly Uberhazy? A quick stop for polenta sticks in the midst of a hectic day—not a time for reflection. Trace Yarrow, who had been Greg's colleague, had come to the set only the day Lark died, and then he had stood along the edge near Kiernan, his attention on Lark. And Jason Pedora had not been allowed on the set at all. But Lark Sondervoil had known Greg. Lark had paused to give the cook a salute before she strode across the set to do her gag and die.

Kiernan stood against the pulled-down metal awning, listening to the metal clanking softly in the wind and thinking of the pictures she'd seen in Lark Sondervoil's notebook: Greg young, confident, full in control. To Kiernan's eyes now, Greg looked every bit of his fifty-some years. To Hollywood eyes he would have been too old and unimportant to focus on.

"A *private* investigator?" Greg said, pulling two cups from a box on the floor. "I'd wash them, but the water's off. The whole place is covered in grease. It's only the rubber mat on the floor that's keeping us both from slipping on our asses. That, and all our training," he added, grinning. He poured the coffee. "So you're not with the police."

"No," she said, taking a sip. It was cold; that didn't matter, she was only drinking it to wet her dry throat. Greg seemed to loom over her, eight inches taller, with muscles visible in his arms and the mound of his buttocks. He was still thin, but no longer the wiry-thin necessary to double an actor who was himself expected to be reedlike. As he moved, his steps were firm but light, so easy and yet controlled that Kiernan had the feeling he could freeze at any point and hold that pose for the next half hour.

But, she reminded herself, she didn't know him. She'd created him from press clippings, wishes, and a hand on her shoulder.

As if reading her thoughts, Greg said, "I didn't kill Carlton Dratz." He said it as matter-of-factly as he might have announced that the polenta recipe hadn't originated with him.

Kiernan nodded.

"Greg, you've had years to ponder this. You didn't orchestrate the switch with Dratz. Who did?"

"I don't know."

Her chest went cold. How could he *not* know? "Who killed Lark?"

"I don't know that, either."

"Greg, you must have some idea. Whoever did it is desperate. And once finds out you're here, he won't have any choice but to kill you. We have to figure out who he, or she, is before he nails us! Think! Lark was going to hold a news conference. She was going to talk about you, wasn't she?"

For the first time he blushed. "I told her not to. She promised me she wouldn't. Nothing I said could convince her I didn't want to be Greg Gaige again. She was talking like a teenage gladiator, ready to resurrect my reputation."

"Just to announce you were alive would have been enough to open an investigation into Dratz's murder."

"Lark never let on I was alive; I'm sure of that."

"Doesn't matter. She'd made it clear she was going to say something about you, your death, or *Bad Companions*. And reporters, who invested the time to come to her press conference, would jump on a lead to a hot story on the movies, or a mysterious celebrity death, or a toxic waste scandal. The person who was involved in the toxic dumping on *Bad Companions* and in Carlton Dratz's death couldn't take chances."

He leaned back against the edge of the stove, took a swallow of his coffee, and nodded thoughtfully, as if he were contemplating murders in a movie script.

She grabbed his arm. "Greg, you don't have time to ponder at leisure. Once the cops know you're alive, they'll say, 'Dratz wanted to do the gag, and Greg Gaige was only too ready to help him die, then to take his own insurance money and disappear. Dratz drove him crazy belittling his ability, and no one wants to give up the thing they've worked all their lives for.'"

He laughed. "That's an axiom in the business. As if ambition didn't exist outside the pictures. Nothing could convince them there's more to the world than pictures."

"Pictures . . . *pictures!* Of course! *Pictures!*"

"What?"

"Greg, Liam McCafferty talked about pictures—about succeeding in politics and having his picture on the wall between Kennedy and the Pope."

"McCafferty?"

"Of course, you don't remember him. He was a drone on the set. No one remembered him except Trace Yarrow, and that was only because they worked together before *Bad Companions*. Worked," she said slowly, "with Yarrow consulting for Pacific Breeze Computer and McCafferty doing the boss's taxes there."

"And McCafferty arranged the dumping? Why?"

"To preserve the place where he felt *alive*. Remember telling me that gymnastics was where we were alive?"

Greg nodded. "You clutch onto those places, and they end up killing you."

"Politics was what made McCafferty alive. But the toxin dumping he engineered for revenge—and money. He wanted to get even with Dolly Uberhazy, in a way that would ruin the thing that made *her* feel alive—her career. And Greg, McCafferty's the one who was in the location office, on *Bad Companions* the guy with the copy machine. It would have been no problem for him to make a new copy of the call sheet and leave it for a gofer to take to the fire house."

"So he engineered the dumping. I can see that. But why kill Dratz?"

"To save his career. He couldn't have it come out that he'd dumped toxins, not in environmental California. In politics that's a liability that could be dug up anytime, forever."

Suddenly, she realized the sound of the metal rattling outside was louder. The door to the canteen opened, and a projectile flew through the door and landed on the stove. The stove burst into flames. The door slammed shut. Kiernan grabbed the handle. The door didn't budge.

"It's bolted on the outside. Open the serving window."

"I can't. It won't move."

Flames shot up from the stove.

CHAPTER 35

THE rags on the stove blazed up. Pieces of cloth burned loose, fell to the floor. Kiernan grabbed the door handle. "It's locked from the outside!"

Greg pushed the awning. "Damn, I bolted that down myself."

All six burners were shooting flames. Beside the stove two of the rags on cabinet handles had caught fire. She yanked them down by the good ends, flung them in the sink and turned on the spigot. Nothing came out. "Water—where's the water, Greg?"

"Turned off."

She looked at the stacks of cardboard boxes, the greasy cloths hanging from cabinet handles. "Greg, this place is going to go up all around us." Unbidden, she pictured Carlton Dratz, facing the wall of fire, unable to get through. She could tell from the look of horror in Greg's eyes that he saw the same thing. But he wouldn't be able to imagine Dratz's corpse. That picture flashed in her mind, the heat-cracked bones, the charred teeth where the fire had burned into his mouth. Her throat closed, her eyes tightened, she felt as if panic were going to swallow her. She shouted to cover her fear. "We've got to get out. How can we get out, Greg?"

"There is no other door."

The air was dry-hot. Snapping sounds came from the stove, and the floor was unsteady. It was moving.

"Goddamned trailer's loose!" Greg shouted as he pulled open a cabinet. "We must be rolling toward the bluff." He yanked out a bag of flour, looked toward the shoots of flame coming from the stove, then turned and threw it on the burning rags in the sink.

Not quick enough. Sparks shot off, to a roll of paper towels. The canteen hit a bump; the towels rolled off the sink onto a cardboard carton by the door.

The canteen rumbled faster. Her breath was coming in fast puffs. *What about the guard?* Kiernan thought desperately. Was there still a guard? Even if there was, he'd be so startled to notice a trailer traveling across the sand that it would be over the bluff before he got himself in action.

"Awning!" Greg shouted. "It's the only way. I'll have to kick it free."

Smoke rose from the cardboard. "That's going to be blazing in a minute!" Kiernan yelled.

"I can't get leverage to kick; there's no place to hang on to."

"The cabinet door. I'll brace it." She pulled it open and pushed her knee in the opening. Her heart was banging in her chest. She'd never been so panicked.

He grabbed it overhead, his back to the cabinet, flexed his biceps, lifting his shoulders to an inch below his hands, and kicked at the side of the awning with both feet. The latch in the middle held, but the metal of the awning gave, then snapped back, like the corner of a lid let go. The recoil thrust Greg back into the door. Into Kiernan's knee. She braced her teeth to keep from yelping from the pain.

He kicked again. And again. Harder. Faster. The metal gave in fractions of inches.

The cardboard boxes burst into flames. Black smoke filled the trailer. She could barely breathe.

He kicked again. The awning opening was four inches at its widest at the corner.

The canteen rolled faster.

"Push with your feet, Greg!"

He braced against the cabinet door and shoved with both feet. The awning bent eight inches. He released. It sprang back. Coughing from the smoke, he let go.

Flames shot from the floor.

"Grease," Greg shouted. "Christ! The propane tank is going to blow."

Shoving him to the side, Kiernan grabbed the top of the cabinet door and braced her feet against the awning. "Get out, Greg. You can squeeze through." Maybe she would make it on her own, but he wouldn't. His shoulders were too thick, too wide.

"No! You go!"

"Greg, we don't have time. Outside, you can stop the trailer; I can't. Go on!"

She pushed with all her strength. The awning gave; the cabinet door smashed back into her fingers. The smoke stung her eyes. Beneath her, flames crackled through the floor mat.

Greg hesitated, then thrust his head and shoulders through the opening. His legs dangled over the sink, then disappeared into the hole and his feet were gone.

Her fingers shrieked with pain. She could barely see for the smoke. A new spout of flame shot up from the floor, singeing her hamstrings. She had to let go. No! The floor was blazing. The trailer bounced but didn't slow. She couldn't get air through the smoke. Her fingers were going numb. She had to get across the aisle, across the counter, and out through the space that looked four inches wide.

She'd get only one chance. If she miscalculated, she'd fall butt-first to the burning floor.

She coughed against the smoky air. Her eyes watered. She could feel the heat of the fire on her legs. Pushing with all her strength, she shoved her feet and legs fast through the opening, pushed off hard, and grabbed for the side of the awning, pulling it toward her, narrowing the opening. Her legs slid through thigh-high. Her face smacked into the hot metal. She pressed her free hand against the ceiling, pulled her chest against the hot metal awning, exhaled, and pushed her legs down the side of the trailer.

The awning scraped her legs, her hips stuck. The ceiling was out of reach.

Something pulled on her legs. Her face scraped down the metal.

The night air hit her like a cool cloth after a fever. Her butt struck the ground momentarily, then Greg pulled her up.

The edge of the bluff was twenty feet away.

The trailer rattled over it. An explosion lit up the jagged knuckles of the bluff.

Greg wrapped his arm around her shoulder. "I have never in my life been so scared."

She let out a squeak that she'd meant to be a laugh. "Me neither."

The guard was running toward them. In the distance a siren cut the night air. Greg said, "Did you really think I could stop that trailer?"

She didn't, she realized. Why had she insisted he get out first? Stubbornness? Gift to an old idol? No. In the safety of the cool air, on hard ground, it seemed ridiculous, but she knew the reason: She couldn't have borne losing him again, not without knowing who he had become. "You did pull me out in time."

"I . . . called in . . . his plates," the guard panted. "I seen him pushing the canteen. I gave chase, but he moved fast for an old guy with a gut on him. Was burning rubber before I could catch him. But I got his plates."

"We could have died in the trailer while you were chasing after him," Greg said.

"You were in the food trailer! Hey, no one's supposed to be in there now. You had no business being in there."

Kiernan and Greg looked at each other and laughed. "The chase," she said, "so much more rewarding than the save."

The guard glared, turned, and strode back toward the parking lot.

"And you," Greg said, "you're not worried about chasing McCafferty? You don't think he'll escape?"

She considered a minute. "No. I barely know Liam, but he's so much like my relatives. And he's not you, Greg. He couldn't go off and leave his life behind like a shed skin. For him, there'd be nothing left. Movie people think 'the business' is all that matters. They're right; they just don't realize theirs isn't the only business. Liam could no more imagine life without his picture between Kennedy and the Pope than Dolly could envision a career managing the local motor vehicle office. He won't run, because there's nothing to run to. The police will find him at home, in his chair by the picture window overlooking Mission Bay, with one of his Waterford crystal glasses on the table beside him, and a bullet through his brain."

Greg shivered, and she had the sense that the reaction was not just for McCafferty but for the path not taken.

CHAPTER 36

IT was after sunrise when Kiernan answered the last question and signed her statement at the police station. "Mr. Gaige finished his a full hour sooner," Officer Melchior chided her as he held open the front door for her. "I want you to be clear on this, Ms. O'Shaughnessy. I'm pleased you did not go off the bluff. I just wish you'd go off . . . somewhere—out of my district."

She patted his arm. "Life is fraught with disappointment, Melchior."

She should have been exhausted. She would be in an hour or two. But now she was running on adrenaline, and the still-startling realization that Greg Gaige was alive. Without gymnastics, but *alive*. And waiting for her at Gliderport. Her stomach quivered, and the smile on her face was so wide, she felt silly.

She forced herself to stop at home to change out of her soot-streaked jeans and sweatshirt. The sleeves were singed, and there were fire holes in the backs of the legs. She doffed her clothes and was in and out of the shower in three minutes. Then she put on her forest-green running suit, brushed beige eye shadow on, and rubbed it off twice before it looked good enough. Looping by the Pannikin, she picked up two double cappuccinos and an assortment of scones, and muffins, and, suddenly unsure of Greg's taste, added two chocolate-covered croissants, and headed to Gliderport.

Winding through the curves of Torrey Pines Road, she grinned at the magenta bougainvillaea cascading over stucco walls, and the orange birds of paradise that seemed poised to take off into the fog. Traffic was still light going toward San Diego, and northbound ahead of her the road was empty. When she turned onto the entrance to Gliderport, patches of fog hung in the branches of the Torrey Pines like discarded illusions. But over the ocean slivers of light slit the fog for an instant before it resealed around them.

There was almost no sign now that the movie set had ever been on the bluff. Only the two trailers remained.

Greg wasn't by them. For an instant she feared he'd disappeared again, or she'd dreamed his reemergence. Then she spotted him, across the warning chain—at the far edge of the bluff, a shin's length from the brink of nothingness. Her breath caught; she started to run, then, taking in his stance, slowed herself to a walk. Greg looked like he was in a gale —the wind was snapping his shirt and hair, breaking off mouthfuls of the bluff itself and spitting them at his legs. But there was nothing unsteady or tentative about his stance—his firm, muscular legs were planted solidly apart. Kiernan couldn't help thinking of Lark Sondervoil —her lithe body wavering, eyes wide in terror, hands grappling for ground that wasn't there. The rise where Lark had gone over was less than forty feet to the north. Slowly Greg turned toward it, and his eyes, already tightened to slits against the wind, pressed shut as if the sight, the memory, the grief, were more than he could bear to take in.

She stopped, unwilling to intrude. Was this, she wondered, as much of a memorial as Lark Sondervoil would get? Then she started forward again, knowing that the acknowledgment from Greg was what would have mattered to her.

Greg opened his eyes, slowly turned toward land. When he spotted Kiernan, he waved. He had changed his shirt. The wind fingered his curly gray hair, whipping a strand loose from the rubber band at the nape of his neck. He had washed his face, but the residue of soot had settled in the crevices across his forehead and formed black lines between his eyes.

She slowed, drinking him in. Her chest felt so full, she could hardly breathe. She barely knew Greg, she warned herself. And emotion was something she'd never trusted. But she brushed all that aside as she came up beside him. She smiled, then laughed to cover the illogic of it all. "You smell like a barbecue pit."

He ran his fingers down the side of her neck, made a show of checking them for soot, and grinned. "You're no perfume ad yourself, briquette."

Three feet from the edge of the bluff she stepped down into the ridge trail worn by the wind and the daring, and sat back on the bare sandy rise, and felt around in the paper bag until she found her coffee. When Greg sat down next to her, she gave him a cup, and rested a hand on his knee. "I'm still so astonished you're alive."

"Astonished as in 'pleased'?"

"Real pleased." Suddenly embarrassed, she removed her hand and passed him the bag of pastries. "There's so much I want to know—about you, who you are, and how you've lived. But first tell me what happened the day of the fire on *Bad Companions*." She had a good idea how McCafferty had orchestrated the result, but she wanted to know what Greg had seen and what he'd deduced after a decade of pondering.

He picked a scone and turned to half face her. She could barely see the blue of his eyes. Earlier he had been squinting against the wind. But now the wind had let up and what he was fighting back was inside himself. "Kiernan, some of what I'm telling you I saw, some I read in the paper; it's all jumbled together for me by now. There've always been questions, but of course, I've never been able to talk about them."

She bit into a croissant and nodded for him to go on.

"In all my time in the business, I'd never once missed a call or been late. But that morning I didn't even wake up until I heard the shouting outside. Even then, I felt sluggish. Normally, if I'd woken up late and heard shouting, I'd have been out of the trailer before the second syllable. But that morning I just felt dazed."

"Drugged?"

"That's what I figured. It would have been no problem to dump a dose of sleepytime into a drink. The location out there in the desert was so small and isolated, we were all in and out of the catering truck, and for dinner there was only the motel café." He chomped down on the scone.

Kiernan sat feeling the post-dawn chill cut against her skin. Something was amiss with that reply. It took her a moment to realize what was lacking. "You're not bitter?"

"It was another life back then. Besides, what good would it have done me?"

A splash of sun came through the clouds from behind them. In an hour the light and heat would press the fog back over the sea, but now it merely turned the sand from dun to red-brown, lightened the lines in Greg's face, and added the first tentative wash of color to his exhaustion-paled skin. "You shared your day wagon—"

"Honeywagon. It was supposed to be a place to relax. Dratz made it X-rated. There was almost no privacy on that set. So when they needed it, Carlton and Jane used my honeywagon. More than once I walked in on them." He shrugged. "It wasn't a crisis. That's Hollywood, too, and everyone's expected to be cool about it. Still, the idea of me wandering in at the moment of orgasm probably wasn't an aphrodisiac for either one of them. A couple of times Carlton lent me his Corvette—like movie money, you know? It was a helluva car. Car crashes were one of my specialties, so I knew cars, and that was a beaut. Out there in the desert there were no cops or speed traps. I could get that baby up over a hundred on the straightaways and lean into the curves at the last moment." Now his eyes sparkled the way she remembered them, and his cheeks bunched in a grin.

She who had been to traffic school twice for speeding understood his glee only too well. "Cut out everything but you and the road, huh?"

"Yeah, exactly. Not a thought in my head, just me and the car and the wind and sun and the next curve coming up fast."

"Didn't Dratz care?"

"About the speed? Had he known"—he grinned again—"he wouldn't have. If I'd crashed the 'Vette he'd have been put out by the inconvenience. His father would have bought him another—and canned me. An insignificant price for him to pay for an afternoon in the sack," he added. "But the day before the fire, he had had a blowout with Jane. He came storming out of the trailer across the hill to the car park, and voilà! No 'Vette! Of course, he had lent it to me, but in the middle of his tantrum he forgot about that. When I got back, he was pacing around, screaming and shaking his fist, yelling about me stealing his car. I should have ignored it, but I didn't. I just blew up at him." He sighed. "Well, the bigwig's kid wasn't used to that. He couldn't let that go unanswered, not with half the crew standing around watching. He carried on and on about how it made sense that Bleeker would get an old broken-down stunt man to do a simple gag like the fire gag. He was pulling out all stops."

Old, broken down. She wanted to rub out the memory for him; instead, she said, "So on the morning of the fire, you heard the screams and jolted up . . . ?"

He took a long swallow of coffee and chewed on the last piece of scone. The sun had gone in behind the fog now, the wind picked up. It flicked the strands of his ponytail like minute lashes on his back. "When I saw the time that morning, I panicked. I'd left my car with Jason, but I still had the keys to Dratz's. I drove to the location; I was lucky it was just dawn and no one was on the road. I was still real woozy, and it's a miracle I made it up that hill at all. Probably just instinct from all the car gags I'd done.

"I could see the smoke before I got out of the car. The whole set was a madhouse. Something had gone wrong with the gag, I could tell. In the state I was, I was sure it was my fault. If I hadn't overslept . . . Cary Bleeker was yelling. The flames, huge, fat flames—no wonder they're called tongues of flame. These could have licked up that little house on the set and swallowed it like a canapé. I couldn't figure what was going on. How could they be doing the stunt without me? Bleeker was shouting for people to help. I remember someone saying, 'Where the hell is Dratz? For once the little bastard could be of some use.' And someone answering, 'Gone off with Jane. I saw her drive out of here last night.' Then I heard a voice, guttural, scared: 'The cabin, it's collapsed! Greg's in there! Get it off him!' And Bleeker: 'Call a doctor.' And then they were all quiet. I could hear birds chirping. It seemed so unbelievable that the birds were starting a day like any other day. Then Bleeker said, 'Oh, my God, what a way to die. God, poor Greg.' "

Kiernan realized she was shaking with Greg's decade-old horror. She wrapped her hands around her coffee cup. The paper sides squeezed inward; she had to look down at her hands to ease her grip.

"Closer, someone whose voice I didn't recognize—probably one of the gaffers—was saying, 'It's a damned shame Greg died and Dratz took off. Damned shame it wasn't Dratz burned to an ember. Greg probably could have killed him, the way he was lighting into him yesterday. Real pity Greg's dead." Greg shook his head slowly. "I couldn't take it in. It was like the words were in Technicolor, but I could only process them in black and white. Me dead? I remember actually thinking 'I'm not dead.' And then wondering if Carlton had gone off with Jane after all.

"But it wasn't me on the set. It was someone else. I wasn't thinking clearly—still, I *knew* that body was Carlton Dratz. After all, he was gone. But I also knew enough about Hollywood to realize how convenient it would be to lay the blame for his death on me. No one would care that he was dead, but his father would make a fuss and need a scapegoat. The studio—Dolly—would jump to join him. She'd sacrifice anyone. Cary Bleeker would be scurrying not to be that lamb. And me, a stunt man at the end of his career, I was real expendable. I panicked. I ran back to the Corvette and coasted down the hill because I was afraid to turn on the engine. No one would have noticed that, of course, not with all the commotion. I was in town before I passed another vehicle—the fire truck." He shook his head slowly, his face as ashen as it must have been back then.

Kiernan stared out at the ocean. Beyond the breakers it looked like old green silk, here faded by time, there in the distance one great fold, swelling almost yellow. She lifted her cup and drank slowly, letting the coffee warm her. "Then what did you do, Greg?"

"I drove east. I was going slowly, carefully. I got near Yuma. I still felt fogged; I didn't dare get stopped by the police, and the idea of the state line checkpoint freaked me out. I turned around and headed back toward El Centro and then north. Sometime in the afternoon, it hit me that if I'd thought I looked guilty earlier on the location, it was nothing to how guilty I'd made myself appear by running off in Carlton's car. I pulled onto a side road and parked out of view and just sat there till it was dark.

"Later, it occurred to me that there were advantages to being 'dead.' There was a hundred-thousand-dollar insurance policy that would go to my mother; I'd know she was okay financially. I wouldn't have to make work for Jason anymore. And most appealing, I'd be clear of *me*." He stared out toward the ocean, pulling his arms in defensively against his sides. "I had lived with a brother who got more paranoid, making up wilder and wilder tales, each year. And I was so absorbed in my art that I didn't even notice until he began to impinge on my practice time. Then I disengaged myself from him tentacle by tentacle, had him barred from sets, got a new practice space, and left him alone to nourish his delusions." He glanced at her and then quickly away. "But being dead meant I could get rid of Jason. And—and I could escape from being the guy who'd stooped to stealing Trace Yarrow's job. It was like someone offering you cash for the smelly sweat shirt you wanted to throw out anyway. Burned to black ash was a real fitting end for Greg Gaige."

Kiernan lifted her coffee, but halfway to her mouth she knew she wouldn't be able to swallow it.

Greg hurried on, as if there had been a break in a levee that was never meant to hold back this volume of distress. "In the foggy, panicked state I was in then, that was enough to assure me I shouldn't go back to the set. After dark I drove to the San Diego airport and left Dratz's car with the keys in it."

"What did you do for money?"

"Money? I never thought of that when I was deciding to escape. I had maybe a hundred dollars on me. I hitched a ride north with the type of guy I wouldn't have trusted to change my oil before. But, you know, you can take chances when you're 'dead.' What've you got to lose?" He laughed. "What's *who* got to lose? Once you don't have any real identity, you ride along in a truck cab or talk to a guy you're painting houses with, and you think you're playing a game with them, hiding behind the mask of the moment. But when you can't talk about gags, or gymnastics, or movies, or L.A., or Baltimore, or anything else at all personal, you lose your grasp on who really is behind the mask."

She let a beat pass before she asked, "And what is there behind the mask?"

He laughed dismissively. "Nothing special. Or at least, someone who's a lot less special than I thought I was—and all the time I was the great stunt man, I *thought* I was a pretty modest guy." The paper bag rattled in the wind; he stuck his hand in and came out with a muffin.

The picture of him in the gym flashed in her mind, flushed with the glow she'd painted on it year after year. The awkward Greg Gaige visiting the gym who'd made a special effort to encourage her; not much else in her life had been that special. It was wrenching to give that up. But this new Greg Gaige—she liked him. Greg Gaige grown up. She could almost not believe she was about to get an answer to her question: "You made your decision to be 'dead' off-balance, too suddenly. But once you got over the shock, what was it like? You were the best in the business. You'd created a Move that no one could copy. What was it like to walk away?" She swallowed hard. "What was it like to live without the thing that mattered to you most?"

Greg took a long swallow of coffee and crumpled the paper cup but didn't let go of it. "Hard," he said slowly. "Hardest thing I've ever done. Stunt work was my life, more important than eating, sleeping, sex. Way more important than sex. It shaped what I did, who I was with, and, more than that, how I thought of things that weren't even connected to it. I never just watched a woman move; I watched *how* she moved, in case there was something about it that I could incorporate in a gag when I was doubling a woman. Not doing, not *thinking about* gags was like being plopped down in a foreign country with a language you can't quite understand and customs that don't make sense. Or like being shunned —you know, the Amish punishment." He stared down at the crushed paper cup and ran his finger along the broken lip. "A hundred times a day I saw something—a movie poster, a wooden horse like the one my father had covered for me to practice on when I was six, or just chalk—and it was like my cells screamed out for the life I couldn't have any more."

When she'd gotten to India after being fired from the coroner's office, she'd felt utterly "other." Then she'd ascribed it to culture shock. Now she felt the bond of worn-out regret between them. She longed to reach out to him, but she couldn't, not the way other people did. Instead she nodded in understanding.

"I guess I did the whole grieving bit—anger, bargaining, et cetera. Then for months I just spaced out. Didn't think, didn't exercise—unless you call long glassy-eyed walks exercise. Didn't talk to anyone I didn't have to. I was more out of shape than I'd ever been in my life; it was like being in a stranger's body. I got a labor job up around Redding. Later, I got some jobs helping a couple with remodeling—even out of shape, I'm stronger than the average man and not afraid of climbing up on slanting second-story roofs." He flashed a wry smile. "You wouldn't believe how rare a quality that is. I took any odd job that wasn't connected to movies or gymnastics. I was real careful not to blow my cover. My cover—it was like that was all I had from my old life. I realized later I was protecting that cover. As long as it shielded my old life, I believed at some level that I could get that life back someday. Ridiculous, of course." He caught her eye and shrugged.

She held his gaze, afraid to let him escape into shrugs and asides. "And the stint of teaching at High Country gym, what about that?"

He put the last piece of muffin into his mouth and chewed deliberately. When he'd swallowed, he said, "It was a mistake. I should never have taken that chance."

A mistake or a death wish? But she didn't ask that.

"I was up in Alturas to see if there was any work with the wild horses. I spotted the gym, like I did every place gymnasts practiced. But this time I went in. I didn't want to teach, I just wanted to smell the chalk and the sweat, to feel the intensity of practice. But before I could stop myself, I was correcting a girl in her uneven bar dismount. I knew from the moment I took the job there, I was courting danger. I kept having to come up with new lies about my 'past.' Kids ask ten times more questions than an adult would. They wanted to know which tournaments I'd been in, which I'd won, which of the great gymnasts I knew, why I hadn't made the national finals. I made the Olympic trials, and I was just lucky that none of them found photo coverage of it, or the poster.

Pitfalls were everywhere. And then there was Lark." Greg nodded slowly, his face paling back to gray. "Lark—God, how can she be dead? It's not my fault, you'll say; everyone will say. But—"

Now she did squeeze his hand.

In a moment he went on. "Lark was so good. She wasn't a natural, but she had talent and drive like I haven't seen anywhere, even in Hollywood. She inspired me. It had been so long since I'd even been able to push off into the Move, I just wanted to *do* it again. It was like discovering a photo of a dead lover: it's not her, but you stare at it so hard, you get caught in the 'pretend,' and for an instant it is her, you know? I knew I would never do the Move again like I did on the screen when I practiced every day and I had the second unit director telling me he could only afford one take. But just to feel the air twisting around me as I did the flip and the punchback . . ." He shrugged. "I thought it would be enough. Like looking at the photo until the spark of life leaves, and it's just a piece of paper.

"But it wasn't. Lark went crazy over the Move. She begged me to teach her. Against all logic I did, because—at least this is what I thought at the time—because I really wanted the excuse to practice again and to assure myself I could still do it." He shrugged.

"And could you? Could you still master it?"

"Not quite. For a while I told myself that it had been seven years since I tried it; I was out of shape; I just needed more practice. Now I had the gym to practice in; I could come as early as I wanted, stay as late, even get a kid with a video camera to record it so I could see my faults. I could *have* it again. But the truth was, I could have it and *not* have it."

"What do you mean?"

"To have it, I had to give it to Lark." He waited till Kiernan nodded in acknowledgment. "I didn't deal with that for a while—you know they always tell us it's getting to the top that's hard." He shook his head. "Climbing's the easy part. Sliding down the other side, that's the hard part. In a couple of months, Lark was doing the Move better than I was. It was really her Move then. That's when I decided Greg Gaige really was dead. That was my great realization. And I knew I had courted danger too long there and I had to move on before someone recognized me."

"And yet you took this job on the set here. Talk about taking chances!" Thinking back to the Baltimore gym, Kiernan smiled. "I remember you going out of your way for a girl who needed it. Did you take this chance now because Lark wanted you to be here to see her Move?"

He shrugged. "Part for Lark, part for me. I didn't just *take* this catering job, I sought it out. It was a stupid idea. I told myself I just wanted to stand in the shadows and see the Move performed again before the cameras with everyone watching and the cast and crew bursting into applause when she climbed out of the catcher. Or maybe I just couldn't resist being near *my* Move again. Maybe I haven't really given it up." He closed his fingers tighter around hers. "I don't know anymore. I just don't know."

She sat unwilling to move. The sky had lightened, but the damp cold had seeped beneath her skin and penetrated her spine. A bolt of sunlight cut the clouds, warmed her face, and vanished. His hand lay on top of hers, but it no longer felt real. "So Greg, what are you going to do now?"

He hesitated. "I don't know that, either. Things have changed again so completely. I've gotten used to being Luke Correra. Now I'll have to be Greg Gaige again and tie up ends I left hanging, *people* I left hanging." He stared out over the water. He hadn't released her hand, and now he tapped his forefinger on it. "But I'll be able to get a passport. That's really great. I can go wherever I want now. Hokkaido, New Milford Sound, Lhasa, Rangoon." He turned to her, his beard twitching as he smiled. "Want to come?"

Greg Gaige really was dead, she thought, and yet he wasn't. She leaned into the crook of his shoulder. Below, the morning light had faded the water to a silky blue-green, the waves swelled, arched, crashed, spreading into a lacy froth and pulled back teasingly. The welcome mat to the world beyond.

There would be more ends to be tied than he suspected, more complications. Nothing was certain. Maybe Rangoon would turn out to be Seattle or Del Mar. After this flash of closeness burned out there might be nothing but embers. Or maybe— But she'd never been deterred by a challenge. Long odds only whetted her appetite and made the prize all the more succulent. Dreams of childhood coming true, what were the odds on that? No matter how long the odds, she knew she wouldn't let go of Greg Gaige.

"You do have a passport?" he said.

She linked her arm through his and felt the warmth of his body permeate hers. "Yes."